ANGEL FIRE

THE SEDONA FILES: BOOK 3

CHRISTINE POPE

DARK VALENTINE PRESS

ANGEL FIRE

ISBN: 978-0-9883348-4-7

Copyright © 2013 by Christine Pope.

Revised version copyright © 2019

Published by Dark Valentine Press

Cover design by Lou Harper

Ebook formatting by Indie Author Services

To Sedona itself, for its beauty, power, and enduring mystery.

CHAPTER ONE

Jeff Makowski leaned over Grace's bassinet, his expression more than a little dubious. "She doesn't look like a half-alien baby to me."

"Quarter alien," I corrected him. "Or something like that, anyway. No one really knows if Grayson was actually half alien or a little more or a little less."

"Still."

I reached past Jeff to pick up Grace, who submitted to my less than expert handling with her usual aplomb. She cooed, blew a milk bubble, and reached out for a piece of my hair as it fell over my shoulder. I hastily scooped the stray lock out of the way. Now I understood why Kara had started wearing her hair in a ponytail most days. I'd just figured it was because she didn't have time to do anything else with it, but I realized she also needed to keep it away from grabby baby hands.

Jeff continued to watch me with a sour expression on his face as I held Grace up against my shoulder and patted her back. Not that I was really surprised by his reaction; Jeff generally tended to look as if he'd just smelled rancid two-week-old leftovers.

What had truly surprised me was his being here in Sedona at all. He'd emailed me just the day before, saying that he planned to come to Arizona for a little while, maybe a week, maybe more. Lance had offered to let him crash at his condo, since it was pretty much vacant now that he'd moved in with Kara. Things weren't really formal yet—they'd had a few more important things on their minds than planning a wedding—but there'd never been any question of them living separately. Not now.

Why Lance didn't just sell the condo, I didn't know, but maybe he figured the market was soft at the moment and so was waiting for a better opportunity. Not really my business, anyway. I was still trying to wrap my head around the way things had changed, how my sister was now a mother and practically a wife, and I was an aunt.

Aunt to a baby unlike any other on the planet. Okay, Grace looked like a normal month-old infant. You'd never guess her father had quite a bit of alien DNA running through his veins. But everyone in our little UFO-chasing group knew better. Human babies didn't go from conception to birth in three months flat.

Funny thing was, after her accelerated gestation

period, she seemed to be developing like a regular baby. The midwife had checked her out thoroughly, and Kara and Lance even allowed a bunch of tests to be run. The upshot was that Grace could pretty much pass any casual inspection. You'd have to do cell-level DNA testing to discover that something not of this world was twisting its way along those double helixes.

So it was decided the adopted Romanian orphan story would float after all, and Grace came home without too much ceremony and went to the pediatrician—who found nothing strange about her—and made her debut at a local MUFON meeting to a whole bunch of cooing and exclamations. If anyone thought it strange that my sister had suddenly gotten it into her head to adopt a baby, no one said anything out loud. Then again, these were people who spent their whole lives thinking about aliens and UFOs. A Romanian orphan barely merited the batting of an eyelash.

"I didn't know babysitting was in your repertoire," Jeff remarked as I went over to the couch, still holding Grace, and sat myself down.

"Or yours," I replied, balancing Grace with one hand as I reached for the remote on the coffee table.

Showing unexpected chivalry, Jeff moved forward and scooped up the remote, then handed it to me. "I didn't come over to babysit. I came over to satisfy my scientific curiosity."

"And?"

He frowned again. "She just looks like a baby."

"Well, what did you expect? Grayson looked like a normal guy." I paused, thinking about the hybrid soldier who was her father. "Well, okay, he looked like a normal underwear model."

Jeff's expression grew even more jaundiced, if that was possible.

"Besides," I added, shuffling through the Apple TV menu until I got to the cache of old *Walking Dead* episodes on Kara's system, "she's not just any baby. She's my niece, so watch it."

For a minute, he didn't say anything. Then, "Are you sure you should be watching this stuff in front of a month-old baby?" He jerked a finger toward the TV, where the series' intrepid survivors looked as if they were about to open a serious can of whup-ass on a herd of zombies.

I rolled my eyes. "Oh, please. Like she's able to process any of it." Still, I grabbed the TV remote and turned the sound down a little.

"How do *you* know what she can process? She's part alien."

Buzzkill. With a sigh, I paused the show and then scowled up at him. "Why are you here, anyway?"

"I wanted to see the baby."

"I mean in Sedona. Yearning for a white Christmas or something?"

"Yeah, about that." He shifted so he could look out the sliding glass window in the dining room, where the landscape lights showed pale little patches of snow from the night before that hadn't completely melted yet. "What's up with this weather?"

"Um, elevation above four thousand feet. If it bothers you, you should've stayed in sunny L.A."

He made a grunting sound that might have been a half-laugh. "Sunny, right. It was pouring buckets when I left."

"Well, there you go. This time of year, if it rains in California, we get snow here. Sometimes. Has to be cold enough, though."

Grace managed to grab a handful of my hair, and I had to spend the next minute extricating it from her clutching little fist. Couldn't really blame her, I supposed; my hair was a shade or two lighter than Kara's, but probably to a baby one lock of long blonde hair looked pretty much the same as another.

Maybe she was missing her mother. This was the first time Kara and Lance had entrusted me with babysitting duties, and it had taken a lot of talking on my part to convince them I was up to the task. I was still sort of shocked that they'd left Grace with me, even though they were only five minutes away at the Heartline Café. Kara wouldn't travel any farther than that, even though, as far as we knew, there was absolutely nothing for her to be worried about.

Things had been normal enough the past few months—well, if you could refer to running your sister's business while she was a state away giving birth to a part-alien baby as "normal." Anyway, the baddies out at the base in Secret Canyon had gone dormant again following their latest setback. None of us knew whether this was just a lull in the storm, or whether they'd finally decided Sedona really wasn't working out for them and had gone elsewhere. But there had been remarkably few UFO sightings in the area this autumn, and although I would much rather have been concentrating on my own web design business, I knew I owed it to Kara to mind the store until she was back up to speed. This dinner at the Heartline Café was the first time she'd gone out since giving birth.

Although Jeff and I had hung out together a good deal, we really hadn't talked much about anything personal, and I liked it that way. I knew our relation-ship was the subject of some worry on my sister's part. I'd tried to tell her it was no big deal, that she was making mountains out of molehills, but some-times it seemed as if Kara's whole reason for being was to worry about stuff, so I gave up. I couldn't even explain the situation to myself half the time. It wasn't as if Jeff was the world's greatest conversa-tionalist. I wasn't attracted to him, that was for sure.

So as to the real reason for why Jeff was in Sedona now—besides wanting to see whether Grace was green or had antennae sprouting from her head or something—I really couldn't say, except I was pretty sure it had nothing to do with my charms. Maybe he just didn't want to spend the holidays alone.

As far as I knew, he didn't have any family. I'd been to his house in L.A. For all its ramshackle appearance on the outside, inside it was sterile and clean and conspicuously lacking in any personality.

No family photos, no antiques that could be heir-looms, not even collections of old books or anything else to show he had a connection to anyone else on this planet. It was possible he didn't. Maybe he was an orphan, just like me.

Okay, if you wanted to get technical about it, I wasn't exactly an orphan. My mother was alive somewhere—Taos, New Mexico, according to the latest intelligence—but she might as well be dead as far as I was concerned. I refused to acknowledge the existence of someone who'd walked out on my sister and me when I was only three years old. Luckily, Kara wanted no more to do with our mother than I did, so at least that was one thing we agreed on.

Still standing at the window, Jeff straightened up from his usual slouch and stared out into the storm, eyes narrowing. "There's something out there."

"I doubt it. Even Mrs. Martinez brings her cats in when the weather is like this."

"I saw something," he said flatly.

I recognized that tone from the times when we'd argued over some minute detail of computer coding. It meant he was the authority and he knew what he was talking about, and that was that.

When the subject was computers, I didn't bother to argue. I knew way more about their inner work-ings than most people probably even guessed, and I could hack in and out of some pretty secure systems, thanks to Jeff's coaching, but he could still code rings around me.

However, when it came to Sedona, or my sister's

house, he didn't know what the heck he was talking about. I set Grace back down in the bassinet and went over to the window, pausing next to Jeff so I could stare out into the blurry darkness. Snow in Sedona was generally dry and light; the flakes floated, delicate as feathers, illuminated here and there by the backyard lights.

I didn't see anything.

It was cold enough that I could actually feel the chill radiating out from the sliding glass doors. I crossed my arms and kept my gaze fixed on the drifting snow.

I still didn't see anything.

But for some reason, I thought I could *hear* something—what, I wasn't exactly sure. It almost sounded like a crowd of people murmuring...or maybe it was just the wind. Sometimes it could really howl down the chimney when it got going.

Then the hair on the back of my neck began to stand up, because I heard something I *could* identify. Gort, Kara's shepherd/Keeshond-mix dog, was growling low in his throat.

Gort hardly ever growled.

He might bark when someone was at the door or if one of Mrs. Martinez's cats had the temerity to invade our backyard, but I couldn't remember the last time I'd heard the dog growl at anyone...or anything.

Something had gotten him going this time, though, and I strained to look once more into the darkness, to see something in the little areas of light around the solar lamps. Even though it was snowing now, the weather had been bright and sunny for most of the day; the lamps were fully charged.

And then they blinked out all at once, and absolute black reigned outside. I couldn't see anything at all, but it was as if some unseen pressure began to push down on me, to press against my throat. I struggled for breath, even as Jeff gasped,

"What the *hell*, Kirsten?"

Without thinking, I reached up and grasped the drapes—Kara had them hanging from those little metal clips attached to rings—and slid them shut, as if those simple lengths of fabric could provide some sort of barrier against whatever was lurking in the dark outside. Almost as soon as I had blotted out the sight of the backyard, the pressure on my throat eased, and Gort stopped growling.

The lights flickered and I tensed, icy tentacles of fear running down my back. God, what if we lost power altogether?

But then the electricity seemed to reassert itself, and the lamps in the living room kept shining as if nothing had happened.

For a long moment, neither Jeff nor I spoke, but only stared at each other, like two little kids who had just discovered that "Bloody Mary in the mirror" wasn't only a slumber-party game.

Finally he said, "Was that...?"

I lifted my shoulders and looked past him to the lengths of heavy rust-colored cotton that blocked the view outside. Finally, I shook my head. "I don't know."

By some unspoken agreement, we said nothing to Kara and Lance when they got home, but only told them Grace had been a perfect angel—the simple truth—and went our separate ways. Since Jeff was staying in Lance's condo, he got to save money on a hotel room while acting as temporary caretaker of the place at the same time. The arrangement made sense, but as I got into the UFO Night Tours van that was my usual transportation around town, I found myself wishing that Jeff had decided to crash on my couch instead.

At least that way, I wouldn't have to drive home alone.

No such luck. I turned the key in the ignition, cranked the heater to full blast, and turned up the ancient CD player as well. Jeff was already pulling away from the curb in his own van. Somehow, it seemed vitally important to follow him as closely as I could, even though we'd only share the same route until we got out on 89A. Then he'd be heading west, while I needed to go east, back through the heart of town, then south a little to my apartment complex off Highway 179.

Better short-term company than none at all, and I backed out a little too quickly, startling when the van's tires slipped on the slick pavement. I cursed under my breath and eased up, but was glad to see that Jeff hadn't gotten all that far ahead of me. He was driving like a ninety-year-old afraid of getting his license revoked. No real surprise—I guessed he didn't have a lot of experience driving in the snow. It wasn't falling all that hard, a few flakes here and there, but it was just enough to make the roads slippery and treacherous.

For some reason, I found myself holding my breath as I stopped at the light, watching as he turned right while I had to wait for the signal to turn green. It wasn't all that late—a little after eight o'clock—but the streets were still almost deserted. Not a lot of tourist traffic on a Wednesday night, and I guessed the weather had kept quite a few people safely in their hotel rooms and rented condos and Airbnbs.

Most of the time, I would've been glad not to have to share the road with a bunch of people unfamiliar with the area, but at the moment, I would have welcomed a traffic jam. At least I wouldn't have felt so alone as I eased the van out onto the highway and headed toward home. And although I'd always appreciated Sedona being a "dark sky city," meaning there was a conscious effort to keep nighttime illumination to a minimum so it wouldn't interfere with stargazing, right then I would have been happy to see blazing billboards and streetlights every ten feet.

Maybe that would have kept my mind from playing tricks on me, kept me from thinking I glimpsed movement out of the corner of my eye when there was nothing to see, or imagining that some kind of massive craft hovered above me, blacker than black against the night sky, when in reality nothing was up there but some quickly scudding clouds. My fingers tightened on the steering wheel as I slowed down for the first roundabout in the center of town.

Normally, I would have gone to the right and turned down Brewer Road so I could avoid the second roundabout, but tonight I stayed on the highway. The shortcut was way too dark, with trees almost meeting overhead. Anything could be lurking down there....

I gave myself a mental shake and muttered, "Get a grip, Kirsten," but even so, I didn't relax my death grip on the steering wheel. Really, the road wasn't totally deserted—just ahead of me was a Chevy Suburban with Oregon plates going almost ten miles per hour below the speed limit. On any other night, I might have uttered a few choice curses about tourists under my breath. Right then, I was just glad to have their taillights to follow. Surely the aliens wouldn't swoop down on me with witnesses so close by?

Well, they'd done a lot worse than that over the years, actually, but nothing happened as we passed Tlaquepaque Village, still with a few stalwart vehicles in the parking lot, then took the roundabout that brought us onto Highway 179. The Suburban, God bless it, turned down my side street, although I knew it must be heading for the Arabella Hotel and not my own shabby little apartment complex just a little farther down. Sure enough, the SUV pulled into the parking lot for the hotel, which was still packed. One of Sedona's most popular restaurants, Elote, was located on the same property as the Arabella, and it was the one place you could always guarantee there would be a lot of people well past ten o'clock.

But the parking lot in my own complex was quiet and still, although lights shone from most of the apartment windows. Not my own, though—I'd been stupid enough to head out to Kara's without leaving even a single lamp on.

"Great," I muttered as I turned off the engine and grabbed my backpack.

Nothing for it, though. I climbed out of the van and locked it, then grasped my keys with the house key sticking out between my index and middle fingers—supposedly you could use your key as a weapon if someone attacked you, although I guessed the self-defense experts who came up with that one were thinking more of muggers and rapists than alien invaders. A cold wind pulled at my hair and found its way past the scarf I had tied around my throat as I made my way to the stairs.

A metallic noise brought me up short, until I realized it was just someone throwing trash into the dumpster behind the Circle K, whose property butted up against the apartment complex. My heart still thumped away uneasily, though, and I found myself bolting up the stairs, running as if a horde of Greys was after me.

Of course, they weren't. I managed to open the

door and get inside with no problem, although my fingers shook as I turned the deadbolt and flicked the light switch. Immediately, the hanging Moroccan-style lamp over the dinette table turned on, flooding the room with a warm, reassuring glow. That wasn't enough, though. I went into the kitchen and turned on the overhead light there as well, revealing nothing more frightening than a couple of empty glasses and plates that I'd been too busy to put in the dishwasher.

Usually this would be the point where I told myself I was acting like an idiot. Tonight, though, I wasn't so sure. I hadn't been imagining that awful pressure I felt at Kara's house. Jeff had experienced the same thing. Something had been lurking out there, something heavy, dark...inimical. Yeah, *that* was a ten-dollar word for you. But it did seem to describe what I'd felt almost perfectly. Something was out there, and it wasn't friendly.

And yeah, go ahead and laugh at me—the girl who wanted more than anything to see a UFO, to experience some of the crazy stuff that seemed to happen to everyone else except her. Persephone and Paul O'Brien had actually been *in* the alien base, and my sister Kara almost had a UFO run her over, for crying out loud, but I'd never seen a damn thing. Oh, I believed, but only in a secondhand way, because nothing had ever happened directly to me.

Except tonight. And I realized I wasn't liking it all that much.

Well, that was just great. So much for Kirsten Swenson, intrepid explorer into the unknown.

Frowning, I stalked through the combo living room/dining area and down the hall to my bedroom. Even though I was feeling more than a little annoyed with myself, I wasn't so irritated that I didn't still flip on the bedside lamp as soon as I entered the room. A swirl of soft cedar incense—my favorite, because it always seemed to say "Sedona" to me—greeted me, instantly comforting, the scent lingering long after the stick had burned out. My apartment, with its mishmash of yard sale finds and consignment store goodies, its Indian textiles and art-glass lamps, seemed the last place an alien would want to defile.

Then again, the ranch house Kara had inherited and carefully decorated in a Southwest style too tasteful to be called kitschy wasn't exactly the most likely place for an alien invasion, either. And even a casual reading on the topic of abductions and visitations was enough to show that aliens went where they wanted to go, whether it was a suburban tract home or a car on an empty country road.

And what had they been after? Had they somehow figured out that Grace was the offspring of one of their hybrid soldiers? Or were they just keeping an eye on Kara after her brush-by with them in August?

I wouldn't flatter myself by thinking they were looking for me. Not much there to interest them, except maybe my association with Kara and Grace, and of course the rest of our group of alien hunters. It was probably naïve to think that they didn't know who we were, and that we had a particular interest in UFOs. For whatever reason, we'd been mostly ignored…until now.

So what had changed?

I wasn't sure I wanted to know.

CHAPTER TWO

THE STORE WAS PROBABLY THE LAST PLACE I FELT LIKE going the next morning, but Kara hadn't come back to work full-time yet, so it was my duty to run the place most days. Things had been glacially slow, and I wasn't looking forward to yet another day of clock watching.

You'd think the weeks leading up to Christmas would be busy for us, but Sedona actually tended to be sort of dead until right after the holiday. People wanted to come into town for the week between Christmas and New Year's, and even right afterward into the first of January, but before then? Not so much. True, there was always the influx of pagan types who wanted to be around the vortexes on the solstice. Unfortunately, they tended to spend all their money on new crystals for their collections and not on UFO literature and alien-motif tchotchkes.

I placed a king-size travel mug filled with green

tea on the counter, then pulled my MacBook Pro out of my backpack and set it up on the counter, plugging an ethernet cable into its designated port. Kara didn't bother with wi-fi, but at least she did have high-speed internet. Since business had been so slow, I worked on my clients' projects in between helping the odd customer here and there. A string of brass bells hung from the shop door, ready to announce the arrival of whatever tourists did decide to show up.

The fears of the night before seemed to have blown away with the clouds and the snow. This morning was fiercely bright, the sun glinting off the patches of snow that still survived. The ridge lines would probably stay white for several days as long as the temperature didn't rise too much, but the slippery streets I'd had to navigate on my way home from Kara's were already a memory.

My newest client owned an art gallery in West Sedona, and wanted a site that would help showcase her art and draw more customers out to that part of town. I was glad I could use HTML5 to build an animated portfolio that wouldn't be a drag on those customers who had slower computers—or not show up at all on devices like iPads and iPhones, which wouldn't even support Flash. Playing with the code helped take my mind off that sensation of unbearable pressure I'd felt the night before, that wave of cold, that sound of hellish voices murmuring words I couldn't understand.

I'd almost called Jeff this morning but decided against it. If he wanted to hash things over, he knew where to find me. Besides, I knew for a fact he wasn't an early riser and probably wouldn't have appreciated a phone call any time before noon.

Maybe I was sticking my head in the sand. Of course I wouldn't bother Kara with this—and I didn't feel close enough yet to Lance to open up to him—but maybe I should tell Michael Lightfoot what had happened. He was always calm, considerate, never judgmental, sort of the uncle I'd never had, a sympathetic ear when I needed one. I somehow doubted Jeff would talk to Michael, although he might decide to say something to Lance.

Great. If that happened, then Lance would probably give me shit for not mentioning the incident to him first. Some days it seemed I just couldn't win with Lance.

The bells on the door jingled, and I looked up from my laptop. A couple of tourists in their thirties, probably from Southern California, judging by the way they were overly bundled up against the forty-degree temperatures outside.

I pulled a smile out of somewhere. "Welcome to the UFO Depot. Can I help you?"

"Oh, we're just browsing," the woman said, giving me the funny side-eyed look I was used to by that point, the look that always seemed to ask, *Do you really believe in this stuff?*

"Okay," I said, knowing better than to say anything else. "Just let me know if you need anything." And I returned my attention to my computer screen, switching to a mindless task like resizing images in Photoshop so I wouldn't completely lose track of what I was doing if they did end up buying something.

And although I'd pegged them as lookie-loos, the husband did actually buy one of the "I Had a Close Encounter in Sedona, Arizona!" T-shirts. His wife didn't look overly thrilled with his purchase, leading me to guess they probably wouldn't be having a close encounter of their own when they got back to their hotel room.

Then they left, and quiet descended once again. Kara tended to play dreamy New Age space-themed music when she tended the store, but I could only handle so much of that stuff. I was pretty sure she wouldn't be too happy if I blasted hard rock, so I went with silence instead. Besides, it was easier for me to concentrate on my real work without a distracting soundtrack.

The bells on the door jingled again. In the middle of saving a file, I said automatically, "Welcome to the UFO De—" And the words sort of caught in my throat, because I looked up on the last syllable and realized that my latest visitor wasn't a tourist at all, but Martin Jones, Kara's erstwhile Man in Black.

Okay, he wasn't really "her" Man in Black the way Grayson had definitely been "her" alien-human hybrid super-soldier, but since she'd been the first one to meet Agent Jones, I'd always sort of labeled him that way in my mind.

Well, when I wasn't privately referring to him as "sex in a suit."

I'd last seen him in August when he'd stopped in the store, looking for Kara. He'd disappeared soon after Grayson performed his sabotage on the alien base in Secret Canyon, and we'd all sort of assumed that he'd gone back to wherever MIBs hung out. Too bad, since he was awfully easy on the eyes.

But now he was here, looking even more gorgeous than I remembered, a long wool overcoat half hiding the trademark black suit, aviator shades covering his eyes. The suit was enough to make him stand out in Sedona, even aside from his good looks; the high-desert town wasn't exactly business-suit territory. Dress shirts and ties for the waiters in some of the higher-end restaurants, and for some of the guys who worked in the local banks and so on, but a full-on suit?

"Hello, Kiki," Agent Jones said, his tone casual, as if dropping into my store out of the blue was no big deal.

"Kirsten," I replied automatically, wishing I'd never bestowed the nickname on myself. Getting everyone to stop calling me that was a Sisyphean battle at best, but necessary if I wanted people to start taking me seriously.

"Kirsten," he repeated, and smiled.

That smile did certain things to portions of my anatomy that I really didn't want to think about. I closed my laptop. "Kara's not working today."

"I know." He moved a little farther into the shop, pausing a foot or so from the counter I was sitting behind. "So, how do you like being an aunt?"

"It's great," I said. I wasn't about to let him rattle me. So sure, he knew about the baby. How *much* he knew about the baby, well...that was the $64,000 question, wasn't it? I mean, you didn't have to be a government agent to know that Kara Swenson, owner of the UFO Depot, had just adopted a baby. It wasn't as if she was hiding Grace under a rock.

"Good." His smile faded a little. "I actually didn't come in here to see Kara. I came here to see you."

"You did?" Normally, I would have been happy enough to learn that a guy of Martin Jones's caliber had come into the store expressly to see me. When the hot guy in question was a Man in Black, though, that sort of statement wasn't necessarily a good thing.

"Yes." He paused and glanced away from me, as if taking in the clutter of alien-themed merchandise, from the crowded bookshelves on the far wall to the stacks of T-shirts and the alien plush dolls on the low tables. God knows what he thought of all that stuff. Taken in aggregate, it did look pretty silly, even though I knew the creatures that had inspired it were no laughing matter.

And I sort of doubted Agent Jones' presence here, the day after those aliens had decided to let me know that they hadn't taken a powder after all, was exactly a coincidence.

The silence stretched out for a minute, but I wasn't about to break it, no matter how uncomfortable it might feel. If he'd come here to tell me something, then he could just tell me. He was going to find out real fast that I wasn't a game-playing kind of girl.

"Been quiet here lately?"

"Oh, well, we're mostly busy right after Christmas," I told him, even though I knew he wasn't really asking about business.

He reached up and took off his sunglasses. The blue-gray of his eyes was a little shocking against his olive skin and dark hair. I'd just assumed he must have brown eyes, judging by his coloring.

Gorgeous as they might be, those eyes were just a little too piercing. "I wasn't talking about the store."

"Oh?"

"Do you want to talk about what happened last night?"

Uh-oh. I cleared my throat and said, "Not really."

"It would be smarter for you if you did."

"Is that a threat?"

He looked a little taken aback at my words. "No. As I once told your sister, we're on the same side."

"Uh-huh," I said, nonplussed. Wow, that was eloquent. To cover my confusion, I reached over for my mug of green tea and took a long sip. "I'm not sure what you want me to say," I went on. "I mean, it sounds as if you already know what happened."

"I know *something* happened. I want to know exactly what it was."

"Well, then, sounds like you're doomed to disappointment, because I don't know exactly what it was, either. If anything."

He just stood there, waiting, watching me with

those improbable blue eyes. I'd never thought of myself as someone who rattled easily, but it was really hard to meet that stare and not want to spill everything.

Then, again, he'd probably been doing this for a while. I wondered exactly how long, and how old he was. Translation: I wondered how much older he was than I. Ten years? Twelve? He looked like he was somewhere in his mid-thirties.

Not relevant, Kiki! I scolded myself. Shrugging, I remarked, "Not much to say. I mean, I could've just been having a galloping case of the heebie-jeebies."

One eyebrow lifted. "'Heebie-jeebies'?"

"Okay, maybe it was a little more than that. But really, it just felt dark and cold and...heavy. The solar lights went out. And I heard something."

"Something like what?" His tone was calm enough, but I caught a little edge to it that I didn't like, as if even Martin Jones the super-cool MIB was hearing something he didn't particularly care for.

"Just...voices." I stopped for a moment, forcing myself to recall that faint but somehow hostile murmuring I had heard at the outer limits of my perception, as if hundreds or even thousands of beings were speaking all at once. "Not words or anything. I couldn't even tell you if it sounded human. Just this weird murmur, rising and falling. Jeff didn't hear it."

"Jeff Makowski."

I didn't bother to ask how he knew who Jeff was.

"Yes. He was with me over at Kara's house. But Gort sure heard it...and he didn't like it."

Martin Jones didn't ask me who Gort was. I guessed he must have met the dog when he came to first question Kara in August, just after she had her buzz-by—briefly celebrated on YouTube before the powers-that-be pulled the plug—from a UFO while trying to conduct a tour.

Needless to say, we hadn't offered any UFO tours since then.

"And how did it make you feel?"

How did it make me feel? What the hell was this, a session with my shrink? I crossed my arms. "Well, it didn't make me feel all warm and fuzzy, that's for sure."

He didn't crack a smile. "It's...worrisome...that they would make their presence known to you like that."

"You're not exactly inspiring confidence here, Agent Jones."

This time, his lips quirked a little. But his expression sobered again just as quickly. "That wasn't my intention."

"So what are your intentions?" The words slipped out before I realized what I was saying, and then I felt a stupid flush spread over my cheeks. *Great, now he probably thinks you're a complete airhead!*

But obviously, a good poker face was as much a part of MIB training as chasing aliens and interrogating abductees, because he didn't even let out a betraying twitch this time. "To keep an eye on things, Kirsten. The time of year is...troubling."

"What, you're not into the whole holiday-spirit thing?"

"It's not the holidays, per se. It's the astronomical event taking place before that."

It was my turn to raise an eyebrow. "Oh, come on. You're not seriously talking about the solstice, are you?"

"Why should that surprise you?"

"Well, because—" I broke off, then made a dismissive gesture with one hand. "I mean, sorry, Agent Jones, but you don't look like the type to be dancing around naked at the solstice with the rest of the pagans." *Although that's something I'd pay to see....*

Expression deadpan, he replied, "True, that's not something I'm in the habit of doing."

I had the distinct impression he was teasing me, so I just said, "But you think the solstice is important."

"I know it's important." He frowned. "Unfortunately, so do the aliens."

"And...?" I told him, annoyed by the way his words seemed to hint at something important but wouldn't actually reveal anything. "What do you expect us to do about it? I mean, thanks for the vote of confidence, but it seems as if we've been doing you guys' work for you lately, so it would be kind of nice if we got a little help, you know?"

His gaze shifted away from mine. "I can't say for sure yet. But if anything else happens, call me." And he reached into his breast pocket and pulled out a card, then laid it on the counter next to my laptop.

I glanced at it quickly, noting the FBI logo at the top, and then saw his name with "special agent" after it, and a Phoenix-area phone number below that. Who knew it would be that easy to get his number? However, I sort of got the feeling he wouldn't exactly be amused if I called him up later and asked him out for drinks.

"Thanks," I said, and picked up the card and shoved it in my jeans pocket. I could transfer it to my wallet later. Looking back up at him, I added, "It's only ten days until the solstice. Cutting it a little close, aren't you?"

"This was the first time they've made any sort of move here in town," he replied calmly. "It may be nothing."

"But you don't think so."

"No, I don't."

A thought struck me as I realized for the first time he'd come here by himself, instead of as part of a team. "Seems like kind of a big thing to take on by yourself. Where's your partner?"

A grim smile. "He was reassigned. Take care, Kirsten."

And he turned and went back out the door, leaving me to stare after him, wondering what the hell his visit had been about.

Ten days to the solstice. Ten days until...what?

I decided then that I'd better talk to Michael Lightfoot, stat.

Actually, "stat" was more like six hours later, after I'd finished a full shift at the UFO Depot and could close the place up and get the hell out of there. I did call Michael not too long after Martin Jones had left, telling him I needed to see him at his place when I was off work, so at least Michael was expecting me.

No cozy summertime chat on his patio this time, with the warm winds in the trees and a fire going in the fire pit. No, the temperature had fallen to thirty-five degrees outside by the time I pulled up in front of Michael's place. I was happy to see smoke billowing out of the chimney and to smell the scent of burning mesquite on the air, so I knew Michael had a good fire going indoors.

He greeted me solemnly and led me inside, to his front room with its mishmash of Southwestern tchotchkes and mismatched furniture and assorted souvenirs. More than once, Kara had made a derisive comment about all the shops in Tlaquepaque Village throwing up in Michael's house all at the same time, but I sort of liked the clutter. Not that I'd want to live with it myself, necessarily, but there was something comforting about it when I went to visit.

Obviously, he'd guessed from my tone of voice that this wasn't going to be an ordinary chat; I spied two glasses of red wine sitting on the banged-up coffee table. Or maybe he'd just psychically divined that I was more than a little freaked out. Either way, I wasn't going to argue with a glass of cabernet...or Malbec, or whatever it was.

"Thanks, Michael," I said as I shrugged out of my coat and hung it on the hall tree by the door. "I really didn't want to bug Kara with this...."

"It's no problem. We are all here for each other, after all."

Some of us more than others, I thought, but I just smiled and went over to the couch, then sat down and picked up a glass of wine. After taking a sip, I was doubly glad that I'd gotten over my beer and tequila phase pretty quickly. There was a reason why its nickname was "ta-kill-ya," and beer just made me feel bloated, but a glass of wine tended to make everything seem better. My palate wasn't developed enough yet for me to say for sure what I was drinking, although I knew it wasn't heavy enough for a cab. Pinot noir, maybe? Not that it really mattered, I supposed.

I waited to say anything until Michael sat down opposite me, but once he was there, it seemed harder than I'd thought it would be to tell him what was going on. We'd all had such a quiet autumn—even with Kara going away to New Mexico to have Grace —and I supposed we all had been hoping that maybe that was the end of it, that this time the aliens had decided to go elsewhere.

No such luck.

Well, a little more wine couldn't hurt. Maybe it would help unfreeze my tongue. I drank again, then blurted out, "I think they're back."

He didn't bother to ask who. "So you felt it, too."

"You did? I mean—last night? That...whatever it was?"

"'Whatever it was' is a good way of putting it." Michael finally lifted his own glass and took a slow, measured sip. "It's interesting that you felt it, though. You might want to talk to Persephone about that."

"I am not psychic," I said flatly. I knew I wasn't. I'd never shown any signs of any kind of telepathic powers, and believe me, growing up in Sedona, you tended to be surrounded by psychic people and people who would be ecstatic if you turned out to be psychic, too. That wasn't me at all. Otherwise, I would've started playing the lottery a long time ago.

Michael's dark eyes were amused. "Did I say you were?"

"No, but Persephone—"

"Persephone is open to many forms of communication. She might surprise you."

"Maybe," I said, unconvinced. Persephone was Kara's friend much more than she was mine. Those two had hit it off like a house on fire. I mean, I liked Persephone, but it would feel strange to go spilling secrets to her when I couldn't be sure that Kara wouldn't end up finding out about it sooner or later. Whereas I trusted Michael implicitly. Of course, I'd known him since I was a kid. He'd been a good friend of Grandpa's, had helped Kara and me get through the rough transition after he passed and we knew we were really alone in the world.

But thinking about my grandfather just made me

feel sad. I knew I didn't have time for that now, so I said, "Okay, I'll think about it. But what do *you* think it was?"

He didn't blink. "You already know the answer to that, don't you?"

Typical Michael, always answering my questions with questions of his own. He was one of the few people I never bothered to argue with, mostly because doing so would be a wasted effort. He never tried to persuade you that you were wrong. He mostly didn't do anything except watch you with those dark eyes of his, a tactic that worked about ninety percent of the time. I sighed and set my glass down on the table, using one of the kitschy sandstone coasters painted with a cactus that Michael had set out.

"Okay…it was *them*. But why now?"

For the first time, I saw the hint of a frown touch the lines around his eyes. "Things are moving. Time is getting short."

I bit back a remark about him saving it for a fortune cookie. Besides, Martin Jones' comments about the solstice weighed heavily on my mind. *Ten days….*

"Well, if they were aiming for 2012, they kind of missed the cutoff a long time ago."

Michael actually smiled at that. "It's not the year itself, but the *time* of year. The winter solstice has always contained a power the summer one does not. For many of us, it is a time of introspection, of inner healing. But there's a darkness to that power as well, one that our visitors may be trying to tap into for their own purposes."

Great. Well, on the first go-round, Persephone had managed to blast the minds of every alien or alien-infected human in the Secret Canyon base, and the second time, we'd had a little help from an alien hybrid soldier who had luckily decided to throw in his lot with the humans—and paid the ultimate price for it. Right then, though, I didn't see a lot of options. Maybe the next time I saw Agent Jones, I'd have to ask him when he planned to send in the cavalry.

"Do you think they're looking for Grace?" I asked suddenly.

The smile disappeared. "They would be looking for her...if they knew she existed."

"Do you know for a fact that they don't?"

Michael's eyes took on a blurry expression, as if he was looking past me, past the cluttered walls of his house, out to the shadowed gullies and caves of Secret Canyon. "Facts are slippery things. But I felt it last night, felt the darkness moving over the city. The lights went out here, but I'm guessing not many people paid it much mind. The power lines in this part of town aren't that reliable, especially in the winter. Whatever they were doing, it didn't feel focused to me. And if they knew about Grace, I have to believe they would be very focused."

I didn't quite breathe a sigh of relief, but I did feel a little of the tension go out of my shoulders. "Well, that's something, I guess. I didn't want to go to Kara with this—she's got enough on her plate right now."

Which was nothing more than the truth. Yes, Grace was an awfully good baby, but even angelic babies cried in the middle of the night and needed their diapers changed and had to be fed regularly.

"Sometimes trying to shield people from things just makes it that much worse when they do find out."

Oh, Michael and his pronouncements. I sort of wished I could just wave off what he'd said, but the truth was that he tended to be right more often than not.

As if in response to my thoughts, my cell phone rang from the depths of my backpack. Usually, I would ignore it, but I hadn't heard a peep out of Jeff all day and was sort of expecting him to call at some point.

I mumbled, "Sorry, Michael," and bent down to retrieve the phone. When I pulled it out of the backpack, though, the number on the display wasn't Jeff's, but Kara's.

Uh-oh.

It could be something totally innocuous, like her asking me to stop at Walgreens on the way home and pick up some diapers. But she had Lance for errands like that—grumble though he might about it—so I kind of doubted that was why she was calling.

For a second, I considered letting the call roll over into voicemail, but I knew that ploy would only work for so long. Cell reception could be kind of spotty around Sedona, especially if the weather was bad. Kara, though, would see right through that excuse, since I'd already used it more times than was probably realistic.

So I touched the little icon on the screen and lifted the phone to my ear. "Hi, Kara."

"'Hi' yourself. So, when exactly were you going to tell me?"

"Tell you what?" Actually, I could figure out from her tone exactly what she was talking about, but I figured I might as well hedge a little, just in case.

"About what happened last night. Jeff said something to Lance..."

Figures.

"...and Lance told me, but you didn't say one word. What were you thinking?"

I was thinking that you were going to get your panties in a bunch...and here you are, proving me right. But of course I knew better than to say that out loud. "Sorry, Kara, but I didn't know for sure that it was actually anything."

"Well, Jeff seems to be of a different opinion."

Jeff, who'd made himself scarce all day. I'd wondered what the heck he'd been up to. I just figured he'd gotten on his computer once he crawled out of bed and found it way more interesting to hash out the latest news in a conspiracy theory chatroom or something rather than hang around at the UFO Depot with me. But obviously, he'd gone blabbing to Lance.

I shrugged, then realized my sister couldn't see me. "That's his opinion. Nothing happened, though.

Things just felt sort of strange. But everything seems to be fine now." *Well, for the next ten days, anyway*....

"I think you should come over."

Getting grilled by my big sister was not high on my list of fun things to do. At the moment, though, neither was going back to my empty apartment and wondering whether they were going to come knocking on my sliding glass door next.

"What about Michael?" I asked, even as he gave me an *et tu, Brute?* look.

"If he's available."

"Okay. See you in a few." I pulled the phone away from my ear and ended the call before she could add anything else. "Looks like I'm getting called on the carpet, Michael. But I'm sure Kara and Lance will be very interested in your solstice theories."

Being Michael, he just shook his head a little. Then he smiled, one of those smiles that seemed enigmatic and rueful at the same time. "Better finish your wine, Kirsten. You may need it."

CHAPTER THREE

WHEN WE GOT TO KARA'S HOUSE—I'D OFFERED Michael a lift, since his ancient El Camino didn't look as if the tires had enough tread to back out of the driveway, let alone go across town with another snowstorm threatening—I saw that both Jeff's van and the Olivers' silver pickup truck were sitting in Kara's driveway. It looked as if she'd called in all the troops, although I thought it was a little early for a full-on council of war.

I only allowed myself a slight head shake as I parked the UFO Night Tours van on the street, since there wasn't any more room in the driveway. Michael got out of the passenger side without a comment, although of course he had to have seen the other vehicles as well, then followed me up the front walk. It still felt sort of strange to go up to the front door, knowing that I didn't live here anymore, that my old bedroom was now irrevocably altered, having finally been made over into a nursery.

But I still had a key, so I unlocked the door and let myself and Michael in. At once, I heard the sound of voices, and smelled the smoke from a wood-burning fire. That was one thing I really missed—of course my apartment didn't have a fireplace.

I saw the gang gathered in the living room: Paul and Persephone on the couch, Jeff in one of the side chairs, Kara standing up and holding Grace, who appeared to be asleep. The one person I didn't spot right away was Lance, but then he emerged from the kitchen with a mug of something for Kara. I noticed then that both of the Olivers had glasses of wine in front of them, although Jeff was drinking a Coke. Of course, Kara couldn't have any wine, not while Grace was still on breast milk, so I guessed Lance had been getting Kara some herbal tea or maybe spiced cider.

"Hey," I called out as Michael and I entered the living room.

Everyone offered up a greeting, although I noticed that Kara was giving me a fairly jaundiced look. Obviously, she still hadn't forgiven me for not telling her about the...whatever it was...last night right when she got home.

"Pepperoni?" asked Lance.

"Um...what?" I guessed I could be forgiven for not getting what he was saying, since the question sort of came from out of left field.

"We thought we'd order pizza," Persephone

explained as she leaned over the coffee table to retrieve her wine glass.

That sounded like a great idea. Much as I wouldn't have minded snagging another glass of wine before the inevitable third degree started, having some ballast to go along with the booze would probably help me last a little longer. "Pepperoni's great," I said. "I'll eat pretty much anything except anchovies."

There was one side chair left, but I figured that should go to Kara, or maybe Michael if she didn't feel like sitting down. I was used to being the one who ended up on the floor, so I lowered myself into a cross-legged position with my back to the fireplace. The heat from the crackling pine logs felt heavenly. I loved the house—it was the only real home I'd ever known—but it could be a little drafty.

"No pineapple," Jeff said darkly, brows lowering, as if he expected me to place an order for Canadian bacon and pineapple the second his back was turned.

Well, "girl" pizza was sort of a secret favorite of mine, but I knew better than to request it in mixed company. So I just scowled back at him and shook my head, as if offended that he'd even suspect me of wanting to eat something like that.

The next few minutes were taken up in placing the phone order and making sure that everybody more or less got what they wanted. But after Lance had taken the phone back to the kitchen and gotten a wine glass for me—Michael apparently had had enough for the evening, and asked only for water— an awkward silence fell.

Everybody was watching me, as if they expected me to go first, but I really wasn't in the mood for that. Jeff had started all this, so he could be the one to talk.

Apparently, he got the point, because after a few more silent seconds passed, he cleared his throat and said, "Well, it seems clear to me that they "—the "they" was accompanied by a shift of Jeff's eyes basically in the direction of Secret Canyon—"are up to something again. Kik—I mean, Kirsten—was acting like it was no big deal, but I could tell she was scared."

I didn't bother to deny it, not with Michael sitting there and watching me. "It was sort of freaky," I admitted, then added, "Michael felt it, too."

At once, everyone's attention shifted to Michael, but of course, he looked imperturbable as always. "Yes. They're active again, asserting themselves. This year, the new moon comes with the solstice. I'm guessing they plan to take advantage of that."

"'The solstice,'" Lance repeated, looking dubious in a way that only Lance could.

"Yes. I began to wonder about that after last night, but Kirsten confirmed it for me today after she told me Agent Jones paid her a visit and told her the same thing."

This time, I was the focus of everyone's stares.

Kara's blue eyes, a shade or two darker than mine, were positively blazing. "What, that MIB came to see you today and you couldn't be bothered to tell me about that, either?"

For some reason, I didn't like her referring to him with that epithet. Oh, sure, we all tossed it around like it was no big deal, but I just kept seeing those blue-gray eyes watching me, remembering the flash of his white teeth against his olive skin. Martin Jones might be a Man in Black, but he was also seriously, seriously hot.

"I wanted to talk to Michael about it first, okay?" I reached for my wine and took my first swallow, which only made Kara look angrier. Hard to say whether she was more irritated by my radio silence or the fact that she was cut off from having a glass of wine for at least another six months.

"Well, we all know about it now," Persephone said in soothing tones. "So, I guess the question is, what are we going to do about it?"

For a minute, no one said anything. Sure, it might have felt better for all of us to get together, to act as if we were being proactive, but I guessed the real truth of it was that everybody probably felt a little rattled. It wasn't as if we could simply arm ourselves and march into Secret Canyon and declare open warfare on the aliens. Whatever they were planning, I guessed it didn't bode well for us humans. Even so, we were sort of ill-equipped to take them on. They had Persephone's number by now, and Grayson was, well, not with us anymore.

I glanced around the group. Jeff was drumming his fingers on his half-empty Coke can, while both

Paul and Persephone looked more than a little worried. Lance had a tense set to his jaw that told me he'd be happy to march out that very moment and hit the base in Secret Canyon with whatever explosives he was currently hiding at the U-Haul storage center at the west end of town. Kara was biting her lip, and kept rubbing Grace's back with her free hand in an unconscious gesture of protection.

And Michael, well, being Michael, he stood there and drank his water quietly as if nothing had ever bothered him and nothing ever would.

"Well, I guess I can try calling Agent Jones," I said. "He gave me his card."

At once, Jeff shook his head. "No way. Bad enough that he's showed up again. We don't need to be dragging the government into this. I mean, we already know some factions were in bed with the aliens before. We can't trust this guy."

If it had been anyone else, I might have suspected Jeff of being a little jealous. But since he didn't trouble himself with such lowly emotions, I knew this was just his usual paranoia talking.

"He told Kara he was on our side," I pointed out, and Jeff gave me a pained glance.

"Well, of course he'd *say* that. Doesn't mean anything."

Lance broke in. "I think I have to agree with Jeff on this. We can't stop this Agent Jones from sniffing around, but that doesn't mean we have to seek him out on purpose. We don't know what he's really here for."

Everyone seemed to be in agreement on this, judging by the nods and little murmurs of assent I heard from the group.

Great. I thought contacting Martin Jones was probably a pretty good idea, and not just because I really, really wanted a good reason to call him. It seemed obvious to me that he knew more than he was letting on, so why not try to bring him on board so I could attempt to pick his brain?

But I knew better than to say anything. That would only get me dog-piled. And if I just happened to call Agent Jones later, maybe for a little advice, well, then, sue me.

After all, better to ask for forgiveness than permission....

The "party" broke up not quite two hours later, after everyone had chewed at the subject for a while but hadn't come up with any real solutions. Vigilance seemed to be the watchword for the day. We all made a pact to report anything strange, even if it was just a case of the heebie-jeebies, and then went our separate ways.

I drove Michael home. Both of us were quiet during the short trip, although he did finally say, just as I brought the van to a stop in front of his driveway, "You're going to contact this Agent Jones anyway." It wasn't a question.

Not looking at him, I replied, "What makes you

say that?"

A flash of teeth in the darkness. "Because I know you."

He got out then, breath puffing in the freezing air as he made his way past the rear end of his El Camino and up the walk to his door. I waited there, made sure he got in okay, before I turned the van around and headed for home.

You know, sometimes it was rough being around people who'd known you since you were three years old.

I didn't have to work the next day, as Kara had gone back to a limited work schedule of two days a week —Tuesdays and Fridays. And though I knew my friend Lindsay was back home for the holidays, taking a break from her "five-year" plan at Arizona State University down in Tempe, somehow I had the feeling that dropping everything and going off to Prescott for a day of shopping and movie-watching or whatever wasn't the best use of my free time.

What exactly I *was* supposed to do with it, I didn't know. I did have that one web design project to work on, but Skye wasn't expecting it until after the first of the year anyway. Besides, it was sort of hard to feel fired up about a long-term venture like that when you had the threat of alien armageddon hanging over your head.

I kept pulling Martin Jones's business card out of

my wallet and staring at it, then putting it back. Really, nothing new had happened, so I didn't have any actual reason to call him. Never mind that I wanted to see him again, wanted to ask him...what? How much he really did know? What, if anything, was the organization he worked for planning?

Well, better that than confessing I really just wanted another peek at those baby blues of his.

Oy.

As I was giving myself a mental kick for being a complete dork, my cell phone rang. I picked it up and looked at the screen.

Jeff.

Okay, so maybe I'd have to settle for muddy hazel rather than baby blue.

"Hey, Jeff."

"Can you meet me at the condo in fifteen?"

"Morning to you, too."

He made a sound of disgust. "No time to bother with that. Can you be here in fifteen?"

Actually, I could, since I'd already showered and dressed and put on some makeup, just in case I decided to say "what the hell" and go shopping with Lindsay after all. "Can I ask why?"

"Don't want to talk about it over the phone. Just come over."

"Okay," I said, figuring that I didn't have anything better to do. Besides, hanging out with Jeff —whatever he had planned—would keep me from obsessing over whether or not to call Martin Jones.

"Fifteen," Jeff warned me, and hung up.

"Asperger's," I muttered as I got up to retrieve my backpack. "That's got to be it."

But I could reflect on Jeff's foibles as I was driving. If he said fifteen minutes, he meant fifteen minutes. I ran the risk of him not being there at all if I shilly-shallied and got there later than I said I would.

It was a beautiful day, clear and cold and bright. I shoved my sunglasses on my nose as I hurried down the steps to the UFO Night Tours van, which looked particularly shabby in the white morning light. Maybe it was time for a new paint job.

Or maybe it's time to buy yourself a real car, I thought as I climbed into the driver's seat and turned the key in the ignition. The engine turned over, but grudgingly, and I wondered if I needed to add a new battery or alternator to that new coat of paint I was contemplating.

To be honest, it wasn't that I couldn't afford a new car. Grandpa had left me a chunk of change, since Kara had gotten the store and the house, and I really hadn't touched that much of it. No, I guessed I could chalk up the whole not buying a car thing to yet another byproduct of my massive commitment issues.

Scowling, I pointed the van up Highway 179 and then swung through the roundabouts so I was heading west, toward Lance's condo. Traffic could get pretty thick around there on a Friday, but it was still early enough that I knew I could make it out to West Sedona well within Jeff's fifteen-minute deadline.

Sure enough, I pulled into the visitor parking lot of the condo complex with almost five minutes to spare. The van was the only vehicle in the parking area; a lot of the condos were owned by people who used them as vacation homes, and most of them wouldn't be arriving until after Christmas.

If there was a Christmas this year, of course.

Okay, that was a little melodramatic, even for me. None of us really knew what the aliens were planning. However, I kind of got the feeling that they'd be much more likely to give the human race a big old lump of coal than candy or toys.

I followed the path back to Lance's condo—it was in the rear of the complex, naturally—and knocked on the door. Jeff opened it at once. He looked annoyed, almost as if he wished I had been a little late so he could give me some crap about it.

But he didn't say anything, just stood aside slightly so I could push past him and go into the living room. I'd been here once or twice before, which was why I didn't need directions, but I'd forgotten how sparse Lance's condo really was. No wonder he'd moved in with Kara so quickly once they'd stopped pussyfooting around their feelings for each other.

The carpet was beige, the walls your typical Navajo white. A black leather couch sat behind a glass and metal coffee table, and a matching entertainment center on the opposite wall held a large TV. The dinette set was pushed up against one wall and had two very uncomfortable-looking straight-backed chairs flanking it. Nowhere was there a single photograph, or piece of art, or even a book. The whole place was even more soulless than a hotel room.

Since Jeff's house back in L.A. was almost equally sterile, I figured he probably felt pretty much at home here. The only evidence that he was even occupying the place was the laptop sitting on the dinette table and a black ceramic mug carefully placed a perfect six inches away.

"Okay, I'm here," I said. "So, what's so important that you couldn't talk on the phone about it?"

"I thought it would be a good idea if we did a little recon."

"Recon? If you think I'm driving back out to Boynton in a van—"

"We're not going to Boynton in the van." He pulled out his phone and glanced at the time. "Come on, we need to get going."

Mystified, but knowing I wasn't going to get any more answers out of him, I followed him through a door off the condo's one short hallway. This led into a cramped single-car garage, currently occupied by Jeff's Astro van.

I squeezed past the rearview mirror and gingerly opened the door, then got in the passenger seat. Jeff backed the van out of the tiny garage with more skill than I had expected, although I winced a little when the mirror looked as if it was going to scrape on the garage door's frame. But then we were out in the alley that ran between two of the condo buildings, and I couldn't help letting out a little sigh of relief.

Stupid, I knew. It wasn't as if we didn't have much bigger things to worry about than a little scraped paint.

We headed east, then turned down Airport Road, taking the winding route up toward the mesa. Jeff's comment about doing some "recon" bubbled up ominously in my thoughts, but even so, I kept hoping that he'd meant something else. Surely he couldn't be *that* crazy, could he?

Apparently, he could. We passed the overlook area, drove past the Sky Ranch Lodge, and pulled into the parking lot designated for the airport or people using the various aerial tourist services— biplane rides, regular plane rides, helicopter rides....

Jeff started to march toward the Sedona Helicopter Adventures building, and I came to an abrupt halt.

"Are you nuts?" I demanded.

He halted, barely looking at me over his shoulder. "What do you mean?"

"I find it hard to believe your short-term memory is so impaired that you forgot about how Lance's friend got himself killed by the aliens because he went snooping where he wasn't supposed to!"

Not even a blink. "Actually, you're referring to my long-term memory, since that happened more than four months ago. Short-term memory is—"

"I don't give a shit what it is! If you think I'm going up in a helicopter after what happened to Brian Henderson—"

"People have been taking helicopter tours all

during those four months, and nothing bad has happened to any of them," Jeff broke in, somehow managing to sound irritated and imperturbable at the same time. "Now, come on. I don't want to be late."

Muttering several choice words not fit for polite company under my breath, I followed him into the office. It was a fairly small room with spectacular aerial shots of Sedona and its environs covering the walls. Behind the desk sat a woman around Kara's age. She wore a pullover with the company logo embroidered on the right side of the chest.

"Makowski. Reservation for eleven," Jeff said without preamble, and she looked a little startled, but then put on a good customer-service smile. I'd worn too many of them myself not to recognize it for what it was.

"Great," she said. "If you and your girlfriend would just sign these forms—" And she pushed a clipboard containing some paperwork toward us, probably stuff protecting the company in the event we did suffer some sort of a fiery crash.

I thought about protesting the "girlfriend" comment and then decided to let it go. Choose your battles and all that.

Surprisingly, Jeff didn't say anything about having to sign the forms, but only added his signature quickly, barely looking at the paperwork. I had a feeling he'd already investigated all that online before he even made the reservation.

So I went ahead and signed as well, and then the gal at the counter asked us to take a seat while she let the pilot know we were here, and that it would just be a few minutes. She went out, and I turned a death stare on Jeff.

"I can't believe you're seriously considering—"

"And I can't believe how much you're overreacting. I would have thought you'd jump at the chance to get some advance intel on these guys."

"If we're sticking to the tourist spots, I'm not sure how that's going to help us," I countered. "We all know it's over in Secret Canyon where everything is happening, and we're not going to get that close."

"Relax," Jeff said, looking bored.

There were few things I hated more than being told to relax, or to chill out. I crossed my arms and stared at an eye-popping shot of Cathedral Rock apparently taken while hovering about a hundred feet above the rock formation's crown. For a second or two, I contemplated simply walking out and making my way down Airport Road to 89A. From there, I could catch a bus back to Lance's condo.

But I knew I'd be even more pissed off if Jeff actually picked up on something and I missed it, so I stayed where I was until a tall man in his forties wearing a leather flight jacket entered the office.

"Hi—I'm Darren Greene, your pilot today."

Jeff and I both stood and mumbled a greeting.

Darren Greene didn't seem too fazed by our lack of enthusiasm. "First time in a helicopter?" he asked.

I shook my head while Jeff nodded, then shot me a look of surprise. I didn't know why my response was such a revelation to him. After all, I'd spent almost my whole life in Sedona, and Grandpa had known all sorts of people who ran the local tourist businesses. I'd had my first helicopter ride when I was only ten years old.

"Okay, then some of this will be old news to you." He went through a quick spiel about safety procedures, told us to make sure we kept our seatbelts and earphones on at all times, then led us to the helicopter.

Even though I'd been up in them three or four times, I didn't know enough about the various types of flying machines to know which kind this one was, except that it had a lot of glass, probably to offer as much unimpeded viewing of the local sights as possible. Jeff and I both got in our seats and belted in, then settled the earphones on our heads.

The pilot got in his own seat and went through his preflight check with unhurried ease. The motors spun up, and even though I knew exactly what it would feel like, I still shivered a little as the vibrations made themselves felt in my bones.

What the hell am I doing? passed through my mind as we rose into the air and hovered above the mesa. I tried to tell myself it was no big deal, that we were just going to do the standard loop over Red Rock Crossing and then out to Boynton—but not close enough to Enchantment Resort to irritate the tourists paying $450 a night for some R&R, and not far enough off one of Boynton's spurs that we'd be getting dangerously close to Secret Canyon. Probably thousands of people had made the same flight in the months since Brian Henderson's death. We weren't doing anything to attract attention, after all.

Right.

My fingers gripped the armrest as we flew west, following the path of Oak Creek. The cottonwoods and sycamores were bare, but the pines were still thick with needles, dark green against the red rock. Here and there, patches of snow glinted in the sunlight. It really was a beautiful day, and I tried to force myself to relax a little.

Through the headphones, I could hear Darren Greene giving a scripted talk that he'd probably repeated a thousand times by now. Since I already knew the landmarks, I only listened with half an ear, feeling myself tense again as we moved away from Oak Creek and to the north, crossing 89A, heading toward Boynton Canyon.

There was nothing here to worry about, of course. The ridge lines were thick with snow, and against the drifts bristled the dark, spiky outlines of pine trees. Beneath us, the red landscape flashed by, with Darren now launching into a short explanation of the area's geology, how the forces of water had eroded the ground to expose the different strata, finally bringing to light the iron-rich earth that made Sedona's landscape so distinctive.

Beside me, Jeff was fiddling with some gadget he had attached to his iPhone. I had no idea what it was, and conversation was mostly impossible, since the only way to communicate was via the microphones attached to our headpieces and anything we said would be heard by the pilot as well. I shot Jeff a quizzical glance, and he shook his head. That could have meant anything from "there's no point in explaining because you won't understand" to "can't talk now, dummy, the pilot will overhear," so I merely lifted my shoulders and turned to look back out the window.

That was when it hit me—a surge of malice so intense, I doubled over in my seat, hands still clenched on the armrests. I let out a gasp, and Jeff glanced over at me, his expression of annoyance morphing quickly into something almost resembling worry.

"What is it?" he asked, apparently forgetting in his concern that anything he said the pilot would hear as well.

I only shook my head, speech deserting me for the moment. It was all I could do to hold on to my seat, to will myself not to pass out as wave after wave of cold hit me. I'd never been in the ocean, had never come close to drowning, and yet that was all I could think of, that the evil emanating from Secret Canyon would fill my mouth and my lungs, drag me down into darkness, suffocate me.

Darren Greene's voice crackled over the headphones. "She all right?"

"Motion sickness," Jeff said hastily. "Maybe we'd better go back."

Even in the depths of my misery, I mentally thanked him for his quick thinking. Because Darren turned the helicopter around almost at once, heading out and away from Boynton, back over West Sedona, back to the mesa where the heliport was located. And as we traveled, I could feel that cold grip on my mind and heart slowly lessening, falling away until I could finally sit up and pull in a real breath, one that went all the way to the bottom of my lungs and reassured me that I hadn't actually drowned in the ocean of evil surrounding Secret Canyon.

Jeff's eyes were filled with questions, but of course, he kept his mouth shut as the helicopter approached the helipad and then landed so gently I could barely feel it. At once, I pulled off my head-phones and set them aside, although I waited until I felt the engines powering down before I undid the seatbelt.

Then Darren Greene leaned back and said, "All clear. You going to be okay, miss?"

I could only nod.

Next to me, Jeff unbuckled his own seatbelt. "She'll live," he said shortly.

I could tell he was more than a little pissed, but whether that was because we hadn't been in the air long enough for him to get a reading on that gizmo he'd been fiddling with, or whether because I'd cut his $200-a-half-hour flight heinously short, I didn't know. All that mattered to me then was getting out of the helicopter, being able to stand on firm ground again.

Maybe sensing my mood, Jeff climbed out and stood aside so I could move past him. Darren Greene got out as well and gave us a puzzled look. He was probably trying to figure out why someone who looked as sick as I did hadn't just thrown up into one of the airsick bags they'd thoughtfully provided in the passenger section of the helicopter.

But now that I was back on *terra firma*, I was more or less okay. Well, okay as a person could be after feeling firsthand how much the aliens hated us, how much they wanted nothing more than our destruction. I gave the pilot a wan smile and headed back to the parking lot, Jeff a pace or two behind me. Even as he walked, he was fiddling with his phone.

"What the hell was that?" he demanded at last, just as I stopped at the passenger door to his van.

"It was *them*," I said, shoving my hands into the pockets of my jacket and wishing that I'd thrown a pair of gloves in my backpack. Some clouds had begun to drift in, blurring the bright day, and the air on top of the mesa had a definite bite to it.

His scowl lessened a bit. "Really?"

"Yeah, really. Can we go? I'm cold."

He shot me a look that seemed to indicate I was being a wimp for someone supposedly used to Sedona's less than balmy winters, but he went ahead and unlocked the door. The interior of the van was blessedly warm from sitting in the sun, even though the temperature outside was probably in the low forties.

Once we were both inside and Jeff had the van moving back down the road to the main highway, he said, "So…what? Are you turning psychic all of a sudden or something?"

"No," I said irritably. "I don't know why it happened. Guess we were just getting too close."

"*I* didn't feel anything," he pointed out.

"Maybe you were just too busy fiddling with that —what the hell *is* that thing on your phone, anyway?"

"Monitoring device. I thought if I got close enough, I might be able to pick up some of their communications."

"With an iPhone."

"The iPhone is just an easy interface."

"So did you?" I asked, glad to shift the focus of the conversation away from me.

"I got something. I don't know if it's a big enough sample to analyze or not. I'll have to download the data I gathered to my laptop."

My friend, the mad genius. Actually, I didn't even know if Jeff was really what you could call a friend. He was…well, he was just Jeff.

"So I guess that'll keep you pretty busy."

"Yes," he said shortly.

Good. Because after this latest encounter, I knew what I had to do. The hell with everyone's concerns about dragging the government into all this. We couldn't face an enemy like this alone. No way.

As soon as I got home, I was placing a call to Martin Jones.

CHAPTER FOUR

I ASKED AGENT JONES TO MEET ME IN THE BAR AT THE Sedona Rouge hotel for two reasons—first off, it would have felt weird to have him come over to my apartment, and secondly, the Rouge was not the sort of place most people I knew would be hanging out. It was very nice, but not really a "locals" kind of place. I figured there we could have some privacy.

He agreed to meet me at five-thirty. As much as I'd wanted a drink after my little incident earlier in the day, I didn't want to give the wrong impression. Bad enough that I had to spend most of the day cooling my heels, waiting until the time I could meet him. It got so bad that I went to a movie alone, something I never did. And at last I sat at the one corner table that was available in the bar, sipping a Perrier with a slice of lime and trying not to look too anxious about scanning the entrance to the lounge every time somebody entered.

My own fault, really—I'd gotten here almost fifteen minutes early. That despite messing with my hair and makeup and changing about three times before I decided on a black riding-style blazer over my skinny jeans and black cowboy boots. Stupid, I knew. This wasn't a date. I doubted Martin Jones gave a rat's ass what I looked like.

He entered finally—okay, exactly on time—paused for a moment to survey the tables in the bar and their occupants, then spotted me and headed straight for the corner where I was lurking. Of course, he looked elegant as always, this time with a black wool scarf knotted around his throat in addition to the heavy black overcoat, making me glad that I'd pitched my usual long-sleeved T-shirts or baggy sweaters in favor of something a little more presentable.

"Kirsten," he said as he sat down across from me.

Having him this close was a little unnerving, and it probably didn't help that my nerves were still rattled from the helicopter flight. "Hi, Agent Jones," I responded, wondering if he would ask me to call him by his first name.

Of course, he didn't. "You sounded upset on the phone."

"Did I? Here I thought I was being all cool and collected."

One eyebrow went up, but he didn't have a chance to reply, since a waiter appeared at that moment and asked what he'd like to drink. He shot a quick glance at my mineral water and said, "Perrier is fine."

"No drinking on the job?" I asked after the waiter had left.

"It's generally frowned on." He unwrapped the scarf from his throat and unbuttoned his overcoat, but made no move to take it off. "Something happened today, didn't it?"

I'd been incredibly vague on the phone. Maybe just more of Jeff's paranoia rubbing off on me, but I hadn't wanted to go into any details until Agent Jones and I could talk in person. I nodded, and sipped at my Perrier so I wouldn't have to meet his eyes.

He sat there, apparently thinking. Or it could be that he was only waiting for the waiter to come back before he said anything. Luckily, our waiter was pretty fast, and returned and deposited the Perrier on our table before the silence could get too awful. Then Agent Jones said, not touching the mineral water, "Tell me about it."

So I went into the whole story, explaining how Jeff wanted to go out in the helicopter even though I thought it was a spectacularly bad idea, and how the trip was cut short when I reacted so strongly to the aliens' presence as we went deeper into Boynton Canyon.

Martin Jones was quiet during this entire recitation, although he did pick up his Perrier and take a drink before he said anything. "This feeling—is it similar to the sensation you experienced the night before last?"

I really didn't want to think about it too closely, but I also knew that now was not the time to be squeamish. Folding my hands in my lap, I replied, "It was colder. Much colder. But sort of the same in that I felt as if I couldn't breathe, as if there was some sort of pressure being exerted on my lungs. That wasn't the worst of it, though."

He waited. It was dim enough in the bar that I couldn't see his eye color as clearly, although I noticed for the first time how heavy his eyelashes were, thick and dark like his hair.

Since there wasn't any way to say it without sounding like a kook, I decided to just go for it. "The worst was the sensation of malice, of evil. You know how some people say they can feel it when they walk into a house where something terrible has happened? Well, I never claimed to have any abilities like that, but I'm guessing this was sort of the same. Except worse, because this didn't feel like it was about something that *had* happened—it felt like something that was *about* to happen."

For a minute, he didn't say anything. Then, finally, "You're right. It is about something that's going to happen...unless you stop it."

"Unless *I* stop it?" I'd intended the retort to come out as an indignant rebuttal, but somehow it turned into more of an undignified squeak. Clearing my throat, I added, "What the heck am *I* supposed to do? I called you because I needed your help."

"Against the wishes of your friends and family, no doubt."

"Well, yes, but—" I stopped short. "How would you know that?"

"I haven't bugged your sister's house, if that's what you're worried about." His tone was amused. "I'd say it's a fairly predictable reaction from a group of people who tend to operate on the fringes. Calling a government agent isn't exactly their style, so to speak."

That was more than true. I could only imagine Kara's reaction when she found out I'd had a clandestine meeting with a Man in Black. Good thing I'd been living on my own for more than a year. Otherwise, she probably would have been sorely tempted to kick me out.

"Okay, yeah," I admitted. "But this sort of thing is way over my head. I think it's way over everybody's heads. Obviously, your organization has been monitoring the situation, or you wouldn't be here. So some help would be appreciated, you know?"

Something about this little speech seemed to make Agent Jones uncomfortable. He looked away, past the half-empty lounge area, to the wide windows that showed nothing beyond utter blackness. Clouds had gathered all afternoon and threatened snow once again, but so far, the weather had held. After an awkward pause, he said, "I'm afraid I'm only here in an observational capacity."

"You're *what*?" I couldn't believe what I was hearing.

"Yes. I'm under strict orders not to get directly involved."

"So, what, coming into the UFO Depot and stirring the pot with me wasn't getting directly involved?"

Even in the dim light, I could see the tensing of his jawline. "No, that still falls in the area of information gathering."

"And so even though you know the aliens are planning something, have a pretty good idea even of *when* they're planning to do it, you're still not going to do anything to help us?"

"I'm afraid it's not as simple as that—"

"It seems pretty simple to me," I retorted, and pushed my Perrier away from me. My heart was pounding in fury. No way I was going to sit there and listen to his excuses. So much for all my hopes that he'd rustle up the MIB equivalent of a posse and ride into town to kick some alien ass. "Enjoy your *observations*, Agent Jones. I guess some of us have real work to do."

And I pushed my chair back and stood, grabbing for my backpack at the same time. Luckily, I was able to find my wallet without too much scrabbling, and I found a ten and threw it on the table even as Martin Jones was rising from his own seat.

"Kirsten—"

I ignored him and marched out. That was something I'd never done before—turn my back on a person and walk away. I halfway expected him to get up and follow me, but he didn't. A cold wind hit me the second I stepped outside, but I knew that wasn't the real reason I was shaking. No, that had everything to do with anger.

Now we were really on our own.

Saturday I was stuck back at the UFO Depot, and it was just busy enough that I didn't have much of a chance to work on my own projects, or even contemplate the alien threat hanging over our heads. Eight days and counting.

My cell phone rang, and I picked it up with almost pathetic haste. I'd been thinking—hoping, actually—that Martin Jones might have had time to rethink his policy of *laissez-faire* and maybe would call me to patch things up. But no. It was my friend Lindsey.

I almost didn't answer, but a batch of customers had just left, and I had the store to myself for the moment. Besides, if she was calling with another offer of shopping or something, I might as well take her up on it. Sitting around and brooding was only going to make me crabby.

"Hey, Miss Antisocial," she said as soon as I swiped the screen to accept the call.

"That's me," I replied. I didn't even have the energy to throw a similar epithet back at her. "What's up?"

"What's up is that my parents went down to Scottsdale for the weekend, so it's party time over here tonight."

A party was probably the last thing I needed. "I don't know, Linds...."

"Oh, come *on*. Stop being such a drone. I mean, I guess you have to help out at the store, but it closes at five, so don't use that excuse with me."

She was right—the store did close hours earlier than any party she'd be having would start, and on Sundays, we didn't even open until noon. It wasn't as if I wouldn't have time to sleep off whatever partying I'd done the night before.

"And Dave Wallace has already offered to be the DD and chauffeur people around, so you still have no excuse." She hesitated, then added, "And you can bring that friend of yours from L.A. if you want."

"Jeff?" I said, and gave a small laugh. "Jeff is *so* not the party type. I can only imagine his reaction if I tried to drag him to a kegger."

"It's not a kegger. Well, okay, we're going to have a keg, but you know."

I did. Lindsey's parties were sort of legendary.

And that decided it. I could sit in my apartment, alone on a Saturday night, and jump at every creak and rattle, or I could go out and try to be a real twenty-three-year-old. "Okay," I said.

"Awesome. Dave will pick you up a little before eight, okay?"

"Got it."

"See ya then."

She ended the call then, and I dropped the phone back into my backpack, wondering if I'd just agreed to something really, really stupid.

Lindsey's parents lived in the Village of Oak Creek, about five miles south from my apartment. I was the last person Dave picked up, since he'd started out in West Sedona and sort of wound his way down from there. Five passengers besides me were squished into his SUV. I knew a couple of them since we'd gone to high school together, but the others were strangers, obviously friends of friends or people Lindsey had met after we graduated.

They talked about sports or movies or concerts they'd gone to, while I sat shoved into a corner of the back seat and began to feel kind of like an alien myself. It seemed as if they didn't have a care in the world, weren't worried about anything in particular beyond their favorite team not making it to the play-offs or whatever. Whereas I....

Well, I had just a little bit more on my mind.

We pulled up into the driveway; obviously Lindsey had made sure no one would take that coveted spot, since Dave was doing her a favor by ferrying people around. There were already cars all up and down the street, and I guessed the neighbors probably weren't too thrilled about the influx of vehicles. Oak Creek was even quieter than Sedona proper.

But the house itself was spectacular, built on multiple levels and with the property backing up to U.S. Forest Service lands, so there wasn't anybody behind it. Lindsay's father was a dentist and her mother a real estate agent, so they did pretty well for themselves.

Music pounded around me as I entered the house a few paces behind the rest of my fellow passengers. Some auto-tuned crap, and I winced. Lindsey and I had never shared the same taste in music. Of course, that made her call me an old lady for liking good old-fashioned rock and roll, but whatever. I told her she was the one with a hearing problem if she actually liked that stuff, but she just laughed it off. Nothing seemed to bother Lindsey too much.

She spotted me from across the living room. "Keeks!" she yelled, strident enough to cut through the quasi-hip hop that was blasting through the house's built-in Bose speakers, and ran over. I noticed she wasn't so drunk yet that she didn't carefully hold on to her cup of beer as she threaded her way through the crowd.

"Hey, Linds," I said, not bothering to correct her on the whole Kirsten/Kiki thing. It wasn't worth the effort.

"You look fab!" she burbled. "So glad you made the effort." She looked past me and blinked. "No date?"

"I told you, Jeff is not the party type."

"Shame on you for having such an antisocial boyfriend."

"He's not my boyfriend."

She blinked again. "Seriously?"

"Seriously."

After pondering that response for a second or two, she grinned. "Well, then, we have got to get you hooked up. What's wrong with the boys in this town? I would've thought they'd be all over you after you and Brad broke up."

I shrugged, wishing she hadn't brought up Brad. Not that I was mooning over losing a love for the ages or anything, but it was actually the first time I'd been the dumpee and not the dumper, and the memory still smarted. Then again, Brad and I had been going out for almost four months when we split. It was coming time for us to break up, since I'd never been with anyone longer than that. Just because Brad was seriously freaked after the whole Secret Canyon alien incident with Persephone and Paul and had taken a powder shortly afterward didn't mean he'd ended anything serious.

Serious was not something I allowed in my relationships.

Neither was hooking up. I'd lost my virginity my senior year of high school because it seemed the thing to do, but the experience hadn't been all that great. It was easy enough after that to have a series of short-term relationships, always breaking it off before things got physical. At least that way no one could ever accuse me of being like my mother....

"No hook-ups," I said sternly. "I'm here because I wanted to see you, and I thought it would be fun to get out. I'm not looking for a boyfriend."

She shot me a disbelieving look. "Come on—it's been what, more than six months since you and Brad broke up? Don't you think that's kind of a long dry spell?"

Well, yes, it was, but I didn't see anything appealing about any of the guys around me, most of whom were already in various stages of drunkenness despite it being barely eight-thirty.

Maybe it's because you've decided you have a thing for older men, my mind jeered at me, and I clamped down on that thought. He might be gorgeous, but Martin Jones was definitely on my shit list right now.

"Why don't we just start with a drink?" I suggested. "Anything besides beer?"

Another one of those incredulous stares. "Like you have to ask. I even got some wine for you, old lady."

"Sign me up for AARP."

Lindsay laughed then and led me over the dining room table, which was covered with bottles of just about every kind of booze known to mankind, including some white wine in a small cooler on ice, and a couple of bottles of red, too. I chose the white just because I'd feel less guilty about spilling it on one of her parents' prized Navajo rugs if someone jostled me or bumped into me.

After that, she sort of abandoned me to go socialize with other people, which I totally understood. She was the hostess, after all. I talked with some acquaintances from high school—Tony Lopez, Angela McGuire. They'd both gone away to college, too, but were back for the holidays. Our conversation was kind of awkward, because I could tell both of them felt sort of sorry for me. I hadn't gone to college. I was still here in Sedona, working at a store. It was clear they thought I'd done nothing with my life.

And I couldn't say anything about what was really going on, what I was really involved in, because they'd only think I was crazy. I also didn't really care about not going to college; Kara had made me apply, and I'd gotten in to both NAU and the University of Arizona campus in Tucson. In the end, though, I didn't see the point. I loved Sedona. I didn't want to leave, and what I wanted to do—play with computers—I could do on my own, and actually was. I had my own business, while my two conversation companions were still students. But I really didn't feel like explaining any of that at the moment.

Angela and Tony eventually drifted off, and I turned around, thinking I'd earned a refill on my wine after that conversation. My gaze fell on about the last person I wanted to see.

Brad.

Our eyes met, and I waited for him to look away first. I hoped he'd just melt back into the crowd and lose himself again, but no, that wasn't Brad's style.

He sent a fake smile at me and walked in my direction, and I knew I'd have to stand there and pretend to have a polite conversation with him.

"Hi, Kiki."

"Hey, Brad." I took a sip of wine and wished I hadn't drunk so much of it while I was talking with Tony and Angela. I had less than an inch left in the bottom of my cup.

"So what have you been up to?"

I shrugged. "The usual. You?"

"I got a job working at Off-Road Adventures."

Well, that was one thing Brad had going for him —he was an excellent driver. And, if I tried to be objective about it, he was cute in a sort of sandy, all-American-boy kind of way. He probably got great tips from the female tourists.

"Congratulations," I said, and wished I could find a way to gracefully get the hell away from him.

"Look, Kiki, things got weird, and—"

"Yeah, I get it," I cut in. "Things were very weird. I'm not blaming you for anything."

"No?" he said, looking relieved. "Because I know you were pissed at me, and—"

"It's all right. Really. But I don't see any need to rehash ancient history. So see you around, Brad." And I pushed past him, intent on refilling my drink if it was the last thing I did.

He stared after me, astonishment clear in his expression, but at least he didn't try to follow me.

I wasn't about to tell him that the real reason I was pissed off at him wasn't because he'd dumped me instead of the other way around. Rather, it was because I'd heard through the grapevine that he'd only put up with my UFO fascination for so long because he was determined to get into my pants, no matter what it took. "Thaw out the ice queen" was the charming way he'd put it, actually.

Screw that. I wasn't an ice queen. I was just…selective.

Unlike my mother.

The evening pretty much went downhill after that. I drank way too much, and Dave Wallace eventually drove me and a similarly inebriated group of passengers home at around one o'clock in the morning. Five miles wasn't enough to really give me time to sober up, but I did feel a little better the farther away I got from Lindsey's house. The freezing air that hit my face as I got out of Dave's SUV helped somewhat, too.

But then I realized I was really hungry, and I didn't have that much to eat in my apartment. The Circle K seemed like the perfect solution. I could go down, grab a hot dog and some chips, maybe get a Coke, even though I normally didn't drink much soda. Sounded like a plan.

I tucked my scarf in more closely around my throat and headed down to the convenience store, walking carefully, since my boots had almost three-inch heels and it was a downward slope from my apartment complex. Of course, there was no one else in the store. But I knew Mike, the clerk, and he nodded at me as I made my selections and went to check out.

"Midnight munchies, huh?" he said as he rang up my purchases, giving my somewhat bleary state a knowing grin.

"Something like that, yeah." I knew I didn't have to explain myself. Mike had probably seen plenty of people stagger in here looking for something to soak up the booze.

I took my bag and went outside, trudging around the corner of the store into the shadowy side of the building. The wind had picked up, finding its way past the scarf I'd tucked into my wool coat, blowing my loose hair and sending it flapping around my face, obscuring my vision. I reached up to push the offending strands away.

When I lowered my hand, I saw a figure standing in front of me. I blinked, vague alarm bells going off in my mind behind that fourth glass of wine I'd drunk. But then I realized it was just a man, bundled like me in a heavy coat, probably in search of another six-pack or maybe a bag of chips.

I sort of gave him a nod but kept moving forward. Sedona was a small town, and a safe one. That didn't mean I was about to engage a stranger in conversation at one o'clock in the morning.

But instead of returning my nod and heading down to the Circle K's front door, the stranger lunged for me, hands outstretched. Without really thinking, I brought my knee up, thinking I could get him in the groin and run before he had time to recover.

Great plan. Too bad it didn't work.

I knew I connected—I could almost feel the sickening thud of my knee into his nuts, but I might as well have given him a hangnail for all the good it did me. Even as I kneed him, his hands were up and around my throat.

No time to think. Of its own volition, my right hand raised the bag of "munchies" and smashed it against his temple. Now, okay, a hot dog wasn't that great a weapon, but a can of Coke smashing into a person's head generally should at least slow them down.

Not in this case. Those icy fingers continued to clamp down on my neck, and white spots began to flare in my field of vision, even as I ripped at his hands with my fingernails, pulled at fingers that might as well have been made of iron for all the difference my struggles made. I stared at my assailant, gasping, stared at the ordinary features, the too-blank eyes. My brain couldn't seem to form a coherent thought. I still tore at him, but weakly. I knew my oxygen-starved brain was going to shut down at any second.

Murdered behind a Circle K. That was a hell of a way to go out.

A flash of blinding blue-white light flared from nowhere, striking my attacker squarely in the side of the head. At once, he let go, and I doubled over, gasping, choking, as the light flared again and the murderous stranger slumped motionless to the gravelly asphalt.

Someone was bending over me. A voice I half recognized said, "It's all right. I've got you."

And strong arms were suddenly around me, lifting me and carrying me away. I blinked my streaming eyes and looked up into Martin Jones's face. "What—?"

"Not here."

My throat felt scraped and raw, although the alcoholic haze seemed to be gone. Funny what a murder attempt and a rush of adrenaline could do to make four hours of drinking disappear just like that.

Maybe I should have attempted to get out of his arms, but at the moment, I didn't know whether my legs would even hold me up. He seemed to know exactly where he was going, taking me across my apartment complex's parking lot and up the stairs to my apartment. A pause at the front door, and I realized he'd somehow managed to scoop up my purse as well.

He handed it to me. "Keys?"

I dug them out with shaking fingers and handed them over with the key to the deadlock extended so he'd know which one to use. Still holding me, he unlocked the door and carried me inside, then set me down on the couch. After that, he moved away, going to the front window and twitching the curtains aside just for a second, as if to make sure no one had followed us.

My hands were still shaking. I pulled off my gloves and then shoved my icy fingers between my legs and the sofa cushions, trying to restore some of their warmth. Martin Jones turned to face me, brows slightly lowered.

I stared up at him. There were roughly a million questions rushing through my mind, and I blurted out the first one that rose to the surface.

"What the hell was *that*?"

CHAPTER FIVE

HE DIDN'T ANSWER AT FIRST. HE WATCHED ME, FACE almost impassive, although I thought I saw a muscle twitch in his cheek, as if he was trying very hard not to betray any emotion. Finally, he asked, "Are you okay?"

"I'm fine," I said, although my voice didn't even sound like mine, raspy and rough, more like someone who'd spent the last twenty-five years smoking unfiltered Lucky Strikes and drinking Jack. I could almost feel those heavy fingers circling my throat, see those blank eyes staring into mine. Giving a shaky laugh, I added, "Strange things are afoot at the Circle K."

Something that might have been the beginnings of a smile twitched at one corner of his mouth. Wow, gorgeous and familiar with '80s cult movies? I hadn't really expected a Man in Black to recognize a quote from *Bill and Ted's Excellent Adventure*.

He didn't reply right away, however. In silence, he went to the kitchen, extracted a glass from the cupboard, and poured me a glass of water. He handed it to me. "What were you doing out there alone?"

"I was getting a frigging hot dog, for God's sake. That a crime?" Stupid as it might have been, I experienced a pang at the loss of my little bag of goodies. Attack or no, I was still hungry.

A shadow passed over his face. "No, but I would have thought you'd be more careful...considering."

That was rich. Here I get attacked by some methed-up maniac behind a convenience store, and yet somehow it's my fault. Talk about victim blaming. I drank some of the water, then cleared my throat. "Well, maybe I wanted to spend my Saturday night feeling like a normal human being. And if that includes a late night run to the Circle K, well, so what?"

"But you're not—" he began, and then seemed to check himself, as if he had been about to say something he realized I shouldn't be hearing.

"I'm not what?"

"You're not being careful."

"Okay, I think you established that already." I sipped the water, then reached up to feel my throat and winced. Good thing it was scarf season, because I had a feeling I was going to be covering up some nasty bruises for the next couple of days. "What you didn't do was answer my question."

He hesitated, then shook his head slightly and

pulled his own scarf from around his neck before sitting down in my one armchair. "Could you be more specific?"

Oh, for Chrissake—"All right. Why did that man attack me? What was that light you shot him with? And, for that matter, how did you happen to be there in the first place? Not that I'm not grateful for the rescue and all, but seriously—have you been following me or something?"

Incongruously, he smiled. "Okay, that's pretty specific. To answer your last question first, yes, I have been...keeping track of you."

""Cause that's not creepy or anything."

"It's my assignment."

"Me?" I demanded incredulously. "Why the hell would you be assigned to follow me? I'm nobody."

His smile disappeared as quickly as it had come. "Don't be so sure about that."

I had a feeling that being important wasn't all it was cracked up to be, especially if said importance included lunatic strangers attacking you in the middle of the night. "So who was that man? And is he...?" I let the sentence trail off. I didn't really want to utter the word "dead." That would make the situation seem even worse than it already was.

"No, he's not," Martin Jones said quickly. "He was only stunned, the thing that was controlling him knocked out of his system. He'll wake up and won't remember anything, except that he left the house to get a six-pack of beer and ended up there."

This explanation didn't have the reassuring effect

Agent Jones apparently expected it to. "The *thing* that was controlling him?" I demanded. "He wasn't on drugs?"

"No." The blue eyes caught mine and held, and something in them made a shiver run down my spine, even though I'd left the heat on in the apartment while I was gone and it was cozy enough in there. "I think you know what took hold of his mind."

I broke away from that gaze and looked past him, out in a general westerly direction. Toward Secret Canyon.

Toward the aliens.

"Will they try again?" The question was almost painful to ask, but I needed to know if I had to be on guard against anyone in the immediate vicinity who looked at all spacey.

"Not in that way," he replied immediately. "Now they know you'll be looking for them. It was a gamble. They'd hoped to catch you alone and unprotected."

And thank God Agent Jones had been lurking in the background. I didn't even want to think about what would have happened if he hadn't been there. My voice dropped to almost a whisper, and it wasn't just because of the throttling I'd suffered a few minutes earlier. "But *why* do the aliens want me dead?"

His fingers clenched on the knees of his dark pants. "I can't tell you that."

Could you be insanely grateful to someone and

still want to throttle them at the same time? "Oh, you can't? Why the hell not?"

"Because I'm not the person who should be telling you."

This conversation was not going at all the way I had expected it to. For some reason, I could still feel his arms as they'd held me, carried me away from danger, feel the rough wool of his overcoat as it scraped against my cheek. And that was just stupid, because he'd only been doing his job. Watching me. Defending me if necessary.

But...why?

I pulled my hands out from where I'd been trying to warm them up under my legs and crossed my arms over my chest. At that point, I realized I was still wearing my overcoat, and that I was actually starting to feel overheated now that I was back inside. So I unbuttoned my coat and pulled the scarf from around my neck, trying not to wince as I did so. Alien-possessed or not, that bastard had some strong fingers.

"Okay," I said, since Martin Jones seemed content to watch me in silence, waiting until I responded. "I'll bite. Exactly who *should* I be asking about why the aliens want me dead?"

"Your mother."

At that reply, I stared back at him, a frown digging itself into my forehead. My mother? Was this some sort of sick joke?

I said, "I have a feeling you know that I'm not exactly on speaking terms with my mother."

"Yes."

"And so why do you think I'd suddenly get the urge to talk to a woman who ditched me when I was only three years old?"

"Because if you don't, the aliens will win."

Okay, he must have lost his mind. It was the only explanation for a pronouncement like that. "You're joking, right? What the hell does Marybeth Swenson have to do with the aliens?"

Face impassive, he said, "You have to talk to her. In person. Once you hear what she has to say, you'll know why she's the only person who could provide that information."

Something in his tone told me he wasn't going to give me any more than that. My thoughts roiled. Marybeth Swenson had gone out for cigarettes twenty years ago, and I hadn't seen her since. And now I was supposed to go waltzing off and drop in on her—in Taos, I recalled. At least, that's where Agent Jones had told Kara our mother was hanging out these days.

"And what about this whole 'time is running out' thing?" I demanded. "You do realize that it's going to take me two whole days just to drive to Taos and back?"

"Yes," he replied, expressionless. "That's why you need to leave first thing in the morning."

First thing in the morning. Now it was almost two, and my head had begun to pound, although whether that was from the adrenaline or the alcohol wearing off, I couldn't say. I supposed it really didn't matter.

For a minute or two, I just sat there, wondering what the hell was really going on, and if there was any way to get out of it. I didn't want to drive to Taos. I didn't want to see my mother—not that I'd probably even recognize her after all this time. What I really wanted to do was go to bed and sleep for about a hundred hours.

But then I thought of Persephone, who had left behind everything she knew to drive to Sedona to rescue the man she loved, and Kara, who'd faced her fears and decided to keep a half-alien's baby, despite not knowing what bearing such a child could do to her. Was I going to drop the ball now just because I was carrying twenty years' worth of resentment toward my mother?

"First thing tomorrow," I said wearily, and stood. "This whole thing is crazy. So do you at least have an address for her, or do I have to start hacking the New Mexico motor vehicle department's database?"

In silence, he reached into his breast pocket and pulled out a business card, then laid it down on the coffee table. "Thank you," he said quietly and went out, closing the door behind him. I didn't hear his footsteps on the stairs. Maybe he was taking up guard position outside my door.

I bent to pick up the business card. It was heavy recycled paper, with a stylized depiction of clouds and birds in a soft gray-blue shade. It read, "Skyheart Designs, Marybeth Swenson-Engle." Beneath that was an address on Bent Street in Taos. I didn't recognize it, of course, since I'd never been to New Mexico, despite it bordering my home state.

Swenson-Engle. So had she gotten married at some point?

I guessed I'd find out more soon enough.

Five hours of sleep was not really enough to make me functional, especially after the night I'd had, but I didn't have much choice. I rolled out of bed at a little past seven, took a long, hot shower, and nuked two breakfast burritos, hoping that I could make up my energy deficit in calories if I couldn't do so with actual sleep.

A few minutes on the computer, and I had a hotel room booked at the Taos Inn. I didn't know anything about it except it was the first place that popped up when I searched on Yelp for hotels in Taos, and luckily they'd had a cancellation and were able to accommodate me. Okay, so I wouldn't be sleeping in my car...which led to my second problem. Transportation.

I knew there was no way the UFO Night Tours van was going to make it all the way to northern New Mexico, especially in the winter. Right then, my bias against buying a new car was really biting me in the ass. True, Lance had a four-wheel-drive Jeep, but if I asked to borrow it, then all the questions would start, and I just couldn't face the third degree right now. The only way I was going to make this work was if I kept at it logically, mechanically, not thinking about the inevitable confrontation at the end of my 500-mile road trip.

Okay, so Lance's Jeep was out of the question, but I'd just done the Sunrise Jeep Rental's website overhaul a couple of months ago, and I thought I might be able to wheedle a vehicle out of Henry, the owner. True, his rentals were mainly intended for tourists going off-roading in Sedona's environs, but he liked me and knew I was reliable. It seemed my best chance. Otherwise, I'd have to see if Enterprise had a truck I could rent, which didn't seem as optimal as a Jeep.

I packed enough for a three-day trip. Even if I didn't encounter any problems on the road, it was still going to take me more than seven hours to drive to Taos, and it would be too late to try seeing my mother by the time I got there. That card was for a place of business, not a house, and if Taos was anything like Sedona, the sidewalks would be rolled up way before I got there around six.

After throwing my suitcase in the passenger seat of the van and making sure my apartment was securely locked up, I headed over to Sunrise Jeep Rentals. It was barely nine in the morning, early for a Sunday in a tourist town, but I knew Henry would be there. A lot of people liked to get an early start for their off-roading ventures, and he opened at eight seven days a week.

As I drove, I called Michael. Normally, I would

never have phoned someone at such an ungodly hour on the weekend. However, Michael was always up with the sun, so I guessed I wouldn't be even close to waking him up. And I had to have someone watch the store while I was gone, since Kara wasn't supposed to be back in until Tuesday. If I was lucky, Michael wouldn't ask too many questions.

He answered on the second ring, and I said, my tone falsely bright, "Hey, Michael. Something's come up, and I need to go out of town for a few days. Do you mind watching the store today and tomorrow?"

Being Michael, he saw right through me, even on the phone. "What's happened?"

"I can't talk about it right now. Just please, Michael—can you do this for me?"

A long pause, and then I could almost see him nod. "It's time for your vision quest. This is necessary, so...yes, I'll come in to the shop for you."

I wasn't about to explain that I only intended to drive to Taos, not wander around in the desert hopped up on peyote and hoping that my spirit animal would come visit me. The important thing was that he had said yes. "Great. We don't open until noon today, so you have plenty of time."

Another one of those pauses. "One thing, Kirsten."

"Yes?" I asked, stopping at a red light. Sunrise Jeep Tours was only a few blocks away now, and I hoped the worry and impatience hadn't seeped into my voice.

"When the truth comes to you, don't turn away from it."

"Um...okay."

He chuckled. "You're dubious. That's all right. Just be open to it when the time comes."

"Okay, Michael, I will." I saw Sunrise Jeep coming up on my left and added, "I have to go, but thanks again."

He didn't say "you're welcome," only, "Be mindful," before he hung up.

Damn straight I'd be mindful. I was about to drive almost five hundred miles in the winter in an unfamiliar vehicle, just because an agent from a clandestine government organization had told me to.

Sigh.

Henry dug his thumbs into his belt loops and rocked back on the heels of his hiking boots as he watched me with too-bright blue eyes. I tried not to shift my weight from one foot to the other like a grade-school student caught wandering the halls when she should have been in class.

"Borrow a Jeep," he said.

I nodded.

"So you can drive to Taos, New Mexico, in December."

"Yes."

The wrinkles around those keen eyes deepened a

little. "Flagstaff's a lot closer if you're planning on skiing."

"No, it's not that." I stopped there, not wanting to say any more than I had to. Henry was certainly no blabbermouth, but word did tend to get around in Sedona. "Just some...personal business. I'll be back no later than Tuesday afternoon. Promise."

He didn't reply at once, but just looked me up and down. I'd made sure before I left the house that my multicolored wool scarf was tucked securely into the collar of my coat, and although I usually didn't wear that much makeup, I'd dotted some concealer under my eyes, since the shadows there betrayed my rough night.

Then he let out a little sigh, unhooked his thumbs from his belt, and said, "Well, yeah, all right. S'pretty slow right now. Not like I don't have vehicles to spare." His eyes narrowed. "You ever drive a 4x4?"

"Sure," I responded at once. "One of my boyfriends had one." I didn't bother to add that the aforementioned boyfriend had been the one from my senior year of high school, and that I hadn't driven a vehicle with four-wheel drive since then. Still, it wasn't that hard, really. With the way newer vehicles worked, you basically kept the four-wheel drive in "auto" and didn't switch over to one of the other options —snow, rock, mud—unless things got really hairy. And it wasn't like I planned to go off-road, was only worried about driving in bad weather on unfamiliar highways.

"Uh-huh." Henry gestured me over to the

counter. "Go ahead and fill out the paperwork, since I'll still need your driver's license and insurance information. Just don't worry about the payment info."

"Thanks, Henry—" I began, but he waved me off.

"Go on, fill out the paperwork. I'll go over your Jeep to make sure everything's okay with it." He shook his head and added, "You can park your van in the back. I figure you'll need someplace to leave it."

I opened my mouth to say thank you again, but he was already out the door. Besides, he was doing me an enormous favor. A couple of meager "thanks" weren't really adequate compensation, but they'd have to do for now until I could think of an appropriate way to show my gratitude.

A half-hour later, I was on the road, heading up 89A through Oak Creek Canyon to pick up Interstate 40 so I could head due east into New Mexico. That route could be a little dicey, since it got closed down more often than I-17 did, thanks to the rock slides that often happened during a bad storm. But it hadn't snowed overnight after all, and today the sky was simply stunning, huge white clouds and deep, deep blue competing for space as the sun slipped in and out, creating fast-moving shadows along the ground.

I didn't have a lot of company on the road. It was still fairly early—not even ten yet—and the tourists tended to get scared off when they saw the huge blinking signs on the interstate warning of possible closures on the winding canyon route. It was safer to just go down Interstate 17, even if it did send you out of your way.

And that Jeep—well, let's just say I was seriously reconsidering my "no new cars" policy, because driving that new Rubicon was like piloting a Lear jet after spending years at the controls of a Cessna. Frankly, I was afraid to touch half the stuff because I didn't know exactly what it could do, but at least the USB port for my iPhone was easy enough to locate. Henry had given me a quickie demo of the four-wheel-drive system.

"Probably won't need to do anything except stay in 'auto,' if all you're worried about is snowy roads," he'd told me, and I'd assured him that I didn't plan to go off-road with it.

He'd seemed satisfied by my reply, and I'd driven off the Sunrise Jeep lot going about five miles an hour under the speed limit, just because I was still trying to figure out how everything worked. As I went through town I gradually gained some confidence, but I was still a little over-awed by the vehicle...and humbled.

Henry hadn't just loaned me a Jeep—he'd loaned me the best vehicle on his lot. I'd known better than to protest, though, because he probably would have said something like, "Better you than some damn-fool tourist who's going to get it stuck in a riverbed because he doesn't know what he's doing." The guy definitely had a unique viewpoint about tourists, considering they provided his livelihood.

Now, though, I followed the switchbacks on 89A as they led me up out of the canyon. Then I was on I40, heading steadily eastward, listening to my mega Foo Fighters playlist on the Jeep's awesome sound system and watching the shifting light and shadow on the ground. There were patches of snow off to either side of the highway, but they gradually disappeared as the road sloped downward and the temperature warmed into the upper forties. Traffic was still fairly light, even on the interstate.

And that was the problem, because with this flawless vehicle taking me east—and not much else to concentrate on—I couldn't help circling around to where I was going. Who I was going to see.

Marybeth Swenson.

In my mind, she was never "Mom." Every once in a while, Kara would slip up and refer to her that way, but I always thought of her as "my mother"…when I thought of her at all. I'd tried pretty hard to excise her from my life. After all, she'd done the same thing to me.

I didn't even remember what she really looked like in person, although Grandpa had kept a picture of her in his dresser drawer until the day he died. When I was little, I'd sneak in and pull it out every once in a while, take a look at it. Marybeth was very beautiful, or at least she had been back then. Actually, the person she really reminded me of was that actress who was murdered by the Manson Family back in the '60s. Sharon Tate, that was her name. No wonder my mother seemed to have no problem finding male companionship.

Grandpa had never made excuses for her behavior, although I'd heard him arguing with Grandma a few times about her. I guess ol' Marybeth really went off the rails when her older brother, the uncle I'd never met because he was gone way before I came on the scene, died in the last year of fighting in Vietnam. She'd apparently settled down enough to get married for a few years and have Kara, but that marriage broke up long before I was born. After that came more wild years, and then somehow in the midst of her partying, she'd gotten knocked up with me and decided to continue with the pregnancy—probably because she was so out of it that she couldn't even get her act together long enough to go get an abortion.

Really, she probably did Kara and me a favor by taking off that one night and never coming back, although at the time, it had been pretty terrifying. Most of the details were now mercifully hazy, since I was barely three years old at the time, but I did remember Kara acting all worried and trying to hide it, feeding me mac and cheese and frozen pizza, then finally refried beans on tortillas she baked in the toaster oven because we didn't have anything else. After the first night alone, she started rummaging around our dingy apartment, obviously looking for something, but it wasn't until our grandparents showed up on the third day and gathered up the two of us and all our belongings that I realized Kara had been looking for a phone number where she could reach them, could call them to let them know Marybeth had finally taken off for good.

There wasn't a formal adoption, but our mother never came looking for us. I got the impression that Grandma sent Marybeth news about us from time to time, but once she passed away, I had the feeling that the pipeline was cut off. Grandpa had never forgiven his daughter for what she'd done to us.

I liked to pretend that it was no big deal, that Kara had fared the worst because she was so much older and remembered so much more, but of course there were scars. We went to counseling for a while, but I didn't see the point. It was like picking at a scab that should have been left alone to heal. And yeah, maybe I had trust issues, but I'd turned into a more or less functional adult, so I refused to worry about it. I'd relegated my mother to oblivion, and sincerely hoped she'd stay there.

No such luck.

No, I was heading toward her at roughly eighty miles an hour, and I had absolutely no idea what to say when I got there. *Hi, Mom, it's been a few decades. I'm here because a Man in Black said you had some super-secret information you needed to pass on to me so I can save the world. How've you been?*

Right.

The drive was pretty straightforward until I got to Santa Fe. I'd stopped once for gas and to use the restroom, and also to get a long-delayed hot dog. The dog didn't sit so well in my stomach afterward, but I didn't know if that was because it had been resting in its little warming case for too long, or because the closer I got to Taos, the more I seemed to clench up.

But then I had to take some kind of bypass road intended to keep travelers from being bogged down in Santa Fe proper, although it didn't seem like that great of a bypass, since the speed limit kept varying widely, going from 65 to 55 and even 45 in a few places. And even when I got past that, the highway itself seemed just as capricious, spitting me out in a lovely armpit of a town called Española where I had to drop to 35 miles an hour and missed just about every goddamn traffic light.

By that point, it was past four-thirty, and the sun was dipping down behind the hills to my left. I knew there was no way I'd make it to Taos before full dark, and set my teeth as I passed yet another Native American casino. As far as I could tell, the main sources of income in New Mexico were casinos or working for the state government, judging by the casinos I'd seen off the highway or the numerous "official" vehicles that had passed me once I crossed the state line.

Then, of course, snow began to fall. Clouds had been lowering all afternoon, but I'd sort of hoped they'd hold off until I reached my destination. No such luck. By that point I was traveling north on Highway 68, twisting and turning as the road paralleled the path of a river I guessed must be the Rio Grande, although there weren't any signs indicating it as such. Totally unlike Arizona, where they'd practically label a ditch if it floods during the wet season.

I felt a slight slip of the Jeep's tires and wondered if I should select the "snow" option. However, it didn't happen again, so I decided to leave things as they were. There were chains in the cargo area, just in case, but Henry had told me I probably wouldn't need them. "Keep her steady, and the gears will do the job," he'd said, and so far he seemed to be right.

The Jeep would most likely get me where I was going, but I knew there was no way I'd make it there before six. More like six-thirty, I revised mentally, as I dropped down to thirty miles an hour. Good thing there wasn't anyone behind me, probably because most people had read the weather reports and decided to stay home.

I didn't have the luxury of waiting for the storm to pass. This trip was already costing me enough time.

Finally, after what felt like hours but was only another forty-five minutes, the road dropped down into civilization, or at least what passed for it in this part of the world. In my mind, I had been expecting something like Sedona, another high-desert resort town, but Taos looked pretty sparse as I headed through a section that trumpeted itself as being Cristobal Somebody-or-other's land grant, and then past the inevitable Walmart and Walgreens and Autozone before I entered what was obviously the older, more touristy part of town.

Here there was more traffic, mostly because there

seemed to be only one main street. I'd double-checked the Taos Inn's location and knew it was right on the main drag, and sure enough, there was the neon sign guiding me in. I had to go around the block to find the entrance to the parking lot, but that was okay. I was here. I had made it, despite the weather.

The parking lot was about three-quarters full. I found an empty parking space, pulled my one suitcase out of the back of the Jeep, and then headed off in search of the lobby. Since I'd guaranteed the reservation with a credit card, there wasn't any problem with my late check-in.

"And you can get dinner right here at Doc Martin's if you're tired from your drive and don't feel like going back out," the clerk at the front desk told me as she handed me my room key.

Not going back out sounded like a great idea. I thanked her, found my room—which, thank God, was located not too far from the lobby—and dumped my suitcase on the little stand in the closet. After that, I stood for a moment, staring at myself in the mirror. I looked like hell—shadows under my eyes, hair messy, lip gloss long gone. Maybe the hotel had room service.

No such luck. I ran a brush through my hair, went back downstairs, and sort of hovered at the hostess desk in the restaurant. I hated the idea of eating alone, and the hostess apparently took pity on me, because she told me I could sit at the bar and order dinner there if I didn't want to occupy a table by myself.

That seemed like a great idea, so I cozied up to the bar, ordered a glass of New Mexico wine just to be different, and got myself a huge plate of portobello ravioli. It was absolutely divine, and just what I needed. And maybe it was because I looked like hell, but no one bothered me or tried to sit down next to me at the bar and chat. I ate quietly, and alone, and tried not to think about what was coming the next day.

CHAPTER SIX

SINCE I GUESSED THAT "SKYHEART DESIGNS" DIDN'T open until at least ten, I took my time the next morning with showering and getting ready, tying my favorite blue and purple scarf around my neck, taking more care with my makeup than I normally would. I'd brought my laptop, but I'd been so tired the evening before that I hadn't even opened it up before falling into bed.

Now, though—after I'd signed on to the hotel's wireless, since Taos appeared to be even more of a digital sinkhole than Sedona—I found about fifty unread messages in my inbox: some spam, some from potential clients, a petulant one from Jeff asking why I hadn't accepted his Facetime request, since he had some important information he needed to share with me. Maybe he'd had some luck with that gizmo he'd designed to pick up alien transmissions. I didn't know, and right then was not the time to get into it.

So I wrote back quickly, saying I'd had to go out of town but would be back tomorrow, and I'd call him when I was available. I had a feeling that response would just piss him off more than ever, but it couldn't be helped. I had more important things to do.

By the time I'd gotten breakfast and then went back up to my room to brush my teeth and repair my lip gloss, it was just a hair before ten. No more reason to delay—by the time I walked over to Bent Street, Skyheart Designs should be open for business.

For some reason, my hands were shaking as I closed the door behind me and shouldered my purse. It was only a few blocks from the hotel to Bent Street, so I wouldn't have to drive. And the day was beautiful—fresh snow everywhere but blue sky overhead, with just a few clouds still crowning the mountains to the north and east of town.

My breath puffed out in front of me as I made my way to my mother's...well, whatever it was. "Skyheart Designs" sounded fairly artsy-fartsy. So was she an artist of some kind? Painter? Sculptor? I had no idea. My grandparents had never mentioned her being particularly artistic, but then again, they really hadn't talked about her much at all. I was definitely going in blind here.

Someone had shoveled the sidewalks, since tourists slipping and falling was probably bad for business. I kept my hands stuffed in my pockets as I walked, and was glad of the bright cotton scarf swathed around my throat. It was a good deal colder here than in Sedona, which made sense, I supposed. Taos was thousands of feet higher than my hometown, so the climate must be closer to that of Flagstaff. Not a lot of trees, though. Up in Flag, you could drive through mile after mile of Ponderosa pines. Here were the usual bare, leafless sycamores and cottonwoods and manzanita, and a few others I didn't recognize, but I had the feeling these had all been planted on purpose. It wasn't like Taos was surrounded by a forest or anything.

And there it was—Skyheart Designs, a small storefront set between a chocolate shop and what appeared to be a real estate office. Through the display windows, I could see a young woman probably around my age setting out intricate pieces of jewelry gleaming in silver and gold, and glittering with semiprecious stones in shades of purple and red and blue and green.

My heart rose somewhere to the vicinity of my windpipe. I choked it back and forced myself to take one step, then another.

You can do this, Keeks.

A string of bells hanging from the door handle jingled as I entered, and for some reason, I had to fight back a wave of treacherous tears at the familiarity of the sound, since we had a similar string of bells hung on the door of the UFO Depot. I didn't want anything here to be familiar. I wanted it to be alien and different, so I could feel comfortable rejecting it.

The girl at the window paused in setting up the display and asked, "Can I help you?"

She was dark and very pretty, clearly Native American. Probably not a long-lost half-sister, then.

I forced the words out. "Is Marybeth Swenson here?"

"She's in back. Let me go get her."

"Thanks." And somehow I managed to make myself stay there and wait as the girl closed the display window and locked it, then went past the counter and through a door into what was obviously the back room.

I heard muffled voices, and then the shop girl returned, followed by a tall, slender woman with pale hair pulled back in a simple ponytail, turquoise drops hanging from her ears and a stylized silver cross studded with turquoise at her throat. She had to be in her middle fifties, but her face bore hardly any lines. The blue eyes that met mine were the same deep forget-me-not color as Kara's.

For a minute, we just stood there, staring at each other, and then she seemed to gather herself and say, quite normally, "Hello, Kiki."

"Kirsten," I said, my tone sounding abrupt even to me.

"Oh—of course." And then silence fell again.

This was going well. Probably, my brain hadn't gotten quite caught up to the fact that she was about the farthest from the meth-raddled, used-up woman of my imagination than she could possibly be. Mindful of the shop girl watching us, I said quietly,

"Could we talk somewhere? I know you're probably busy, but—"

"Of course." Just a repetition of her previous words, as if she couldn't quite figure out what other phrase to use. Then she looked over at her assistant and said, "Carla, can you watch the store for me for a while? I need to go out for a bit."

"Sure, Mrs. Engle."

Mrs. Engle. Well, what else had I expected? I'd seen the name on the card for myself.

I waited while Marybeth—my mother—went into the back room again and came out wearing a very chic brown suede coat, a teal scarf around her throat. She moved past me, and I caught a whiff of some soft scent. Not floral. Sandalwood, maybe?

She opened the door for me, and I went out into the bright morning sunshine. We took a few steps so we were out of view of her store's windows, and then she stopped and asked, "Why are you here?"

Not the greatest welcome in the world, but I hadn't expected one. I stared back at her, at a face that was half-familiar to me, as if something remembered from a dream. "Someone told me I had to talk to you. He hinted you knew something about me, something that could help me fight the aliens in the base outside Sedona."

I almost expected her to burst out laughing at that explanation. After all, if you tell most people that you're trying to defeat a bunch of aliens in a secret base, they'll either sniff your breath for alcohol or call up the men with the straitjackets. Laughter was a pretty distant second to those possibilities when it came to a bad response to my statement.

But Marybeth didn't laugh, or start calling for help. No, her mouth tightened, and her gaze shifted away from me. Then she seemed to nod and straighten her shoulders, as if gathering herself for a confrontation she'd half dreaded and half expected. "We shouldn't talk here. I'd thought we could go for some coffee, but now…now I think you'd better come back to the house."

"Where's that?" I asked. Somehow, I didn't quite like the idea of going with her to her house. Surely we could just go back to my hotel room if a diner or coffee house wasn't private enough.

"A few miles up the road." I must have looked suspicious, because she added, "Don't worry. I've been an upstanding member of society for quite a few years now."

There being nothing I could say in response to that without sounding petty or grudging—although I had every reason to be, frankly—I only nodded. "Okay. But maybe I should go back and get my car and follow you—"

"It's really all right," she cut in. "My car's just parked around back."

I decided not to protest anymore. If she wanted it her way, fine. But I was going to make a careful note of the route we took, just in case I ended up having to walk back.

She led me to a parking area behind the row of businesses and over to a shining white Range Rover.

My eyes bugged out a little at the sight of that vehicle. Not that I knew everything there was to know about cars, but I did know that a Range Rover—especially a new model like the one she was unlocking now—cost the equivalent of a small condo. Business must have been going really well for her, or she'd found herself one hell of a sugar daddy.

I climbed in and buckled my seatbelt while she did the same. Then she backed out of her spot and pointed the big SUV back to the main route, and took us northward out of the heart of town.

It was like riding on silk, despite the recently plowed roads. As she drove, I stole a quick look at the rock on her left hand. Two carats? Three? I wasn't educated enough on such matters to be sure. The ring seemed to go with the Range Rover, with the quietly expensive coat she wore. I couldn't begin to piece together how my mother—the hard-drinking, chain-smoking woman who could barely scrape the rent together—could end up living in apparently the lap of luxury.

To cover my confusion, I stared out the window, watched the white-blanketed landscape flash by. We crossed a river, then turned onto a road that seemed to be heading up toward one of the ski areas in the mountains. But then she took a hard left, and we wound down a narrow lane that could barely accommodate the Range Rover. I sucked in my breath and hoped we wouldn't meet anyone coming the other way.

A minute or two later, we inched our way down a

steep drive and into the center bay of a three-car garage. I didn't get a good look at the house, but the one glimpse I did have was of a large lodge-style residence, more imposing than I wanted to admit.

Marybeth stopped the car and said, unnecessarily, "Here we are." Maybe she hadn't been too thrilled with my silence on the way over, but really, what *was* I supposed to say?

I got out and followed her through a door that led into a kitchen like something out of *House Beautiful* or *Architectural Digest*—high-beamed ceilings of natural wood, granite counters, stainless-steel appliances. Despite myself, I couldn't help contrasting the luxury around me with my own small apartment with its patched-together garage-sale finds, or even with Kara's house, which, while nice, was still a modest ranch-style home built in the mid-'60s, not someplace that looked as if it should be in a magazine.

Marybeth went through the kitchen without a second look and brought me to what appeared to be the family room. Saying, "Go ahead and make yourself comfortable," she went over to a huge slate fireplace, added some wood to the grate, and touched off a couple of those waxy little starter blocks to get things going. I wanted to call this affectation, a way of stalling me, but it was cold in the house, even though I guessed the heat must be on.

So I sat on a plump brown leather couch and looked around, at the Navajo rugs on the floor, the polished juniper coffee table, the paintings of local landscapes on the walls, which were tinted a soft burnt-biscuit shade. The air smelled of wood smoke. It should have been homey, comforting...but of course it wasn't. This wasn't my home. Maybe it was the home that should have been mine, if things had been different...but they weren't.

"Coffee?" my mother asked.

I shook my head. "I'm not much of a coffee drinker. Do you have any green tea?"

"Sure," she said, and went out. I heard her busying herself in the kitchen and realized it wasn't just hospitality driving her—the longer she rattled around with those sorts of tasks, the longer she could put off actually talking to me.

So I sat there and watched the fire grow, eventually filling the space with warmth. About five minutes later, Marybeth came back into the room and handed me a sturdy mug with a deep red-brown gaze. I noticed she had gotten coffee for herself. It smelled wonderful, but, in my humble opinion, coffee only tasted about a tenth as good as it smelled.

She sat herself down on the couch opposite mine and wrapped her fingers around her own mug, as if she needed its warmth, despite the room being quite comfortable now. "So...." she said at last.

"So," I said. A deep breath, then another. "Look, I know it sounds crazy, and I wouldn't have come here to bug you if it wasn't really important, but—"

"'Bug me'?" she repeated. "Kirsten, don't ever think that you're bothering me. I've dreamed of this day—" She broke off and shook her head. "That is, I hoped maybe one day you'd forgive me, come see me. Seeing you now, seeing what a lovely young woman you've become—" Again, she stopped herself. "I suppose I never stopped to think you'd come asking questions I didn't want to answer."

I couldn't think of what to say in reply, so I only hung on to my own mug like a lifeline, not drinking from it, but merely reassuring myself with its solidity. "So you do know what Agent Jones was talking about."

"Agent Jones?"

"He's—well, I guess he's what you'd call a Man in Black. So he knows things that other people don't know. But he wouldn't tell me what was so important. He only said I needed to hear it from you."

She still had a light tan, despite the season, or maybe it was just a careful application of bronzer. Beneath it, though, she seemed to pale. Almost under her breath, she said, "He was the most beautiful man I'd ever seen."

"Huh?"

A hint of a tight smile before she glanced away, seeming unable to meet my eyes. "Your father."

"My *father*?"

"Yes." Deliberately, she took a large swallow of her coffee, as if she needed the caffeine to brace her for what was about to come next. "I know there's no way of excusing my behavior back then, so I won't even try. It's one thing to be free with yourself— that's your own business—but the drinking, the drugs...." She shook her head. "I had no business dragging you girls into that."

Damn straight. But I only asked softly, "How long have you been sober?"

"Seven years," she said, pride in her tone. "And I wanted to make it up to you two, make amends, but my father wouldn't hear of it. He told me I'd burned my bridges, and that was it. So I backed off, and then he was gone, and I just sort of let it go. Maybe it was the wrong thing to do, considering...." The word trailed away into nothingness. "Anyway, I can't fix that now. And you deserve to hear the truth. Kara knew her father, if only for a little while, but you didn't even have that."

I sat quietly, hardly daring to breathe. Maybe I was afraid that if I interrupted her, I would break the flow of her thoughts, destroy the air of quiet intro-spection that seemed to have surrounded her.

"My best friend back then was Josie Hendricks. We had some good times, Josie and I. Too good, a lot of people would probably say. Anyway, one night we went to this club in Scottsdale that had just opened. Very upscale, not really our kind of scene, you might say. But Josie thought it was time to give classy guys a try." A rueful smile. "Sometimes the booze makes you a little less than discriminating. But I'm guessing you don't know too much about that, thank God."

No, I'd definitely swung that pendulum far in the other direction. I managed a small shake of the head.

"So there we were, having guys with Rolexes buy us Cosmos, and then this man came up to me and asked me to dance. Of course I said yes—he was amazingly good-looking. Tall, blond hair, blue eyes.

Looked like a Norse god or something. He said his name was Gabriel. He stuck by my side for the rest of the night as we drank and laughed and talked about nothing much in particular." Marybeth paused for a moment, staring past me, as if seeing in her mind's eye that night so many years ago. "Of course, I brought him home with me—I think Josie took a cab home, but things were a little fuzzy after that. And Kara was staying at a friend's house that night, so I knew I'd have the apartment to myself. No need to go into details, of course, but he stayed the night, and in the morning, he was gone."

"And that's unusual how?" I asked, and then wished I'd kept my mouth shut. Not the most politic thing to say, even if it wasn't anything more than the truth.

She didn't look angry, though. Her mouth pursed a little, and I realized I'd seen that exact expression on Kara's face when a jab got through to her and she didn't want to respond. But then Marybeth shrugged and replied, "It's not unusual at all, actually. What was strange was how he got out."

"I don't understand."

"My apartment had one of those deadbolts that you had to lock with a key from the inside," she said. "Pain in the rear, but it was supposed to be more secure or something. And after having one or two of my 'dates' let himself out before I'd slept it off, I'd taken to hiding the keys when I got home—in my lingerie drawer, in my makeup bag in the bathroom.

You'd have to do some serious rummaging to find it."

"But he must have found it if he was gone."

She shook her head and drank from her coffee again. "No. When I got up the next morning and he wasn't in bed, at first I thought he was in the bathroom or out in the living room or kitchen or something. But no—he was gone. The door was still locked, and my keys were still hidden in the top drawer of my dresser, underneath a pile of bras. If he'd gone in there to get the keys out, things would have been disturbed. I would have noticed—by then, I'd sobered up. It was as if he'd never been there."

I wanted to say that maybe she'd just imagined it, that she'd been so wasted, she couldn't remember what she was doing, but I held my tongue. After all, my existence was pretty obvious proof that something had happened with somebody. Whether or not it was this mythical "Gabriel" was another matter.

It was hard to tell how Marybeth interpreted my silence. She paused for a moment, then said, "Even stranger, Josie had no memory of him at all, even though she'd kept telling me all night how hot he was, how I'd really scored a classy guy this time. And yes, you could say she was too drunk herself to remember anything clearly, but Josie wasn't like that. She never forgot anything...but she forgot Gabriel. It was almost as if those memories had just been...erased."

That sort of thing was common enough in UFO circles, but I'd never heard of aliens using the technique to erase the memory of a one-night stand. Then again, most aliens weren't the type you'd really want to be hopping into bed with, although I'd heard that Persephone's spirit guide Otto, when he was in his true form, wasn't exactly the type you'd kick out of bed for eating crackers.

"So...what are you saying?" I asked, not sure I really wanted to hear the answer.

"I think you know," she said steadily, meeting my eyes for the first time since she'd begun her narrative. "When you were born, the nurses were amazed, because you didn't cry. Just looked at everything as if you were analyzing it. And you didn't cry when I brought you home. I actually did sober up for you, for a while. But it was too hard—and I didn't know what to do with you. I thought I knew what to expect. I'd had Kara, after all. I thought another daughter would be easy enough. But then you didn't talk until you were almost two, and everyone was worried something was wrong with you. When you did start talking, it was in complete sentences, as if you'd spent all that time absorbing everything, processing it, so that when you did begin to speak you'd get everything right. Again, okay, not conclusive. And I suppose it wasn't conclusive that I got pregnant with you even though I was on the pill at the time."

Just like Kara, I thought. Maybe I had more in common with my half-alien niece than I really wanted to admit.

Marybeth said, "And tell me this, Kirsten—have

you ever been sick? Even one day? Because you weren't as a child. Ever."

I didn't want to tell her. I'd listened to all these revelations with mounting dread in my heart, not wanting to hear the truth in her words, not wanting to admit to myself that there just might be something very strange about my origins. Probably you could explain one or two of those things away, but when all of them were taken in aggregate—

Somehow, I made myself answer. "No," I said, staring down into my now-cold mug of green tea. "Never missed one day of school. It kind of sucked, actually."

At that comment, she gave a nervous little laugh. "I can imagine. Then one day you came into the kitchen and asked me out of the blue if I was sad because I'd had the dream about Uncle Steve again, the one where the people in the bushes shot him, and I...I lost it. Because I'd had that dream the night before, Kirsten, that same nightmare I couldn't seem to get rid of, no matter how much I drank, no matter how many pills I took. That's the night I left."

Her words shook me more than anything else she had yet said. In barely a whisper, I retorted, "I am not psychic."

"Maybe you're not now. Maybe what happened to you when I left was so traumatic that you repressed it. I have no idea—I'm not an expert in that sort of thing." Her hand shook as she drained the rest of her coffee. Something in her face told me she wished the mug had held something a little stronger.

From what I'd heard, it wasn't as if the urge to drink really went away. People just got better at managing it.

I didn't feel any pity for her, though. "So, rather than trying to figure it out like a normal person, you just took off? And what about Kara? Okay, maybe I was a little Damien freak or something, but Kara didn't deserve what you did to her."

"Neither of you did," Marybeth said, again looking away from me. "I knew Kara, knew she was a smart girl and would call her grandparents. I knew things would get taken care of eventually."

Eventually. In that moment, I hated her. I hated that she somehow managed to look like one of those older models in a Ralph Lauren magazine ad, the ones with the perfect cheekbones and flawless silvery hair, who all looked like they'd gone to Vassar or something, instead of a woman who'd spent a good decade and a half drinking like a fish and not caring about anyone other than herself. When the going got tough…Marybeth Swenson sure got going. Right out the door.

But I couldn't give in to any of that resentment right now. Maybe later I could scream and yell and throw things, but in the meantime, there were aliens to be defeated and not a whole lot of time to do it in. Michael's words came back to me: *Be strong enough to recognize the truth when you hear it.*

So I supposed the truth was that my father had been some sort of otherworldly being. Alien? Angel? With a name like Gabriel, that didn't seem out of the bounds of reason, but the whole thing was so crazy, I didn't know what I was supposed to think.

"Okay," I said at length, as Marybeth watched me carefully with that expression which told me she ached for a hit of something to make this moment a little less real, a little less painful. Too bad. If I had to tough this out, she sure as hell would, too. "So you walked out and left your weird little girl behind, and then went on to your perfect life here in Taos. I'm guessing Mr. Engle isn't exactly hurting for cash?"

"No," she replied, a line forming between her brows for the first time as she frowned. "Ken has been very good to me."

"Good for Ken." I set down my untouched mug of tea and stood. "Okay, now that you've told me what happened, I guess I can see why Mart—why Agent Jones thought I should talk to you. What I'm supposed to do about it, I don't know for sure, but I guess that's not your problem. Can you take me back to my hotel? I've got some alien ass to kick."

"Kirsten—" Marybeth's face was white.

"No, really," I said. I didn't want to hear any excuses or half-assed explanations for her behavior. "Time's a-wasting. Now I've only got seven days until the solstice, and I'm going to have to use up part of one driving back to Sedona. So I really just want you to take me back, please."

As if realizing that any further argument was pointless, she put down her mug as well and rose. "If that's what you want."

"It is."

The drive back was even more awkwardly silent than the one to her house had been. I stared out at the landscape as it passed by, thinking it looked a lot like I felt—bare and windswept, bleak. Maybe there was some beauty here, but I sure hadn't found it.

I wondered who this Ken Engle was whom she'd married, whether she'd gotten sober first, or whether he'd met her while she was still drinking and was the one to get her on the straight and narrow. It probably didn't matter one way or another. Not now. Thinking about that kept me from thinking about anything else, though, so the idle speculation did have its uses.

As we'd climbed into the Range Rover, I'd told her that I was staying at the Taos Inn, so she knew where to drop me off. When she pulled into an empty space in the hotel's parking lot, she began, "Kirsten—"

"Don't," I said. "Really, it looks like you've made a great life for yourself here, and I'm sorry I had to interrupt that. But now that I've heard what you were supposed to tell me, I've got to go." I reached out for the door handle.

"Just—" she began, and hesitated. Then, "Just be careful."

Not really trusting myself to reply, I nodded and got out, then hurried away from the SUV. I didn't bother to look back.

CHAPTER SEVEN

BECAUSE I HADN'T BEEN THINKING ALL THAT CLEARLY when I made the reservation, I'd booked my room for two nights. As I hurried up the stairs at the Taos Inn, though, I knew I had to get out of there right away. I didn't want to stay away from Sedona one second longer than I had to. I went in and packed up the few items I'd left out—toothbrush and toothpaste, the hairbrush I'd dropped on the bathroom vanity as I hurried to leave the room to meet Marybeth.

I grabbed my suitcase and went down to the lobby. "I need to check out," I told the front desk clerk, and slid my key across the counter.

She took it, looked me up on the computer, and frowned. "You're not staying tonight?"

"Something's come up."

Another frown. "Well, I'm not sure if I can give you a refund with such late notice—"

"It's okay," I told her. Of course there was no way

I could let her know what was really going on, that giving up an extra hundred and fifty bucks over a late cancellation was really not going to make a difference in the grand scheme of things.

She bit her lip, worked on the computer, and said, "I can do a partial refund of fifty percent. Is that all right?"

"It's fine," I said. All I wanted to do was to hit the road, put Taos and Marybeth Swenson and her revelations behind me.

Of course, I knew it wasn't as simple as that. I waited while the clerk closed out my bill, then signed the invoice, shoved my copy in my purse, and gathered up my suitcase. She stared after me with puzzled eyes, as if she could tell something was very wrong but didn't quite know how to put her finger on it.

The sky was beginning to cloud up again. I stowed my suitcase in the back of the Jeep, got in, and started it up. With my luck, it would start snowing again as I was driving, but I wasn't going to worry about that now. I glanced over at the clock on the dash. Eleven forty-two. Pretty sad that it had taken less than two hours for Marybeth Swenson to turn my life upside down all over again.

No. Don't think about that now. Just drive.

But I couldn't help thinking about it as I headed south once again, driving at least ten miles over the speed limit. That voice was back in my head again, the one that seemed to keep whispering, *Hurry, hurry, hurry.* Getting a speeding ticket would only slow me down further, though, so I eased up on the gas pedal just a little.

You didn't talk until you were almost two...have you ever been sick a day in your life?...you asked me if I'd had that dream again....

How I wished I could get her voice out of my head, come up with some way to forget the things she had told me.

Ironic how I had just told Michael a few days earlier that I knew I wasn't psychic.

Guess this lady was protesting just a little too much.

And Martin Jones had known. I couldn't begin to figure out how, and for some reason, that made me angry. Maybe being angry was good. If I was angry, then I'd be less likely to be scared.

Who was Gabriel? What had led him to that club in Scottsdale almost twenty-four years ago? Just some old-fashioned alien slumming?

My brain was doing a pretty good job of flogging me, and I'd barely managed to crawl my way through Española, which didn't look any better on a cold Monday morning than it had on a late Sunday afternoon. Scowling, I plugged my phone into the Jeep's stereo and turned up the volume, but the Foo Fighters weren't giving me much reassurance, either.

Run and tell all the angels that everything is all right...

No, everything was definitely not all right. And I wasn't too happy with the angels at this moment, if this mysterious "Gabriel" turned out to be one of them.

The day turned darker as I went south, but it wasn't until I was back on Interstate 40 and crossing the Continental Divide that rain began to hit the windshield. Mouth tightening, I turned on the wipers and told myself to be glad that I was at an elevation where the precipitation was only rain and not snow.

Easy to say. I wasn't feeling too glad about anything at that moment.

I didn't know exactly what I *was* feeling, though. Okay, so booking the room for two nights had been pretty stupid. Maybe in the back of my mind, I had thought that Marybeth and I would have a teary reunion, and she'd apologize for all the terrible things she'd done, and somehow she'd be my mother again, and we'd spend hours catching up before she gave me the one convenient little piece of information that would help me defeat the aliens once and for all.

Not terribly realistic on my part; life didn't work that way. It was pretty clear to me that, despite her saying she hoped one day to be part of Kara's and my lives, she really didn't want that. She had her beautiful house and her rich husband and her pretty little shop, and dealing with the daughters she'd abandoned twenty years earlier would only mess up her perfectly ordered world.

I didn't even have the energy to hate her anymore. As Michael probably would have pointed out, I had more important things to do with my time.

Okay, so, according to Marybeth, there was more to me than met the eye. That just didn't compute. I didn't feel different—I just felt like me. Maybe I'd sensed the malice coming from the aliens, but I was no psychic. I wasn't like Persephone, getting weird feelings about things all the time and having visions and talking to a spirit guide. There had never seemed to be anything terribly out of the ordinary about me. Yes, I'd never been sick, but I knew two other kids at my high school who also had perfect attendance, so my obvious good health never seemed strange. I was a good student. So were a lot of other kids. No signs of genius IQ, nothing to show that my father had contributed anything all that stellar to my DNA.

I was so busy brooding that at first I didn't realize the rain on my windshield had begun to turn to snow as I made the slow climb up to Flagstaff. Then I felt the slightest slip of the tires and really focused, seeing the pavement of the highway starting to blur behind the drifting flakes.

"Well, shit," I said aloud, letting off on the accelerator so I could slow down to a safer speed. Of course, the chains were in the back if I really ended up needing them, but the thought of having to pull over to put them on didn't exactly thrill me.

By then, it was starting to get dark. No chance of getting the Jeep back to Henry before he closed at five; it was pushing four-thirty now, and I was still at least an hour and a half away from Sedona. More, really, because I knew with the weather like this, I wouldn't chance going down through the canyon. I'd have to take the long way around on I-17 and come up through Sedona from the bottom, through the Village of Oak Creek, which meant tacking on another half hour at least. Wonderful.

One good thing about the foul weather, though—it made me shift focus from my turbulent thoughts to the treacherous driving conditions. Of course I'd driven in snow before. But up here it was much worse than it would be in Sedona. I'd have to hang on until I got through Flagstaff and part of the way down the interstate before things improved much.

By the time I reached the interchange, I'd dropped my speed even further, down to about forty miles an hour, and everyone around me was doing the same thing. Not that there was a lot of traffic, even though by that point it was going-home time for a lot of people. I clutched the steering wheel grimly and thanked Henry under my breath for the loan of the Jeep. No way I could have pushed the Night Tours van through this.

And as I crept southward, I began to feel a mounting chill that the heater couldn't begin to combat. I cranked it up a little further, but even so, icy shivers kept running down my back, and I began to imagine I was hearing that ominous murmur of voices again, pitched so low you could almost pretend it wasn't there, almost tell yourself it was just road noise.

I knew better.

This was crazy, though—I was just passing the turn-off for Schnebly Road, and so wasn't anywhere close to Sedona. Well, not really. In the summer, you could take a four-wheeler along Schnebly down some pretty serious goat paths, and eventually end up at the traffic circle right in front of Tlaquepaque Village. As the crow flies, it was maybe fifteen miles or so. But had the aliens gotten so much stronger in the time I'd been gone that I could sense them all the way out here?

During most of the drive, I'd done a pretty good job of not thinking about how vulnerable I was, a girl alone in a very expensive vehicle on some fairly obscure roads. Now, with the darkness seeming to press on all the Jeep's windows, I couldn't help obsessing over it. The glass seemed pretty flimsy protection from whatever was lurking out there, but at the moment, I couldn't do much about it. I tried to tell myself that I wasn't completely alone—there was one vehicle probably a quarter-mile in front of me, and a pair of barely visible headlights in my rearview mirror. If something happened, it wasn't as if there wouldn't be any witnesses. Faint comfort. I'd read too many UFO cases to know that I couldn't be snatched right up under the noses of multiple witnesses if that was what the aliens wanted to do.

Even so, I tried to match my pace to the vehicle ahead of me, just so I wouldn't lose sight of its taillights. It seemed as if the person behind me was doing the same thing, too. Those other drivers might not be suffering my particular attack of the heebie-jeebies, but I doubted any of them wanted to feel completely adrift in the darkness and the falling snow.

When I saw the turn-off for Sedona, I almost wept with relief. Of course, there could still be aliens lurking in the bare manzanita and scrubby juniper that lined Highway 179. But at least I knew that road like the back of my hand. Also, the snow began to lighten as I made my way toward the Village of Oak Creek until it was little more than a flake or two blowing across my windshield at any given time. A few minutes later, I saw the lights in the Village, and uttered a silent prayer that I'd made it this far. Of course, there was still a five-mile gap between Oak Creek and Sedona proper where the aliens could get the jump on me if they felt like it, but there were almost always people going back and forth along that route, no matter what time of day or night it might be.

Sure enough, a big Ford truck pulled out from a gas station about a car length in front of me as I followed the last roundabout at the top of the Village, and I practically hugged his bumper all the way home. By then, the devil's chorus in my head had subsided, along with the sensation of cold that had accompanied it. When I finally pulled into my assigned parking space at my apartment complex, I felt almost normal.

Well, as normal as anyone could feel after a nine-hour drive and learning that their father might or might not be an alien. Or an angel. Or something.

I knew there was no chance now of getting the

Jeep back to Henry tonight; it was almost nine o'clock. So I lugged my suitcase out of the back and patted the Jeep on its rear bumper, thanking it for its good service in getting me home safely, before I went upstairs.

Everything looked the same. Apparently, the aliens hadn't come in to "toss" the place in my absence or anything like that. I set the suitcase down by the coffee table and took off my coat and scarf, and hung them from the hall tree in the corner, since the apartment was too small for me to have an actual coat closet. Then I ran my fingers through my hair and let out a relieved sigh.

Weariness weighted my limbs. It had been a hell of a day. Logically, I knew that I should put my things away, grab something light to eat, and then do the usual face washing and teeth brushing before going to bed.

However, logic and I weren't really on speaking terms at the moment. I grabbed my purse, pulled Martin Jones' business card out of my wallet, and dialed the number.

If he was surprised by the call, he sure didn't show it. Then again, maybe he'd guessed that I would want to grill him after receiving Marybeth's not-so-welcome "news."

He showed up approximately five minutes after I called, which meant he was either lurking around to see if I was going to get jumped by any more alien-possessed people, or his hotel was fairly close by.

I'd barely shut the door before I said, "You knew all along, didn't you?"

The blue eyes didn't blink. "I suspected."

"You suspected."

"It was a strong suspicion."

I stared across the room at him to where he stood by the sliding glass window to the balcony, and something inside me seemed to break. Without even realizing what I was doing at first, I launched myself at him, getting close enough to pound his chest with my fists, even as I repeated over and over, "You knew! You knew!" before my words devolved into outright sobs.

And then somehow his hands were grasping my wrists, keeping me from hitting him again, and from there his arms closed around me as I wept into his chest, wept for realizing I had lost my mother all over again, and worse, had lost something I didn't even know I had until it was gone. Over the years, I had often wondered who my father might be, wondered if anything about me was like him—the color of my eyes or the shape of my chin or the way I laughed. Anything.

But now that faceless father wasn't just some unknown man my mother had slept with on yet another in a long series of drunken nights, but a mysterious being of unknown origins and powers. And it seemed he just might have passed some of those powers on to me.

At last, I came back to myself enough to realize I was standing there with Agent Jones's arms around me. Maybe I should have pulled away, but I also realized that I liked the feel of those strong arms encircling me, despite how angry I had been with him just a few minutes earlier.

Oh, Jesus, I really was messed up.

I pulled away then, sniffling. "Sorry about that," I muttered.

"You don't really think I minded, do you?"

Looking up, I saw him watching me, noticed a gentleness in his expression that I hadn't seen before. But there was something more than that—a warmth, maybe. Yes, it must have been that, because something in his gaze made the blood in my veins seem to run a little hotter, my heart beat a little faster. And that was really crazy. Sure, I'd made jokes to myself about Martin Jones, the hot Man in Black. But something about the look in his eyes told me that what I was feeling was no joke.

"I—I don't know," I replied in faltering tones, and dragged my gaze away from his. "I'm acting like an idiot. Sorry."

"You're not an idiot." He looked over at the couch. "Maybe you should sit down."

That sounded like a great idea, considering my legs were roughly the consistency of rubber at the moment. I went to the sofa and basically fell onto the worn cushions. I wondered for a second or two whether he would come and sit next to me, but he remained at the window, almost as if he was standing guard.

"All right," I said wearily, once I realized he had no intention of moving from his post, "I went and got the great revelation. I went on my vision quest, as Michael Lightfoot put it. Now will you please tell me exactly what the hell is going on and what I'm supposed to do next? We don't have a lot of time."

"No, we don't." He paused, then added, "But it's not safe to talk here, and you're tired."

"What do you mean, 'it's not safe to talk here'? Are they…listening?"

"In a manner of speaking. It would be better for us to talk tomorrow at the place I'm staying."

If it had been someone else, I might have tried to read something into that statement. So he wanted me to meet him at his place? But even if what I'd seen in his eyes was real, he had no reason to try to get me alone. We were alone right now, after all.

"Okay. Where?"

"I'll call you." He finally moved away from the window, but instead of coming toward me, as I halfway hoped he would, he headed to the door. "The best thing you can do is get some rest. You're going to need all your strength." With those ominous words, he let himself out, slipping away into the night.

Great. Well, at least he'd offered me a shoulder to cry on, even if it was only for a few minutes. Fighting back a sigh, I pushed myself off the couch and went to secure the deadbolt and the chain latch on the door, although I was pretty sure neither one of them would do much to keep out the aliens if they really wanted to get in.

But I did somehow find the energy to limp into the bathroom, to clean myself up a little so I could go to bed. Martin Jones had told me to rest, so I would try my best, even though my brain didn't want to shut itself off. As I lay down, reassured a little by the soft glow of the stained-glass nightlight on one wall, I tried to push back the images of my mother's still-lovely but troubled face, the sound of her voice telling me that I'd seen her dreams, that my father couldn't possibly be an ordinary man.

I rolled over and squashed my pillow, attempting to find a more comfortable position. It didn't help that when I forced my mother's face out of my mind, it was only replaced by that of Martin Jones—the firm chin, the mouth that I found just a bit too distracting. How was it that I'd lived in this apartment for a whole year and slept alone that whole time without it ever bothering me, and yet now all I could think about was how it would feel if I had him next to me, had him to hold me close and keep the dark and the cold and the fear at bay?

Okay, now you're being completely stupid, I told myself. *Go the hell to sleep.*

I shut my eyes, willed away Martin Jones and Marybeth Swenson and the aliens in Secret Canyon. Time enough for that tomorrow. At least there would be a tomorrow. I didn't know about what would happen five days from now....

Because reception had been so bad on the drive back from Taos, I'd put my phone into "airplane" mode and basically forgotten about it. When I staggered out of bed the next morning, though, I saw I had four texts from Jeff in escalating tones of annoyance, culminating in "I can't believe you would leave w/o talking to me first. Call me!" That was Jeff—he refused to use textspeak even to save letters.

That wasn't the worst, though. Those were the messages from Kara, also expressing her dismay that I would skip town without discussing my plans with her, along with the added bonus of her guilting me about getting Michael to cover my shifts at the store. "He's not a temp agency, you know," she snapped during the last message before hanging up.

I found that a little rich, considering that she'd used Michael a time or ten to watch the store when I wasn't available. Not that I didn't understand her worry, but still.... I decided to chalk it up to hormones but knew I'd have to talk to her. It wasn't fair to keep from her where I'd been, who I'd spoken to. And probably better to do that first and get it out of the way so I'd have the rest of my day to talk to Martin. I'd have to hope that he planned to spend a little more than ten minutes talking to me. Our exchanges lately had been pretty brief.

After a long shower and two cups of tea, I felt a little more human...or at least as human as my questionable parentage would allow me to be. I even went to the Secret Garden Café and treated myself to a slice of their heavenly quiche lorraine, figuring that if I was about to get ripped a new one by Kara, at least I could do it on a full stomach. My plan was to drop off the Jeep after I ate and retrieve the van, then hit the store about fifteen minutes before it opened at ten. At least that way, Kara would have a finite amount of time to yell at me.

Henry was already at Sunrise Jeep when I got there, of course. He looked a little surprised when I came in just past nine-thirty, since I'd told him I probably wouldn't be back in Sedona until the late afternoon.

"Small change of plans," I said as I handed him the keys. "I filled up on the way over. I didn't have time to get it washed, but I figured with the weather the way it's been, that's not too much of a problem."

"No problem at all. The tourists like the dirt— makes the Jeeps look like they've been well used." A quick glance, as if he could tell something was wrong but couldn't quite figure out what it was. "Drive went okay?"

"Oh, yeah, flawless. Anyway, I've got to run."

He let me go without further inquiries, thank God. I was less than thrilled about having to go and get a lecture from my big sister, but frankly, after confronting our mother, Kara didn't seem quite as scary.

Driving the UFO Night Tours van was a little like having to steer a Coke can on wheels after that Jeep, but I told myself to suck it up. Maybe after the alien apocalypse was averted, I'd have time to worry about whether or not I should buy a new car.

In the meantime….

I pulled into the UFO Depot's parking lot, noting that Kara's Prius was already sitting there. Great. There went the element of surprise. But at least I had my own key and so could come in through the back entrance, the one that opened into the shop's minuscule storage room.

Not that it did me any real good. Kara was still waiting to pounce.

"I can't believe you would take off like that without telling anyone!"

First rule of sibling guerrilla warfare was to always have a comeback ready. "I did tell someone. I told Michael."

She crossed her arms over her chest. Just like Grace had been the miracle baby, Kara was sort of the miracle mom. Sure, that chest was a little bigger than usual, but overall, the baby weight had fallen off her like it did those Hollywood stars who were back to a size four less than a month after giving birth…except that Kara didn't have a team of trainers and nutritionists working for her. I didn't know quite how she'd managed it, unless the weight loss was another byproduct of Grace's part-alien DNA.

"Telling Michael isn't enough. You should've called me." Kara paused to catch her breath, then looked at me a little more closely, as if seeing something of the strain of the last two days in my face. "Where *did* you go, anyway?"

Moment of truth. I sucked in a breath and let it out. "I went to see Marybeth." Somehow, after that encounter, I'd stopped even mentally referring to her as my mother.

"You *what?*"

"I went to see her in Taos."

"In Taos," Kara repeated, as if that was the pertinent element of my reply. "In this weather?"

"I borrowed a Jeep from Henry at Sunrise."

My sister usually wasn't at a loss for words, but I could tell I'd flummoxed her. She turned away from me and went to the table where the T-shirts were stacked, reaching out to straighten them—even though they were in perfect order—as if that was the only thing her brain could handle at the moment. After a long pause, she said in a low voice, "How is she?"

"Great," I said. "She looks like a Ralph Lauren model. Married some rich guy. You should see her house—and her shop."

"'Shop'?" Kara echoed faintly.

"I think she does jewelry design or something. Very ritzy. I'm guessing the resort crowd just eats that stuff up."

"I need to sit down." Abruptly, she moved away from the table and sort of collapsed in her chair behind the counter. "Kiki...why?"

I ignored the use of my old nickname, figuring I should forgive the lapse in this moment of stress. "Because Agent Jones said I should."

At his name, her head went up, just the way

Gort's did when he heard something he didn't quite like. "Agent *Jones*?"

"Turns out his instincts were right. Marybeth had some interesting information for me—namely, that she's pretty sure my father wasn't just your run-of-the-mill barfly but some sort of otherworldly being. She didn't know whether he was an alien or an angel, but I guess that doesn't really matter so much. Oh, and apparently I have some sort of weird psychic powers that I've been repressing all this time. Who knew?"

During this speech, Kara's eyes kept growing wider and wider. Finally, she managed, "But you're —you're—you're my *sister*."

"And Grace is your daughter," I replied. "Doesn't change the fact that there's something a bit freaky about her DNA if you look close enough."

"But you've never—I mean, there isn't anything extraordinary about you."

"Gee, thanks," I said, planting my hand on my hips.

"Oh, come on, Keeks, you know what I mean. You're beautiful and you're smart, but so are a lot of other people. It's not as if you've been walking around reading minds or bending spoons or—"

"Or getting visited by spirit guides," I supplied. "Yeah, I know. Believe me, I'd rather be normal. Normal was working out okay for me. But lately...."

"Lately?"

"I keep sensing *them*," I said, with a quick jerk of

my chin in the direction of Secret Canyon. "It's getting worse."

She paled. "Worse?"

"According to Agent Jones, the shit's really going to hit the fan on the solstice." I figured I might as well tell her; it was going to be all hands on deck pretty soon. "And he seems to think I might be able to do something about it."

"How?"

"I have no idea. That guy's tighter-lipped than a clam." Maybe I shouldn't have said anything about his lips. Because then I started thinking about his mouth, and his face, and everything his head was attached to...and that was a distraction I really didn't need at the moment. Fighting the heat I knew was rising in my cheeks, I added, "He said he would talk to me today. So maybe I'll have more to tell you later."

"But Keeks—" She broke off with a guilty look at the clock above the counter as the door to the shop rattled and an irritated-looking couple of faces peered in. "Oh, crap. You'd think people would have something better to do on a Tuesday morning."

"It's okay," I told her. "I really need to check in with Jeff. I think he was also kind of pissed that I took off like that."

"But what about the solstice, and—" She couldn't quite bring herself to say the words, but gave a significant nod westward, toward alien country, even as she hastened to the door with her keys.

"We still have a few days. Let's try to get

everyone together tonight. I'm not sure when I'm meeting Agent Jones, but I hope it will be this afternoon at the latest."

"Okay," she said, and opened the door, murmuring apologies even as a small group of tourists hurried in, grumbling about being locked out in the cold.

I knew we wouldn't have a chance for any more conversation after that, so I just gave her a quick smile as I pushed past the tourists and headed for the van.

Well, I'd survived that confrontation without getting my ears chewed off too badly. I'd have to see if I fared as well with Jeff.

CHAPTER EIGHT

"DO YOU HAVE ANY IDEA WHAT WE'RE UP AGAINST here?" Jeff demanded.

Probably a better one than you do, I thought, but I only shrugged. I knew his annoyance stemmed from my not being around to appreciate his brilliance in hacking the aliens' transmissions, not because he'd been worried about me or really cared what I was up to. I sat back in the other dinette chair in Lance's cramped dining area and replied, "Enlighten me."

One of Jeff's patented scowls spread across his face. "Okay, so I managed to isolate the frequency they're using—"

"Really high, I bet."

"No," he said, now looking a little pleased to prove me wrong. "Low. So low that it almost sounds like background radiation emissions or something. I'm sure they're trying to make sure it blends, make it seem as if it's something natural. Only it isn't."

I nodded, a little impressed despite myself. Jeff could be trying at times—okay, most of the time—but I would never dispute his brilliance. "Can you understand anything they're saying?"

"Not yet. That is, I've detected a pattern, but I haven't cracked the code yet. But I will. It's just a matter of time."

"That's something we don't have a whole heck of a lot of," I said.

Jeff's sandy eyebrows drew together. "What do you mean?"

"Because according to Agent Jones, they're going to draw on the power of the solstice to do…whatever they're planning on doing. Kara's calling everyone in for a pow-wow at the house tonight."

"She hasn't called *me*." Jeff sounded distinctly petulant.

"I guess she figured I'd tell you. Anyway, that's beside the point. I'm hoping to get more info out of Agent Jones, but in the meantime, you've got to work on cracking that code like nobody's business. This is Enigma and World War II all over again."

At those words, Jeff brightened—for him, anyway. "It's a worthy challenge."

"I'm sure you'll kick its ass. Just try to make sure you do it in the next four days."

The scowl returned as Jeff glanced down at his laptop's screen and starting pounding away at the keyboard. I wondered how many of those things he went through in the course of a year.

But then my phone rang, and I pulled it out of my

purse and checked the number. Phoenix area code. I knew who that was. "Gotta take this," I said.

"Uh-huh," Jeff muttered, not even bothering to look up from his keyboard.

I wished I felt a little calmer as I touched the "accept" button on the screen and put the phone to my ear. "Hi."

"Hello, Kirsten."

He had such a nice voice, too. Warm and deep, but not too deep. It reminded me of the caramel-y burnt-sugar topping on crème brulée.

"Are you free now?"

"Sure. I mean, I can finish up with what I'm doing." I hoped that didn't sound too over-eager, like I was just dying to drop everything I was doing so I could run to be by his side.

"Good. I'm staying at the Creekside Inn. The Sovereign Suite. Do you know where it is?"

"Sure," I replied. No wonder he'd been able to get over to my apartment so quickly the night before. You could practically throw a rock out my apartment window and hit the B&B where he was staying. Okay, maybe that was a slight exaggeration, but still. "Give me about twenty minutes."

"Of course." He hung up.

"Jeff."

He didn't look up from his laptop. For the first time, I noticed he had an earbud in his right ear. Maybe he was listening to his audio capture of the alien transmissions.

"Earth to Jeff!"

That time, he did glance up, but he didn't look too thrilled at the interruption. "What?"

"I'm heading out. Kara didn't give me an exact time, but I'm guessing six o'clock at her place, since she won't be getting out of the shop until after five."

He grunted something and went right back to his laptop.

I decided to take that as a yes. Shouldering my purse, I let myself out of Lance's condo and went back to the van, then drove over to the Creekside Inn. Their parking lot wasn't very big, and I hoped it was okay to leave my van there. Then again, they must have some accommodation for people coming to visit guests.

Luckily, there were pretty little signs pointing the way to all the various rooms, so I didn't have too hard a time finding the Sovereign Suite. Somewhere below me, I heard the soft chatter of the creek running over its stony bed. It never got cold enough here for Oak Creek to actually freeze over, so it flowed all winter long.

I knocked on the door, and Martin Jones opened it at once. "Hello, Kirsten," he said, then stepped aside so I could enter the room.

"Wow," I remarked once I was inside and had gotten a good look at my surroundings. Not exactly the sort of $69-a-night motel that you'd expect a government agent to be holed up in. "My tax dollars at work, huh?"

"This location is…important."

"Hmm." The place was almost the size of my

apartment, with a little freestanding fireplace and French doors that opened to a private patio. It was too cold to sit outside and enjoy it, of course. I tried my best not to look at the enormous Victorian-style king bed. It was a little too easy to imagine being in it with him.

I reached up to remove the scarf from my throat, but Martin said at once, "No, keep it on. We can't talk here."

Mystified, I stared back at him. "Then why did you ask me to meet you in your room?"

"Follow me." He crossed the room to the French doors and opened them, indicating as he did so that I should step outside.

I did as he requested, and paused on the little herringbone-brick patio while he secured the doors behind him. As I waited, I noticed there was a stone path leading away from the patio, and that was where he ended up taking me. The path wound down through bare cottonwoods and sycamores, and I could see patches of snow gleaming here and there in the shadowy spots. As we walked, the sound of the creek got louder, until we came to a small wooden bridge that crossed the water at a narrow point.

Here he halted, and so I stopped as well, then gave him a questioning look.

He pointed at the water with a black-gloved finger. "It's the creek," he explained. "The water blocks their instruments. They can't listen to us here."

"Are you saying they're listening everywhere else?" That was not the sort of revelation I really wanted to hear.

"Not that they necessarily *are*, but that they *can*. Your friend Michael's house offers the same protection because of its location."

This made me wonder whether I should call Kara and tell her to move tonight's meeting to Michael's place. It would be cramped, but it's kind of silly to have a council of war if the enemy has a direct pipeline to everything you're saying.

"Okay," I said, trying to ignore the cold seeping up through the bottom of my boots. If I'd known we were going to be hiking around in the semi-wilderness, I would've put on my waffle-stompers, not these thinner cowboy boots. "So, you've got me in the cone of silence. What exactly do you expect me to do next?"

Those storm-blue eyes scanned my face carefully, as if looking for his own answers there. "I expect you to defeat them."

I couldn't help it. I let out a laugh before I realized he was being deadly serious. "Okay, Agent Jones—"

"Martin."

Not sure exactly what to do with that, I stumbled on. "Okay, Martin, thanks for the vote of confidence, but I don't know what you expect me to do."

"I expect you to tap the powers within yourself to drive them from here once and for all."

This conversation was not going the way I had expected it to. All right, I actually didn't know for sure what I *had* expected, but somewhere in the back of my mind, I had probably hoped that he'd offer assistance, would say the entire MIB brigade was about to descend on the town at any minute to do a clean sweep of the alien horde. Nice fairy tale, but it didn't seem to bear much resemblance to my current reality.

I shoved my hands in the pockets of my coat. "And how am I supposed to do that? I have to warn you, I'm not a very good shot. Just last month, when Lance took me shooting at the range over in Cottonwood, he told me I couldn't hit the broad side of a barn."

Incongruously, Martin smiled at that remark. But the smile faded quickly enough, and he turned away from me to gaze down at the creek as it burbled and chattered a scant yard beneath our feet. "It won't be that kind of battle. Because of the powers you've inherited from your father, you're the one who must confront the aliens. This is your world, your place… and your fight."

As reassurances went, that one was a little lacking. "What powers *are* they, anyway? And how come you seem to know all about them? Or is this sort of thing common knowledge at Man in Black Central?"

He didn't answer for a moment, just kept staring into the clear waters of the creek as if they could somehow provide their own answers. Finally, he looked away and faced me once again. His expression was bleak, as if he knew he had to tell me something important but worried I might not react all that well to it.

"No, it's not," he said, the words slow, as if he was turning each one over in his head before he let it escape his lips. "You see, I haven't been entirely truthful with you—or even the people who think I'm working for them."

"The people who—" I broke off and peered up into his face, trying to understand what he was saying. "Are you telling me you're *not* a Man in Black?"

"I've been working for that organization, but only as it suited me...suited the situation." Another hesitation. I could see the muscles in his jaw tense before he went on, "You see, I'm of the same race as your father."

It was too much. I stared at him, thinking he couldn't possibly mean what I thought he'd meant. "You're—you're an *alien*?" Even as I asked the question, I couldn't believe how silly it sounded.

But he nodded. "Yes. We've been observing your world for many years now."

If my father was really the same race as "Agent" Jones, then I wanted to retort that dear old dad had been doing a bit more than just observing, if you know what I mean. All I said, though, was, "Then why not help us? You've got to have more of these 'powers' than I do, if I'm half human."

Martin let out a very human-sounding sigh and shook his head. "It's not that easy. We are supposed to observe, and occasionally instruct—as Otto does with Persephone—but we can't interfere directly."

"Oh, great, Otto's one of you, too?" I didn't wait for him to reply, since the answer seemed clear enough. "So, you're going to be my Obi-Wan Kenobi or something and show me the ways of the Force so I can defeat the evil Empire?"

"If you want to put it in those terms, then yes."

I almost stormed off the bridge then and there. No way had I signed up for anything like this. But something in his eyes kept me rooted on the spot, something that looked almost like pleading, as if he knew I wanted to call the whole thing off.

Don't give up on me, that look said.

But...an alien? Then again, as Grayson had proved, there were aliens and then there were *aliens.* Of course, anyone who's made a study of UFOs and the races people had encountered while dealing with them knew it wasn't just the Greys or the Insectoids or the Reptilians. Many people had reported being visited by aliens who looked like extremely beautiful human beings. I'd always halfway dismissed those stories as wishful thinking, but maybe there was more truth to them than I'd realized.

I gripped the wooden railing of the bridge, almost as if I knew I needed it to keep me there, to prevent me from staggering under the burden Martin had just placed on me. Keeping my own gaze fixed on the ever-moving water, on the little moss-covered stones and the creek bed of red mud, I asked, "If you're not supposed to interfere, then why was one of your people club-hopping in Scottsdale and banging random women? Scientific research?"

"Kirsten."

His tone was gentle. Too gentle. I didn't look up but just stood there, fingers clenched on the rail. The bridge creaked a little as he stepped toward me and came to stand beside me, very close. I could almost feel the heat of his body, a welcome relief from the chilly air.

"It's difficult to explain. My people—your people, too—can see the shifts and twists of time itself, of possible futures. We don't pretend to predict it, because one chance decision can change everything. However, that doesn't mean we can't see the most probable future. Your father saw this day coming, knew that humanity's best hope was to have a defender who shared both worlds...and he paid a very great price for it."

At those words, a chill went through me that had nothing to do with the frosty December air. I tilted a sideways glance at Martin. "What do you mean?"

He wouldn't meet my eyes. "The penalties for interference are harsh, even if the interference is spurred by good intentions."

"They didn't...." I let the words trail off, not wanting to say out loud what I was thinking. Funny how I could be so worried about this father I had never met, who hadn't bothered to stick around to see if I would be okay.

"Oh, no," Martin said quickly. "My people don't believe in capital punishment. But many feel that what happened to him might as well have been death." His mouth tightened, and I had a feeling he wouldn't give me any more information on that subject even if I asked for it.

"So...this," I ventured, guessing it was time to redirect the conversation away from my father. "Isn't what you're doing the same thing as interfering?"

"No more than what Otto does when he sends a suggestion Persephone's way. Guiding and instructing is permitted. Personally dropping the hammer on the intruders in Secret Canyon is definitely forbidden."

And what about the way you looked at me last night, held me? Isn't that getting a little close to fraternizing? No way I'd ask Martin that, though. Since I didn't have the alien etiquette handbook on me, I didn't know if a half-breed like me was off-limits or what.

I found myself hoping that I wasn't, which was probably crazier than anything he'd yet told me. Now I knew he wasn't of this world...and I found myself not caring all that much. He looked too human, sounded too human. Those arms that had held me last night definitely felt human, too, no matter what his DNA might have to say on the matter.

He was probably waiting for me to respond, but I couldn't find the right words. I knew I should probably ask him what the first step in this "training" was, and how on earth he was going to awaken powers that had been dormant in me for years. But asking those questions would push me over a threshold, put me on a path that would lead to...what? A kind of confrontation I'd never dreamed of, that was for sure.

Just the smallest shift of weight, and my arm was brushing against his. His hand reached out for mine, gloved fingers twining around one another, and then he was pulling me against him, his mouth coming down to touch my lips. His flesh was warm, so warm compared to the icy breeze that tugged at my hair. And his touch was like a shockwave going through me, sending heat down into my chilled limbs, making my whole body almost cramp with need.

Before then, I'd never really believed the myth that when you kissed the right person, you'd know it. I'd kissed a random sampling of guys, some of them better at it than others, and while it was fun, I'd always had a sort of "take it or leave it" attitude about the whole thing.

What an idiot I'd been.

Because kissing Martin Jones—if that was even his real name, which I sort of doubted—made me understand at last how another person's touch could set your blood on fire, make you feel as if you'd been sleepwalking through your life up until that point. I tasted him, smelled some kind of smoky, spicy scent on his skin that could have been wood smoke or cologne or just tantalizing alien chemistry. It didn't matter. None of it mattered, except that I never wanted this to stop.

But of course, it did. A minute later, he lifted his mouth from mine, very gently.

"Was that part of my training?" I asked, and that flash of a grin came and went again. It lit up his whole face, making him seem almost like a different person.

"No," he replied. "That was me doing something I shouldn't have but very much wanted to."

A little of the afterglow faded. "Are you going to get in trouble?" What a stupid question. It sounded as if I was asking whether he was going to get detention.

"That's nothing you need to worry about."

Which was a fairly elegant way of sidestepping my question. "But—"

He smothered my mouth with his again, this second kiss having an urgency about it that made my body respond even more. I wrapped my arms around him, pressed myself against his chest, opened my mouth to his, and let him kiss me hard, kiss me in a way that made my head buzz and the world seem to tilt around me.

The consequences of what we were doing—if there were even going to be any—seemed very far away at that moment. It didn't matter who he was or where he'd come from, only that I wanted him with every cell in my body.

"Oh, wow—sorry!" came an unfamiliar voice, and Martin and I broke apart.

Somehow, I managed to focus, and saw an older couple bundled up in puffy coats and mufflers hesitating on the path. Obviously, they'd wanted to cross the bridge, but we'd been, well, blocking it.

The heat in my face then had nothing to do with passion. "No problem," I mumbled, and took Martin by the hand and dragged him past them, back up to his suite.

As we went, I thought I heard a whispered convo of disapproval, something about a man his age messing around with a girl like me. I supposed it did look sort of bad, especially since Martin was still wearing his long wool coat over his black suit and looked way more "official" than I did. We sure didn't fit the profile of a vacationing couple.

I waited until we were back in his room before I said, "Guess that path isn't quite as private as you thought it was."

He shrugged and began unbuttoning his over-coat. It was fairly warm inside. "I suppose more than one suite here has access to that path. The probability of someone going down there in this cold was fairly low. A miscalculation."

"Oh, really?"

His eyes took on a wicked glint. "Yes, really. Are you embarrassed?"

"No," I replied. "I'm not the one they were calling a dirty old man."

Instead of smiling, he sobered abruptly. "I am a good deal older than you."

"So what? Lance is twelve years older than Kara."

"It's not quite the same thing."

No, I supposed it wasn't. Persephone had always spoken of Otto as this apparently ageless being, and he'd been visiting her for almost twenty years. Going by appearance alone, Martin looked as if he had the same dozen or so years on me that Lance had on Kara, but that didn't mean much.

I realized I didn't want to ask Martin how old he was. That might change everything, and I didn't want it to. I only wanted him.

Something in my face must have shifted, because he dropped his overcoat on one of the side chairs and came to me, pulling me close, holding me against him. I felt his lips brush the top of my head before he said, "We can stop this here, if you wish. This must all be very strange to you—"

"Well, that much is true," I said, interrupting him. "But you can hold up right now with this talk about stopping things. Don't kiss a girl like that if you don't mean to follow through."

A small chuckle. "I have to say, I'm glad you feel that way."

I wanted to stay there in his arms forever, but I knew we didn't have forever. Not even close.

After pulling away slightly, I asked, "So what's next? I mean, I'd love to plop down on that couch there and spend the rest of the afternoon making out, but I'm guessing that's not going to help much when it comes to booting those aliens out of Secret Canyon."

"No, probably not." He shoved his hands in his pants pockets, seeming to think. "I have a back-up plan. I chose this place because of its proximity to the creek and to your apartment, but I also reserved another location, just in case."

"Where?"

"A place called Forest Houses."

I knew exactly where that was. Forest Houses was a collection of cabins about six miles out of Sedona proper, up along 89A as it wound its way toward Flagstaff. For isolation, it really couldn't be beat—and since the cabins themselves ranged up and down the creek itself, there wasn't much chance of alien eavesdropping. I'd never stayed there, but Lindsey's former boyfriend got them a cabin for New Year's there once. Supposedly it had been pretty romantic. Not romantic enough, however, since they'd broken up about a month later, although I doubted their stay at Forest Houses had much to do with that.

Being holed up in a cabin alone with Martin Jones didn't sound too bad. But....

"I need to be back at Kara's by six," I said, then added, "or wherever we're having our meeting." It probably would be a good idea if I texted her or something to tell her it would be safer if we all got together at Michael's house.

If Martin was surprised by my *non sequitur*, he didn't show it. "That's not a problem. It's just a little past noon now."

His mention of the time made me realize I was hungry. "Well, if you're going to take me up there to teach me to walk on water, could we get something to eat first? It sounds like I need to charge my batteries before we get started with this 'training.'"

"Sure," he said easily, and his eyes glinted a little. "I'll just expense it."

I grinned, because I knew he was getting me back for my "taxpayers" comment earlier. "Well, in that case, you can take me someplace fancy."

The gleam didn't leave his eyes, even as he said in tones of mock concern, "Fancy? For lunch?"

"It's okay," I told him as he gathered up his coat and put it back on. "I have a cunning plan."

CHAPTER NINE

ACTUALLY, I DID HAVE A PLAN. ALTHOUGH IT WAS great to live in a small town where your family is sort of a fixture and a lot of the locals know you, it can be a real pain if you ever want to do anything on the down-low. So I decided it would be best to eat in Uptown Sedona, mostly because it was the really touristy part of town and there was always a good deal of "churn" in the wait staff at the various eating establishments. My chances of being recognized were a lot lower there. And while I wasn't embarrassed to be seen with Martin *per se,* I knew people would start chattering if they saw me having lunch with an older man...especially one who looked like a younger, handsomer Blues Brother. Minus the hat, that is.

I explained as much of this as I felt comfortable with to Martin, who agreed that discretion was always preferable. He followed me back to my apartment so I could leave the Night Tours van there, and then I climbed into the front seat of his black Ford Taurus.

"Seriously, have you guys ever thought of driving something that doesn't scream 'unmarked law enforcement vehicle'?" I asked as I buckled my seat-belt and Martin pulled out of the parking lot, heading north toward Uptown.

His brows drew together. "This is the vehicle they assigned me. It seems adequate, given the limitations of your technology."

I reminded myself that he must have a seriously different perspective on this world and everything in it than I did. "Well, I wouldn't know that much about 'adequate,' but you should really try changing it up sometime. Maybe a Camaro or something."

"I'll pass that on," he said, and even in profile, I could tell he was amused.

So many things I wanted to know. Exactly how long had he been a mole in the MIB department? I supposed a being from a race as advanced as his wouldn't have any trouble faking the background checks and physical tests required to have a job like that, but still, it didn't sound like much fun.

"What happened to your partner?" I asked.

"I told you. He was reassigned."

I shifted in my seat, then arched an eyebrow at him and gave him my best "don't bullshit me" look.

A lift of his shoulders under the heavy overcoat. "I knew he shouldn't be here this time. Frankly, he'd only get in the way."

"So he's not…one of you?"

"No. Human, born in Gary, Indiana, actually."

"And he never guessed you weren't who you claimed to be?"

"Would you have guessed, if I hadn't told you?"

He had me there. "Probably not."

"Well, then." Martin shrugged. "In Agent DeSalvo's case, it was easy enough to manufacture a situation where he'd be assigned a new partner and sent elsewhere."

"Elsewhere being?"

"Lake Okoboji, Iowa."

I laughed and shook my head. "Like in the *X-Files* episode?"

Martin shrugged again. "It's a known UFO hotspot. And a thousand miles away from Sedona. It wasn't too difficult for me to persuade my superiors that I could do a simple check-in here on my own."

Exactly what form that "persuasion" had taken, I probably didn't want to know. I had a feeling that members of Martin's race could push the bounds of that whole "no interference" policy when it suited them.

I had to hold my questions for a few minutes, though, because we'd pulled into the parking lot behind the building where our destination, the Open Range Grille, was located. Even with the chilly weather, the sidewalks up here were fairly crowded. I knew Kara would have killed to have that kind of foot traffic nearby, but at least she owned the building where the UFO Depot was located, and so her overhead wasn't that high. Up here, you'd have to have serious walk-in business just to cover the rent.

The restaurant had a large patio with an absolutely amazing red rock view, but even I wasn't crazy enough to try *al fresco* dining when it was barely forty-five degrees out. Instead, we got a table in a cozy corner and divested ourselves of our overcoats. The girl who led us to our table was a stranger, with an accent that told me she'd probably come here to Sedona recently; she sounded as if she wouldn't be out of place serving barbecue at a Texas roadhouse. Good.

I ordered hot tea, and Martin asked for water when our waiter showed up—another stranger. Of course, it wasn't as if I knew everybody in Sedona, but if I'd waltzed into, say, the Secret Garden Café with Martin in tow, I knew I would have had a lot of 'splainin' to do.

Neither one of us said much of anything until the waiter came back with our drinks and then took our food orders. I noticed that Martin didn't seem to have any problem with ordering a bison burger and fries. So much for advanced races being vegetarians. I got the same thing, mostly because it sounded good.

A silence fell that was more than a bit uncomfortable. Maybe it was the memory of the kisses we'd shared hanging over us, or maybe it was just that Martin guessed I was about to launch into more questions.

"So how do you get a gig like this, anyway?" I asked after stirring some honey into my tea.

"Like what?"

"*Faux* Man in Black. I mean, how come you're pretending to be a government agent, while Otto gets the whole spirit-guide gig? Not that pretending to be a dead Turkish eunuch sounds like it's a ball of laughs, either."

I'd thought that Martin might smile at my comment, but instead, he frowned and used his fore-finger to trace through some of the condensation from his water glass on the wooden tabletop. "We're not all that different from you, in many ways. We have our strengths and weaknesses. Otto is very good at perceiving the time threads, and that makes him a good spiritual advisor. I happen to have some facility at interacting with humans and emulating their behavior, so it makes more sense for me to be stationed where I am."

"'Stationed'?" I repeated. "So you're all given assignments by someone higher up the food chain?"

"'Stationed' is probably not the best word for the situation," he said, although I noticed he didn't quite meet my eyes as he said it. "I certainly made the choice to come here. I could have gone to a different posting if I'd wanted to."

"But you didn't."

"No."

Again, I got the sense that he was concealing a lot more from me than he was telling. I guessed I shouldn't be all that surprised. He'd been dealing in secrets for quite some time, apparently. "And you've been a Man in Black for how long now?"

"Five years."

His straightforward answer surprised me. I'd expected more equivocating. At least he hadn't said something like, "Oh, since before you were born."

Then he added, "That's when the base in Secret Canyon was first established."

"Really?"

"You sound surprised."

It was my turn to shrug. "Well, there've been reports of UFOs there for years and years, so I just figured—"

"Some of those were advance scouts. Some were what you might refer to as 'friendlies.' But as the situation developed further, and the group in Secret Canyon made their beachhead, it became clear we needed someone on the inside. So here I am."

It was stupid of me to feel reassured that he'd only been hanging around this planet for the past five years or so. It was a comfortingly normal time-line, and one that matched his physical appearance, more or less.

Never mind that he could have lived a thousand years before he ever got here.

At that moment, the waiter showed up with our food, so the conversation came to an abrupt halt. And although I wanted to get more out of Martin while he was still apparently willing to talk, it didn't seem too smart to let my burger get cold while I gave him the third degree. I took a bite, which told me it would be doing that burger a grave injustice if I ignored it while trying to pick Martin's brain. So I ate in silence for a few minutes while my mind churned away, trying to decide which questions were mostly likely to get answers.

It didn't help that every once in a while, I would shift in my seat, or Martin would move in his, and our knees would brush against one another, sending a whole new set of hot shivers up and down my body. Obviously, my lizard brain, the one that controlled those lower functions, didn't care whether the man sitting next to me was human or not.

Kara must have had a way more obvious "off" switch when it came to that sort of thing. Then again, she'd been in love with Lance for years before Grayson came along. Grayson was the distraction, not the other way around. And while I really didn't get the whole Lance thing—although he did have a certain tough-jawed Clint Eastwood vibe going on—I couldn't fault Kara for going with her heart.

But I sure as hell hadn't been mooning after anyone. Just the opposite, in fact. No doubt a shrink would have told me that my avoidance of relationships was a direct reaction to my mother's promiscuity, and maybe he or she would have been right. It hadn't bothered me all that much. And now —

Now I knew what I'd been missing all this time. Whatever was going to happen, however impossible the situation, I saw something in Martin, felt a connection with him that I'd never felt with anyone else. I knew he sensed it, too. I sort of doubted that getting mixed up with me was part of the grand plan.

But he'd kissed me anyway, despite the consequences.

Whatever those might turn out to be.

"You're quiet," Martin said, setting down his bison burger and reaching for a fry.

"Oh, I was just wondering if you were going to make me dodge a remote-controlled training device that's going to shoot laser bolts at my ass."

For a second, he looked puzzled, and then I saw him nod as the *Star Wars* reference apparently sank in. "No, nothing like that. It's more about concentration at this stage. You'll see when the time comes."

I didn't know if I liked the sound of that, but there wasn't much I could do about it at this point. So I only nodded and went on to finish the rest of my meal. I had a feeling I was going to need all that protein to get me through the rest of the afternoon.

Martin's "backup" retreat was a small cabin called the Bridge House at the Forest Houses resort. I could see why he'd chosen it—the place was right on the creek, so near that apparently the whole house had gotten flooded during the heavy rains of '93, according to the Forest Houses website, which was full of little anecdotes like that. It was very close to a second, slightly larger cabin, but that cabin wasn't rented out at the moment.

"I made sure of that," he told me, a comment that

could have been ominous or completely innocent, depending on how you wanted to look at it.

"It's great," I said, after climbing the stone stairs to the front door and taking a quick look around at the scene below me. There were patches of unmelted snow here and there in the shadows of the trees, and my breath rose in the frosty air, but somehow I felt sheltered and safe here in a way that I hadn't back at the Creekside Inn.

"I thought you might like it." He unlocked the door and went inside, leaving it open for me to follow when I chose.

I lingered on the stoop for a moment. Maybe I was just trying to delay the moment when I would have to begin my training for real, or maybe I only wanted to drink in the scene, let the stillness of the place sink into my bones. Somehow it seemed important for me to be here, though, to allow the magic of the creek to work on me, prepare me for what was ahead.

Then I took in a deep breath of cold, clean air, and went inside.

Martin had already gone to the fireplace and was stacking the wood within—quite expertly, too, from what I could tell. Good thing, since it was very cold in the cabin. It didn't feel as if the heat had been on at all. Or maybe its only heat source was the fireplace.

I kept my overcoat on until the fire really took hold, sending its warmth out into the room. The place wasn't very big—there were a couple of over-sized chairs, a kitchenette, and a king-size bed—so it didn't take long before it was warm enough inside for me to unbutton my coat and sling it on the bed. It was the closest piece of furniture to the fireplace, but I thought sitting down on it might not be a good idea. Instead, I took a seat in one of the chairs and waited for Martin to do the same.

He also took off his coat and laid it on the bed next to mine, then ignored the one empty armchair and instead grasped one of the oak farmhouse-style chairs and settled it in front of me before sitting down, facing me. His expression was calm, but serious. "Are you ready?"

"I don't know," I said honestly. "I don't know what you're about to do."

"It won't hurt. I promise."

I bet you say that to all the girls. But I kept my thoughts to myself, and forced myself not to react as he reached out and took my hands in his. My fingers were chilled, even though I'd been wearing gloves outside, whereas his were warm and friendly. They didn't look extraterrestrial—they just looked like a man's strong hands, with close-clipped fingernails and the smallest dusting of dark hair along their backs.

"Have you ever done any sort of meditation?" he asked, his voice gentle, quiet.

"A little. I mean, I've tried. I'm not that good at getting my brain to shut up."

A smile flitted across his face before disappearing again. "That's fine. Just breathe in and out, slowly but deeply. Close your eyes."

I did as he requested, even though it felt strange, even though I could sense my body beginning to react to his touch on my fingers. That old lizard brain was saying it didn't want to meditate—it wanted to pull him over onto that nice king-size bed and indulge in a little rumpty-tumpty.

Crap. That was not going to get my mind to anywhere near a meditative state. I breathed in and out, forcing my thoughts to stillness, to something quiet and gentle and innocuous, like the gentle ripple of the creek only a few yards away from where I sat. Okay, that was better. Some of the pulsing heat retreated from my midsection, leaving me tranquil, contemplative.

"Good," said Martin, as if he had somehow sensed the ebb and flow of my thoughts. Maybe he had. "Now I want you to reach out with your mind. Feel the patterns of energy all around us."

Easy for him to say. I wanted to tell him that if I knew how to do that, I'd be doing psychic readings for people instead of building websites for the people who did the psychic readings. But then it was as if I sensed some strange shift in my consciousness, felt it with almost a physical twinge, and the darkness behind my eyelids flared to sudden strange light.

The light source closest to us was also the strongest, a twisting ribbon of brilliant green that I knew had to be Oak Creek itself, alive with all the myriad insects and fish and birds and mosses and everything else which composed the ecosystem that made Sedona so vibrantly alive. Past it were the more muted skeins of energy running through the woods, of the trees and the animals that moved amongst them. And beyond that was the energy of the town itself, the people bright sparks against black, all moving, all intent on their own business, weaving in and around one another in a pattern so complex and yet so beautiful I almost wanted to weep when I saw it, because in that instant, I realized nothing was random, that everything had an order to it, even if we couldn't always see it for ourselves.

But then....

It pulsed with its own dark light, like a lava flow that hadn't hardened all the way, or like tired blood moving sluggishly under a half-healed scab. The wrongness was something I'd never experienced before, and behind it was a sense that whatever had created that wrongness wanted to have it spread everywhere, so there was no more light, no more green.

My mind recoiled, and my eyelids fluttered open. I hung on to Martin's hands as if they were the only thing keeping me in this world. As I stared at him, I realized my cheeks were wet.

He reached out and brushed the tears away with a gentle finger, still holding on to my other hand with his left one. "You felt them."

I nodded, not trusting myself to speak yet. Yes, I had felt that first wave of cold at Kara's house, and then again as I was driving through the storm on I-17, but that was like turning on a shower and realizing there wasn't any hot water, compared to being thrown into the middle of the north Atlantic in the dead of winter.

After blotting his damp finger on his pants leg, he took both my hands in his again. "It's terrible. I know. But you have to know them before you can face them. Do you understand?"

"Yes," I whispered. "I mean, I'm trying to understand." I pulled in a shaky breath, noting for the first time how my hands were trembling within Martin's warm grasp, as if I'd taken a chill I couldn't shake. "Who are they, Martin? *What* are they?"

His fingers tightened around mine. "They are an ancient race, but in their case, with age did not come wisdom. Their home world was depleted of its resources long ago, and so they moved on. That's what they do—go from world to world looking for a new planet to exploit once their current one is used up. They are brilliant, and strong, but in this case, they may have finally made a fatal error."

It was a story I'd heard before—rampaging aliens determined to suck Earth dry were a staple of sci-fi action films. Too bad the concept wasn't merely fiction. "What error is that?" I asked.

"They've underestimated the resiliency of the human race. Persephone dealt them a horrible blow, even if she wasn't powerful enough to eradicate their base completely. They couldn't believe that one of their own would turn on them, but Grayson did, the humanity in his genetic material overcoming the alien DNA. And now—"

"Now?"

"Now there's you, Kirsten. Again, a blend of two worlds, a combination they didn't foresee and don't know how to fight."

Those words only made me feel colder. Okay, so I'd opened my mind enough to really sense the aliens, to know that they were just as alive as I'd feared. But it was a long way from that to somehow making sure none of them ever harmed anyone or anything on this planet again.

"I'm scared," I said.

At once, he let go of my hands and came to me, reaching out and lifting me from my chair so he could enfold me in his arms. "I know," he said. "There's nothing wrong with being frightened—as long as it doesn't keep you from doing what needs to be done. You can't let it paralyze you, because then they have all the power."

Logically, I understood what he was saying. Trying to deny the fear wouldn't make it go away. But surrendering to it would be even worse. And beneath the fear was the beginning of a tiny spark of anger, fury at these beings for coming here and thinking they could do whatever they wanted with our planet. Sure, we'd done enough already to screw it up, but it wasn't so far gone that it couldn't be saved. And I knew it was worth saving.

"Okay," I told him, feeling braver than I would have otherwise, simply because it didn't seem as if anything could go too terribly wrong while he held me in his arms. "So what now?"

"Now you rest, and then I take you back into

town so you can meet up with your friends and family."

Was he joking? I pulled away from him slightly and stared up into his face. He looked serious enough, those gorgeous eyes of his meeting mine directly.

"I don't need to rest. I can do more." As I spoke, I realized that I did feel as if I had much more energy to expend. "We've only got five days left."

The corners of his eyes crinkled a little, as if he was amused by my statement but trying hard not to show it. "The sort of focus you just learned requires more energy than you might think. And it certainly takes a lot more time than you know."

"Oh, come on—" I began, but then I glanced down at my watch and almost let out a yelp. Five-thirty? Seriously? I'd closed my eyes and gone into that trance or whatever you wanted to call it at a little past two. So I'd been lost in that strange darkness for more than three hours?

"Yes," Martin said gently. "Time functions differently in the world of the mind. I didn't want to rouse you, not when you were doing so well, but now I need to get you back."

"No kidding," I said, noticing for the first time how stiff I felt, as if I'd just stood up from watching *Avatar* or some other three-hour epic. "Kara's already on edge, so I know she'll flip out if I'm not there on time."

"Well, we can't have that." He leaned down and kissed me then, his mouth warm and welcome.

Any stiffness or weariness I might have been feeling disappeared immediately. I wished with all my heart that we could stay here in this cozy cabin, keep the fire going...and progress to better things. Any suggestions on that front would probably be shot down, though, so I didn't bother. I only let him kiss me and kissed him back, letting him know just how much I loved the feel of his mouth on mine.

When we pulled apart, I could tell he was thinking that it would be nice if we didn't have to worry about alien invasions and all that crap. Well, I'd just have to hope for the best. If by some miracle we actually won, then Martin and I would have all the time in the world to enjoy one another. And if the aliens managed to defeat us, well, then, I guessed we wouldn't be worrying about much of anything, because we'd be dead.

Cheery thought.

Spirits somewhat dampened, I went to retrieve my coat, and Martin did the same. He banked down the fire and placed the fire screen in front of the hearth. I waited while he performed these tasks, then let myself out the front door, standing in the freezing air as he locked the place up.

The drive back into town was a quiet one. I wanted to text Kara, tell her that she should move the meeting to Michael's house, but I didn't get a signal until we were practically back in Uptown. Finally, a few bars appeared on my phone at a scant fifteen minutes until six, and I sent the text then. Very late notice, and I had a feeling my sister would be less than thrilled about the whole thing. That didn't matter, though, as long as she followed my advice and didn't still attempt to have her council of war in a place where the aliens could eavesdrop on the whole thing.

A thought struck me then, and I shifted in my seat so I was facing Martin as best I could. "You keep saying the aliens can't hear us when we're near the creek, that something in its energy disrupts their equipment."

"More or less, yes."

"So how come they didn't listen in this summer, when all that was going on with Grayson? For that matter, why didn't they know Persephone and Lance and Michael were coming for them that first time back in March?"

Martin didn't look over at me as he swung the car through the first traffic circle. "Because they had no reason to."

"Huh?"

This time, he allowed himself a small smile at my confusion. "That first attack caught them completely unaware. Don't get me wrong—they knew about the UFO Depot, and they knew about your little group of UFO hunters. But of course, they didn't perceive you to be any kind of a threat, so there was no reason for them to waste resources on you. Then, over the summer, they were focused on trying to find Grayson. Their minds aren't well-suited to concepts of charity and compassion, so they never imagined that a human would take in their lost soldier and care for him when there was no profit in it. They did continue to keep a close eye on Persephone and Paul, but as they settled into a quiet life and didn't appear to be up to anything much, the aliens left them alone, too. It was more important to focus on rebuilding the base, on getting back to an operational level where they could exploit the coming solstice and its power."

"But then?" I prompted. "Something changed, right?"

"You changed," he replied.

"I what?"

We approached the second roundabout, and were getting closer and closer to my apartment. "Your father's blood was in you, even if you knew nothing about it. As you got older, it started to manifest—in ways you probably didn't even notice at the time. You had a birthday recently, right?"

"Yes," I said reluctantly. Not that it had been a birthday for the ages or anything. Kara's and my birthdays were only three days apart, and we always had celebrated them together. Two against the world and all that. But this time she was over in New Mexico, hiding her pregnancy and waiting for Grace to make her appearance, so I'd sort of limped along with those few of my friends who were still living in town and tried to make the best of it. After all, it was just birthday number twenty-three; it wasn't some milestone like twenty-one or twenty-five or—yikes—thirty.

"Well, then," Martin told me, as if that explained everything.

Yeah, right. "So, what, as these powers I didn't know I had started growing, the aliens were able to pick up on it?"

"Something like that. At first, I doubt they could tell exactly where they were coming from, but that was bound to change."

Lovely. So I had some kind of homing beacon in my blood, broadcasting to the aliens my whereabouts and what I was doing every moment of the day?

"That kind of stinks," I told him, then added, "If it's something about this race you and my father are from, then how come they're not tracking you, too?"

"Because I've been trained to block them. It's something I can show you, too, but first I had to get you to open up, to experience what it's like when your consciousness expands."

I had some acquaintances from high school who probably knew all about expanding their consciousness —they were always talking about their mushroom trips —but of course I'd stayed far away, not wanting to be Marybeth Swenson part deux. Although she generally stuck to pills and booze. You know, the high-class stuff.

"Well, I hope it's something you can show me soon, because I'm not thrilled about the aliens tracking my every movement."

"Soon," he said, his tone placating. "All things in their time."

Time. The one thing we were running out of.

Martin pulled into the parking lot of my apartment complex. There was an empty space next to the van, so he parked there.

"Maybe you should come with me," I told him. Beyond the obvious hormonal reasons, I just felt better with him around. Safer. The thought of the aliens knowing where I was going and what I was doing almost paralyzed me.

"No, I don't think so."

"Why not?" I demanded. "I know you could explain all this much better than I ever could."

His expression was unreadable, stony—just as I imagined a real MIB's would be. "It's not my place to do that. I'm here to help you, guide you. But you're the one it comes down to in the end." Finally, a trace of a wry grin pulled at his mouth. "Besides, do you really feel like explaining me to Kara right now?"

"Probably not," I admitted, and leaned over and gave him a swift kiss on the cheek. "Although, being Kara, she'll most likely figure it out anyway."

He gave a philosophical shrug. "We can deal with that when the time comes. But now—" And he glanced at the digital clock on the dashboard. Five fifty-eight. I was going to be late no matter what, but no point in stalling any further.

"Now I have to go. I know." I began to turn away, but he caught my hand and pulled me toward him, burying my mouth under his, tongue touching tongue even as his fingers twined themselves around mine.

Then he broke it off and said, "Be careful."

All I wanted to do was reach out to him and kiss him again. And again. And again. But I knew I had to go.

"I will," I said, even though I knew it was an empty promise.

After all, if the aliens really wanted to come get me, what could I do to stop them?

CHAPTER TEN

THE ALIENS MUST HAVE HAD BETTER THINGS TO DO WITH their time, because I made it over to Michael's house without too much trouble. Oh, I guessed they were probably watching me, but I came and went at Michael's place usually at least once a week, so there wouldn't be anything that odd about my movements. And really, although I knew for a fact that people got abducted all the time, the aliens probably didn't want to do it with a built-in audience. Sedona was way too public when it came to that sort of thing, since so many of its visitors were there to actively look for UFO activity. Better to scoop up your anal-probe victims in East Bumfuck, Kansas, or something.

I saw Lance's Jeep and Persephone's red Volvo and Jeff's battered Astro van ranged up and down in front of the house, so at least I knew Kara had gotten the word out. Since there wasn't any room on the street directly in front of the property, I had to park almost a block away. As I did so, I cast a suspicious glance up at the sky. No weird lights, but the clouds were getting thick. We'd probably have more snow before dawn.

No reason to knock; I didn't think Michael ever locked his front door. I let myself in and saw that everyone was clustered in the over-cluttered living room. Paul and Lance sat on a couple of folding chairs, since Michael didn't have enough real furniture to accommodate everyone.

"Sorry I'm late," I said, preemptively apologizing so Kara wouldn't have a chance to give me crap for my tardiness. "I'm glad you all got the message about meeting here."

"Yeah, about that." Lance straightened in his borrowed chair and gave me a penetrating look. "Care to elaborate on how you got this intel?"

I hesitated, but I knew I was going to have to mention Martin sooner or later...even if I wasn't about to tell the whole story. "Agent Jones warned me that Kara's house might not be the safest place for this conversation."

At my mention of Martin, I saw Kara's head go up a little, as if she'd caught something in my inflection that didn't smell quite right. Jesus. If I couldn't hide anything from her, how the hell was I ever going to manage to conceal my doings from the aliens?

"Oh, yeah, our visiting MIB," Lance drawled. "He drop any other pearls of wisdom?"

It didn't take a rocket scientist to figure out that

my brother-in-law was less than thrilled at what he perceived as governmental intrusion into the situation. "Um…a few things," I hedged, and then shot a questioning glance over at Kara. I wasn't sure how much she'd told the others, if anything. After all, she'd been stuck at the shop all day.

She gave a small shake of the head, apparently indicating that everyone except her was still in the dark. Great. I really didn't feel like having to spill my personal secrets in front of everyone, but it seemed that I didn't have much of a choice.

"Well, he hasn't given me much in the way of particulars, but the aliens are planning their final push for the solstice. That's this coming Sunday," I added unnecessarily, since I was pretty sure everyone listening to me knew when the solstice was, if not down to the second. Come to think of it, I didn't, either. I'd have to follow up on that when I had a spare moment.

Not a whole lot of reaction from the crowd, although I thought I saw some sympathy in Persephone's expression, as if she was able to sense something of what I was feeling. Too bad she couldn't just reach into my brain and pull everything out so I wouldn't have to stand there and spill my guts in front of everybody.

"So…." I let out a sigh and realized I hadn't even put down my purse or taken off my coat. So I did both those things, and hung the coat on Michael's now-crowded coat rack. It was a stalling tactic, but I needed some time to figure out how best to phrase what I needed to tell them.

Then I realized there was no way to say any of it without it sounding crazy. Good thing the people watching me with expectant faces sort of specialized in crazy.

"It turns out the father I never knew was some kind of an alien or something," I announced.

I could tell no one was expecting that particular revelation, not even Persephone the psychic. Widened eyes and shocked looks greeted my remark —even from Jeff—and I saw Lance give Kara a narrow glance when she didn't respond with similar astonishment. It was pretty clear that she'd already known what I was about to say, and he was none too happy about being left out of the loop.

Well, they could work out their domestic problems later. I knew I had to forge ahead if I was ever going to get through this. "Anyway, I guess because of that, I have some powers that might help with defeating the aliens."

"What kind of powers?" Lance asked.

It figured he'd be the one to ask that question. "Well, I don't know for sure yet. I mean, I've been sensing the aliens more and more, and I guess being tuned to them is the first step…. Anyway, Agent Jones is helping me with figuring that out."

"Why would he know anything about that?" Paul asked, his expression frankly curious.

Oh, crap. I had gotten the distinct impression that Martin really didn't want the facts of his true identity spread all over the place, so I'd have to figure out a way to make this sound believable. "He's—well, he's been tracking the aliens for the past five years. So he knows a lot about their movements and the way they think."

I hoped that explanation sounded plausible enough. Paul's eyebrows drew together, as if he was analyzing the likeliness of the situation, while next to him, Persephone cocked her head to one side and stared slightly upward, looking like she was getting advice from on high or something. Maybe she was. I'd heard via Kara that Otto hadn't been coming around as much lately, although I wondered if he would decide to drop in now that things were soon coming to a head.

Lance, of course, appeared suspicious, but since he tended to look that way a majority of the time, I wasn't all that worried about it. Michael gave a small nod, as if accepting my explanation at face value. And Jeff—well, he was scowling, which wasn't strange at all, since that was his default facial expression anyway.

My sister wore an odd look of her own, as if she was doing some mental calculations and trying to see whether my story fit in with them or not. Oh, well. I knew she and I were going to get into it at some point, probably, but as long as it wasn't here in front of everybody, I'd just have to count my blessings.

"Anyway," I went on, knowing I needed to get off the topic of Agent Jones as soon as possible, "Jeff was just telling me this morning that he'd figured out the frequency of the aliens' transmissions. Any closer to cracking the code, Jeff?"

As I'd hoped, all attention transferred itself to Jeff, who appeared decidedly not happy at being put on the spot.

"And when exactly were you going to mention this?" Lance inquired. His irritation only appeared to be getting worse.

"When I had something concrete to report," Jeff replied in tones of equal annoyance. "I can track their transmissions now, that's true, but if I can't figure out what they're saying, that doesn't help us very much, does it? Besides, I knew trying to have a meaningful conversation about it while you were babysitting was probably a futile endeavor."

"Boys," said Persephone. She sounded calm enough, but there was sufficient steel in her tone that they both subsided…somewhat.

Despite everything, I had to fight to keep a smile off my face. She'd sounded just a little too much like Ms. D'Antonio, my eighth-grade English teacher, who'd always been able to strike fear into even the most hormone-crazed thirteen-year-olds.

"Well, if you can come up with anything, that would be really helpful," I said. "Because right now, although we have a date, we don't have much more to go on than that. I'm going to work on picking their brains from my end, but coming at it from both sides might get us to a solution a lot faster."

"Working on it," Jeff mumbled. "Would've still been doing that if you hadn't called us all here."

Although I was tempted to fling a retort back in his direction, I held my tongue. Jeff and I had fallen into a pattern of bickering like an old married couple most of the time, but there falling into that behavior now would only waste more time. "I know you are," I said, hoping that my tone of conciliation read as more or less genuine. "Because I did learn one thing today, and it's that these aliens aren't taking any prisoners this time. They want this world for themselves, and they're going to do whatever they have to in order to achieve that goal. No more messing around with mind control and trying to turn us into slaves—they're going for the whole scorched-earth thing."

"How do you know that for certain?" Paul asked.

I noticed that Persephone had reached out and was gripping his hand, as if to reassure herself that he was there. And Kara clutched Grace a little closer to her, one hand cupping the baby's head. Her expression was worried, but also somehow fierce. The old mama-bear instincts coming out in the face of danger, I supposed.

"I just do," I replied, not wanting to say much more than that. "I sensed it today, felt something of what they intend to do, even if I don't have all the details." Okay, so that was only partly true. A lot of my information had come from Martin, but I really didn't feel like going into all of that at the moment. Some misdirection wasn't that big a deal, as long as everyone got the point that the aliens were done messing around with fun stuff like mind control and possession and were going straight ahead to total global domination.

"It doesn't matter how she knows it," Michael put in, speaking for the first time. "The important thing is that she sees the truth of the matter."

I wanted to hug him. But Lance still looked far from convinced.

"Okay, so the truth of the matter is that things are going sideways fast," he said. "What can we do about it? I think we're all agreed that another assault on the base is out of the question."

"Of course it is!" Kara exclaimed. "They'd see you coming from miles away."

"Kara's right," I said. "The thing is, I'm not sure how much any of you *can* do. Agent Jones made it pretty clear that this one is on me. "

My sister made a sound of protest, but I just shook my head at her. I knew she only wanted to protect me—after all, she'd been doing that very thing for most of her life—but I was beginning to realize I couldn't be sheltered forever.

"What I want you all to do," I continued, my voice picking up a strength and confidence that startled even me, as if I was channeling some energy not entirely mine, "is to stay together, and stay safe. Their power is in darkness, in isolation. I'm not asking you all to bunk here at Michael's or anything—"

"Thank God," Lance muttered.

"—but I do think Jeff at least should come and stay here, or maybe take the spare room at Paul and Persephone's or something."

Persephone looked aghast for a second or two before she could adjust her features into something a little more socially acceptable. Jeff was giving me a narrow glare, as if he was trying to figure out why I didn't just offer to have him come crash on my couch. But I knew that would never work, not with Martin coming and going at unexpected intervals. I really wanted to keep those two out of one another's orbit for as long as possible.

"He should be here," Michael said. "He's working on a sensitive project. Better that he be here by the creek where the aliens can't tap into what he's doing."

This sounded very sensible, and I nodded. "You're right. And don't give me that look, Jeff. I don't think it's safe at the condo for you. It's the farthest west of all our houses, and closest to, well... you know."

The scowl disappeared from Jeff's face as he appeared to chew on that piece of data for a few seconds, and he almost looked afraid. It was pretty obvious to me that he hadn't thought about the downsides to crashing at Lance's condo.

"Okay," I went on, "I'm not saying we all have to turn into hermits or anything—in fact, it's probably safer to be in public places as much as possible. Shopping, the movies, whatever. But Kara, I won't be able to go back to the store until this is all over."

She gave me a look of outright consternation. "But—"

"I can't babysit the UFO Depot and train to

confront the aliens at the same time. No way in hell. And I think the survival of the human race is just a little bit more important than your receipts."

Almost as soon as I made that remark, I wished I could take the words back, because the anger in her face melted away, to be replaced by something dangerously close to embarrassment. It really wasn't her fault; she'd lived and breathed the UFO Depot for the past six years, and stressing about keeping the business going had to be a constant background noise in her head.

"You're right," she said. "We have more important things to focus on."

I could tell the rest of the group was made a little uncomfortable by watching this exchange, and I didn't really blame them. But at least now we'd gotten that out of the way. I had a feeling the "closed for family emergency" sign was going to have a repeat engagement on the front door of the shop real soon.

"All right," I went on, trying to sound as brisk and matter-of-fact as possible. It felt weird for me to be the one addressing the whole group, being the person in charge, but that was what appeared to have fallen to me on this particular go-'round. "Michael, can you go with Jeff to pick up his stuff at the condo and bring it back here?"

He nodded.

"Kara, Lance, just hang tight as best you can. You need to be watching out for Grace. Some goes for you guys," I added, looking over at Paul and Persephone.

He leaned forward a little in his rickety folding chair. "It's okay if we have people over, though?"

It seemed like an odd question to me. Paul and Persephone weren't exactly the partying type. "Um… you planning on throwing a wild solstice bash or something?"

At my question, Paul looked almost embarrassed, but Persephone spoke up then, pride clear in her tone. "Some scouts from the Discovery Channel are coming into town tomorrow to talk to Paul. They're interested in having him host a show about the paranormal."

All at once, the room got very noisy as everyone started offering their congratulations. Paul waved them off and said, "It's very preliminary. I really didn't want to say anything until things were a little further along in the process. And a TV show definitely takes a back seat to what's going on here."

Despite everything, I couldn't help being excited about the possibility of knowing a real-life celebrity. Okay, Paul was certainly well-known in UFO circles and had a lot of dedicated fans, but that still wasn't the same thing as having your own television show.

"That's awesome, Paul," I told him. "I don't think you need to cancel your appointment or anything. I mean, I'm pretty sure the aliens aren't going to do anything if there are people hanging around your house with TV cameras and stuff. You know how publicity-shy they are."

He nodded, and both he and Persephone couldn't

hide their relief. I couldn't blame them. Talk about your once-in-a-lifetime opportunities.

I'd just have to make sure they'd be around to enjoy their fame.

The gathering broke up soon after that. Kara and Lance insisted on walking me to the van, as if they thought the aliens were going to swoop down at any moment and beam me right up. I kind of doubted that would happen, but I knew better than to argue. Michael's street was only lit by the lamps on the houses themselves, so it was pretty dark outside.

"This Agent Jones," Lance said abruptly, just as I was turning my key in the van's door lock. "Can you trust him?"

Trust him? I thought. *I think I'm falling in love with him.*

Since I knew that answer would only open the mother of all cans of worms, I settled for what I hoped was a nonchalant shrug. "I've got no reason not to. It's pretty obvious he's doing all he can to help me defeat the aliens."

"'Everything'?" Lance repeated. "Doesn't sound like he's doing much to get his own hands dirty."

"Because it's not his fight!" I retorted, then realized in my haste to defend Martin, I'd let something slip that I really shouldn't have.

"Not his fight?" Kara asked, tugging the hood of Grace's tiny sweatshirt farther down over her forehead as protection against the chilly night air. "He told me once he was on our side. So how can this not be his fight?"

"Well—" I floundered for a second, then said, "I mean, he knows he doesn't have the powers to take the aliens on. So the only real 'fighting' he can do is train me. That's all I meant."

Even on the dimly lit street, I could see how dubious both Lance's and Kara's expressions were. Neither of them seemed too inclined to push it, though.

"Okay," Kara said. "We need to get Grace inside. I guess we can talk about this later."

"Sure," I replied, thankful for Kara's motherly hovering. At least this way, I'd have enough breathing space to come up with a better story, should she decide to push it the next time we talked. "Be safe. I'll send you a text when I get home, just so you know I'm okay."

"Great." I could tell she was relieved by that small olive branch. "'Bye, Kiki." And she gave me a quick hug, sort of squashing me against Grace, who made a tiny mewling sound of protest but didn't cry, because she was just that good.

They headed back toward Lance's Jeep then, and I got into the Night Tours van and wheeled it around so I was pointed in the right direction to get back to the highway. By then, both Persephone's and Jeff's vehicles had disappeared from their parking spaces. Thank God Jeff was coming to stay with Michael. He'd probably bitch and moan about it, but at least he'd be safe.

For now, anyway.

CHAPTER ELEVEN

I'D BARELY LET MYSELF IN AND LOCKED THE DOOR behind me when I heard a knock. Although I wasn't expecting him, I knew right away who it must be.

"Lurking again?" I asked as I let Martin in, then locked up once more.

He didn't crack a smile. "We prefer to call it 'surveilling.'"

"Whatever." I did grin, just a little, but hid it by looking down to unbutton my coat and remove my scarf. And if I smiled more because I was glad to see him than because of his maybe-quip, well, who could blame me? Around him, I didn't feel as if I had to hide anything. "Just couldn't stay away, huh?"

"No," he answered, watching me steadily "Also, I felt it would be safer if I were here."

I hesitated. Was he saying what I thought he was saying? For all the attraction I felt toward him, I didn't know if I was quite ready to take that step.

"On the couch," he added, and although he didn't exactly smile, I could tell from a certain light in his eyes that he was amused by my assumption.

Oh, man. I hoped he couldn't see me blushing; I'd only turned on the torchiere lamp in the corner, so the room wasn't all that well lit. Hanging up my coat and scarf seemed a good way to cover my confusion, so I did that before I turned back to him and said, "Why don't we just go back up to the cabin? I'm off the hook for sales duty at the UFO Depot, so my schedule just opened up."

"That's good. But I think it'll be okay if we stay here tonight. Then in the morning, we'll head back into Oak Creek Canyon."

"Sure, if that's what you want to do." Truthfully, it did seem a lot more appealing for me to catch a decent night's sleep here, then pack up any necessities in the morning and head out to do...well, whatever we ended up doing. More mental gymnastics, sounded like.

I wasn't about to let myself consider the other kind of gymnastics we might get up to if we were sequestered together for any amount of time. Oh, sure, my brain was telling me I wasn't ready, that I had about a million other things to do before I could even consider jumping in the sack with Martin...but my body told me something different every time I looked up into those eyes, the color of a sea I'd never seen.

If he caught anything of my mental turmoil, he didn't show any sign of it. "How'd the meeting go?"

"Fine. Jeff's going to bunk at Michael's, just to be safe, and, as I said, I got Kara to release me from Depot duty so I could concentrate on more important things."

"All good. I'm glad everyone is taking the situation seriously."

"Well, they were all here for rounds one and two, so they already know the aliens aren't messing around. I think the biggest problem is that they all wish they could be doing more."

"They'll do enough, when the time comes." His eyes searched my face, and he moved closer to me. "What about you? Are you holding up all right?"

I closed the gap between us and pressed myself against him, felt his arms encircle me and hold me tightly. Just being there, hearing his heart beating and letting his warmth envelop and fill me, was enough to bring some energy back to my weary limbs. It wasn't until that moment that I realized how tired I really was, as if I'd spent all day hiking around the red rocks instead of mostly just sitting quietly and using my mind instead of my body.

"I'm okay," I murmured. "Probably because so much of this doesn't even feel real to me. Except you," I added. "You feel *very* real."

He bent and kissed me then, gently, the touch of his lips so tender, it almost made me want to cry. I wasn't used to being treated like this. Maybe it was because he was a man, not a boy like all the guys I'd dated previously, or maybe it was because his race was so much more advanced than mine...half of mine, anyway.

Or maybe it was simply because he was Martin, and nothing else really mattered.

At some point, we sank down onto the couch, with me leaning into him and his hand stroking my hair as we lengthened the kiss into something I'd only imagined up until then. That hand moved from my hair to my neck, fingers brushing against my skin, sending shivers all through my body.

It was crazy. How could I feel this way, react this way, toward someone I'd only known for a few days? Okay, technically I'd met him back in August, but our interactions then had been extremely brief. His focus had been elsewhere.

Whereas now...

He finally lifted his mouth from mine and regarded me carefully. "You don't feel that I'm pressuring you, do you?"

I chuckled. "Are you kidding me? I was having impure thoughts about you from the first time I laid eyes on you."

"Really? You hid it well."

"Mostly because I didn't want to look like a total idiot."

"I don't think that's possible."

Another kiss then, and I wondered if we actually were going to give the couch a workout. But Martin pulled away and said, "I really didn't come over here for this."

"You could have fooled me."

He did smile then, and shook his head before he moved away from me and stood up. "It's getting late. I think the best thing for you now is to get a good night's sleep. We have much that needs to be accomplished tomorrow."

I didn't know if I really liked the sound of that, but I did know that playing kissy-face on my sofa, while infinitely enjoyable, was not going to do much to defeat the aliens. So I didn't bother to argue, but said only, "You're seriously going to sleep on my couch?"

"It's not exactly sleeping. We don't need sleep the way humans do. More like a meditation that refreshes, but still keeps me aware enough...just in case."

Obviously, I took after my human mother when it came to the whole sleeping thing. Any time I had to roll out of bed before around seven-thirty, I got cranky. Whether having a not-quite-sleeping/sort-of-meditating Martin Jones on my couch was weirder than having him passed out and rolled up in some borrowed blankets, I didn't quite know, but I decided to let it pass for now.

"Okay," I replied, then wondered if I should tell him about the bathroom facilities before I decided to let that go for now. I really didn't want to know whether his physiology was *that* different. "Then I guess I'll go ahead and get ready for bed, since you're probably going to want an early start tomorrow."

He nodded, and I went back to the bathroom and

did my usual washing and brushing and flossing, and pulled my big flannel sleep shirt off its hook on the back of the door. If Martin thought he was going to catch a glimpse of me running around in a flimsy nightie, he was going to be very disappointed. Come August, it would be a different story, but now I cared more about warmth than titillation.

Speaking of which—

I called out a goodnight to Martin, and he said, "Sleep well." And that was it. I knew going back out to him would only lead to more snuggly-times, and even if I was wearing a *Little House on the Prairie*–style nightshirt, there still wouldn't be any bra in the way if we started kissing…and that could set off a whole series of events I wasn't sure I wanted to deal with right then.

So I crawled into bed, noting that he'd switched off the torchiere in the living room and instead had turned on my little Moroccan-style light over the dining table. That light was even dimmer than the torchiere, and sent a soft reddish glow down the hallway toward my bedroom.

It could have been because I was so damn tired, or simply because the lighting created a womblike atmosphere conducive to slumber, but I fell asleep a lot faster than I thought I would. The blackness surrounded me, sucked me in, and I slipped into it gratefully, glad for a chance to rest.

At first, my sleep was so deep that I dreamed of nothing, thought of nothing. But then at the borders of my subconscious, I seemed to feel a wrongness, a red-tinged glow at the edges of the blissful black all around me. Something in my brain tried to tell me to wake up, but I couldn't seem to move or do anything except lie there as that blood-colored light flooded through my mind, somehow paralyzing me while at the same time making me painfully wakeful.

The voice was like acid dripping through my veins. *You will not defeat us.*

Somehow I knew who—*what*—that voice belonged to. The enemy. The alien leader.

It could have been because of the connection I'd created earlier that day, when I truly saw them for the first time with that mysterious mind's eye that Martin had helped me to open. I didn't know. And although some part of me was whimpering, "Oh, God, oh, God, let me wake up," I knew it wouldn't be that easy.

Somehow, I managed to rally myself. *You go on telling yourself that, buddy.*

I don't have to convince myself of something I already know. You are a child. You know nothing.

Apparently, I could add "raging assholes" to the list of sterling qualities the aliens seemed to possess. *I know enough. I know that you have no place in this world, and I'm going to make sure you get sent back to whatever hole you crawled out of.*

I heard something that might have been the alien equivalent of a laugh, although it sounded more like the shriek of metal against metal. Shivers rushed up and down my spine at the horrible noise.

So sure of yourself, when you have nothing to be

certain of. You cannot imagine what we have in store for you.

Oh, really? my sleep-self challenged him. *Try me.*

And then...it was as if unseen hands were moving over my body, touching me, in a way I wished I could say wasn't sexual, but somehow, nauseatingly, *was*, clawed hands trailing over my flesh as if to show that they could possess me, take me, and I would be powerless to stop it. In my sleep, I writhed against that touch, knowing somehow that he—*it*—wouldn't let me escape, would hold me down, violate me in a way I'd never thought possible
—

Moans of protest rose in my throat, a scream of negation. *No—no—no—NO!*

Hands were touching me then, human hands, warm and reassuring. "Kirsten! *Kirsten!*"

My eyelids flew open, and I looked up into Martin's face. I managed to get out, "Oh, God!" before I buried my face in his shoulder and began to cry hysterically.

"What was it?" he asked, his tone far more urgent than someone merely inquiring about a possible nightmare should have been. "What happened?"

At first, all I could do was shake my head and continue to cry. After a minute or so, I recovered myself enough to whisper, "It was *them*."

"In your sleep?" His tone was bleak, revealing little, although I somehow sensed he was more disturbed by this facet of the situation than anything else.

"Yes. I heard him. *It*. Whatever. At first it was just your usual Bond villain threats." I gulped back my tears and began to cough. In silence, Martin let go of me, went to the bathroom and filled the cup there with water, and brought it back to me. I took it from him and drank greedily, not even caring that the water tasted faintly of toothpaste. "But then—" I broke off. It was too horrible. I didn't want to tell Martin what the alien had done to me, even if none of it had been real.

He sat down on the edge of the bed and waited. Maybe he knew what was coming, or maybe he was just trying very hard not to push me.

I swallowed the rest of the water, then set the empty cup down on my bedside table. Reaching out, I took his hand in mine and clutched it, trying to reassure myself with the touch of his warm fingers. "He—*it*—was touching me. *Touching* me, Martin! It was vile." His fingers tightened around mine as I whispered, "Why would he do that? They're aliens. I mean, *alien* alien. Not like you."

Grim-faced, Martin pulled me against him and held me close, his hand stroking my tangled hair. "You know that rape isn't about sex. It's about domination. He was trying to strike you where you were vulnerable."

Strangely, his using the "R" word made me feel a little stronger. At least this hadn't been that kind of physical violation. It could have been worse. "So that's all it was—mind games. Of course, the aliens would never—"

I'd been expecting him to chime in and say *oh, no, of course not, the aliens don't have any interest in humans that way*...but he didn't. Instead, he drew away slightly and took both my hands in his.

"No." I shook my head. "I can't believe that—"

He frowned. "Why is that so impossible to you? My people were aware of these things even before I infiltrated the MIB unit, but once I was there, I saw the reports, the case studies. With your own interest in ufology, of course you must have come across these reports as well."

"Well, yes, but—" I pulled one hand from his and made a feeble gesture skyward. "I guess I figured that people had to be making that sort of thing up. Oh, sure, seeing lights in the sky and having physical evidence of UFO activity...of course I believed that stuff. But it just seemed so far-fetched to think that aliens were coming down here just so they could boink a bunch of abductees. It always sounded a bit too *Mars Needs Women* to me."

"It's unfortunately all too true." He spoke slowly, as if weighing every word before he let it escape his lips. "For dominance, for cruelty—these things are part of their nature. And human DNA is a very malleable, adaptable thing. They soon discovered that crossbreeding was possible. From there, they took the problem to their labs, as those first human/alien offspring were often weak, not suited for their purposes. They wanted a race of soldiers who could pass as human, and those unplanned crossbreeds were anything but human in appearance."

Bile rose in my throat. I choked it back, not wanting to give the alien leader even that much power over me. Yes, the whole situation was sickening, but Martin had been here to wake me before things could progress any further.

I wouldn't let myself think about what might have happened if he hadn't been around.

"So what do we do now?" I asked, dismissing the aliens and their sexual perversions. If I let myself think about it too much, I really would get sick.

"Obviously, it's not safe here, not even for one more night." He got up from the bed and turned on the lamp on my bedside table. "We're going back up to the Forest Houses. Pack enough clothing to get you through"—a brief hesitation, and he continued—"well, to get you through the next few days."

Spent as I was from that horrible nightmare-that-wasn't-a-nightmare, relief flooded through me at the thought of getting out of here, going someplace where the creek itself would shelter me, hide me from the aliens and their malice. "Good." And I pushed back my bedcovers and got up, going to my closet so I could pull out the battered old suitcase I used for the rare occasions when I actually left Sedona. Funny how I'd barely been back here a day before it was pressed into service again.

Warm clothes, of course—jeans and sweaters and long-sleeved T-shirts, thick socks, a couple of scarves. I'd wear my waffle-stompers, and pack my favorite broken-in cowboy boots, which always felt as if they'd been custom made for me. After that, clean underwear and a couple of my flannel sleep shirts. I'd have to save the silky Victoria's Secret stuff for warmer days...if I was around to see them, of course.

As I went into the bathroom to pack up my toiletries and other necessities, Martin spoke. "You're taking this very well."

"What am I supposed to do?" I asked, leaning into the shower so I could retrieve my shampoo and conditioner. "We both knew this was a possibility. Okay, I didn't know brain-rape was a possibility, but you made it clear enough that we'd be ending up back at the cabin at some point."

"Still—"

I emerged from the bathroom with my cache of personal-care items, dumped them into the suitcase, and then latched it shut. "In a way, I'm relieved. Something bad happened, I survived it, and now we're going on to the next phase."

He didn't say anything in reply to that, but only gave a sort of grim, approving nod before he took the suitcase from me and headed out to the living room. I shut off the lamp in my bedroom and trailed after him.

I didn't have a cat or a dog, or even a goldfish, and my plants were of the type it was almost impossible to kill—pothos and snake plants, mostly. There was nothing here that couldn't survive being left alone for days or even weeks.

So why did it feel so weird to retrieve my purse

and fish out my keys, then follow Martin as he went outside? As I locked the door, I had this odd sense of finality, as if I would never see the place again.

Who knew? Maybe I wouldn't....

We decided it would be better if I drove the Night Tours van to the UFO Depot and left it there in case Kara needed it for some reason. She had a spare set of keys, so it wasn't as if I had to hand them off to her or anything. After that, I slipped into the passenger seat of Martin's black Taurus—we'd already stowed my suitcase in the trunk—and leaned my head back and watched the dark town pass by outside the car windows.

Midnight had come and gone, so the streets were deserted. Even the places that stayed open late in Uptown had shut down for the night by that hour, and so the place had a weird, almost post-apocalyptic feel to it, as if the aliens had already done their worst and eradicated the entire human population.

I must have made some sort of sound, because Martin glanced over at me and asked, "You all right?"

"I think so." I shrugged and shifted in my seat. "Guess I just feel off, what with that dream and being out this late. I stay up late sometimes in the summer, especially if we're running tours, but...."

At first, he didn't reply, but only took us through the last stretch of shops and hotels before we got to the dark road that led up into the canyon. "You'll feel better once we're at the cabin. Fifteen minutes at the most."

That sounded good. Although some part of me didn't want to fall asleep ever again—not if I had *that* waiting for me on the other side—I knew I had to get some rest, some real sleep. And Martin had promised me I would be safe once I was tucked back into the cabin.

So I only nodded and stared out the window, not seeing much except the little reflectors along the roadside, since of course there were no streetlights out here. Once, a truck passed us heading south into town, and I wondered what business it was that took the driver into Sedona at this time of night. Heading home after a swing shift in Flagstaff? Possibly, although most regular commuters took the main highway because you could never count on the canyon road to be open at this time of year.

These sorts of idle thoughts kept my mind occupied until we pulled onto the narrow lane that led down into the Forest Houses resort. Because of the way the place was laid out, we still had a slight hike from the parking area to the cabin, but I found I didn't mind. The air was bitterly cold, and yet it felt fresh and clean in my lungs, helping to clear out the lingering dregs from my nightmare. Somewhere off to my left, I could hear the creek chattering its way over the stones, and that reassured me as well. The creek would protect me. I was safe here.

Martin unlocked the door and let me inside. The

fire had settled down into barely burning embers, but it was still alive enough that he was able to stir it back to crackling goodness in a few minutes. I set my suitcase on the floor of the small closet, and went ahead and took off my coat.

Then I stood there and sort of awkwardly stared at the bed. Since I'd already done all the face washing and toothbrushing hours ago back at my apartment, I really didn't have to do anything except climb into one of my nightshirts and try to get some real sleep this time.

Except for the part where Martin stood there by the fire, seemingly occupied with setting it up so it would keep going through the rest of the night. Somehow I knew better, though, knew that he was also just a little tense about being here with me like this. Earlier in the day, I might have thrown caution to the winds and pulled him down onto that bed next to me, but not now, not with that horrible nightmare still fresh in my mind. I didn't want anyone touching me that way.

Not even Martin.

So I knelt down and opened my suitcase, dug out one of the shirts, and disappeared with it into the bathroom. Despite the fire, the place was still awfully chilly, and I wondered whether I should sleep in some of my socks or not. Then I told myself that was a terrible idea. *You want to sleep alone tonight, but not for the rest of your life. Don't scare him off!*

I grinned and shook my head at myself, then folded my discarded clothes and went back out into the room. By that point, Martin had taken off his own overcoat, and even loosened his tie.

"Well, guess I'll try this again," I told him, and casually turned back the bedclothes as if I'd done that in front of him a hundred times.

"You should have a much better outcome this time," he replied.

I slipped in between the sheets and choked back a small yelp. They hadn't had a chance to really warm up yet, and they felt like ice against my bare feet. "I hope so, because I get really cranky when I haven't had enough sleep."

"I'll have to remember that." He came over to the bed and bent down, then placed a small, chaste kiss on my forehead. "Good night, Kirsten."

Okay, maybe I wasn't quite as off sex as I thought, because I really wished he had kissed me on the mouth instead. But I also knew getting all riled up at this point was stupid. I'd need all my mental energy the next day, and I was already up way past my bedtime.

So I reached up and touched the sleeve of his coat, just a whisper of my fingers against the fabric, as if reassuring him that I still wanted him, and shut my eyes before saying, "'Night, Martin."

Whether it was because of his presence, or the quiet murmur of the creek just a few yards outside the building, this time I felt sleep come up around me in a wordless embrace. I fell into it, and hoped it would make me whole.

CHAPTER TWELVE

THE FIRST THING I SAW WHEN I OPENED MY EYES THE next morning was Martin, but I had to blink once or twice to reassure myself that it was him.

While I'd slept—been comatose, to be more precise—he'd gotten rid of the perpetual black suit, black tie, and white shirt, and had changed into a dark gray sweater over a white T-shirt and a pair of faded Levi's. He looked so different in this getup that I even shook my head, wondering if I was dreaming.

A good kind of dream this time. Who knew the man would look so good in a pair of jeans?

"Okay, where's Martin Jones, and what have you done with him?"

He actually laughed, a real laugh with nothing forced about it. For the first time, I noticed he held a glazed stoneware mug in one hand. Wisps of steam curled up from it.

"I seem to recall you like tea," he said. "There was

only English Breakfast in the cupboard, not green. Hope that's all right."

"It's perfect," I told him. And it was. I drank green tea during the day because it had just enough caffeine to keep me going without making me totally wired, but I preferred something stronger to kick-start me in the morning.

He handed me the mug and I wrapped my fingers around it, glad of its heat. I'd been cozy enough under the covers, but as soon as I sat up, I realized it wasn't all that warm in the cabin. Not uncomfortable if you were dressed for it, like Martin was, but far cooler than I kept my apartment.

His dark hair still looked a little damp, and I guessed that he must have showered and dressed while I slept. Normally, I wasn't that heavy a sleeper, but the previous day had been anything but normal. And I wondered then if he'd been watchful all through the night, making sure I had no more nightmares, or whether he'd allowed himself to slip into the "meditation" he said his people used instead of sleep. Hard to say for sure; he certainly appeared rested enough.

I realized then that the sunlight coming through a crack in the curtains was bright and white, making it much lighter in here than it had been the night before with just one table lamp lit. And I also realized the daylight was showing me in all my no-makeup, sleep-mussed-hair glory.

Well, my appearance couldn't be helped. Setting down the mug and fleeing for the bathroom would only show I was worrying about stupid things like my appearance instead of the real matter at hand. So I lifted the tea to my lips and drank, and hoped Martin's eyesight wasn't as good as I knew it had to be.

Hah.

"So what's on the docket for today?" I asked.

"Today, I want to show you how to block them, how to protect yourself. That's necessary before we go any further."

That was for sure. I wished he'd showed me that little trick the day before, but apparently there was an order of operations that had to be followed. "Breakfast?" I asked hopefully, because I'd hardly eaten anything since the lunch we'd shared the day before.

"I thought we'd eat at the cafe down the road. Junipine?"

"That's only for guests of the resort," I pointed out. There wasn't a hotel or restaurant within a twenty-mile radius of Sedona that I didn't know the particulars of.

The glint was back in those storm-blue eyes, which somehow looked even bluer now that he wasn't wearing stark black. "You really think a detail like that is going to stop me?"

"Mmm...probably not." I took a large swallow of tea, then another. "Okay, let me shower and get ready."

"Sounds good."

I set down the mug and slipped out of bed, glad of the worn Navajo and oriental rugs that covered the wooden floor. A quick stop at my suitcase to get the necessities, and then I let myself into the bathroom and started the water running. The shower was small, matching the scale of the rest of the cabin, so that quelled any thoughts of future hanky-panky in there. Probably just as well.

It seemed strange to be climbing out of my clothes with Martin hovering in the next room, but it couldn't be helped. I tried to focus on the feel of the water, the smell of my shampoo. The sensation of washing away the last vestiges of that nightmare, with the unclean feeling that had come along with it.

At least the alien leader hadn't returned to my dreams. I had no idea whether he'd even tried, but my sleep had been undisturbed, to the best of my recollection. One confused dream about chasing cows down the middle of Highway 179 in front of one of the posh art galleries there, and I kind of doubted that one had any secret meaning—unless it was my stomach trying to tell me that it hadn't eaten for more than twelve hours.

I finished rinsing off and got out, then rubbed myself down with the towel. Clothes first, followed by a quick round with the blow dryer. In the summer, I would have gone out with damp hair to save time, but doing that when the temperature outside hovered above freezing was just asking for trouble.

Even so, I was out of the bathroom in around a half hour, which wasn't too bad. I dug my watch out of my purse and strapped it on; it was a little before nine. So I hadn't gotten a full eight hours, but the sleep I did get seemed to have done the trick, as I felt alert and refreshed enough. All I needed now was some food.

"I'm ready," I announced.

Martin got up from where he'd been sitting in one of the room's two armchairs. His black overcoat had been draped on the other chair, and he reached down to gather it up and pull it on. I followed suit, getting my own coat out of the closet and buttoning it up even as I followed him out the door.

It was a beautiful morning, the sky blue, but with fluffy white clouds drifting lazily along. Far above, on the ridge line, I saw the snow glint like fractured diamonds.

Hard to believe that someone would be willing destroy all this loveliness.

We were both silent as we got into the car and drove the scant half-mile down the road to the café. I still wanted to see how he intended to pull this one off, since I knew for a fact that they checked your name against a list of guests when you went to eat at Junipine. If you weren't staying at the resort, then forget about it.

But after we'd parked and gone inside the building, Martin merely sailed up to the hostess and said, "Jones, room twenty-three."

She smiled. "Take any seat you like."

And off we went. Martin selected the last empty table by a window, where we shrugged off our coats and took our seats. Outside, I could see a patio with an outdoor kitchen that probably got a lot of use during the warm months, but it was closed to guests right now.

"How the hell did you do that?" I whispered. "Jedi mind trick?"

A quick flash of those blue eyes. "You can call it that if you like."

"Okay, Obi-Wan."

He shook his head, smiling a little, and then a server came up and asked what we'd like. Since I'd already had tea, I requested orange juice, while Martin ordered coffee.

Neither one of us said anything. I didn't know what he was thinking, but although I had more questions, I wanted to wait until the waitress—who looked like she was working through her holiday break from high school—brought us our drinks and took our orders. True, Sedona was the one place where you could be overheard discussing aliens and UFOs and not get some serious side-eye, but it never hurt to be careful.

Luckily, the waitress was fairly prompt; she took our breakfast requests and disappeared once again. The café wasn't all that crowded; I saw a family of four finishing up what appeared to be a fairly chaotic meal, and the other two window tables had their own occupants—a married couple in their fifties and a couple of women who looked like they were doing a girls' outing—but they appeared to be wrapped up in their own conversations. Well, mostly. I noticed one of the women at the table past ours giving

Martin an appreciative once-over, and tried not to bristle.

"So...." I said, and sipped at my orange juice. Now that we had a chance to talk, I really didn't know where to start.

Also, now that I was rested and sitting here across from him, I was struck again by how good-looking he was, how those black lashes circled his eyes and made them look that much bluer, how the heavy dark hair waved back from his forehead. His jaw was lightly dusted with stubble, indicating that he hadn't shaved. Did godlike aliens have to shave, or did they just make their facial hair come and go at will, depending on their mood?

I had no idea. Martin looked human, sounded human, felt human...tasted human. But despite all that, he wasn't, and I found myself trying to figure out the best way to wrap my brain around that concept.

"So," he repeated, and sipped from his coffee. I noticed that he hadn't put any cream or sugar in it.

Right then, I was kind of regretting not getting something hot to drink. My fingers felt chilled, and wrapping them around a glass of orange juice wasn't going to help much. "I guess I'm a little confused."

"By what?"

Everything, I thought, but I only said, "The aliens. I just sort of assumed we were dealing with the Greys here, but that—*thing*—in my dream was definitely not a Grey."

"No," he said. "It's a common misconception that

it's the Greys running things because they're the most commonly encountered aliens."

"So they're not actually in charge?"

Martin ran a hand along his jaw, absentmindedly scratching at his stubble. It made me think that maybe he wasn't used to having it, so I guessed he actually did have to shave like a normal man, even if he wasn't one. "Not really. They're—well, I suppose one way to think of them is as biological robots. They're designed to do information gathering, collect abductees, conduct experiments. Some of their brain functions are very high-level. But they're not the ones making the command decisions."

"Who is?" I asked, but I thought I knew, recalling the touch of scaly alien skin with a shiver.

"What you call the Reptilians," he said. "As I told you before, they're an ancient race, but one that has learned very little about how to coexist peacefully in this universe. They only plunder and move on. There's still enough left on Earth worth taking... which of course will be easier most of the humans out of the way and the rest enslaved."

That remark didn't do much to dispel the chill that seemed to have settled over me, despite the warmth of the room. Of course, I knew about the Reptilians, had even met a few people who claimed to have been abducted by them rather than the Greys. I remembered now that those encounters were described as having distinctly sexual overtones.

This time, I couldn't repress my shudder, and Martin watched me with both worry and understanding in his expression. "So you know something of them."

"Enough that I really wish we were being invaded by something a little more friendly, like Godzilla."

That comment actually elicited a chuckle. While he was laughing, the waitress came by with our plates, and I was relieved that she'd shown up during a relatively normal moment and not when we were discussing how to welcome our new lizard overlords.

She left, and I started to pick at my omelette, my appetite having taken a sudden tumble. But I knew I had to eat, so I scooped up a forkful of eggs and cheese and bacon, and put it in my mouth. It did taste good, so I ate some more.

Martin followed suit, but then paused after one mouthful, hash browns dangling off the tines of his fork. "And you know why they're here."

"You just told me—to take all the good stuff and leave scorched earth behind."

"No." He ate the hash browns from his fork, then set it down. "I meant here here, in Sedona."

Two words came to mind immediately. "The power."

He nodded. "What does that mean to you?"

I put down my own fork, my thoughts racing back to August, to Grayson's look of anguish while he was under hypnosis, the truth being somehow dragged from him during Persephone's questioning. Even months later, I could remember how the cords had stood out on his neck, the perspiration on his forehead, even though Paul and Persephone's air conditioning worked great. "We thought it must be something about the vortexes, but we could never really figure out why."

"Why does it surprise you that the vortexes would be involved?"

The waitress came by to top off Martin's coffee right then, so I waited until she was gone before replying, "I don't know." I felt myself shrug and added, "That is, they're a great gimmick to bring in the tourists, and I guess you can get a natural high from being in one if you're attuned to it or something, but it's not like we're sitting on a nuclear reactor or something."

"Really?" His tone was mild enough, but I thought I saw something challenging in the way he stared at me over the rim of his coffee cup as he held it to his lips and blew on it gently.

"Well, I've been to most of the vortexes more than once, and I can't say I felt much of anything." *Except a need to get away from the tourists who were trampling all over them*, I added mentally.

"I think you'll find that you'll have a very different experience now that your powers have begun to awaken."

I wasn't sure I liked the sound of that. "So, what, are we going on a vortex field trip today?"

He shook his head. "First things first. I have to make sure you can protect yourself before we go any further."

No way I was going to argue with that, not after last night. But I could feel the unease creeping over me all the same. Now it was Wednesday. It was going to be a bang or a whimper come Sunday, and I just hoped that Martin knew what he was doing, that all this Zen stuff of the proper things in the proper times wasn't going to end up with me being able to protect myself but unable to do jack shit to save anybody else.

"Kirsten."

I looked up and met his gaze, saw the concern there. "You don't think I would let anything terrible happen to you, to the people you love?"

"I don't—I don't think so. But how can you help me and not interfere at the same time?"

At that question, he reached across the table and laid his hand on mine where it rested next to my discarded fork. Even with all the worry and doubt crowding my mind, still I felt a rush of heat go over me at his touch, at the warmth of his flesh as it seemed to soak into my own chilled fingers.

"Do you trust me?" he asked.

What a loaded question. I *wanted* to trust him—so far, he had done nothing but protect me, be there for me when I needed him to quite literally preserve life and limb. But I couldn't shake the feeling that he hadn't told me the whole story, that he was still beholden to some unseen masters wherever he had come from, and I found notion that more than a little worrisome.

Unable to hide my hesitation, I answered slowly, "...yes."

"Not very convincing, Kirsten." He didn't sound angry as he said this, but calm, as if stating a simple fact.

"I want to," I told him. "I guess I'd be more clear about it if I didn't get the impression you weren't telling me the whole story."

A shadow passed over his face then, and he let go of my hand rather abruptly and went back to his neglected omelette. I did the same, forcing the food into my mouth even though my appetite, so hearty earlier this morning, seemed to have deserted me.

"But which whole story?" he asked then. "There are parts of it that aren't germane to the matter at hand."

I couldn't believe he'd actually used the word "germane" in a sentence. I thought that was reserved strictly for vocabulary tests. "Okay, then, let's get to something 'germane.' You and me."

His eyebrows went up at that remark. "I don't follow."

"Why me? I mean, is this some alien *La Femme Nikita* thing where you seduce me into becoming your bad-guy killer or something?"

For a few seconds, he didn't say anything, his face still as he apparently attempted to process the reference. "No, of course not. I'm here to help you defeat those who want to destroy your world. No secret subtext. As for the rest...." He let the words trail off, then lifted his shoulders. "Kirsten, you're intelligent and courageous and beautiful...and occasionally funny. Why do you think it strange that I would be attracted to you?"

This response was so not what I had been expecting that I only sat there and stared at him, stunned. Then I cocked my head to one side and asked, "Only 'occasionally funny'?"

"All right...often funny." Again, he reached across the table, this time enveloping my left hand in both of his. "It's not what I intended, if that makes you feel any better. When I first saw you last summer, I thought...." Once more, he paused. "That is, when I saw you again, I knew."

"Knew what?" Oh, how his touch made my blood race, made me forget that only thirty seconds earlier I'd been more than a little irritated with him.

A disarming smile. "Knew that I was in a lot of trouble."

Somehow, I knew that wasn't quite it, that there was something else he wasn't saying, but I decided to let it go. Really, sitting at a table at the Junipine Café probably wasn't the optimal location for heart-felt revelations.

"And how are we doing here?"

I jumped a little at the sound of the waitress's voice. Martin, though, only sent her one of his most charming smiles and said, "Great. I think we're about ready for the check, though."

"Got it!" she chirped, and went on her way.

Secretly, I was glad that she looked to be only around sixteen or seventeen. That was a little too young to be ogling Martin the way the woman at the next table had been.

He paid the bill as soon as she returned, laying down two twenties and saying, "Keep the change."

My eyes widened a little—talk about your forty-percent tip—but I refrained from comment and instead shrugged into my coat once again, and picked up my purse once I was all buttoned up. Martin put on his own overcoat but didn't bother to fasten it.

Once we were outside, I said, "So what now?"

"We go farther up the canyon, to West Fork."

I nodded, but then frowned a little. In a way, it made sense. West Fork was one of the most popular hiking trails in the Sedona area, a stunningly beautiful trail that actually crisscrossed the creek at several points. In the summer, it was definitely not the place for any kind of quiet meditation, as you were likely to get trampled by tourists while trying to reach enlightenment. On a Wednesday morning in mid-December, we probably wouldn't encounter too much foot traffic.

More importantly, it was supposed to be quite a vortex.

"I thought we weren't doing vortexes yet," I remarked as I climbed once more into the passenger seat of Martin's Taurus.

"The vortex aspect is secondary. There's a strong protective power in that spot. It should be the best location for today's training." He flashed a quick look over at me, his eyes now shaded by dark sunglasses.

"But if you do really well, we may move on to vortexes."

"Gee, thanks, teach." I reached into my purse and pulled out my own sunglasses, since the day was getting progressively brighter, even down here in the canyon.

A head shake, and he piloted the car back up the road, past Forest Houses, twisting and turning and gradually moving higher. About five minutes later, he pulled into the turn-off for the West Fork parking area, flashed a Red Rock pass at the Forest Service attendant on duty, and eased to a stop in a space fairly close to the trailhead. There were only two other vehicles there, a Jeep much more battered than the one I'd borrowed from Henry, and a sleek little Audi two-seater that looked distinctly out of place.

We both got out and made our way over to the trail itself, which wound down away from the parking area, toward the creek. With so few cars in the parking lot, I guessed we wouldn't have to worry too much about getting intruded upon by tourists, but even so, it seemed as if Martin was intent on taking me as far away from the sections where we'd be likely to meet people as possible. We actually did pass one couple in their thirties, who I guessed must belong to the Audi. They both wore new-looking North Face gear, and the woman's expression told me that she'd much rather be back in town getting a massage or a facial.

Wouldn't we all, I thought, gamely plugging along the muddy trail in Martin's wake, glad that I'd worn my heavy trail boots today even though they weren't exactly the height of fashion. Too bad he was wearing that overcoat, though. It deprived me of the pleasure of watching his rear end in those blue jeans.

But then we came around a bend and emerged at the first of the water crossings, and it was as if it hit me in a wave. A surge of life, of energy, wrapping around me, so buoyant and joyful, I almost felt I could have fallen on it and it would have lifted me up.

"We're here," Martin said unnecessarily.

"I kind of got that," I replied, my voice breathy and not sounding much like mine.

"So you feel it."

"And then some."

He looked pleased by that response, as if he'd had some lingering worries about my ability to come up to snuff when the time came. "Good." There was a fallen log lying half in the water, and he pointed to it. "Go ahead and sit down there. It's probably wiser if you don't try to do this standing up."

Mystified, I did as he directed and sat down on the log, hoping it wouldn't be too damp. Even while performing these mundane movements, it seemed as if clouds of energy swirled around me, a gentle cushion of light and warmth. Once I was seated, I noticed several pairs of tracks in the red mud of the creek's bank, tracks that went into the freezing water and came out again on the other side of the shallow crossing. Apparently, the occupants of that Jeep back in the parking lot were dedicated hikers. With any luck, we'd be done here before they came back down the trail.

"All right," Martin said, looking down at me. The sun was almost directly behind his head, casting his face in shadow, but also making it almost look as if he had a halo. Which was silly. He was an alien, not an angel.

...or at least, I didn't think he was.

I told myself to focus. Not paying attention to what he was saying could have far graver consequences than blowing off an econ lecture.

"I want you to close your eyes," he went on, and I did as he said, making myself concentrate on the warm tone of his voice, as soothing in its own way as the murmur of the creek at my feet. "Imagine a white-gold light surrounding you, enveloping you, creating a perfect barrier against all harm, against anything that might wish you ill."

If it had come from anyone else, I would have probably laughed at such a suggestion. It sounded way too much like something one of the psychics-for-hire in town would say to someone who was having personal problems. But now I had that white-gold light all around me, the energy from the creek encouraging me, telling me that it wasn't all woo-woo.

It was as easy as resting my palms face up on my knees and letting the energy flow over me, wrap around every limb, drift across my face like the caress of a warm summer breeze, looking almost like an extension of my own pale blonde hair as it flowed around me. Encased in that cocoon of pure light, I knew I could come to no harm.

Martin's voice seemed to come from far away, as if transmitting from a distant radio station. "Very good. Keep that focus."

Not a problem. I can do this all day.

And then I saw the same blinding blue-white light that had struck down the alien-possessed man who'd attacked me behind the Circle K—only this time, it was headed straight for me. Without thinking, I flung up my hands, and a wall of white-gold light flared into being in front of me, blocking the bolt of energy and sending it skittering off harmlessly into the creek, where the water sizzled as if it had been struck by lightning.

"What the *hell*?" I burst out, once I had determined that I hadn't been flash fried. The wall of light sparked away into nothingness, although I could still feel the energy quiescent within me, ready to be called forth at a moment's notice.

"That was…impressive," said Martin as he came toward me. He sounded almost breathless, as if he'd been the one fending off Emperor Palpatine–style lightning-bolt attacks instead of me.

"Oh, really?" I planted my hands on my hips and glared at him. "You might have warned me that you were going to be trying to burn me to a crisp."

"I would have backed off if I thought your shield wouldn't hold." He didn't appear concerned in the slightest; in fact, he looked about the happiest I'd seen him yet, the corners of his eyes crinkled in a smile.

"Who put a nickel in you?" I asked, wondering why he should be so buoyant.

"You did." He reached out and took my hands in his. Again, I wished it wasn't mid-December, that it was a warm day so we could be touching flesh to flesh, not his leather gloves to my admittedly ratty cobalt-blue angora ones. "Kirsten, I've never seen anyone put up that kind of a defense on the first try. Frankly, it was...extraordinary."

"Oh?" His words mollified me...a little. "So I might have a real career as an alien ass-kicker after all?"

"You just might."

"And that—that light you sent at me. It's the same force you used against that guy behind the Circle K, isn't it?"

"Similar."

I slanted a look up at him. "Can you teach me how to do that?"

He laughed then and pulled me against him, folding me in his warm embrace. "Yes. Soon. But not quite yet. Remember—"

"All things in their proper order. Yes, I remember." I snuggled against his chest, glad to be in his arms, especially in this place where the air itself seemed charged with some kind of magic. Of course, he wouldn't have done anything to hurt me. And he'd said I was extraordinary.

The feeling was definitely mutual.

"Okay," I went on, pushing away just slightly so I could look up into his face, "what now? Are you going to fling more lightning bolts at me?" I asked the question in a half-teasing manner so he'd know I didn't really mean it. All right, only halfway meant it.

"No, I think that's enough for one day." He studied my face for a moment, and his expression sobered, some of the light going out of those blue eyes. "No, your next exercise is not quite as showy, but no less important. While it's always possible you'll have to defend yourself from a physical attack, it's more likely that they'll try to approach you again as they did last night...through your mind."

That didn't sound appealing at all. I pushed away from him a few more inches and crossed my arms. "I hope you're not suggesting I try to fall asleep right here so you can attack me in my dreams or something."

A rueful head shake. "No, that's not necessary. All I need you to do is sit down again and close your eyes."

With a sigh, I stepped away from him and resumed my seat on the fallen log. Somehow, I had a feeling that this next exercise wasn't going to be nearly as thrilling as the last one. I closed my eyes, letting myself draw on the energy once more, wrapping it around me like a warm blanket on a cold winter night.

And then I began to feel...something. At first, I couldn't even say what it was, although it somehow made the flesh crawl on the back of my neck, giving me that twitchy feeling you get when you can hear a fly buzzing around but don't quite know where it is. Then it shifted from a fly buzz into a feeling of pressure on my skull, as if someone or something was trying to bore its way into my brain. Not even sure of exactly how I was doing it, I pushed more of the light toward my head, letting it surround me with a glow that seemed to intensify the more pressure was put on it.

This silent battle went on for...minutes? Seconds? I didn't know for sure. But the pressure finally lifted, and I opened my eyes to see Martin watching me with an expression of approval...and something else. Awe?

No, that was silly. He did appear fairly impressed, though.

"From the look on your face, I'm guessing I did okay," I remarked, then stood. My legs wobbled under me, and I sucked in a breath of cold air and willed them to steady themselves. That war of wills had taken more out of me than I thought.

"More than okay." A few swift strides, and he was next to me, his hand on my elbow. "Don't worry if you feel a little weak. That's completely normal."

"Normal for whom?" I retorted, but I didn't try to move away from him. No, I liked the feel of his hand on my arm, the knowledge that he was there to support me if I should stumble.

The sound of voices coming down the trail made Martin's head snap up, and I saw his eyes narrow behind the sunglasses. In that instant, I could see why he'd done such a good job of infiltrating the MIBs. He looked like a Secret Service agent about to throw himself in front of the President to take a bullet.

No such extreme measures were necessary, however, as the source of the voices came into view a few seconds later. Another couple, probably around my age, and a lot scruffier than the man and woman with the Audi. At the sight of them, Martin relaxed visibly.

They seemed to notice us about the same time we noticed them. The young man, with a patchy beard and a disreputable-looking knitted cap, raised a casual hand at us from across the creek and then splashed cheerfully through the water as if it wasn't a few degrees above freezing. His companion, a girl with long dark braids under her own woolen cap, flashed a smile at me as they passed and said, "Beautiful morning, huh?"

"Yeah," I replied, inwardly thanking God or whatever powers were looking after Martin and me that the pair hadn't come along just a few minutes earlier. That could have been awkward.

Then they were gone, and I glanced down at my watch. Damn. I could have sworn it was only about ten-thirty in the morning. Instead, the numbers on the dial told me that it was almost two.

"Is this going to keep happening?" I asked Martin in plaintive tones. "Because it's really hell when you're trying to keep any kind of schedule."

"It will get better as you learn to control things."

At that moment, my stomach growled, and he grinned. "Sounds like I need to buy you lunch."

"Probably," I agreed, then paused. While having Martin wine and dine me all over Sedona sounded like fun in theory, it wasn't very practical. The cabin had a small kitchenette. It would make a lot more sense for us to run into town and get some supplies at the store, then come back up here to prepare whatever meals we needed.

I explained this to Martin as he led me back up the trail toward the parking lot.

"That makes sense," he said. "Besides, having to explain all this dining out on my expense reports is a real nightmare."

Raising an eyebrow, I shot him a *give me a break* look, and he laughed.

"Okay, you got me. But it is a good plan. The less time we waste, the better."

Time, always time. I tried not to brood on the hours and days slipping away, the shrinking window in which I could get up to snuff as an alien defender. No, that didn't sound right. I wasn't defending the aliens, after all, but—I hoped—defending the people I cared about from them.

Well, the bad aliens, anyway. Martin was an entirely different class of alien. One might even say classy alien, considering he always opened the car door for me, the way my grandmother said a gentleman should.

A gentleman and an alien. I supposed I could do worse....

CHAPTER THIRTEEN

THE PROBLEM WITH GOING SHOPPING IN A TOWN WHERE there were only two main grocery stores—tempting as Whole Foods might be, I knew that loading up on expensive organic cheese and vegan brownies wasn't very practical—was that you always ran the risk of running into someone you know. In this case, that someone at Safeway just happened to be my sister.

We did almost literally run into one another, since she was coming up the baby products aisle just as Martin and I turned the corner from the produce section to the meat department. The front of her shopping cart collided with mine, and she began to say an automatic, "Oh, I'm sorry—"

Then she looked up and actually focused on who she was talking to. Recognition flashed over her face, and she started to smile at me...until her gaze moved past me to rest on Martin, who was a pace or two behind me. Then the smile sort of froze halfway in place, giving her a strange lopsided look.

Oh, crap.

"Hi, Kara," I burbled in a cheery voice that wouldn't have fooled anyone, least of all my sister. "We're just grabbing a few things. Is Grace home with Lance?"

"Yes," she said, the smile gone completely. Her eyes were still fixed on Martin. "Hello, Agent Jones. Out of uniform today?"

He glanced down at himself, at the sweater and jeans clearly visible under his overcoat, which he hadn't buttoned up. "I'm off duty," he said easily.

"Ah." Her eyes were a brighter blue than either Martin's or mine, and when that stare returned to me, I felt as if it was boring right into my brain. "Hey, Keeks, can I have a word?"

"Um...sure." This was not going to be good. "Martin, why don't you go on ahead to the meat department? Boneless skinless chicken breasts always work...ground beef...."

"I've got it," he said. He gave me a look that seemed to ask, *You going to be okay?*

I nodded infinitesimally, and he came up next to me and took the shopping cart from under my nerveless fingers. I hadn't even realized I was still holding on to it.

Kara maneuvered her own cart a few feet away, into the leeward side of the clearance rack of odds and ends shoved into a corner, then crossed her arms and stared at me. "So it's 'Martin' now, is it?"

"Yeah. So?" I really didn't know what my best approach to the whole situation should be, but "wounded little sister" always worked pretty well.

"What do you mean, 'so'? He's a Man in Black, Kirsten, in case you hadn't noticed. What the hell are you doing playing house with him?"

That remark hit a little too close to home. Of course, she could have no idea that he and I actually were shacked up at the Forest Houses resort. No, I was sure she'd just been referring to the grocery shopping expedition, which probably looked bad enough.

I didn't say anything for a moment, trying to decide how I should respond.

Of course Kara, being an older sister, took the opening as an opportunity to jump in and continue her attack. "And you left the UFO Tours van at the store without saying anything to me, and you haven't been answering your phone all day—"

"I was someplace where the reception wasn't good."

"And where was that?"

"Up the canyon," I replied. I figured that was vague enough that it really wouldn't give anything away. We could have been doing anything from shopping at the Native American marketplace at the Dairy Queen to having red-hot sex at one of the resorts.

Judging by Kara's expression, it was pretty obvious what she thought we'd been up to. "Even ignoring all that, don't you think he's a little too old for you?"

"Look who's talking," I retorted. "Lance didn't just pass his driver's test, you know."

Her mouth thinned. "That is totally different."

"Different how?"

"Well, for one thing, I was almost thirty when Lance and I got together. There's a big difference between thirty and twenty-three."

I couldn't help replying, "Only seven years," even though I knew that wouldn't go over well.

"Jesus, Kiki, you know there's a huge difference between where you are emotionally at twenty-three and where you are at thirty. I'd gone to college, run a business, been engaged—"

"Okay, I get it. I'm just some stupid little girl who doesn't know what she's doing. Not that you even know I'm doing anything."

At once, her expression softened. Just a bit, but it was something. "I don't think you're stupid. And I know that Agent Jones is supposed to be helping you with—well, you know," she amended quickly. No one had come by to rummage through the clearance items, so we were pretty much on our own. Even so, it was one thing to have a conversation overheard where it sounded as if you were giving your little sister crap for her romantic choices, and quite another thing to bring up alien invasions and impending doom. "Anyway," she went on, "I know you said he was important to everything, and that you needed his help, but—"

"But what?"

"But...I saw the way he looked at you. I wouldn't call it exactly professional."

My ears perked up. No way I was going to pass up a chance to get some outside confirmation that Martin wasn't just using me for his own ends. "How did he look at me?"

Her gaze slid away from mine, but at least she answered. "He looked at you the way Lance looks at me. Like I'm some gift he can't quite figure out how he earned. So, just be careful, okay?"

"Okay."

My assent didn't seem to reassure her. She frowned and pushed a stray strand of hair back behind her ear. "And for God's sake, call Jeff while you're still someplace that has reception. He texted me because he said he'd been trying and trying to get hold of you. He almost sounded worried, if you can believe that. I've got enough on my plate without having to babysit Jeff Makowski, too."

"I will," I said automatically. "I'll check in once we're done here."

A nod, and then she grasped her shopping cart and pushed it away from mine, heading into the refrigerated section where the bagged salads were kept. I noticed then that her cart was full, which meant she's been wrapping up just as we were getting started.

I wondered what Jeff wanted that was so damn urgent, but I guessed I'd find out soon enough. In the meantime, I needed to get back to Martin.

By the time I caught up with him, he'd finished with the meat department and had gone on to the dairy section. I looked down at the neat packages of meat and fish and chicken in the cart, at the almost dizzying array of cheese and yogurt, and wondered if he was stocking up for Armageddon.

Actually, maybe that was exactly what he was doing.

He turned to me, a carton of two-percent milk in one hand. "Glad to see you're still alive. Kara looked like she was about to breathe fire."

"It's okay. She was just being a big sister." I glanced at the milk carton. "I'm lactose-intolerant, you know."

His face fell.

"I'm kidding," I told him, and plucked the carton from his hand and put it in the shopping cart.

"That wasn't funny."

"It's your own damn fault for not remembering that I had two kinds of cheese in my omelette this morning."

A head shake, and he headed off toward the bakery section. My favorite.

Martin watched in astonishment as I dumped containers of blueberry muffins, brownies, and croissants into the cart, then picked up a loaf of wheat bread and a bag of sourdough dinner rolls and added them to the pile. "You can't possibly be thinking of eating all that."

"Watch me," I said. I'd never met a carb I didn't like, and it never seemed to matter what I ate—I was always just the size I was, which leaned toward the thin side. Yeah, the girl you loved to hate, although in this case, I guessed I could blame my enviable metabolism on my father. Then again, Marybeth hadn't plumped up over the years, either, so maybe I got it from both parents.

"This should be interesting," he muttered, and followed me into the condiment aisle, where I got my favorite sweet-hot mustard and some salad dressing.

"That should do it," I announced after dropping a bottle of Newman's Own into the cart and pointing it toward the checkout stands.

Martin cast a grim eye over the jam-packed shopping cart. "I would hope so."

"Worried about the total?" I inquired, and started to reach for my wallet. "I mean, I'd hate to make the bean counters at MIB Central's heads explode."

"It's fine," he said, moving past me, his own wallet already in his hand.

I grinned, but still pulled out my rewards card and gave it to him. "This should help ease the pain a little."

He took it without further comment and swiped it, then handed it back to me. Elise, the check-out person, knew me, of course, and I saw her eyebrows tilt a bit as she glanced at Martin, then at me, and back over at him again. It was fairly obvious from the items we'd selected that this was a stocking-up sort of trip and not just a party-food run, so God knows what deductions she was making from all that. Couldn't really be helped, though.

Fortunately, she kept up a breezy stream of chatter about the weather, and if Martin noticed her noticing him, well, he didn't give anything away, but only thanked her as she handed him the receipt. I trailed after him, my cheeks hot, which was probably stupid. I was an adult, after all. If Elise wanted to think I was shacked up with Martin, let her.

Actually, I supposed I was sort of shacked up with him, if not in the strictest sense of the phrase.

We loaded all the groceries into the trunk. By then, it was pushing five o'clock, and the skies had already begun to darken toward twilight. Remembering Kara's remark about Jeff, after I'd gotten in the car and buckled my seatbelt, I fished my phone out of my purse and double-checked my messages. Three texts, asking me to come over to Michael's—and sounding progressively more annoyed—and then a voicemail that ended with Jeff saying testily, "I didn't come to Sedona expecting you to pull a disappearing act on me. Geez."

I still didn't know exactly why Jeff had come here in the first place, so his having any expectations of me was a bit rich. Still, I experienced a pang of guilt when I thought about him cooped up at Michael's house. A place that cluttered had to be anathema to Jeff's overly precise soul.

Pulling the phone from my ear, I let out a sigh. "I may have to babysit Jeff a little tomorrow. It sounds like he has something he wants to talk about. Maybe he's made some progress in decrypting the aliens' transmissions."

Martin didn't take his eyes from the road. "If you think it's necessary. Better you do it first, in the morning, so we can have the rest of the day uninterrupted."

"Okay," I replied, and wondered what was scheduled for tomorrow. Vortexes? Maybe. Jeff was no more of an early-morning person than I was, but around ten should be safe. So I picked up my phone and tapped out a quick text: *Sorry I bailed. See you tomorrow at 10.* I knew better than to use textspeak with Jeff; I'd done that once out of haste and then got a fifteen-minute lecture on the deterioration of the English language.

The message had hardly been sent before my phone chimed, signaling his reply. *Tomorrow at 10. Don't be late.*

And what are you going to do if I am? I thought, but only texted back: *Okay.* Besides, I knew I wouldn't be late. The sooner I could get that over with—whatever it was—the sooner I could get back to the important stuff.

To Martin.

It was full dark by the time we reached the cabin. We had to make two trips to haul all the groceries from the car, and it took another fifteen minutes or so to unload everything and put it in its proper place. By then, my stomach was really protesting its emptiness, even though I'd sneaked a cookie out of its container and eaten it back in the store. One chocolate chip cookie, however, was not enough to replace all the energy I'd used up that morning.

So, we rattled around companionably in the tiny kitchen space, putting together some quickie "three-way" chili using the Carroll Shelby mix's recipe and some pasta and cheese. It was a meal I remembered from my childhood; Grandma used to make it a lot in the winter, and it was always one of my secret comfort foods. I was a little surprised at Martin agreeing to eat it, though.

"This doesn't really seem like your thing," I remarked as I stirred the pasta.

"Why not?"

I shrugged. "I don't know…I guess three-way chili just isn't high on my list of things I expect highly evolved alien races to eat."

He laughed and reached up to a shelf to retrieve a couple of glasses so he could take them over to the table. A bottle of a local red wine was already airing out; I hadn't seen those wine bottles when I started loading things into the shopping cart, but I had to admit I was kind of happy Martin had slipped them in there. "I've been here for five years, remember? Even in the MIB department, you still have to be one of the guys and go out for burgers and 3 a.m. doughnut runs. I managed to keep up with most of it, although I'm pretty sure I'm going to do whatever I can to avoid menudo in the future."

That wasn't one of my favorites, either, and I

fought back a grin. "So, did you not like it, or did it not like you?"

"Both, unfortunately."

"But chili's okay."

"Definitely okay."

Then it was ready, and I dumped the pasta into a bowl I found in the cupboard while Martin did the same with the chili itself. He'd already grated the cheese and put it in a separate, smaller bowl, so all that was left was to settle ourselves at the little table for two, where the flatware and glasses were waiting. I sort of wished we had a candle, just for some mood lighting, but I had to admit the fire was doing well enough for that. Besides, with everything we needed crammed onto the little dinette table, there wasn't even room to accommodate a votive.

I sat down, and Martin poured some wine into my glass before taking his own seat and getting some for himself. After I scooped some pasta onto his plate and ladled chili on top, I did the same on my own plate. He sprinkled cheese on both mounds of chili, then reached for his glass of wine.

"To you," he said.

"Me?" I replied, a little startled. "Why?"

"You did very well today. Far exceeded my expectations. I'm...hopeful."

I took a large swallow of the wine. It hit my empty stomach in a rush, and I wondered whether I should have started with a few mouthfuls of chili instead. *Can't be helped now.* "So you weren't hopeful before?"

He drank some wine as well before saying, "Let me rephrase that. I suppose I was hopeful at the beginning. But now I'm cautiously optimistic."

"And that's better?"

"Much better."

Mindful of my stomach, I dug into the three-way chili and ate for a minute in silence, letting the simple, hearty food do its work. "What's it like?" I asked.

"What is what like?"

"Where you come from."

At first, he didn't say anything, although he did look across the table at me, directly meeting my gaze. He picked up his glass and watched the dark garnet-colored liquid inside pick up interesting glints of amber and ruby from the fire in the hearth. "Imagine this world," he said, "but with no hunger, no disease, no pollution. No war, no conflict."

"So you're from heaven, then," I replied.

To my surprise, he chuckled. "No, although I suppose some people on this planet might see it that way. No, we've just had much longer to conquer the demons humanity is still struggling to overcome. But this is why it's so difficult for us to deal with the evil of the Reptilians—it's been millennia since we sought to conquer, or make war, and therefore we have a hard time understanding those urges in others."

"So your people never get angry, or tired, or worried?"

"Of course they do." His expression clouded, and

I wondered what he was thinking about. "But we have better mechanisms to handle it."

"And since you don't have wars of your own, you won't interfere with the ones the Reptilians start." My tone sounded bitter even to myself.

"Unfortunately, no. The help I'm giving you—the help Otto gives Persephone—is the most we're allowed to do. And even that isn't entirely applauded. There are some on our world who think we should keep ourselves entirely separate. Luckily, that mindset isn't universal, and there are other races out there who deplore the depredations of the Reptilians as much as we do, but who lack the resources to fight them directly." He took another sip of wine, then added, "The Reptilians also are clever, and exploit worlds on the outer fringes of the galaxy, in places where their destruction is more likely to be overlooked."

"But not here." By that point, I figured I'd had enough chili; I needed more wine. I reached over to the bottle and topped off my glass.

Martin's eyes narrowed a bit, but he didn't comment. "Your world is unique in several ways."

"Glad we have something going for us."

At that remark, he did frown, then said, "You have many things going for you. I told you before of the adaptability of human DNA. It's unique, and leads us to wonder whether your world was actually the source of all humanoid life, which then somehow was dispersed across the galaxy."

"Oh, the old star-seed theory?"

"You've heard of it?"

I gave him a disbelieving look. "I grew up in a household that lived, breathed, and slept UFOs. I read *Chariots of the Gods* instead of *Little House on the Prairie*. I've probably been exposed to every implausible theory there is on the subject of UFOs and aliens, secret bases, you name it. So yeah, I've heard of the star-seed theory. It would explain you, your people, wouldn't it? I mean, you obviously look like a human, and although I've never seen him, I've heard Otto does, too, when he's in his true form. I guess the Reptilians and the other humanoid life-forms I've not yet had the pleasure to encounter strayed from that, but they're still bipedal and have two eyes, a nose, and a mouth, right?"

Martin nodded. "More or less."

Judging by the expression on his face, I probably didn't want to know what that "less" meant. "Okay, so we have über-DNA. What else?"

A lift of his chin toward the window, as if to indicate the landscape outside. "The vortexes."

"Oh, come on," I said, and ate another mouthful of chili. "I've read that there are energy vortexes all over the place, if you know where to look for them."

"That's partially true, but the concentration of vortexes here, and their individual powers, isn't repeated anywhere in the known universe. No wonder the Reptilians came to Sedona—they wanted to tap into the power of the vortexes while also helping themselves to some human DNA along the way."

I reflected that sometimes it wasn't all that great to be special. If we'd been just a regular medium-sized desert town, like Taos or Prescott, we could have been overlooked completely. "I guess that makes sense. But if they came here to tap into the vortexes, why haven't they done so before this? I mean, it's not as if they just showed up three months ago."

"The Reptilians are advanced technologically, but they're not infallible. It's taken them this long to determine the best way to access and utilize the energy of the vortexes. That's why they need to make such a big push on Sunday, on the solstice. At 11:14 a.m., to be precise."

Knowing the exact time cheered me up a little. I supposed I should have looked it up, but I'd been a little busy. "Eleven o'clock in the morning? At least I'll be able to confront the aliens on a good night's sleep."

At this remark, Martin sat upright and frowned, as if trying to recall some important piece of data. "Sorry. That's 11:14 Greenwich time. Here it'll be 4:14 a.m."

I groaned. "Great. So I don't even have four more days after this. Saturday night is the apocalypse."

"Sunday morning, actually."

That comment earned him a very evil stare. "If it happens before seven o'clock in the morning, it's still night in my book."

At another time, he might have smiled. Instead,

he watched me carefully, eyes darkened by the dimness of the room. "You'll be ready."

"So you say." Good thing he was feeling so confident, because, despite my performance this morning, I couldn't see how on earth—pardon the pun—I was supposed to defeat a base full of Reptilians single-handed.

"You will."

I didn't really feel like arguing with him, so I just picked up my wine and had a few more healthy swallows. By that point, I could tell it was starting to get to me—not that I was drunk or anything close to it, but I did feel a little bit swimmy, with a light-headed, floating sensation that wasn't at all unwelcome. It felt good to be a bit disconnected, what with everything that was going on. "I'll take your word for it."

"Good." He dumped some more pasta and chili on his plate, then sprinkled cheese on top. Alien or not, that man could eat when he wanted to.

It was probably the wine that prompted me to ask, "And us?"

A forkful of three-way chili stopped approximately an inch from his mouth. "Us?"

"You." I pointed at him with my own empty fork. "Me." And I turned the fork around so it was roughly level with my chin. "How do we fit into all this? At breakfast you said, 'The first time I saw you,' and then you tried to make a joke about it, but I don't think you were telling me the whole story, were you?"

"I didn't want to frighten you off."

At that comment, I did laugh, although the rusty chuckle I gave didn't sound all that amused. "'Frighten me off'? Believe me, if I was sufficiently freaked out, I would have bolted a long time ago. So what aren't you telling me?"

He was silent for so long that I began to worry he didn't intend to say anything after all. Then he finished the wine in his glass and poured some more —not a lot, about a third of the way up the glass. "Probably one reason our world is so at peace, so harmonious, is that we all have one lifemate, one person to spend this existence with. We always know when we meet this person, because we see our other self in them. For some, this happens early in life, and for some, a good deal later. For a rare few, it doesn't happen at all. Otto is one of those, which is part of the reason why he's here pretending to be a sixteenth-century Turkish eunuch."

"Poor Otto."

"He says he sees it differently…something about being glad to be free of all the sighing and weepy eyes and declarations of true love." Martin's lips quirked, as if he was trying to repress a grin at Otto's expense. "At any rate, I'd thought I had the same destiny in store for me. I didn't mind being assigned here, since I had no one to leave behind." The blue eyes caught mine, and I didn't think I could have looked away if I'd wanted to. "And then I saw you that first time at the UFO Depot last summer, and I knew."

"You knew...." I let the words trail off. My heart had begun to race in my chest, telling me what he was about to say before he even said it.

He didn't blink. "I knew you were the one. Improbable as it was, the lifemate I thought I'd never find was here, on this world, in this town."

"B-but you didn't say anything—"

His hand went up to run through his hair, mussing it, the disarray somehow making him look even more handsome...if that was possible. "What was I supposed to say, Kirsten? I was in the middle of a case, and anyway, what would your reaction have been if I'd gone up to you and said, 'Hello, Kirsten, you don't know me, but I'm your destined lifemate. And oh, I also happen to be an alien. Hope you don't mind.'?"

I wanted to argue, but I knew he was right. Even hearing it now shook me, shook me to my core. That wasn't the sort of declaration I'd been expecting, and as much as Martin's revelation explained a good many things, it still didn't explain everything. "Okay, I probably would have freaked," I admitted. "I'd like to say that I wouldn't, but...."

"Exactly. At least now we've spent some time together." He paused and studied my face, as if searching for an answer he wasn't sure he wanted to find. "But still—I don't know what this means for you."

Good question. I hesitated, unsure as to how best to articulate my thoughts. Even discounting the whole alien lifemate thing, I wasn't used to guys making open declarations of their feelings. Oh, sure, the boyfriend of my senior year in high school once used the "L" word, but in hindsight, I was pretty sure that was just his way of guaranteeing that I'd sleep with him. But this—I saw the terrible hope in Martin's eyes, knew he must be wondering if I shared those feelings. We'd kissed, of course, but he'd spent enough time here to know that among us Earthlings, that didn't always mean that much.

What I did know was that I'd had a physical reaction to him early on, of an intensity I couldn't really explain to myself. Yes, he was extremely good-looking. It was more than that, though. As he said, it was as if something in me had responded to something in him, even though at the time I had no way of knowing what that really meant.

I reached out and touched his hand, reassuring myself with its very familiarity. "It means that now I know I wasn't crazy for feeling drawn to you from the very beginning. Here I just thought I was being mesmerized by your good looks, when all along it was actually some crazy alien chemistry thing."

It's hard to say exactly how it happened, but one minute I was touching his hand, and the next he was standing, pulling me to my feet so he could wrap his arms around me, touch my lips with his. He tasted of the wine he'd just drunk, and maybe a little of cheddar cheese, and that also seemed so reassuringly normal that it was the most natural thing in the world for us to stumble away from the dinette table and the remains of our dinner, to fall onto the bed, his weight on me, his hands moving over my body, touching me in a way I'd only dreamed about.

Suddenly, it seemed far too warm in there, with the fire crackling away in the background. As if he'd had the same thought, Martin took hold of my sweater and pulled it and the T-shirt I wore underneath up and over my head in one swift motion. I did gasp then, because the air was colder than I had expected. But that was all right, because in the next instant, he pulled off his own sweater, and I was treated to the sight of a wonderfully sculpted torso, his abs taut and defined, the muscles on his arms larger than I had expected.

He didn't give me much time to stare and admire, though, because he drew me toward him again, bare flesh meeting bare flesh, a heat building in me that had nothing to do with the fire blazing a few feet away. I wrapped my legs around him as he kissed me again and again, drinking in the taste of my mouth like a man dying of thirst in the desert would drink from an unexpected spring. Then I realized both of us still wore our jeans, and it seemed silly to have them on when we both knew where this was going.

I reached down and fumbled with his belt buckle, then got it undone and reached for the button of his jeans underneath. At that point, he lifted his mouth from mine and whispered, "This is—this is what you want?"

A big question. Ever since that one fumbling experience in high school, I'd avoided sex, partly because I couldn't see what all the fuss was about, but also because I didn't want to do anything that would have people comparing me to my mother. I was on the pill, mostly as a "just in case" sort of thing, and also because I liked that it knocked my period down to three or four days, but I hadn't thought I was going to put it to the test during the alien apocalypse.

Now, though...now I knew I wanted nothing but Martin. I wanted to give him that part of myself I'd been holding back for years.

"Yes," I breathed. "Oh, yes. More than anything. Please."

And that was all it took, because his hands were reaching behind me, undoing the clasp of my bra, then moving over my bare breasts, awakening shivers in me unlike anything I'd ever experienced before. I think I was murmuring "yes, yes, yes" over and over, but it was hard to say for sure, as the heat in the center of my body seemed to be expanding ever outward, enveloping me in a supernova of need. The next thing I knew, he'd undone my own jeans and pulled them down, dragging my underwear with them, but I didn't care anymore, didn't care about anything but the feel of his hands and mouth on me, his fingers reaching between my legs and stroking, concentrating all that heat and desire in my core.

Good thing no one was staying at the cabin next door, because as he brought me to the release I'd denied myself all these years, I cried out, gasping, digging my nails into his shoulder as he took me to the brink of ecstasy and right over the cliff.

I collapsed on the mound of pillows, gasping, and while I was attempting to recover myself, he took off his jeans and threw them somewhere on the floor. His underwear—black boxer briefs—followed immediately afterward. Wow. He definitely looked human all over...or at least like my ideal of a human male.

Then I didn't have time to think about comparative anatomy, because he was on the bed next to me, his hard shaft pressed against my leg as he took me in his arms again. His mouth found my nipple, tracing circles around it, and I was crying out again, pressing myself against him, wanting to feel as much of his skin against mine as possible.

He shifted his weight, positioning himself above me. Even in the dimly lit room, I could see the gleam of his eyes. "We don't have to go any further—"

I let out a little moan. "Don't you dare. I want you. Now. Please."

A sharply indrawn breath was his reply, and then I felt him pushing against me, felt the hardness of his flesh entering me, taking away an emptiness I hadn't even realized was there until he filled it. His breath was hot on my neck as he moved in and out, and I rocked my hips along with that rhythm, the whole thing as easy as breathing, as if I had done this with him hundreds of times before.

Time spun away from me. There was only this warm darkness, the heat of our bodies taking away the December chill as if it had never existed. And in that eternity, I felt the climax overtake me again, my entire being shuddering as he reached orgasm as well, our bodies locked together in a perfect puzzle that only the two of us could solve. At last, we collapsed on the bed, Martin reaching for me so he could pull me close, hold me as the aftereffects rippled through me, mini aftershocks following a quake that had shaken me to the foundation of my being.

He reached out and touched the corner of my eye, where some unexpected tears had pooled. "Are you —was that all right? I didn't hurt you, did I?"

"No," I replied at once. The last thing I wanted was for him to get the wrong idea about what had just happened. "God, no. That was...better than anything I could have imagined."

No reply but him holding me even tighter, his mouth leaving light kisses on the top of my head, on my temple, at the edge of my cheekbone. So tender, so unlike the frenzied passion of a few minutes earlier.

In that small piece of eternity, he had given me yet another reason to go on fighting.

CHAPTER FOURTEEN

WE DOZED FOR A WHILE, THEN AWOKE AN HOUR OR SO
later and reached for one another again, bodies
locking in passion as if drawn together like iron
filings to a magnet. After that, I managed to stumble
out of bed, reclaim my underwear and my T-shirt,
make an effort at brushing my teeth and washing my
face. When I crawled back under the covers, Martin
drew me to him again, joining his body warmth to
mine. I fell asleep for real that time, knowing I was
safe, and loved.

It should have been awkward the next morning
but somehow wasn't; I awoke and saw him gazing
down at me, something beautifully tender in his
expression. Over his shoulder, I could see morning
sunlight peeking around the edges of the curtains.

"What time is it?" I asked, reaching up to rub the
sleep from my eyes.

"A little past eight." He pushed a lock of hair back

over my shoulder. "You were quiet all night. No dreams?"

I shook my head. "Nothing. It was wonderful." I realized then that he'd put on a T-shirt and a pair of sweat pants, and that the remains of our dinner from the night before had been cleared away. A freshly laid fire snapped in the hearth. "Wow, I really was out cold, wasn't I?"

"Well, you did exert yourself quite a bit yesterday."

"I'll say." I smiled, remembering the perfection of our lovemaking. Because that's what it had been. Perfection. It went far beyond mere sex. But that thought made another one cross my mind, and I frowned.

"What is it?" Martin asked, obviously catching the shift in my expression.

"Well, it's just—" I sat up a little straighter in bed and watched him carefully. "You told me last night that your people had only one lifemate."

"Yes." The word had an edge of questioning to it.

"If that's the case, then what was it between my mother and my father? I mean, he took off before the night was even over. I wouldn't exactly call that 'life-mate' kind of behavior. But obviously he didn't have any problem going to bed with her."

Martin settled himself on the bed next to me and took one of my hands in his. I noticed the way he traced along the lifeline on my palm with one finger, as if reassuring himself that this business with the aliens was merely a blip and that we'd have a long lifetime together afterward.

"When I told you about lifemates, I didn't mean to give the impression that we only were physically intimate after we bonded with our lifetime partners. Of course, my people reach out for one another for pleasure, for companionship, as it suits them. It's only that we know these joinings aren't meant to last."

How very practical. Something in my mouth seemed to sour. "So my father was just looking for companionship, something to while away the time while he was stationed here?"

Martin's eyes looked very blue in the pale morning light. He held my gaze as he said, "I already told you that he spent that night with your mother for one reason. You."

True, he had told me that, but something still nagged at me. "And you—have you had a lot of 'companions' while you were here?"

To my surprise, he grinned, then reached out and pulled me against him, his breath warm on my cheek. "No, I haven't," he murmured. "Fraternizing with the locals is frowned upon. Besides, you really don't know much about the MIB unit if you think its agents are out there looking to hook up."

"'Hook up'?" I repeated, amused. "Who've you been hanging out with?"

"I thought that was the standard phrase for it these days."

"It is…I guess." I kissed him softly on the side of

his face, glad that no other woman's lips had been there before mine...at least, not lately. "It's just funny to hear you say it."

"Well, I'm glad I can amuse you from time to time."

"Oh, you do a lot more than that." I remembered the heat of his touch from the evening before and contemplated a third go-'round, but glanced at the clock and realized that idea was a non-starter. I still had to shower and dress and eat something, and then have Martin drive me all the way over to Michael's house, which would take at least a half-hour.

My regret must have been obvious, because Martin pressed his lips to mine, but gently, as if to reassure me rather than arouse me. Then he pulled away and said, "We'll have plenty of time. You need to meet with Jeff and see what he wants."

I nodded and pushed myself out of bed so I could go get ready. At the same time, though, I couldn't help wondering if Martin was being overly optimistic.

It could very well be that we didn't have much time at all.

Michael's car wasn't in the driveway when I arrived, which surprised me. But maybe he'd wanted to give Jeff and me some privacy while we talked and had invented some sort of errand to get himself out of the way. At any rate, I didn't see much sign of life as Martin pulled to a stop in front of the house.

"I hope this won't take too long," I told him. "But I'll call you when I'm ready."

"No need to do that," he said.

"Huh?" I stared at him, mystified.

And then it was if he spoke again...only this time his lips didn't move at all. He watched me, his words clear enough in my head as he said,

This is the easiest way to reach me.

"What the hell—" I began, but he laid a finger across my lips.

Not like that. Like this.

Concentrating, I thought back at him, *How is this possible?*

It's how lifemates can communicate, after they've been joined physically.

Wow. I paused for a moment, trying to absorb this strange and beautiful talent I'd suddenly acquired. *You might have warned me.*

I had to wait and see if it would even work. You're half human. I can't always count on your talents being exactly like those of one of my kind.

In this case, it seemed pretty clear that they were. *Well, this will definitely cut down on my cell phone bill.*

In reply, he leaned over suddenly and kissed me, kissed me with an unexpected passion that left me gasping as he pulled away. His smile warmed me even as I opened the car door, letting in a wash of chilly frost-laden air. Much as I would have liked to stay there and kiss Martin over and over again, I knew I had to get inside and see what Jeff wanted.

Call for me when you're ready, and I'll be here.

I nodded, still a little unsure of this newfound gift for nonverbal communication, and shut the car door. A few seconds later, Martin pulled away from the curb. I didn't know where he planned to wait for me. Maybe he'd just hang out at the Starbucks inside Safeway, get a latte or something.

That thought made me grin and shake my head. Somehow I couldn't really picture Martin doing anything quite so *normal*.

After hurrying the rest of the way up to Michael's front door, I knocked, then hoped Jeff wouldn't take too long to answer the door. The sun was dancing in and out of the clouds, and the day hadn't warmed up as much as I'd hoped it would. I didn't really want to be cooling my heels out here because he had his earbuds jammed in as he hacked code or something.

Then the door banged open, and Jeff scowled down at me. "You're late."

"Five minutes."

"Still."

Shrugging, I pushed past him and into the warm, wood smoke–scented confines of Michael's house. The fireplace kept the main rooms warm, and wall heaters in the bedrooms did the rest.

The clutter had been cleared off the old drop-leaf dining table so Jeff could put his laptop there. Next to it was his black mug, which traveled with him everywhere, it seemed.

"So what did you want to tell me?" I asked, reaching up to unwind the scarf from around my throat. Then I remembered that Martin had left a few marks there on top of the fading bruises from my would-be attacker at the Circle K, and I paused awkwardly, pretending that I had only wanted to adjust the scarf slightly.

"Who was that?" Jeff asked in accusing tones.

"Who was what?"

"You got dropped off by someone in a black Taurus. It looked like he was *kissing* you."

Jeff Makowski was about the last person I expected to be snooping on me through the curtains like a latter-day version of Mrs. Kravitz, the nosy neighbor from those old *Bewitched* reruns that my grandmother had loved so much. Even so, I could feel the heat flood my cheeks as I realized the interior of that car, foggy windows or no, wasn't quite as private as I'd thought.

"A...friend," I replied, glad that Jeff had never actually seen Martin, only heard Kara talk about him.

"Uh-huh," Jeff said, and stalked over to his laptop, shutting it with a slam that was very unlike him. Rude and brusque he might be, but his computers were his babies. People he would definitely abuse, but not a laptop. "*Which* friend?"

"What difference does it make? I needed a ride. So what?"

He crossed his arms over his chest. Obviously, he was having some issues with our nippy winter weather, because he was wearing his usual beat-up army jacket over a black sweatshirt, and under that, I thought I saw the neck of a light gray T-shirt. Besides that, though, he looked tired, his eyes smudged and his hair even more of a mess than usual. "Is that who you were with yesterday? *Him*?"

Okay, this conversation was not going at all how I'd thought it would. If I didn't know better, I would have said Jeff sounded jealous, but that was nuts. Jeff was not the jealous type. Jeff barely seemed to notice that I was even female.

"What difference does it make?" I asked. "Sorry I missed your messages, but you know how spotty cell coverage can be around here."

"That's not the point. I came here to Sedona—"

"— Totally out of the blue," I cut in. "You still haven't told me exactly why. I mean, yeah, you wanted to see the alien baby in the flesh, but there had to be more to it than that, right?"

His hands balled into fists in the pockets of his oversized jacket. "I came here to see you," he mumbled.

My ears had to have stopped working properly. That was the only explanation for what he'd just said. "Um...what?"

"You heard me. Don't make me repeat myself." His fingers drummed on the closed laptop case.

This conversation still wasn't making any sense. In all my interactions with him, I'd never gotten one hint that he really cared one way or another if we spoke or not. He wouldn't email me for days or even weeks sometimes, and then only get in contact again when he had a piece of information he wanted to share, or to respond to me after I'd initiated the contact because I needed to pick his brain about some piece of programming minutiae. I shook my head and told him, "Yeah, but what I heard you say was that you came here to see me, and I don't get that at all."

And then the world went kind of sideways, because the next thing I knew, he'd sort of launched himself at me, had taken my hands and was pulling me toward him, kissing me with an awkwardness all the more objectionable because I'd shared such a wonderful kiss with Martin not five minutes earlier. For a second or two, I was so shocked, I didn't do anything at all, but then my brain cells started firing again, telling me that this was not what I'd signed up for, and I wrestled my arms out of his grasp and took a step or two backward, still shaking my head.

"What the hell, Jeff?" I spluttered. "Why would you—what did I—what were you *thinking*?"

Of course, being Jeff, he didn't look embarrassed, but rather supremely annoyed. "What was *I* think-ing? All these months we've been in contact—'oh, Jeff, how do I get that packet routine to work?'—and 'but Jeff, I did compile the code the way you told me to. Why isn't it working?'—what else was I supposed to think?"

I was beginning to feel more than a little annoyed myself, not just at his presumption, but at the irri-tating way he'd pitched his voice higher in an attempt to imitate me. "Did it ever occur to you that maybe I just wanted to learn how to code better?"

"Oh, please," he said dismissively.

Okay, I had enough crazy stuff going on in my life already. I did not need to deal with a lovesick hacker, of all things. Not that being lovesick had made him any more charming. "Um, Jeff, I hate to break it to you, but really, that's all that was going on with me. I can't speak to what was going on with you, but if I led you on in any way, then I'm really sorry. Besides," I added, hoping to soften the blow, "you really don't want to get tangled up with me. I'm half alien, remember?"

"But that makes you even hotter," he said plaintively.

Jesus Christ. Now sounded like a really good time to try out those newfound talents of mine.

Martin, I think it would be great if you came and got me. Like, now.

The response was immediate. *On my way.*

I planted my hands on my hips. "So is that your idea of a compliment?"

He looked simultaneously confused and angry. "Why wouldn't it be?"

Obviously, the smartest thing to do here was to switch topics. Immediately. "So do you or do you not have any new information on the aliens' transmissions?"

A frown. Clueless and antisocial he might be, but Jeff was not stupid. "Avoiding the topic. Very mature."

"Look, Jeff, we don't have time for this. Again, apologies if signals were misdirected, but our love lives are really not the issue here!"

"Oh, they're not? Then who was that guy sticking his tongue down your throat?"

"He was not—"

Someone knocked at the door. At the same time, I heard Martin's warm voice in my mind.

I'm here.

Thank God.

Jeff looked as if he planned to ignore whoever was at the door. Maybe he thought he didn't need to answer the knock because it wasn't his house. But since I knew who was waiting out there, I didn't have any such scruples. I turned my back on Jeff and strode to the door, then opened it. Martin smiled down at me.

"Hello, Kirsten."

"Um, hi." I could practically feel Jeff peering over my shoulder to see who the stranger was. In that moment, I decided to go for broke. After all, Kara already knew I was with Martin, and if she knew, then Lance knew...which meant it was only a matter of time before Jeff found out anyway. Serve him right for mauling me like that without any provocation whatsoever. "Jeff, this is Agent Jones."

Jeff looked past me to Martin, and then past Martin to where the Taurus was parked at the curb. It didn't take him very long to put two and two together. "You were with *him*?" he demanded.

"He's been helping me get some insight into how to defeat the aliens."

"Oh, is that what you call it?"

"Hello, Mr. Makowski," Martin said, both sounding and looking very proper and official, even though you could see the jeans peeking from underneath his overcoat, rather than the suit pants one would expect from a Man in Black.

"'Hello' yourself," Jeff sneered. "Who do you report to, anyway? I think your superiors might be interested to know that you've been corrupting a minor."

"Oh, come on," I snapped, even as Martin's eyebrows lifted and he gave Jeff a startled look. "No one is corrupting anybody, and I haven't been a minor for five years. I can drink legally and everything." *Although what we did last night did feel awfully sinful....*

Jeff's mouth opened as if he was about to let fly another salvo, but Martin, showing great forbearance, said quietly, "We do need to get going if we're going to make that appointment."

"Right," I said. "Can't miss that appointment —not with time getting so short." Thanking God that I hadn't taken off my coat or even set down my purse, I stepped outside, leaving Jeff standing in the doorway, a look of pure thwarted anger on his face. "And Jeff, if you do hack those transmissions, make sure you call Lance or Paul. I'm going to be out of cell range for most of the day."

"Well, I sure as hell wouldn't be calling *you!*" he retorted, and slammed the door in my face.

Oh, boy. Martin's eyebrows were still raised, but he refrained from asking any questions until we were both safely back in the car. He pulled away from the curb and had us headed toward the highway before he said, "Want to fill me in on that?"

"You can't read minds?" The question came out much snippier than I'd intended, and I sighed and reached up to rub my forehead. Barely ten-thirty, and I already felt tired. "Sorry, Martin. I think some of Jeff must have rubbed off on me."

"Poor girl." He lifted his right hand from the steering wheel and squeezed my left one gently. I noticed that he didn't try the nonverbal-communication thing with me—maybe he figured I was too upset to do it properly. "What happened?"

It seemed so silly now. "Oh, apparently Jeff wanted to use this opportunity to profess his undying love for me."

"*What?*"

"Okay, slight exaggeration," I said quickly. "He wanted to see me so he could give me the worst kiss I've gotten since Mike Mulcahey tried to stick his tongue down my throat during an out-of-control spin-the-bottle incident in sixth grade."

By that point, we were back on 89A, cruising east, so apparently Martin thought it was safe to take his eyes off the road long enough to give me an incredulous look. "You're joking."

"Do I look like I'm joking?"

He studied me for a few seconds more, then said, "No." He stopped at a red light. "I wasn't aware that Jeff Makowski had...feelings...for you."

"That makes two of us." I realized my hands were shaking a little, and I wedged them between my knees to get them to stop. Stupid. If I could let Jeff manage to rattle me, how was I going to handle fighting off a battalion of Reptilians? "Frankly, Jeff's always seemed so asexual that he makes Sheldon Cooper on *The Big Bang Theory* look like Hugh Hefner."

Another one of those pauses. I could practically see Martin leafing through the pop-culture database in his head until he got a hit. "I can see why that would have thrown you a bit."

"I'll say." A small pang went through me as I recalled the hurt, angry look on Jeff's face. I certainly hadn't meant to upset him, or wound him, but really, could a guy be that smart about everything else and yet so clueless when it came to women?

Apparently, he could.

"Anyway," I went on, "I just have to hope he'll get over it. There isn't much I can do about the situation. I mean, it's not as if I reciprocate those feelings."

"No," Martin agreed. He didn't say anything else, which could have meant anything.

The silence in the car felt more than a little awkward, and perversely, that made me even more irritated. Martin and I should be enjoying the afterglow of our night together, not having to worry about whether Jeff Makowski's poor tender little hurt feelings were going to throw a monkey wrench into our alien-fighting plans.

"So where are we headed now?" I asked, hoping that would do the trick in changing the subject.

"Down to Bell Rock. That's the best place for you to work with vortexes, I think. I'm ninety-five-percent certain the aliens are going to be utilizing an upflow vortex, and the one at Bell Rock is very powerful."

So I'd heard. Well, at least it was a Thursday, and a December one at that. We might be able to find a spot in which to work that wasn't overrun with hikers. "Why do you think they'd want to use that sort of vortex? From what you've told me about the Reptilians, they don't seem like the uplifting type."

That remark got a smile out of him, and I relaxed somewhat. "It's the direction of the energy that's key. They want to take the energy that's already moving upward and outward. It's easier to harness that way."

"And what are they going to do with it once they've harnessed it?"

The smile faded. "You don't want to find out. That's why it's imperative that they be stopped before they get the chance."

For some reason, I shivered, even though the car's heater was on. "So why wait? Isn't there some way to get the drop on them now, days before the big event?"

He didn't exactly sigh, but he did expel his breath in a way that seemed to suggest that would never work. "Well, first off, you're not ready yet. Second, there's a reason why you have to engage the enemy at the solstice. In order to tap into the energy, they have to open themselves to it, making themselves vulnerable. It's only during that small, sensitive time that you'll have a chance of succeeding."

"Great. Now you're probably going to tell me that the exhaust port is only two meters wide."

A look of mystification swept over his face, and I almost laughed, despite everything. Apparently, there were limits to his store of geek data.

"*Star Wars*," I explained. "It's okay. So we go to Bell Rock, and I get a feel for this sort of vortex, and...what? Is that where they're going to make their stand?"

"No. There's a reason why they're located in Boynton. The vortex there is very strong as well, although it's a slightly different type, a mixture of upflow and inflow. Not quite as powerful as Bell Rock, but they'll want to work from a position of safety and security." His jaw tightened, although I noticed he kept his eyes on the road and didn't look over at me. "You'll have to confront them on their home ground."

Better and better. I reflected that once this was over, I was going to hole up in some resort with Martin, order room service for a week, and not stir out of my suite except to get a mani-pedi and maybe some really expensive reiki or hot rock massage treatments or something. It sounded like I was going to have earned it.

"You really know how to inspire a girl," I remarked. "Any other lovely little tidbits you'd like to share?"

"I think that's enough for now," he replied, and something in his voice sounded more relaxed, as if he was relieved that I seemed to be taking the bad news in stride.

Well, I'd had my share of bad news in this life already. I'd kind of gotten used to dealing with it. Even so, I hoped Martin didn't have any more bombshells he was going to drop before the day was over.

There were a few cars parked at the Bell Rock Pathway trailhead, but not enough to make me worry about the area being overrun. We got out of the car, and Martin offered me his hand. I didn't really need it—I'd hiked this area before—but I took it anyway. I wanted to feel his fingers wrapped around mine, know he was there for me.

A brisk wind blew. I didn't pay it much mind; it was almost always windy in Sedona. However, I did sort of wish I'd brought a rubber band or a scrunchie or something to get my hair out of the way. It kept whipping into my eyes, and I had to continually push it back with my free hand. The lower levels of the trail were easy enough and hardly involved any climbing, which relieved me somewhat. Not that I couldn't manage even an advanced trail, but that spat with Jeff had taken something out of me, and I knew my day was just getting started.

It didn't help that, as Martin led me around to the eastern side of the enormous rock formation, I began to feel…something. A pressure, maybe, although that didn't seem quite right. No, a sensation of something moving around me and above me, something that wasn't the wind at all. It took my breath away and at the same time invigorated me, giving me the impression that I could jump to the top of Bell Rock in a single bound, if I only knew how.

"You feel it, don't you?" Martin asked, blue eyes keen as they searched my face.

"Yes," I said, sounding short of breath, even though the climb so far really hadn't been that strenuous. "I don't get it—I've been here lots of times before."

"Before all your senses were fully awakened."

He stopped and faced me. We stood in a sort of small grotto formed by a natural rock wall on one side and several fallen boulders on two of the others. Bare clumps of manzanita sprouted from behind the rocks. It was sheltered and quiet, away from the main trail. I saw a patch or two of unmelted snow in the leeward side of the boulders.

It was colder in there out of the sun, and I moved closer to Martin. As if recognizing my need, he reached out to me and drew me close, held me against his chest as I huddled into his warmth. Even while I did that, I could still sense the energy swirling around me. Not warm, no, but crackling with power. It seemed to tell me I should reach out and take it, mold it to my own uses.

I spoke to Martin then with my mind. *It's so strong. I can't believe this was here the whole time, and I never felt it like this.*

His arms tightened around me. *Most people never do. It's all right. What's important is you being able to use it now.*

How do I do that?

You are a child of this place. It wants to work with you, just as it will fight against the aliens when the time comes. That's why they have to do their work at the solstice, when the power of your world is at its lowest ebb. Reach out to it, and it will show you the way.

I didn't want to leave the shelter of his embrace, but I knew I'd have to for what was to come next. Taking a few steps away from him, I raised my arms —glad even then that we'd stopped someplace where most of the casual hikers wouldn't come and see me standing there like some goofy new-age sun worshipper—and stretched them outward, feeling the power of the vortex ripple through me, surging along my veins, bright and terrible as molten gold.

And then the boulders moved.

Only a few inches, not enough for anyone to notice, or if they did, they'd probably just chalk up the shift in position to natural erosion or movement due to rainfall. But I knew that wasn't what had happened. I'd moved several tons of rock with only the power of my thoughts.

Well, that, and the energy of the vortex, still snapping and crackling through me, ready to be used, feeling almost playful somehow, like a dog running around my legs and wagging its tail, happy to see I'd come home.

I looked over at Martin, grinning, and he smiled back at me. For the briefest second, I thought I saw a shadow at the edges of that smile, as if not every part of him was overjoyed at my achievement, but I told myself that was silly. Of course, he'd be happy to see that I was able to work with the power of the vortex so easily.

"You continue to amaze me," he said, running a gloved hand over one of the boulders.

"Well, I do my best."

A head shake, but then he came over to me and took me in his arms, his mouth on mine, and I knew then that I didn't have to worry about anything as long as he went through this with me. The heat surging in me right then didn't have much to do with the vortex, only that delicious energy known as sexual attraction.

As much as I wanted to say that it looked as if I had this part of my training buttoned up, and we should just go back to the cabin for some quality alone time, I had a feeling that wouldn't go over very well. So I let myself enjoy the kiss, knowing that was all I was going to get for a while. I tasted him, caught a brief trace of clean soap smell from his skin, let the closeness of his body envelop me and reassure me with its very solidity.

After a minute or two, he lifted his mouth from mine. "I'm letting you distract me too much."

"You say that like it's a bad thing." I gulped in some cold air to steady my head and wished we'd brought along some bottled water from the car.

"In this situation, distractions could be deadly."

What a way to kill the moment. I looked down at the scuffed toes of my boots. "But you say I'm doing well."

"You are."

"But not well enough."

"I didn't say that."

This time, he hadn't bothered to hide the frustration in his tone. I raised my head and watched him carefully. He didn't look away, but I could see the strain in the fine lines of his jaw and mouth. Oh, that mouth....

He went on, "It's just—I can feel time slipping away. There's so much you need to know, and I can only help you so much before...." The words trailed off.

"Before the solstice?"

A nod, although again I had the feeling he wasn't telling me everything.

Since I knew that trying to pry secrets out of him would be an exercise in futility, instead, I planted my hands on my hips and said, "Okay, so show me what else I need to do."

CHAPTER FIFTEEN

THE REST OF THE DAY I SPENT WORKING ON MY CONTROL of the energy from the vortexes. Moving rocks was one thing, but Martin told me when the time came I'd have to do much more than manipulate physical objects—I'd have to reach out with my mind, insert my own will and my own power between their dark energies and the pure flow from the vortex.

"So is Boynton stronger than Bell Rock?" I asked.

We were taking a breather in the Taurus, where Martin had stowed bottled water and trail mix and some sandwiches. He hadn't been cooling his heels in Starbucks while waiting for my *tête à tête* with Jeff to be over, but had instead been stocking up on supplies for what was turning out to be yet another long day. By the time we broke for lunch, it was already almost two o'clock.

"Boynton is different," he told me after taking a swig from his bottle of water. "There, the energies are more balanced. In a way, that will make it more difficult, because you'll need to be able to separate them to focus on the upflow, which is what the aliens will be trying to tap into."

"But it's strong."

"Yes, but not the strongest."

"So which one is? Bell Rock?"

"No." He put the cap back on his bottle of water and pointed past the formation where we'd been doing our energy work to the imposing bulk of Courthouse Butte. "Courthouse is the strongest vortex in Sedona. But because it's so visible, it's useless to the aliens. No place to hide there."

That was true. Although it didn't have the same odd striations, from some angles, the butte had always reminded me of the Devil's Tower formation in Wyoming, the one from the end of *Close Encounters*. Its steep sides went straight up and were mainly bare of vegetation. Most of the top was flat enough, but you'd need a helicopter to get up there. And, as Martin had pointed out, there was no chance for stealth at the top of something so windy and exposed.

I shivered a little, although it was warm enough in the car. The sun had come out from behind the clouds, giving us a nice greenhouse effect to combat the wind-chill factor. That sensation of inevitability came crashing down on me again, making my tone more irritated than I'd intended as I asked, "And how am I even going to get into Boynton? I know the path—it's not the sort of place where I'll be able to sneak in. Persephone and Lance and Michael really lucked out that first time in Secret Canyon, but I have a feeling the security's been beefed up a little since then."

Part of me really didn't want to be talking about this stuff, but I knew I'd have to confront the reality of the situation much sooner rather than later. Besides, by focusing on the frightening things, the very real eventuality of my marching into Boynton and facing the Reptilians, I could almost distract myself from paying too much attention to the way the pale winter sunlight slanted through the car windows and turned Martin's blue eyes almost silver. Or the strong bones of his hands, now with the gloves removed, and how those hands had moved over my body the night before....

All right, so much for distracting myself.

If Martin noticed my preoccupation, he didn't give any sign of it. "You'll know when the time comes."

I didn't know if that was alien/angel double-speak for "all will be revealed in time," but I didn't like it much. All this psychic stuff was new to me. Maybe putting my trust in fate and letting the way be shown me when the time came was what other people did, but it had never been my *modus operandi*.

"If you say so," I replied, and took a bite of my sandwich. I had no idea how Martin had known to get me my favorite from the deli near Safeway, but God bless him for bringing me that delectable roast beef with the roasted red peppers and the provolone cheese. Funny how a good sandwich could do a lot to improve your outlook on life. With regret, I ate the last bit of it, then folded up the wax paper wrapping and put it inside the bag we were using for trash. "So what's next on the agenda?"

"The most difficult exercise so far."

I gave him a hard look, just to make sure he was serious, and as far as I could tell, he was. Those dark-lashed eyes gazed back at me directly without blinking.

A sigh wouldn't have sounded terribly profes-sional, so I settled for taking a bracing swallow of cold water before I put the bottle back in the cup holder where it had been resting. "Okay, then. Might as well do this on a full stomach, right?"

His fingers tightened on the bottle of water he held. "I wouldn't exactly say it's a laughing matter."

"I'm deadly serious," I told him. "Food settles my stomach. So I'll have to make sure I load up on Saturday night."

"Kirsten—"

I didn't want to discuss it anymore. He hadn't said what he planned next, but I guessed it was going to be something a little more complex than levitating a couple of rocks. "Let's go, Martin. As you keep telling me, time's a-wastin'."

No reply, except a tightening of his mouth as he patted his coat pocket to reassure himself the key fob was still in there and climbed out of the car, then locked it. A few more cars had come and parked while we ate, and I had to hope none of the newcomers had decided to take up residence in our grotto and do some *plein air* painting or meditate on the nature of the universe, or indulge in some good old-fashioned necking.

Actually, that was what I really wished the two of us could be doing, but Martin didn't seem too amorously inclined at the moment. Maybe he'd loosen up once he was satisfied with my progress for the day.

Although we did pass a few hikers as we made our way back to our secret little spot, they all seemed to be staying on the more established trails. The weather was unpredictable enough at the moment that I figured most people wouldn't want to venture too far off the beaten path. Well, unless they were borderline crazy, like Martin and me.

We scrambled our way back to the place that had sheltered us during my morning exercises. No sign of anyone having been there in our absence, which relieved me somewhat. I didn't think we'd left any evidence of what we'd been doing, but you could never be sure.

"All right," I said, once we took our positions in the grotto, me with my back to the biggest boulder, Martin a pace or two away from me, partially blocking the "entrance"—if you could call it that, since it was really just a gap between two very large rocks. "Let me have it."

A frown pulled at his dark brows. "Is it all right if I explain what you need to do before I 'let you have it'?"

"Sure," I said, lifting my shoulders. I hoped he could tell that my flippancy stemmed from nerves, and not because I didn't take the situation seriously. It didn't help that every time I looked at him, a little thrill rippled down my spine and settled in my stomach. All right, maybe a little lower than my stomach. I wanted him. I wanted to drop everything and go back to the cabin and let him love me all over again. That activity, while certainly enjoyable, probably wouldn't help much in defeating those pesky lizards out in Secret Canyon, and I told my libido to take a hike for a while so I could concentrate.

Martin watched me for a second or two, then nodded so slightly, I almost didn't catch the movement. "All right. I told you how you'll only have seconds to strike while the aliens are opening themselves to the upflow power of the vortex. They'll be vulnerable, but that doesn't mean they'll be helpless. Once they sense what you're trying to do, they'll do whatever they can to defend themselves. That means you have to protect yourself while at the same time using your own communion with the vortex energies to press the attack."

"Got it," I replied. "Like that little trick you showed me up in Oak Creek."

"Exactly." He didn't smile, but I thought I caught a glow of approval in his eyes. "Ready?"

Not really, I thought. I didn't broadcast the words to him mentally, though, but only said, "Yes."

Then I opened myself to the vortex's energy once more, letting that brilliant white-gold light flow through me again, sparking out to my fingertips. It almost felt as if I could scoop it up and throw it at any marauding aliens in the vicinity.

But I didn't have much time to enjoy the sensation, because in the next instant, I sensed that painful buzzing pressure in my mind, the one that told me Martin was forcing the sort of mental attack he knew the aliens would bring to bear. This time, it was much stronger than up at Oak Creek, almost blinding in its brutal force. I flinched, throwing up my hands even though I knew this attack was not physical at all. It ground into my brain, painful as I imagined a migraine must be. Of course, I'd never had one.

All I knew was that my mind seemed to be shattering under the assault, the shimmering energy from the vortex slipping from my fingers. Behind the ferocious pressure, I sensed an odd vibration...almost one of triumph.

Not so fast, buddy.

I gathered the vortex's power back to myself and flung it outward, using it like a battering ram against the pressure in my mind. The attack eased somewhat, and I pressed my advantage, coaxing the white-gold light to build on itself, pushing, pushing....

From somewhere very far away, I heard something that sounded like a cry of pain, and I opened my eyes to see Martin slumping against one of the red rock boulders, fingers of one hand wrapped around an outcropping as if it was the only thing holding him up. At once, I let go of the energy and ran to his side.

Oh, God, what if I'd actually hurt him?

But when I panted out a worried question, he only shook his head and sucked in a deep breath of the cold air. "I'm fine." A pause, and he added, "That is, I'll be fine in a minute." He shut his eyes, his lashes a sooty shadow on his cheeks, and breathed deeply again.

"Guess I don't know my own strength," I told him, the joke sounding lame to me even as I said it.

"Nothing to feel bad about," he replied. His voice had begun to sound a little stronger, and he pushed himself upright. "I guess I wasn't expecting quite that level of defense."

"But that's good, right?"

"Very good." He reached out and took my hand in his, leather brushing over the soft angora of my knitted gloves. "Don't worry, Kirsten. You didn't do any irreparable damage, and you showed me you can definitely hold your own."

I decided it was okay to let myself feel somewhat relieved. Not all the way relieved, but enough so I didn't have quite the weight of formless fears bearing down on me that I'd had a few minutes earlier. "So, we can call it a day?"

One dark eyebrow lifted.

"Damn," I said. "I suppose you want to do that all over again."

"More or less." This he looked almost amused. "Don't worry—this is a lot harder on me than it is on you, apparently."

Maybe that was true. Then again, the last thing I

wanted to do was wear him out so he wouldn't be any good tonight. My plans for the evening didn't exactly include passing out on the bed face-first at eight-thirty.

Well, I'd just have to hope for the best.

———————

Martin did call a halt to things at a little before five. By then, it was starting to get dark, and we still had to hike back to the car. We both staggered and wove our way down the parking lot, looking as if we'd been drinking something a lot more potent than bottled water.

If only.

I fell onto the passenger seat with a sigh, and Martin edged his way onto his own seat with a visible wince. "Holding up okay, old man?" I inquired, and unscrewed the cap on a fresh bottle of water and held it out to him.

"'Old' is right," he replied, taking the water from me. He lifted the bottle to his lips and drank almost half of it down in one huge gulp.

"Leave some for the rest of us, okay?"

He didn't reply, but merely handed the water bottle back to me and pushed his finger against the ignition button. We were almost the last ones to leave the parking lot; I saw one lone F-150 through the rear window as we pulled out onto the highway, but the rest of the hikers had obviously called it a day. I knew the feeling.

I'd sort of had visions of us going out for a drink as a reward for all that brutal effort, especially since we were close to the Village of Oak Creek and therefore close to PJ's Pub, a place I used to hate because it was strictly twenty-one and over, and now loved for exactly the same reason. Also, their street tacos were divine. At the moment, I felt as if I could have inhaled a whole plateful.

But that was not to be, as Martin had us headed north, back up to the Forest Houses and our secluded little cabin. I slumped down in my seat and told myself it was better that way. We could cocoon there for the rest of the evening and heal up for the next day...and whatever he had planned for then, he hadn't told me. Friday. It didn't leave a lot of time to get ready for the big showdown Saturday night. Sunday morning. Whatever.

A sleety, spattery rain started to fall, telling me that it would probably turn to snow by midnight if the temperature kept dropping. We drove in silence, both of us too tired for conversation. The uptown shops and restaurants slid past, the sidewalks still crowded despite the weather. Holiday decorations glittered from street lamps and signposts. All so normal. None of those people had any idea of what lay ahead.

Come to think of it, neither did I. Not really.

Then we were curving up through Oak Creek Canyon, the trees a dark canopy overhead. The entrance to Forest Houses could be hard to see when approaching from the south, especially after nightfall, but Martin swung unerringly into the narrow opening as if he'd done it a hundred times before. Who knows, maybe he had. He still hadn't gone into much detail about his time in the MIB unit and what he'd done during those five years he was undercover. I sort of doubted he would, considering we had more important things to worry about at the moment.

He parked and we both climbed out, neither one of us all that steady on our feet. Always a gentleman —I wondered if his people were just like that, or whether the behavior was something he'd picked up on Earth—Martin came around to lend me a hand as we negotiated the increasingly muddy path to the front door of our cabin. Once I was safely indoors, I dropped my purse on the floor just inside the door and collapsed on a chair.

"I'd say you know how to show a girl a good time, but I'm not sure how much fun that really was."

"It wasn't meant to be fun," he said sternly as he unbuttoned his overcoat and went to the closet to hang it up.

I kept mine on, because it was uncomfortably chilly in the place after it being vacant for so many hours. But Martin was right on that, going to the hearth and getting a good fire going in a remarkably short amount of time. In about five minutes, I decided it was warm enough for me to take off my coat and get rid of the muddy boots I wore. I unlaced them and then took them into the bathroom to wipe them down before I tracked dirt everywhere.

By that point, I was starting to feel a little more human. It might have been the quiet of the car ride here, giving me a chance to rest and recharge, or maybe the growing warmth in the room, with that delicious smell of wood smoke. Or maybe it was just being here with Martin, seeing him straighten from tending the fire, only to give me a glance that told me he wasn't quite as tired as I'd thought.

A heat that didn't have all that much to do with the fire flickered somewhere deep in my belly. I got up from my chair and padded in my stocking feet to the kitchen, where I pulled out the heavy tumblers we were using as wine glasses before asking, "Chianti or cab?"

He appeared to consider. "Hmm…what are we eating?"

"Considering how tired we both are, I'm guessing it's frozen pizza."

"Chianti, then. Definitely."

I grinned and got out the corkscrew, and he came into the kitchen to offer assistance. Not that I couldn't pull a cork with the best of them, but I didn't mind letting him do some of the work. As he busied himself with cutting the foil and then pulling out the cork, I asked, "So do you have these sorts of things on your world, or do you just really enjoy slumming?"

The cork came out with a satisfying *pop*. Martin set it and the corkscrew aside. "What sorts of things? And no, I wouldn't say I was slumming."

I waited until he had poured me a glass and I had

taken my first sip before replying, "Wine and pizza and burgers. You know."

"Ah." He helped himself to a measured swallow of chianti, shut his eyes for a moment, and sighed. "Frozen pizza, no. Burgers…not really. Wine? Unfortunately, no. Something we drink in somewhat the same manner, but wine is an earthly invention that many of us have come to enjoy."

"I'm glad to hear we have something of value to offer." Realizing that guzzling too much chianti on an empty stomach, especially after the afternoon we'd had, was not the wisest thing to be doing, I went to the oven and turned it up to 400 degrees, getting it ready for the pizza. In the meantime, I got out a box of crackers and a slab of smoked Gouda we'd picked up with the rest of the goodies while we were at Safeway. "To tide us over," I explained, after peeling the plastic away from the cheese. "We only have a butter knife to cut it, though."

"That's fine." He picked up the knife and sliced some cheese for both of us.

I popped some in my mouth sans cracker, enjoying the smooth, smoky flavor of it in contrast to the deep fruitiness of the chianti. The oven made little popping noises as it heated up, adding to the warmth of the fire. Outside, I thought I could hear the patter of rain on stones, and was glad we'd gotten indoors before it really decided to open up.

Again, I was struck by how homey and cozy it was here. Easy to pretend that Martin was my boyfriend and that we were just taking an extended weekend away from it all. But that sort of thinking wasn't safe. I couldn't forget we were here because this was the one place where I didn't have to worry about the aliens invading my mind while I slept. Besides, the man before me wasn't really my boyfriend. Stupid word, really. It wasn't as if I was still in high school.

Lover?

Maybe. Mentor, teacher, associate…who knew. Trying to put a label on such an impossible relationship probably wasn't the wisest thing to be doing.

"You're quiet," he said.

"I suppose I'm trying to talk myself out of being scared shitless," I replied. Somehow, it seemed easier to discuss the situation with the aliens than to admit I was attempting to analyze our affair and not having much luck.

"Fear is nothing to be ashamed of." Martin reached for a piece of cheese and ate it slowly, as if contemplating its flavor. "Fear can give you a healthy respect for your adversary, as long as you don't let that fear get out of control."

"It's kind of hard not to, don't you think?"

"Not really. You did extremely well today. I would think you'd be feeling encouraged by that."

I paused. In one way, he was right. I'd faced another challenge and overcome it, and had shown increasing mastery over these strange powers that a few days ago I didn't even know I had. However, how much did that really prove? Martin was the one training me, and he couldn't be completely impartial. Somewhere in the back of my head, I couldn't help wondering whether he was throwing his punches the tiniest bit, just to make sure he didn't hurt me.

Or to make sure my confidence didn't flag.

To cover my hesitation, I went to the small refrigerator and pulled out the frozen pizza. Unwrapping it and putting it in the oven gave me a little grace, but not all that much. I could tell he was still waiting for me to give him some sort of answer.

I shut the oven door and checked my watch, noting when I'd need to take the pizza out. Finally, I said, "Encouraged...a little. It's just that on Saturday night—Sunday morning—I'm not going to be fighting *you*. I'm going to be fighting a bunch of aliens. If they're all as strong as you are, I don't stand a chance."

He set down his glass and came to me then, drawing me into his arms. I burrowed my face into his shoulder, smelling the scent of wood smoke that seemed to cling to the fine wool of his sweater. This —this was what I'd been wanting, to feel his arms around me, to breathe him in, let his warmth surround me and support me.

"They're not as strong as I am," he murmured, stroking my hair, pushing it off my brow. "Collectively, they can be quite strong, but individually? Their mental powers are not as developed as those of my—of *your*—race. And remember, the very power of your world struggles against them. That's something on your side as well."

"I suppose so," I said, my tone dubious, and his arms tightened around me.

"You don't think I'd ask you to do this if it was hopeless, do you? You have a chance—a good one. A better one than I'd even hoped for. So you shouldn't, as they like to say here on Earth, borrow trouble. I'm not saying it will be easy. All I'm saying is that it's far from impossible."

His words did reassure me, if not completely. After all, what could he or his people get out of it if there was absolutely no chance of me succeeding? Again, I had to wonder at their whole "no interference" policy and its decidedly blurred lines. Apparently, highly advanced races were just as good at rationalization as the rest of us mortal schmoes.

"All right," I said, "you've convinced me. I have absolutely nothing to worry about. So how about you kiss me until that pizza is ready?"

"I think I can manage that." And he bent and pressed his mouth to mine, lips parting, tongues touching, sharing the sweetness of the wine and the smokiness of the cheese, and the heat of our bodies running together, bringing us to a perfect moment when the whole world seemed to stop and it was only his arms around me, only his mouth on mine.

Luckily, I wasn't so far lost in his embrace that I couldn't smell the cheese on the pizza as it began to burn. "Crap," I said, and pulled away. A frantic search turned up a couple of well-used pot holders in the bottom drawer, and I grabbed them before opening the oven door and pulling out the pizza.

It was a little crispy around the edges, but the center still looked gooey and more than viable.

"Close call," Martin commented with a grin.

"Your own damn fault for distracting me like that." I set the pizza down on the countertop, glad it was tile and not Formica so I didn't have to worry about scorching it. "Plates?"

"Of course." He retrieved them from a cupboard and set them on the cramped counter so I could dish us up.

Of course, there was nothing as civilized as a pizza cutter in the clutter of old utensils in the drawer, but I did find a fairly sharp knife shoved toward the back and used that to saw the pizza into more or less equal slices. After this operation, we collected our plates and our wine—Martin expertly grabbing both the bottle and his glass in his left hand—and went to sit in front of the fire.

Somehow, it seemed the most natural thing in the world to settle on the worn rug there as we used the end of the bed as a backrest, our feet stretching toward the hearth and the wonderful heat coming from it. We ate quietly, watching the flames, as the rain outside the window gradually shifted to snow, light and feathery and lovely. It wouldn't last; snow here in Sedona rarely did. But something about it seemed to increase my sense of shelter, as if the weather itself was wrapping a protective cocoon around us, giving us some grace, a chance to relax.

It came to me then that I felt as if I belonged here, sitting next to Martin, in a silence that had nothing of awkwardness in it. Belonging. A concept I'd always had a hard time wrapping my head around. It was as if there had been this little piece of me that never felt as if it fit in, as if there was something about me that always kept me on the fringes. If I stopped to think about it at all, I blamed it on my mother abandoning me at such an early age. Sure, my grandparents had given me a loving home and had taken care of everything I—or Kara—might need, but deep down, that didn't erase the feeling that there had to be something wrong with me for Marybeth to walk out like that.

I'd had friends, but I'd never been what you'd call popular, even if I looked like I should have been on the cheerleading squad or something. Kara had, but Kara worked at it, just as she worked hard at everything. I'd found it easier to play with computers, to read books and graphic novels and hang out at the store, listening to the wild tales spun by some of Grandpa's friends when they thought I wasn't paying attention. Boyfriends, sure, here and there, but we all know how well those relationships had turned out.

But now....

Scary, what I was feeling for Martin. Sure, he could dress it up in talk of lifemates and all that, but even so, the thought that I could be in love with him —could *love* him—when I'd only known him for a few days frightened the hell out of me. It was easy to sit back and be flip and be "kooky Kiki," the girl who dyed a blue streak in her hair one day because she felt like it and spent her weekends looking for UFOs. That girl didn't have a care in the world.

I didn't think I recognized her anymore.

And what scared me even more was that I loved Martin, even though I knew next to nothing about him. What I did know was that when he held me, when he kissed me, touched me, I didn't want anything else. One glance from those sea-blue eyes, and I was lost. Not exactly what I'd expected of myself, when I'd decided several years back that I just wasn't the romantic type and had little patience for all the swooning and heavy breathing and drama I saw going on with my friends who were in relationships.

I set down my pizza rind and picked up my glass of wine. Martin was staring into the fire, shadows dancing over his fine profile, which looked like something that should be stamped on a coin. I couldn't begin to guess what he might be thinking.

Tentatively, I reached out with my mind, still unsure of this new talent. *You're not saying much tonight.*

His mouth lifted slightly at the corner. *Neither are you.*

True. I drank the one swallow left at the bottom of my glass, and he silently poured me some more, filling it about halfway. *Guess I'm just tired.*

How tired?

I caught the hint in the unvoiced question. *Well, not that tired.*

And although I wasn't quite sure exactly how it

happened, I found the glass plucked from my hand, and Martin was lifting me as easily as if I weighed nothing, carrying me to the bed, his hands urgently pulling the sweater over my head, fingers working at the button on my jeans. Normally, I would have reached out to him, but for some reason, I found myself content to lie there as he tossed my clothes onto a chair, unhooked my bra, pulled down my panties.

You're beautiful.

So are you, I thought back at him, and he grinned and stripped off his own clothes, thus proving me right. That body looked like it should be on a billboard.

After that, I didn't have much chance for rational thought, because he was on top of me, mouth trailing from my breast to my stomach, moving lower, and he was tasting me, tongue doing things I'd never even imagined were possible. All I could do was twine my fingers in his hair, feeling the heat in my body swirling in my core, bringing me to an orgasm that had me screaming into the quiet cabin, gasping for breath even as he moved into me, filled me once again, our bodies rocking together. And then somehow we were rolling in the bed, with him shifting the two of us so I rode on top of him, fingers tangled in one another's, clutching with all our strength as we rocketed to a shared climax, light and shadow swirling around us, taking us with them, until I collapsed next to him and he pulled me close, drawing the covers over us.

My weariness caught up with me at last, and I began to slip away almost at once. Even so, I thought I saw his lips moving, and I thought I knew what he'd said.

I love you, Kirsten.

CHAPTER SIXTEEN

No rest for the wicked, of course. I did sleep the sleep of the just, only to wake up to a scent of sausage that turned out to be pre-fab breakfast burritos. Better than Pop Tarts, of course, but I would have killed for some bacon and an omelette after yesterday's...exertions. Yes, that was a nice catch-all phrase for everything I'd done.

As before, Martin was already showered and dressed. I admired his efficiency while at the same time cursing the sloth that made me sleep through his preparations, thereby missing the opportunity to watch him walk around naked. Oh, well.

I climbed out of bed, glad that he'd built the fire back up again, and snagged one of the burritos from the plate where it sat. "So where are we off to today, O Zen Master?"

He only shook his head and set a mug of English Breakfast down next to the burrito plate. "We'll go to

Cathedral Rock. It's a good place for you to learn to separate the inflow and upflow energies."

That didn't sound too frightening. Also, Cathedral Rock and the area around it were some of the most beautiful landmarks in already beautiful country. I could think of worse ways to spend my day.

I could tell from his tone that he needed me to be all business. Maybe a small pang as I imagined climbing into bed with him and snuggling all morning, but we didn't have time for that. I'd just have to hold last night's memories to me and hope for a repeat this evening.

"Sounds good," I said, my tone deliberately neutral.

After that, I ate quickly and hurried into the shower, right after I pulled my phone and charger out of my purse and plugged them in. It was true that there was no reception up here, but I had a feeling there would probably be a ton of messages waiting for me once we got into town where I could pick them up. Having a dead phone would only make matters worse.

Lather rinse, but no repeat, because I'd washed my hair the day before and didn't have time. Quickie toothbrush, blow-dry, mascara, lip gloss, underwear, jeans, T-shirt, sweater.

Thus ready for the day, I left the bathroom and checked the charge on my phone. Seventy-two percent. It would have to do.

Martin didn't exactly smile as he saw me, but I thought I saw a certain light in his eyes as I came toward him and gave him a quick kiss on the cheek, then wiped away the smear of lip gloss I'd left behind. "Okay, ready."

Instead of opening the door, though, he bent down and gave me a real kiss, one that tasted of hot chocolate, and said, "Today should be easier."

I knew he meant to reassure me. In my mind, I couldn't help wondering if he was taking it easy on me today because the big showdown was going to take place in less than thirty-six hours. All I said, though, was, "That's a relief," and I let myself out of the cabin.

The sun was up, the clouds of the day before mostly gone, and with the rising of the sun, most of the snow from last night had already begun to melt. I trudged along the muddy path to the car, then scraped off my boots as best I could on one of the large rocks that bordered the parking lot. Martin went around to his own side of the car and did the same before he got in.

I glanced at the clock on the dashboard. Eight-thirty. Not too bad. There weren't many cars passing us headed north as we drove down into town, and I wondered if the snow from the night before had closed the highway up into Flagstaff. It would have been much heavier there.

After that, I didn't have much time to worry about it, because we came down into Sedona proper and immediately my phone started chiming, alerting me to all the emails and text messages and phone calls I'd missed the day before. I shot Martin a brief apologetic look and waggled the phone next to my ear, signaling that I really needed to get my messages. He gave a philosophical shrug and returned his attention to the road, which luckily wasn't that crowded, since the stores weren't open yet.

Oddly enough, the first voicemail message was from Persephone Oliver, of all people. "Hi, Kirsten. I know you have a lot on your plate right now, but I need to talk to you in person. Call me, please." She hung up after that—no explanations, no clarifications. Just weird. Something in her voice told me I'd better call her, though.

Later, I told myself. She might not even be up yet. Which was probably a cop-out, but I didn't know Persephone well enough to guess whether she was a morning person or a night owl. Considering she was married to an astronomer/astrophysicist, I would guess more the latter than the former, but you never knew.

After that, I had a call from Kara, of course, urging me to further caution and telling me I should really come by and talk. Why, so she and Lance could both dog-pile me? No, thanks. I had the feeling she would really flip out once she discovered Martin and I had taken our relationship to the next level, as it were, and I had enough to deal with as it was.

That was it for voicemails, thank God. Texts from my friend Lindsey, wanting to know if I had time to go shopping this weekend.

Yeah, sure, Linds...let's get together Sunday if the world's still here.

I thought that probably wouldn't go over very well, so instead I just texted back: *Working all weekend. Rain check?* and sent it off. Then I remembered the "Closed for family emergency" sign stuck to the door of the UFO Depot and hoped Lindsey was busy enough that she wouldn't come by to check on me. That could be bad.

Nothing from Jeff, of course. I wanted to be relieved, but underneath my irritation toward him, I did worry...a little. Brilliant he might be, but his emotional development left a lot to be desired. I couldn't help feeling guilty over the way we'd left things, especially with him stuck there at Michael's place with not a lot to do. I could only hope that his work on cracking the aliens' transmissions was keeping him busy enough that he didn't have much time left over to mope about me.

And after that were a bunch of junk emails, and a couple of questions from my client whose project was outstanding, along with a query from someone else who wanted a site done after the first of the year. My calendar was getting pretty full. It would be nice if I was actually around to enjoy the fruits of all these commissions.

"Everything all right?" Martin asked as I shoved my phone back in my purse.

"More or less. Persephone wants to see me about something, though. Think we'll have any time today?"

"Is it important?"

"She sounded like it was."

"Then we'll make time."

That response didn't reassure me quite as much as I'd hoped it would. So was the work we were doing today not as important as Martin had made it sound?

I glanced at the clock again. Five minutes until nine. I knew that once we got off the main highway and started hiking back toward Cathedral Rock, the phone would most likely drop out again. I'd have to risk calling and hope for the best.

Persephone picked up on the second ring. "Hi, Kirsten."

She didn't sound particularly worried or stressed out, but that didn't mean much. Psychic she might be, but she'd been a therapist before she became a professional psychic, and so I knew you couldn't always tell what was going on with her just from her tone of voice.

"Hey, Persephone," I said. "You wanted to see me?"

At that question, she did pause. "Yes. I'm glad you called me back. Do you have any time today?"

I pulled the phone away from my ear and shot a questioning look at Martin. "Time?"

One o'clock, he responded silently.

"How about one?" I asked Persephone.

"That sounds great. I'll see you then."

"Okay. I'll be there at one." I ended the call, wondering what exactly I'd just signed up for, then shifted in my seat so I more or less faced Martin. "You'll need to drop me at Persephone's. Is that all right?"

"Of course it is," he replied, sounding amused. "I like being your chauffeur."

"You do? Because I could probably pick up the van—"

"No, it's fine. Really."

I had to be content with that. What he'd do with himself while I was making this secret but apparently important social call at Persephone's, I had no idea, but her place wasn't too far from some shops and restaurants. He could always put his feet up at the nearby pub and hang out until I was done.

By then, we were at the extreme south end of Sedona proper. We pulled onto Back O' Beyond road and followed the signs to the trailhead. I'd done this hike before, but never in the winter, so I had no idea what shape the trail would be in after the snow of the night before. Well, I supposed I'd find out soon enough.

As he'd done the day before, Martin brought along a small backpack with bottled water and some trail bars. I wondered if that was all I'd have to live on until I went over to Persephone's. Or maybe he'd told me one o'clock because he planned to feed me after our excursion to Cathedral Rock. A girl could hope, anyway.

Since the trail was steep, I didn't have a lot of energy left over for talking. I trudged along behind Martin, watching my breath puff out in the chilly air, trying to hold the memory of last night's warmth close to me. It seemed as if that ecstasy had happened long ago, to some other person.

As we climbed, I did begin to feel what Martin had been talking about, how the rock was a vortex for two different kinds of energy. Upflow, because of the spires of rock that seemed to pierce the sapphire sky, but I could sense how the power moved downward as well, channeling itself through the saddle cut into the enormous formation.

Those twisting energies were beautiful but difficult to track, whispering and winding around me from all directions. It didn't help that I had to keep most of my own energy focused on the treacherous trail. Ahead of me, Martin moved forward, each step deliberate and sure. Obviously, he was having no problem negotiating the difficult ground. As the trail veered ever upward, though, he reached back and took me by the hand, lending his strength to me. I clung to his strong fingers, glad of the assistance. Actually, I was mostly glad that he'd noticed my difficulty and had reached out to help me without a second thought.

At last, we reached the second saddle point between the upthrust spires of rock. Here, the energies were stronger than ever; my whole body seemed to buzz with them. It was good that we'd stopped, because I needed to catch my breath if I was going to have any hope of sorting through those intertwining streaks of light and power. As I concentrated, I could see that the upflow energies were the familiar white-gold I'd seen at Bell Rock the day before, while the downflow energies had a cool blue tinge, as if they'd picked up some of the inky shadows between the rocks.

"You see it, then," Martin said quietly.

"I-I think so. But they're so knotted up together!"

"Focus on the upflow energy. That's what the aliens will be attempting to harness."

I did as he instructed, closing my eyes, letting that inner sense or power or whatever it was follow the upward movement of the gold-hued light. In a way, it almost reminded me of the time when I was ten and a friend of Grandpa's had brought in some illegal fireworks from New Mexico. There had been cones that sent out showers of starry sparks in shades of the palest wheat, and that's what I saw now.

These fireworks would be even more deadly in the wrong hands than those illegal ones.

But now that I had something solid and real to latch onto, it was easier to let the bluish light flow downward and away, out of my field of vision. It had its own power, of course, just not one the aliens apparently meant to tamper with. It seemed almost to fade out, while the white gold light grew stronger, sparking and sizzling.

"I think you've got it," came Martin's voice, warm with approval.

I opened my eyes and grinned. "Really?"

"Really. I told you today would be easier."

The actual energy work, sure. The hike? Not so much.

It didn't help that we were far more exposed here than we had been in our little grotto on the leeward side of Bell Rock. The wind blew strongly from the north, and although I'd bundled up and the sun shone brightly above, we were mostly in shadow here, and it was cold. Really cold.

"Th-then c-can we get down now?" I asked from between chattering teeth.

His answer came in the form of him pulling me against him, holding me close, lending me some of his warmth. "Yes. It's almost lunchtime anyway."

"D-damn." More of the weird time dilation that seemed to happen whenever I went inward to work with these new powers of mine. I pushed my sleeve up a fraction and saw that it was ten minutes until twelve. Good. I still had almost an hour. I shot a hopeful glance up at Martin and asked, "Did somebody say lunchtime?"

We couldn't go too far for lunch, since I'd promised Persephone I'd be at her place at one, and it took us almost twenty-five minutes to get back to the car. But we grabbed burgers at the Irish pub off 179, and nothing had ever tasted so good. Or maybe it was just getting something warm inside me after standing out in the cold for hours I didn't even realize were passing.

Afterward, Martin drove me to Persephone's

house and said, *Call me this way when you need me to come back.*

I will, I promised, and leaned over and gave him a hearty cheeseburger-flavored kiss. *Hopefully, this won't take long.*

He squeezed my hand, then watched as I opened the car door and got out. After waiting for me to cross the driveway and approach the front door, he slowly pulled away from the curb and turned the car around, heading back down to 179.

Taking a breath, I leaned over and pushed the doorbell. A wreath of fresh pine boughs, topped with a red ribbon, hung from the door, and a small potted pine trees adorned with more red ribbons stood sentinel to either side. Somehow the trappings of the holidays felt jarring, what with everything that was going on.

Persephone opened the door at once. "Thanks for coming, Kirsten," she said, and stepped out of the way so I could move past her into the foyer.

That house was truly a thing of beauty. If I was going to be completely honest about it, I was a little envious of the way Persephone and Paul had gotten settled here so quickly. I'd say their house felt like a model home because of the furniture and the way everything always looked just so, but it was too warm and cozy for that. I also liked that Persephone had gone for a sort of Tuscan farmhouse feel instead of the ubiquitous Southwest vibe that seemed to dominate interior decorating in this part of the world.

She indicated that we should go into the living room, so I followed her lead and sat down on the overstuffed couch. A couple of mugs of spiced cider sat on coasters on the coffee table, adding their perfume to the holiday-scented potpourri she had out in several small bowls. All in all, it was a wonderful, welcoming atmosphere.

So why did I feel a shiver of apprehension run down my spine?

I asked as we both sat down on the couch, "How'd it go with the Discovery Channel people?"

Something tense in Persephone's face seemed to relax a little. "Great, really great. It sounds like it's a go. We won't get the formal word until after the first of the year, but...." She trailed off, and I could tell she was wondering if they were even going to be around to get good news after this weekend.

"Everything's going well," I told her, hoping she'd be a little more receptive to my work with Martin than Kara had been. "Martin—that is, Agent Jones is really impressed with how I've been doing. He's...hopeful."

My words were meant to reassure her, but that tension I'd noticed earlier returned to her mouth and jaw. "Well, about that...."

Again, she hesitated and then shook her head, her heavy curls sweeping over the dark green wool of the sweater she wore. When I first met her, I'd envied that hair a good bit, since it seemed to have a life of its own, instead of my own pale, straight locks.

"Look, it's probably better if we both acknowledge that this is a little weird," I told her. "But obviously you have something you need to say, so...just say it."

She folded her hands over her jeans-clad knees. The big diamond Paul had given her sparkled in the pale wintry sunlight streaming through the windows. "It's—well, I've heard from Otto."

"Oh, really?" That surprised me. From what I'd heard Kara say, dear old Otto hadn't been very available to our resident psychic lately. And now, knowing what I knew about Martin and Otto, I had a feeling his latest contact with Persephone wasn't exactly a coincidence.

"He's...well, he's concerned."

"He should be," I said. "Considering our reptile buddies are going to attempt the mother of all hostile takeovers this weekend."

Her eyes widened a little. "So that's who they are."

"You didn't know?" That remark had surprised me. I'd sort of figured, being psychic, she had access to all sorts of inside information that the rest of us didn't.

"No. When I was in the base, they were still possessing their human hosts. I've never really...*seen*...them."

I wanted to say she wasn't missing much, but I hadn't actually seen them, either. Not really. At the moment, I figured that was a good thing, and I couldn't completely contain the shudder that went though me at the memory of those scaled fingers brushing against my body. "Anyway," I went on, banishing the nightmare to the dark where it belonged, "so what has Otto so worked up he'd actually deign to visit you again after all this time?"

For some reason, she wouldn't quite meet my eyes. "Well, you, actually. Or rather, you and Martin Jones."

Oh, for Chrissake.... "Doesn't Otto have anything better to do than interfere with other people's love lives?"

She didn't seem surprised by what basically amounted to an outright admission that something was going on between Martin and me. Then again, she was psychic. Or Kara had gone babbling to her. I supposed it didn't really matter how she knew.

"I don't think he sees it that way," Persephone said mildly, and finally reached over to pick up her neglected mug of cider.

I followed her lead and had some of my own cider. It felt good going down, especially since my throat was a little raw after being out in all that cold air earlier. "Really?" I replied after I'd set my mug back down again. "Exactly how *does* Otto see it?"

Again, she glanced away from me. It was pretty obvious that she really didn't feel like getting in the middle of this. "He says that Martin is too involved, that he is creating great personal risk for himself by letting himself get so close to you. It's not what he was sent here for...according to Otto, anyway."

While I certainly didn't like the concept of putting Martin at "great personal risk"...whatever that meant…I liked even less the idea of Otto butting into our business, especially since we were running out of time and options. "Well, too bad," I said, not bothering to curb the acid in my tone. "Martin's only trying to help me before it's too late. I don't see anyone else stepping in to lend a hand. If Otto's so concerned, maybe he should get up off his fluffy white ass and pitch in."

"I'm afraid that's impossible," a new voice broke in. "And, for the record, my ass is far from fluffy."

Persephone got up abruptly and I found myself doing the same, even as my mouth dropped open and I stared at this new apparition.

He stood in the middle of the Persian rug, watching me with puckered eyebrows and a cast of disapproval to his perfect mouth. Tall, like Martin, and dark-haired like Martin, but this being, who must be Otto, would never be able to pass for a regular human the way Martin did. His skin was smooth and marble-pale, more perfect than any skin I'd ever seen, and he wore pale robes that seemed to shift through a spectrum of pastel colors, as if woven of extruded opals.

Somehow, I found my voice. "Otto, I presume."

He nodded and looked past me to Persephone. "Thank you for bringing her here."

She gave an embarrassed lift of the shoulders, as if trying to apologize to me for putting me in the middle of this…while also acknowledging Otto's thanks.

But then his dark stare fastened on me, and something about it made me want to simultaneously stand up straighter and suck my stomach in—and sock him in the jaw for looking at me like something he'd just found crawling across his pants leg. Not that he was wearing pants.

"Kirsten."

I decided that I really didn't like the way he said my name. I crossed my arms and stared back at him. "Otto. I hear you have something you want to say to me."

"So human."

"Half, anyway."

A flicker of annoyance passed over his perfect features. "I have a feeling it's the dominant half."

"Is that supposed to be an insult?"

"Children," Persephone said, her tone mild enough, but I could tell she'd had enough of the pissing contest.

"Very well." Otto gaze sharpened, if that was even possible. It already felt like it could cut through steel plate. "I will make some allowances, since you are obviously ignorant of the consequences of Martin's meddling, but matters as they stand between the two of you cannot continue. He's shown you what must be done, and that is all he will be allowed to do."

"'Allowed'?" I repeated. "Is he a child? Can't he make his own decisions?"

"You don't understand what's at stake. We cannot interfere, not at the level he's done. Perhaps if he stops now and allows things to run their course, then the situation will right itself."

Godlike being or no, all I wanted in that moment was to tell him to go screw himself. I had a feeling that kind of remark wouldn't go over very well, and most likely would only result in more pronouncements on my ignorance and general human deficiency on a variety of levels. I had no idea how Persephone had managed to put up with this guy buzzing in her head for so many years.

"It sounds like you should be talking to him, not me," I replied. "After all, he's the one who approached me and told me what had to be done."

"We are talking to him," Otto told me, and something about the way he said it made me distinctly uneasy. "But he is being stubborn. You must make a break now, and use the knowledge he's given you to take your stand against the invaders."

"For someone who's not supposed to be interfering in human affairs, you're showing a sort of unhealthy interest in my love life, don't you think?"

Persephone sucked in a breath, as if she couldn't believe I'd just said that. At the moment, though, I was feeling fearless. Maybe it was the memory of Martin's body against mine, or the way he had mouthed *I love you*. I just knew he would never walk away from me, no matter what pressure his people might put on him. Hadn't he told me I was his lifemate?

Otto pulled himself up. He was very tall...and those robes made him look even taller. I could see why some people would confuse these kinds of aliens with angels. "As Martin is not human, and you are only half, I daresay my interference here is entirely within the boundaries of expectation."

Well, he did have me there. I scowled. "Tell you what, Otto. If Martin walks away, I'll drop the whole thing." I felt confident enough in making such an offer, since I knew Martin wouldn't leave me voluntarily.

A flicker of surprise passed over Otto's perfect features. "You would do that?"

Now was not the time to show any hesitation. I recalled the light in Martin's eyes as he looked at me, the way he'd reached down to help me navigate the treacherous trail at Cathedral Rock. We might have only known each other a few days, but somehow, that didn't seem to matter. We were right together. Nothing would keep us apart. Not even meddling multidimensional beings.

"I would," I said steadily.

"I've heard enough," he replied, and then he was gone, disappearing from the room in a brilliant flash of light.

I blinked, seeing dancing sparks behind my eyelids, after-effects of Otto's Vegas-worthy exit. Then I looked over at Persephone, who stood a few paces away, brow puckered in worry.

She cleared her throat and asked, "Are you sure that was wise?"

"I trust Martin." Her expression didn't change, and I went on, "I know you all have the impression that I'm some silly girl who doesn't know what she's doing—"

"I didn't say that."

"No, but you were probably thinking it." I shoved my hands in my pockets and sent her an imploring look, practically willing her to understand. "Didn't you feel that way about Paul, that you knew you were supposed to be together even though you'd only known each other for a few days?"

At that question, her mouth softened. "Yes. Yes, I did." She was silent for a few seconds, and I wondered if she was reaching out somehow, trying to get more of a grasp on the situation by using her own unique abilities. A small nod, and then she added, "I get it, Kirsten, I do. Your sister isn't very happy—"

"Of course she isn't. She thinks I should be seeing someone closer to my own age. Never mind that Lance is just as many years older than she is as Martin is older than me."

"Than Martin *looks*," Persephone corrected me. "We can't apply our same standards to them. Of course, he never came out and told me, but I always had the impression that Otto had to be at least hundreds of years old."

"Then you'd think he would've learned better manners by now," I snapped. Yes, I'd been wondering from the time Martin revealed his alien nature how old he really was, but having Persephone point it out to me somehow made it more real.

She almost smiled. "No, Otto was never very good at being tactful, unfortunately. I guess I've just gotten used to it over the years." Her expression sobered. "And I guess part of me is just as irritated as you are. I'll admit I have no idea what their rules are, beyond the whole 'no direct intervention' thing, but being so concerned about your relationship with Martin when we mere mortals are facing a very real danger seems like a massive case of misplaced priorities."

"That's for sure." It did hearten me to know that Persephone was thinking some of the same things I was, and she definitely wasn't being as judge-y about the whole situation as Kara had been. "But I seem to have pacified Otto for now, so I should probably have Martin come get me so we can get back to work."

"And he really is hopeful?"

"Yes." Persephone's tone had been steady enough, but it didn't take psychic powers to know she was frightened. Not that I blamed her. I didn't know if I was trying to reassure her or myself as I added, "And he's got a much better idea of what we're up against than I do, so if he thinks we have a chance, then we probably really do."

"Good." She let out a little breath and hesitated, as if trying to decide whether she should say anything else. Then, in a rush, "I've been trying not to think about it too much, but it's even harder now because I just found out—well, turns out I'm pregnant."

"Wow—congratulations! I didn't know you guys were trying."

Her fair skin turned faintly pink along her cheek-bones. "Well, we weren't *trying*, trying, if you know what I mean, but...."

"You can spare me the gory details," I said with a laugh. "But I get it. The stakes just got higher."

"But no pressure." She looked almost rueful.

"It's okay." And strangely, it was. Martin had said I was doing very well. He was hopeful. I was fighting for him and for Kara and Grace and Lance and Michael, and now Persephone's unborn child, along with everyone else I cared about. It was going to be all right. "But I really need to get going."

"I understand." And one of her hands went to her stomach, even though it was perfectly flat still. She was probably less than two months along, if she'd only just found out.

But I could worry about all that later. I closed my eyes and called out to him. *Martin.*

Nothing. I could feel myself frown, but I took a breath and tried again. *Martin, I'm ready. You can come get me now.*

Only silence, and the thin, thready edges of panic on the borders of my mind. I refused to let myself give in to it, and instead opened my eyes and went to my purse where I'd left it sitting on the floor by the couch. Maybe he was too far away. He'd never really mentioned how far that strange telepathy of ours reached. So I dug out my cell phone and pulled him up in my contacts, then hit "call."

His phone rang and rang, and finally went into voicemail. *You've reached Special Agent Martin Jones of the Phoenix office of the FBI. Please say your name slowly....*

I touched the "end" button and looked up from my phone to see Persephone watching me with sympathy in her hazel eyes. "Must be out of range," I said, my tone casual, although what was the point of lying to a psychic?

She reached out then, gave my hand a squeeze. She didn't say anything, and she didn't have to.

Apparently, Otto had gotten to him.

Martin wasn't coming.

CHAPTER SEVENTEEN

KARA WAS THE ONE WHO CAME AND GOT ME. I DIDN'T know what Persephone had said to her, exactly, but whatever it was, my sister was fairly subdued, and didn't start in on how I'd been stupid to get involved with Martin when I knew nothing about him, or any of that sort of thing. No, she just asked if I wanted to go home, and I nodded without speaking. Never mind that a lot of my day-to-day stuff was still up at the Forest Houses cabin. I had a spare toothbrush and some sample sizes of shampoo under the sink in my bathroom. I'd make do.

It wasn't that far from Persephone's place to my apartment. As Kara parked her Prius in an empty spot in front of the stairs to my unit, I was overcome by an enormous feeling of inevitability. So much for that sensation I'd had as I left with Martin several days ago, the one that told me I might not be coming back. Oh, I was back all right.

Kara followed me up the stairs, and I was too tired and heartsick to tell her not to come. I realized then that she probably should have driven me to the store so I could pick up the van, but for some reason, the thought of having to drive it made me want to burst into tears. Maybe it was because I had a flash of Martin smiling at me, saying, *I like being your chauffeur*.

Yeah, right.

I turned the key in the lock and pushed the door open, then stopped dead.

"Holy crap," Kara said from behind me.

It looked as if a whirlwind had blown through my apartment—if the whirlwind in question was talented enough to dump the contents of every drawer on the floor, slash open the couch, and even pull my pretty Moroccan lamp from its hook in the ceiling and smash it against the dinette table. Vaguely, I registered my old iMac desktop computer torn apart on the floor, screen shattered and electronic guts strewn every which way. Thank God I'd taken my laptop with me. Of course, said laptop was still resting in my suitcase up at the cabin, since I hadn't wanted to lug it with me when I was hiking up Cathedral Rock.

And it was the thought of my MacBook sitting up there alone, waiting for me, that finally brought the tears. I slumped over, sobs tearing through me, and then I felt Kara's arms go around me, heard her shut the door. Somehow, she guided me back down the stairs and into her car. She pulled out of the parking lot and headed toward West Sedona, back toward her house. All the while, I wept, the scene outside blurring, a surreal smear of red rocks and green trees, a kaleidoscope of cars and buildings and people, none of it making any sense.

Then we were in her garage, and she was leading me inside. I heard her say a few murmured words to Lance, and we went past him, on into her office, which was now mainly a guest room, since Grace occupied the bedroom that had once been mine.

Kara sat me down on the daybed, disappeared for a minute, and then came back with a box of tissues and sat down next to me. "I suppose there's no point in calling the police, is there?"

I shook my head and wiped my eyes with a tissue. "N-no."

"It was *them*?"

"P-pretty sure." I wadded up the damp tissue and pulled another one out of the box. Residential burglary wasn't unknown in Sedona, especially in the big expensive vacation houses that stood empty for months out of the year. Those were easy pickings, despite their alarm systems. But I could tell nothing had been taken from my apartment. Whoever had ransacked my apartment, they'd done it with the intent to destroy. To send a message.

Kara rubbed my shoulder. "At least you weren't there. Things can be replaced. You can't."

Cold comfort. *When did they break in?* I wondered. My first night away, angry that they could no longer attack me mentally, sheltered as I was by the soothing energies of Oak Creek? Or later, once they began to figure out what I might be up to?

I had no idea. Not that it really mattered at this point.

"I need my stuff," I told her.

She raised an eyebrow. "It's okay, Keeks. I can run to Walgreens and get you some things for tonight, and you can borrow some of my clothes—"

"No," I said, and added, "I mean, Martin and I were staying up at Forest Houses. My laptop and some spare clothes and toiletries and things are there. He may have ditched me, but that doesn't mean I can't get my stuff back."

"Sweetie, how do you know your things will even be there?"

I didn't, of course, but something inside was driving me to go out there. Maybe in the back of my mind, I was hoping that Martin would be at the cabin. There had to be a rational explanation for his defection. Maybe he was hiding out there because it was the only place he was safe from retaliation by his own people. "They're there. If you don't want to drive me, then take me back to the store so I can get the van—"

"No way am I letting you drive, not when you're in this state of mind."

Her tone told me there wasn't much point in arguing, which was good, since I didn't have the energy for it. I yanked a fresh tissue out of the box and stood. "Okay, then let's go."

Frowning, she rose from the bed as well and went

out into the hall, where I heard her have a brief muffled convo with Lance. I shoved a couple more tissues in my pocket, just in case, then headed out of the guest room and toward the garage. Kara followed me, giving Lance a quick kiss on the cheek.

Surprisingly, he didn't look angry or annoyed by the situation, but actually worried. I would have thought he'd be ready to break out the "I told you so"s, but I supposed I hadn't given him enough credit. But then Grace started making fussy noises from inside the nursery, and he went in to check on her.

Just as well. I didn't think I was really up to an in-depth conversation with Lance right then.

Kara and I got back in her Prius, and she pulled out of the garage without saying anything. In fact, we went all the way back through Uptown Sedona and out into the wilderness area north along 89A without speaking. I really didn't know what else to say, and she was doing that thing she always did when she was worried—drumming her fingers on the steering wheel as if in time to music only she could hear.

Then, finally, "You don't really think you're going to find him up here, do you?"

"Maybe. No. I don't know." I continued to stare out the windows at the passing trees, some bare and cold-looking, like the winter-naked cottonwoods and sycamores, the pines and junipers still dense dark green. It was easier to watch them than try to pick apart the tangled jumble of emotions inside me. "But

I need my laptop back no matter what. My whole life is on that thing."

She didn't reply, but gave a little nod. I think we both knew I was using the laptop as a crutch, an object I could focus my mental energies on so I wouldn't have to think about Martin's apparent abandonment. All my files were backed up to the cloud, and I had the money to buy a new laptop if necessary, but that wasn't the point. I needed to have something solid to hang on to right then. Martin was gone and my apartment was destroyed, and now I had less than thirty-six hours before all hell broke loose, but dammit, I was going to get that MacBook Pro back.

Obviously not as familiar with the turn-off as Martin, Kara almost drove past it. She hit the brakes —luckily, there was no one behind us—and did a not-quite U-turn into the driveway. By then, it was almost three, so while the sun was still up, it was already behind the high cliffs to the west, and the parking area blanketed in shadow.

I opened the door and got out, and Kara did the same. Since Martin had arranged for the cabin, I didn't have a clear idea of where the Forest Houses office was located, but luckily there was a sign, so I went in the direction it pointed, my sister following a pace or two behind me.

The man sitting in the chair behind the old oak desk looked up as I entered the office. He raised an eyebrow. Of course, he probably had no idea who I was, since Martin and I had come and gone to the cabin directly and hadn't had any interactions with the people running the place. It probably wasn't going to be a lot of fun trying to convince him to let me into the Bridge House so I could reclaim my belongings.

But I'd barely opened my mouth to say, "Hi, I'm Kirsten, and—" before he interrupted me.

"He said you might be back for your things."

My mouth somehow refused to shut. "He —what?"

The man's gray-frosted eyebrow remained lifted, even as he pushed a key across the desk toward me. "Mr. Jones. Told me you might be coming by. So here's the key."

Feeling at right angles with reality, I nonetheless reached out and picked up the key. "Did he—did he say anything else?"

A head shake, accompanied by a look that might have been one of pity. "Nope. Seemed to be in a hurry."

I'd bet. Since I really didn't want to reveal anything more of my private life than I already had, I said only, "Thanks."

He gave a sort of affirmative grunt and turned back to his copy of the *Red Rock News*.

Still not sure exactly what was going on, I left the office, Kara in my wake. She waited until we were a few steps away from the building before asking, "How did Martin know you were coming back here?"

I shrugged. Precognition? Uncanny awareness of my attachment to my laptop? Who knew.

We got to the Bridge House and climbed the steps to the porch. Every other time I'd come to this door, Martin had been with me, and I hated that he wasn't here now. Nothing to do but unlock the door and go in, though.

At least we'd left the place clean and tidy, dishes washed and put in the drainer next to the sink, bed made, toiletries lined up neatly on the counter in the bathroom. I went to the closet and retrieved my suitcase as Kara looked around while trying not to appear as if she was looking around. But as I moved to gather up my shampoo and toothbrush and makeup bag from the bathroom, I paused.

Kara glanced over at me, clearly noting my hesitation. "What is it?"

"I don't know. It's just…." I let the words drift away, trying to figure out how to articulate what I was thinking. "That is, Martin brought me here in the first place because he said it was safe, that here the energies of the creek protected me from psychic attacks by the aliens. I won't have that at your place." I crossed my arms. "Maybe I should just stay here."

Her response was immediate. "Oh, hell, no. Alone? With no car? You're miles away. What if something happened?"

All those were very valid concerns. Maybe I'd made the suggestion because somewhere in the back of my mind I'd hoped that Martin would come back here, would seek me out to make his explanations. And Kara was right about the car.

"I don't know," I replied, and my tone sounded wild even to myself. "I just—I'm *scared*, Kara. Martin showed me how to protect myself, and maybe that will be enough, but you don't know what it's like— they come to you in your sleep, worm into your dreams…do terrible things."

Her eyes widened as I said this. Of course, she had no real idea what had been going on with me for the past few days, and I didn't want to give her the gory details. Whatever else, though, she needed to know that the stakes had gotten higher…and were only going to get worse over the next day.

When she spoke, I could tell she was shaken. "All the more reason for you to be with your family. I'll be there, and Lance—I know you and Lance have had your issues, but you can't tell me he wouldn't be there to help you if something happened."

I couldn't argue with that. Whatever else you might say about him, Lance was a warrior, and he'd do whatever it took to keep Kara and Grace and me safe. When I thought about it like that, I knew my sister was right. Sitting here alone in the cabin was only inviting disaster. Besides, with the final confrontation looming ever closer, it made more sense for me to be with everyone. Martin had been vague about exactly what he expected me to do when the time came, and he apparently wasn't going to be around to share his wisdom. We'd have to do this the way we always did, by pooling our resources and making a stand together.

"Okay," I said, and went ahead into the bathroom to collect my things. "You're right. It was just a thought."

She waited until I had dumped the various toiletries, et al. in my suitcase before coming to me and giving me a brief, fierce hug. "We're all here for you, Keeks. Never forget that."

I wouldn't. They were all I had right then.

Much as I would have liked to crawl into Kara's spare bedroom and hide there for the next seven or eight years, I didn't have that luxury. On the way back to the house, I told her to call everyone to gather at Michael's for what might be our last council of war, then added,

"Just make sure Jeff and I are seated on opposite sides of the room. That way, we won't kill each other."

She shot me a sideways glance, and I gave her a brief summary of what had happened the previous morning between Jeff and me.

"And don't say 'I told you so,'" I warned her. "I'm about at my limit right now."

"I wouldn't dream of it," she said, but there was something about the way her mouth quirked that told me she'd been thinking that very thing.

I hated it when she was right.

When we got back to the house, Lance was in the living room watching a football game, with Grace gurgling contentedly in his arms. Despite everything that was going on, I had to smother a smile at seeing Lance, the hard-ass ex-Special Forces guy, being the very picture of domesticity.

But since I knew better than to say anything, I gave him a half-hearted wave with my free hand and went into the guest room, where I unpacked my meager belongings and set up the laptop on the desk. After all the drama of retrieving it, maybe it was a little anticlimactic for me to boot it up and find that the only emails I'd missed out on were some more correspondence from my clients, and a bunch of junk mail from the various retail sites I'd signed up with so I could get coupons and sale offers and other things that seemed spectacularly unimportant at the moment.

I sighed and shut the MacBook, and wondered if I'd been leading myself to hope that maybe Martin would have sent me an email explaining what exactly he was up to. Did highly advanced multidimensional beings even have email?

Probably not.

It took a supreme effort of will to push myself back out to the living room, where Lance silently handed Grace to me, as if knowing I needed the kind of comfort that holding your one and only niece would bring. So I held her close and inhaled her sweet baby scent, and let her tug on my hair. She cooed and batted her amazingly long, dark lashes—

her father's lashes—and in that moment, I knew I would do whatever it took to protect her...to protect everyone.

Kara was on the phone, making her calls to Persephone and Paul, and to Michael, which meant Jeff by extension. I was so not looking forward to that encounter, but this was no time to be acting like a couple of feuding high school kids.

Outside, the sky was turning bloody, onrushing clouds seeming to shadow the city. I hoped that wasn't a harbinger of things to come.

Paul and Persephone were already at Michael's when we got there. I recalled what she'd told me, about learning she was going to have a baby, and I sent her what I hoped was a reassuring smile. I noticed how her gaze lingered on Grace almost hungrily, as if she wasn't quite sure she'd be around to hold her own child in her arms, the way Kara was now.

Oh, yes, you will, I thought. *Even if it's the last thing I ever do.*

Not that I really wanted to admit it, but it very well might be the last thing I ever did.

I wondered if Kara knew about Persephone's condition as well, since they seemed to exchange a significant glance before Kara sat down on one of Michael's rickety chairs. Jeff was already slumped down in the easy chair by the couch, refusing to meet my eyes. I pretended that I didn't care, and took a seat on a folding chair that looked as if it had been left outside all summer. You could barely see the gray-beige paint because of all the rust.

At least Jeff had his laptop with him, which meant—I hoped—that he'd made some progress and had some sort of intel that could help us. Without that, I didn't know what the hell we were going to do.

Lance had apparently measured my mental state and decided that I wasn't in any shape to lead the meeting. Once we were all more or less settled, he said, "Looks like we're flying solo on this one, so we need to figure out a plan of attack now. Kirsten, what's your latest intel?"

I almost wanted to laugh. Guess you could take the guy out of Special Forces, but you obviously couldn't take the Special Forces out of the guy. "Probably not much more than you all know already. The solstice is less than thirty-six hours away, and the aliens are going to make their move then. They're going to tap into the upflow energies in the Boynton vortex to harness the power they need to…well, you know. Destroy mankind and take the planet for themselves. All that fun stuff."

Kara frowned at my brittle attempt at humor, but she didn't take me to task for it. "Anything else?"

"Well, Mar—that is, I've been training to tap into the powers I got from my father, and it's been going better than expected. I may have a shot at shutting them down…if we can get everything else to line up."

"That's where we all come in," Lance said, his sharp gray eyes roving over the assembled company. "Jeff, what's your progress on cracking that code?"

Jeff had his laptop open and didn't look up from it as he replied, "Getting there."

"'Getting there'?" Lance repeated, frowning. "You're going to have to do a little better than that."

Those words obviously wounded him, because Jeff lifted his eyes from the laptop long enough to shoot daggers with them at Lance. "You're welcome to try hacking through these algorithms if you want. I guarantee you won't have any better luck."

"Arguing isn't the solution," Michael put in mildly. "I've seen him working—barely sleeps two hours a night, if that. Give the boy a break."

Lance's scowl only deepened. "Well, I'd love to be all relaxed and forgiving about this, but the aliens aren't going to give me that opportunity."

Since no one could really argue with that comment, an uneasy silence fell. Persephone cleared her throat and ventured, "How much can we do without better information on their plans?"

"Enough," Paul said. I noticed that he had his left hand on her right, holding it tightly. I didn't even want to think about how he must be feeling, with so much to look forward to, and no way of knowing whether he'd be around the day after tomorrow to enjoy it. He appeared to gather himself and went on, "We have a rough idea of where they are, and we already know the time. It's just a matter of getting Kirsten there when she needs to be in place."

"Oh, is that all?" I said, but then regretted the sarcasm in my tone. "I mean, I have a feeling they're not going to let us just waltz in there."

"No, probably not," Paul said mildly. "But how close can we get?"

Lance appeared to consider. "Fairly close. The resort is a good cover. We can stage from there. The aliens are used to people coming and going from that location all the time. Not to say that they haven't been surveilling us, but I have an idea about that."

"You do?" Kara asked. She shifted Grace to her other shoulder; the baby didn't stir, her eyes shut in slumber.

"Yes." He paused and gazed around the circle, his silver-bright eyes resting on me for a few seconds before he continued. "The Jeep tours go out to Enchantment all the time. I've already booked us a room there. We'll drive to Uptown, leave our cars in one of the parking structures, then take a Jeep tour to the resort. Hard to trace, and they won't be looking for us that way. We'll stay at Enchantment until the witching hour, then head out into the canyon on foot. Since the aliens are going to be tapping into the vortex, they won't be in their base, and we won't have to infiltrate it."

That was true; I hadn't even stopped to consider that we'd be meeting on semi-neutral ground. Their base was back in Secret Canyon, well hidden from the world, but the vortex itself was in Boynton, and well-traveled by hikers and tourists and those seeking inner vision. Not that there would be many of those out tromping around at 4 a.m. on an icy December morning.

"That could work," I said cautiously. "So who's the 'we' you're referring to?"

The barest of hesitations, and then he replied, "You, of course, and me, and Michael."

That announcement was met with an eruption of voices, with Persephone protesting that she should be coming, too, since we might need her psychic powers as well, and Paul telling her that Lance knew what he was talking about, and Jeff breaking in to say that just because he hadn't cracked the code yet didn't mean he wouldn't, and we were going to need him, and—

Only Kara remained silent. Her eyes, watching Lance, then me, were frightened but calm. She knew he was vital to our mission succeeding, and of course there wouldn't be a mission if I didn't go. Two of the people she cared most about in the world going to confront the aliens with nothing more to protect us than those few skills Martin had taught me before he disappeared.

I raised my voice. "Persephone, I appreciate the offer, but I really wouldn't be able to concentrate with you there. I'd be too worried about something happening to you. Please."

She subsided at my words, although I could tell by the set of her mouth that she wasn't happy about the situation.

Looking over at Jeff, I said, "Jeff, Lance and Michael have abilities you don't. This isn't going to be like last time, when you hacked the aliens' computer systems to get everybody out of the base. I appreciate you wanting to be there, but I think you'd be much more help here."

He didn't quite meet my gaze, but he sounded a little less sulky as he said, "I'm just trying to help."

"I know you are. We all know that. I just think you'll help us more by staying off the front lines and continuing to work on those codes."

It was obvious he didn't like the sound of that. I held my breath, waiting for more arguments. To my surprise, he lifted his shoulders and said, "Okay, then."

That was almost too easy. Maybe even Jeff realized that arguing with me in front of the others had the potential to let slip more truths than he really wanted to reveal.

I shifted my attention to Lance. "Sounds like we've got that part worked out. Anything else?"

He seemed surprised that I was willing to ask his advice. "For the moment, no." A bit of a smile touched his mouth. "Well, except ordering dinner. Any requests? Remember, this could be one of your last meals."

The joke fell flat, of course—everyone exchanged uneasy glances. I looked over at Persephone, wondering if she was starting to experience any nausea or food cravings, but as she didn't volunteer anything, I went ahead and said,

"Anything but pizza. I've had Italian for the past two nights. Why don't we get Indian? I wouldn't mind going out with the taste of lamb korma on my tongue."

Kara shook her head at my comment about "going out," but she only asked, "That okay with everyone?"

Since no one disagreed, she handed off Grace to Lance and went into the kitchen, where she kept all the takeout menus, and made the call. The rest of us sat in the living room, no one wanting to say what we were probably all thinking, that our chances weren't that great, and we were all fooling ourselves to think that any sort of planning would help us when push came to shove the next night.

At least, that was what I was thinking. I swallowed, wondering if I would be able to do it—face the aliens with only my powers to help us. Michael and Lance had their talents, but they were only human.

Only human. How I wished I could be that again.

CHAPTER EIGHTEEN

EVERYONE ENDED UP STAYING AT MICHAEL'S UNTIL around ten or so, as we were all clinging to these few moments when we could still be together. Lance had said that the next day we would need to keep to our normal patterns as much as possible so as not to attract attention, and that meant Persephone and Paul back at their house, and Michael at his with the unhappy Jeff in tow. And with my apartment trashed, the obvious thing would be for me to stay with my sister, so even the aliens shouldn't see anything untoward in that.

The daybed in the guest room wasn't particularly comfortable, but that wasn't the real reason why I had trouble falling asleep. I lay there, feeling the emptiness of the bed, wanting Martin next to me. Not that the two of us probably could have squeezed into the narrow twin-size bed, but its very narrowness only served to remind me that tonight I slept alone.

How it could be possible to miss someone so much after spending only a few nights together, I didn't know. I'd never experienced anything like this before. As much as I hurt from his betrayal, I still wanted Martin, needed him. Surely if I could just see him, he'd be able to tell me why he'd disappeared without a single word.

Across the hall, Grace began to wail, and a minute later, I heard Kara hurry in and murmur soothing noises. A few hiccups and whimpers, and the baby subsided. I lay there, wondering if she was going to start crying again, but she didn't make any more noise. Kara padded back down to the master bedroom, and I let out a sigh. Grace was a good baby, but I knew she wasn't sleeping through the night yet. Not surprising, considering she was only a month old.

Maybe I should have crashed on Michael's couch.

Sighing, I rolled over on my side and scrunched the pillow, trying to get it into a shape that more or less matched what I was used to. I needed to sleep. Tomorrow was going to be—well, I couldn't really imagine what tomorrow was going to be like, but I did know that it was going to be much worse if I didn't face it with at least seven hours of sleep under my belt.

I shut my eyes, trying to clear my mind of all doubt, all worries, envisioning that pale gold light surrounding me, creating a protective cocoon.

Sleep...sleep....

The drift into darkness was so gradual, I didn't

even notice it. No dreams, nothing but that calm, still place where I could gather my strength, where yesterday and today and tomorrow all blended, washing away the burdens I felt I had been carrying for far too long.

It began as a pressure on my throat, my chest. Drowning in sleep, I tried to move, but all my limbs were pinned in place, held down by an invisible force. Icy waves of terror flooded through me as his voice penetrated my skull.

Stupid girl. You should have stayed where you were safe.

Again, I attempted to free myself from whatever hideous power kept me immobilized, but I might as well have been trying to lift Bell Rock. Now I could feel the cold strength of scaled fingers wrapped around my wrists, feel the weight of him on top of me. And I could do nothing but lie there, paralyzed by the force of his will.

You cannot win. You wished to know what will come tomorrow, with the solstice? Then see.

I couldn't close my eyes, because they were already shut. And I saw fire and storm sweeping down on the town, blowing away houses and trees and people and cars, looking like the onslaught of a nuclear blast, only I knew this wasn't nuclear. No, it was the power of the vortexes, twisted and perverted to the aliens' purposes. All destroyed, all dead. Save one. I saw them tear Grace from Kara's lifeless arms, and knew they wanted the baby because they were going to experiment on her, find out what was buried in her DNA, how Grayson's hybrid chromosomes had mingled with Kara's human ones.

And Grace was screaming, screaming, and I could do nothing to save her, because he still held me, fingers like ice across my throat, across my breasts, and his voice was in my ear, saying, *If you are good, then perhaps I will keep you as my pet.*

Then it wasn't just Grace screaming, but me, a ululation of *no, no, no, NO* bursting forth, erupting from me as I gasped for air, gasped to be free of his touch, and then Kara and Lance were there, shaking me, telling me to wake up, to wake up now.

My eyes opened, and I saw their worried faces hovering over me, illuminated by the light pouring in from the hallway. I drew in a shuddering breath. It had only been a dream. I was safe.

But I knew it hadn't been a dream. Not exactly. An intrusion…a vision of what could happen. Would happen, if we didn't prevail tomorrow.

More crying filled my ears, and I realized Grace was screaming from her crib, ear-splitting shrieks that were completely unlike her. Lance muttered something under his breath and hurried off to her room, leaving Kara to stay with me, to push the sweat-soaked hair off my forehead and ask, "What was it, Keeks? A dream?"

The use of my old nickname almost started me sobbing again, but I made myself suck in a deep breath, then another. "Not—not a dream. *Them.*"

Her eyes widened and her hand stilled, resting near my temple. "How?"

"I told you—they have ways of getting in. I tried to protect myself, but it wasn't enough. I should have stayed up at Forest Houses. I would have been safe there." As I spoke, deep shudders started to wrack my body, as if I'd been thrown naked out into the cold night air.

"Shh," Kara said, trying to soothe me. "It's all right."

"No, it's not." I pushed myself up to a sitting position and clasped my knees to my chest, trying to still my body's shaking. "If you won't take me back up to Forest Houses, then at least let me sleep over at Michael's. It's safer there."

"I don't—" she began, then stopped herself after she got a good look at my face. "Okay. Let me make the call." And she got up from the bed and went out toward the kitchen, presumably to get the phone.

I glanced over at the clock, at the red numbers glowing in the semi-darkness. Three-thirty. So I had gotten some sleep, although not enough. Not by a long shot. I had no idea whether I'd sleep at Michael's, either, but at least there I knew the power of the creek's waters would keep *him* out of my brain, if only for a while.

Grace's wailing began to subside. Was she only crying because she'd heard me screaming, or had they invaded her thoughts as well, sending terrifying visions of what they hoped would come to her with the solstice? I didn't know, and although she was an exceptional baby, it wasn't as if she could tell me what had just happened.

I heard the murmur of Kara's voice on the phone and crawled out of bed, my rubbery legs making the procedure a lot harder than it should have been. The clothes I'd worn the day before were still draped over the back of the desk chair, so I grabbed them and pulled them on. I hadn't unpacked anything except my laptop, so I thought the move to Michael's place should be easy enough. Well, physically, anyway.

Kara came back and paused in the doorway. "Michael said to come on over. Jeff's already on the couch, but Michael has a cot he's putting out for you in the spare room."

"Okay." My voice quavered a little, and I swallowed. "Sorry about the disruption."

Incongruously, she laughed. "Kirsten, I've got a month-old baby. Nighttime disturbances are pretty par for the course around here." A pause then, as her expression clouded and she looked at me more closely. "Are you going to be all right?"

"Sure." That was a lie, but I knew they were all depending on me; I couldn't let Kara see me fall apart. "I'll just feel better once I'm at Michael's."

Lance stopped outside the doorway. He was dressed, wearing a brown leather jacket and a scarf wrapped around his throat, and I realized he was going to be the one driving me. At first, I didn't like that idea, not at all, because I wanted my sister with me, wanted the comfort of her presence. A second later, I realized that of course Lance would be the one to take me. Lance had a chance of fighting them off. Kara was too easy a target.

I swallowed again, and bent to pick up my suitcase. "I'm ready," I said, glad that some of the shakiness had left my voice.

He nodded but didn't reply, just led me past Kara, who gave my hand a quick squeeze, and then on into the garage. In silence, we got in the Jeep and backed out into the dark night. Overhead, the stars blazed down on us, cold and indifferent. Well, I supposed the stars would still be around even if the rest of us weren't, but that was cold comfort.

And I realized, as I looked at the clock on the dashboard, that at this same time tomorrow, I'd be out in the dark and the chill night air, making a stand with Lance and Michael, three against I didn't even want to know how many. Maybe the number didn't matter so much. From what I could tell, only one of them seemed to be in charge.

I shivered, and Lance sent a quick look over at me before returning his attention to the empty streets around us. "Bad, right?"

"Very bad."

He made a sort of "hmph" sound deep in his throat. What that was supposed to mean, I didn't know, but I was glad he didn't ask any other questions. Bad enough that I'd woken up screaming like a banshee. I knew I'd never want to divulge some of the details of that hideous nightmare to anyone, let alone the grim-faced man who was my brother-in-law in all but name.

I heard Martin's voice in my head. ...*For dominance, for cruelty—these things are part of their nature....*

Yes, they certainly were.

I stared out the window and tried to think of nothing. Everything else hurt too much.

Jeff wasn't even asleep on the couch when I got to Michael's, but instead was hunched over his laptop at the ancient drop-leaf table. He looked up as Michael let me in, eyes shadowed with weariness, but he stayed silent.

Lance said nothing before leaving, except "Sinagua Plaza, three o'clock," which I assumed was going to be our rendezvous point the next day.

Today. That's right. Today is Saturday.

So tired. I let Michael guide me into his spare room, which seemed to be mostly a repository for the excess junk that wouldn't fit in the living/dining room areas. But he did have a cot set up for me, and I settled down on it, so exhausted that all I did was pull off my coat and boots before collapsing on the thin, lumpy mattress and drawing the old wool blanket over myself.

I slept, and this time, nothing disturbed that sleep.

Hours later, I rolled over and stared up at the water-stained ceiling above me. It took a few seconds for me to remember where I was, and then I sat up, heart beating a little faster as I realized that I had less than a day to go before…

…well, before.

I got off the cot and knelt down, scrabbling through my suitcase so I could find my hairbrush. Maybe it was silly for me to care what either Jeff or Michael thought of how I looked, but brushing my hair made me feel better, made me glad I could exert just that tiny bit of control over my existence.

When I went out to the living room, Jeff was still glued to his laptop, appearing not to have moved since the last time I'd seen him. But this time, sunlight was pouring through the living room windows, showing a day of serene beauty, not a cloud in the sky. The flash of white I caught at the edge of my vision was only the last bits of snow remaining on the ridge tops.

The smell of coffee filled the air. Michael emerged from the kitchen, a mug in his hand. "I can get some tea for you, if you want. I know you don't drink much coffee."

"Actually, coffee is fine," I replied. "Today, I feel as if I could use something with a little more kick."

Michael nodded, then looked over at Jeff. "Refill?"

Jeff mumbled something I guessed was supposed to be an affirmative. Quietly, Michael reached down and retrieved Jeff's mug from the tabletop, and took it into the kitchen. I followed, mostly because I could tell Jeff was making a concerted effort not to look at me, and his avoidance just made the whole situation that much weirder.

Although the kitchen was just as cluttered as the rest of the house, it was sparkling clean. I wondered how Michael kept all the copper Jell-O molds and decorative earthenware dishes and baskets hanging on the walls so free of dust and grease.

He went to an old-fashioned cowboy-style coffee pot sitting on the stovetop and filled a heavy stoneware mug with the brew. "Milk? Sugar?"

"Both, please," I said. I knew I'd only be able to swallow the stuff if I watered it down to the approximate color and flavor of coffee ice cream.

Not quite smiling, Michael got me a carton of milk from the fridge, and pointed to where a little bowl of sugar sat. I noted the bowl was a souvenir, probably '50s vintage, from the nearby Meteor Crater national landmark. Somebody probably would have killed for that thing on eBay.

After I finished doctoring my coffee, I leaned against the counter and blew on it. I was acutely aware of Jeff working out in the front room and figured the kitchen was neutral territory, someplace where Michael and I could talk more or less privately, as at least Jeff had his earbuds jammed in.

Michael refreshed his own coffee before asking, prosaically enough, "Do you want a bagel? There are some in the fridge."

I nodded. "Sounds good." I realized I was sort of hungry, as if my body knew it needed the sustenance even though my brain was occupied with other things. I watched for a minute as Michael got a bag of bagels out of the refrigerator, split two apart, and stuck them in a toaster oven that looked older than I was. Just as he was closing the toaster door, I blurted, "Michael, don't you ever get scared?"

He set the timer before turning and regarding me with a pair of very calm dark eyes. "Of course I do," he said easily. "Everyone does."

"Even Lance?" I asked, only halfway sarcastic. He'd been steady as a rock this whole time. Special Forces training, I guessed, but rather than his steadiness being reassuring, sometimes it was downright irritating.

"Especially Lance." Michael drank some coffee and added, "You think he's not frightened for Kara, for Grace...for a life he never thought he'd get to live?"

I hadn't really considered that angle. There was some rough stuff in Lance's past, no doubt about it, and although inwardly I might grin at his newfound domesticity, I knew from some things Kara had let drop that he considered it a minor miracle he'd ended up where he was now.

"Okay," I allowed. "So...how do you manage it? Because right now, I'm scared so shitless, I don't know what I should be doing."

He set down his coffee mug, and leaned over and laid a gentle hand on my shoulder. It was firm and heavy, something about it as permanent and enduring as the red rocks that ringed the town. "It's okay to be scared. Just don't let the fear become bigger than you are."

Martin had said something similar once, as we shared the cabin up at Forest Houses. Thinking about him wasn't a very good idea, though, because I could feel my throat begin to close up with the realization that in about eighteen hours, I'd be facing down the aliens without any help from him.

He'd left me.

As if noting my mental struggle, Michael said softly, "We're all here for you...for each other. Remember that death is nothing to fear. Persephone would tell you the same thing if she were here. She knows a new life waits for all of us on the other side."

"Okay, as a pep talk, this isn't really doing it for me," I told him, my voice shaky. "I mean, if you start talking about death, then I just begin to automatically assume that you think we're not going to make it."

"I don't think that at all. I just want you to know that the thing you fear the most isn't as terrible as it seems."

Oh, but you don't know what I fear the most. It's not death—whether that's going to a new plane of existence or just a long black sleep—but enslavement, torture, the agony of knowing you've lost everything and everyone you care about.

Despair.

But I realized I couldn't tell Michael that. I didn't want him to know the depth of the evil we faced. If he did, then he might decide he was pretty damn scared after all.

———————

It was a very long and very strange day. Eventually, I showered in Michael's cramped bathroom and got cleaned up and dressed and all the normal things you're supposed to do. We had a place and a time, and there wasn't much to do except wait around until we could leave.

Jeff still didn't want to talk to me, which was just as well. I didn't think I could have managed the awkwardness of that conversation, given how depleted I felt. He kept working away, his laptop's screen filled with all sorts of strange numbers and symbols, lines of code so complex that even I, who thought she had a handle on that sort of thing, couldn't begin to decipher what it all meant.

We ate sandwiches for lunch, watched some flickering TV—Michael didn't have cable and relied on an aerial on his roof—and waited. There was no point in me trying to prepare myself, because I still didn't know exactly what I was supposed to do. Yes, Martin had trained me to recognize the vortex energies, but he'd stopped short of explaining how to use that knowledge to stop the aliens. I had to hope that when the time came, the strange powers within me would know what to do.

Put that way, it didn't seem like a very good plan.

At two-thirty, we gathered our things. I was

taking my suitcase, since we were supposed to look as if we were staying at the Enchantment Resort, and Michael had a duffel bag—with what in it, I wasn't quite sure, since we weren't actually staying there, only using it as a convenient place from which to stage our assault on Boynton Canyon.

I paused by the table where Jeff was working away and cleared my throat.

He didn't look up.

Typical. I tapped him on the arm. "Jeff."

With an exaggerated sigh, he stopped typing and kind of lifted his gaze from the screen, although I noticed he still wouldn't look at me directly. "What?"

"We're going."

He stared at me without replying.

Man, he wasn't going to make this easy, was he? I took a breath and said, "Look, I don't know—I don't know what's going to happen. But I'm sorry we argued, and I—I'm sorry if I let you misinterpret things between us. Keep in touch with Paul if you come up with anything." And before I lost my nerve, I bent down and kissed him on the cheek, trying not to notice the expression of startled hope that crossed his features.

Then I grabbed my suitcase and hurried out the door.

Michael's old El Camino was slow to start, and I worried whether we were going to end up having to call an Uber to get us to Sinagua Plaza or something. But eventually the car coughed and turned over, and he backed out of the driveway with care, as if worried that going over a bump too fast would knock loose a vital piece of wiring and strand us on the road on the way to Uptown.

Saturday afternoons were always busy along the main drag, and today was no exception. We pulled into the structure behind Sinagua with barely five minutes to spare, and caught up with Lance in front of the Crystal Vortex shop. He looked annoyed, which I supposed he had every right to be.

All he said, though, was, "Let's go," and picked up his own rucksack and hurried down the street toward the Jeep tour company's storefront.

If the driver was a little surprised to see the three of us appear with various bags and suitcases in hand, he didn't show it. He was probably about four or five years older than I was, but I didn't know him. Not all the tour guides were locals. With a quick grin, he showed us where to stow our bags so they wouldn't get in the way of the other passengers—the Jeep seated six—and then started up the vehicle and headed us back out west, toward Boynton Canyon and the Enchantment Resort.

As we drove, I could feel the pressure building all around me, almost like the one and only time I went up in a jet and could not get my ears to pop, no matter what I did. And of course, I couldn't let any of what I was feeling show in my expression. No, I had to pretend to *ooh* and *ah* over local sights I'd seen a thousand times before, all while gripping the seat cushion beneath me and praying that I wouldn't get sick.

At last we made it to the Enchantment Resort, where we all got off. Normally, the tour stopped there for a brief spell so people could stretch their legs and get a drink or whatever before driving back into town, but this was our final destination. The tour guide did look startled when we said we were going to be staying, but Lance just made a brief comment about taking another tour bus into town earlier today, and the guide let it drop. Sedona was the sort of place where you had to learn to roll with the punches.

Check-in went smoothly enough, with Michael and me hanging back while Lance took care of the paperwork. The "rooms" at the resort weren't really rooms, but small suites in freestanding buildings. Ours was at the edge of the property—by design, I was sure. And if the bellhop thought that Lance, Michael, and I made an odd group to be sharing one of the suites, well, he kept his thoughts to himself as he accepted the folded twenty-dollar bill Lance handed him.

"So," I said, after Lance shut the door behind the bellhop, and we were alone again. "What now?"

"We wait," he replied.

"I've been doing an awful lot of that today," I told him, and he shrugged.

"Well, get ready to do some more. Earliest we should head out is around two-thirty. We'll get some room service in a while. If you can sleep, that might be a good idea."

I didn't think that was a good idea at all. Some of

the pressure in my head had eased as I became acclimated to the mounting negative energies in the canyon, but that didn't mean I was going to risk sleeping here. Not after what had happened the night before.

Lance pulled out a bulky-looking device that turned out to be a satellite phone. "No regular cell reception back here," he explained. "I have this so Paul can keep in touch. He's running point. I want him and Persephone and Kara and the baby to go to Michael's where it's safer."

That made sense. Although if the worst did happen, how long could the sheltering strength of the creek protect any of them?

I didn't say that, though. I sort of nodded and picked up the room service menu, scanning the offerings, wondering if I'd be able to choke any of them down past the mounting queasiness within me. Michael settled himself in a chair, pulled a book out of his duffel bag, and perched a pair of cheap dollar-store reading glasses on his nose. I almost laughed, the sight was so incongruous, but then I realized he was reading the Bible and I sobered up real fast.

Lance took the satellite phone into the bathroom with him and shut the door. Most likely, he wanted some privacy so he could talk to Kara without being overheard, but for some reason, his actions still annoyed me. Shouldn't we be out here making plans? Or maybe he knew exactly what he wanted to do, and just expected us to follow orders when the time came.

Following orders might not be so bad. At least that way, I wouldn't have to think.

I climbed onto one of the beds and took the TV remote from the nightstand. Michael looked up briefly as I started flipping through the channels, and I almost thought he was going to tell me to turn the TV off again. Then he gave the smallest of nods, as if understanding that I needed the sound from the television the same way he needed the words of the book he held.

For comfort...for strength...for something to blot out the echoing, fearful voices inside our heads.

At length, Lance came out from the bathroom and shot a contemptuous glance at the TV. I sucked in a breath, readying myself for an argument with him over whether it should be on or not, but he only picked up the room service menu from where I'd dropped it at the foot of the bed and scanned it briefly.

"Have you picked out something? Because we might as well call it in."

I hadn't, but I took the menu from him anyway. "Chicken sandwich," I said listlessly, since it seemed the most likely to stay put in my stomach where I needed it.

Lance's gaze sharpened at my tone, but he didn't say anything.

"Same for me," Michael put in, and returned his attention to his Bible.

And that was that. Lance made the call, and we waited some more. Rather, I waited, staring at the

TV with the sound lowered so Lance could have a lengthy convo with Paul about standing by, and how to follow the creek down through Red Rock Crossing if necessary, to some sort of hidey spot Lance knew about but I'd never heard of. I didn't bother to tell him that was all an exercise in futility. If we failed, everyone else would be dead almost immediately.

The food came and I choked it down, wishing we'd ordered some wine, knowing that wasn't a good idea at all. And then I actually did doze, slipping in and out of the upper ranges of sleep, jerking awake whenever I felt myself beginning to go too deep. Michael did sleep, still sitting up in his chair, Bible spread open across his chest. I wondered which chapter he'd been reading, and what it meant to him.

Then I felt Lance's hand on my ankle and my eyes flew open, fleeing the hazy edges of slumber.

"It's time," he said quietly.

My heart began to pound in my chest, but I nodded and pushed myself off the bed. Michael set down his Bible and reached for his heavy sheepskin coat, buttoning it up, settling a multicolored scarf worthy of Doctor Who around his neck.

I went and pulled on my boots, which I had discarded earlier, and got my own coat and scarf. All this I did numbly, almost without thinking. It was probably better if I didn't think too hard. Finally, I got out my blue knitted cap and jammed it on my head, just as Lance pulled a pair of 9mm pistols out of his rucksack and stowed them away on his person.

"You really think guns are going to help?" I asked.

He didn't look at me as he slipped several spare clips into his coat pockets. "Never hurts to be prepared. It might be enough to slow them down. Sometimes, seconds can make all the difference."

Maybe that was true. I'd never been in combat; he had.

Without replying, I pulled on my gloves. For some reason, I grabbed my wallet out of my purse and jammed it in my back pocket. Stupid, of course. It wasn't as if the aliens were going to check my I.D.

They already knew who I was.

None of us said anything as we slipped out the door and headed across the resort's grounds. The pathways were set off by low-slung landscape lights, and we followed these for a ways. I realized Lance wasn't heading back toward the front gate, where there was a guard on duty, presumably twenty-four/seven. No, we were taking a roundabout route to the northeast, and eventually through what looked to be a service gate. It was locked, but Lance pulled out a set of lock picks, and quietly and efficiently had the lock off the gate in less than two minutes.

Despite myself, I was impressed, and vowed to wheedle him into showing me how to do that...if, of course, we were around after tonight to even worry about picking locks.

There was no moon, but strangely, the massed starlight was bright enough that it was easier than I'd thought it would be to pick our way over the rough ground, around junipers and patches of manzanita and cactus, to avoid the larger rocks, although here and there I slipped on scree and found myself very, very glad that my boots had such a sturdy tread. And all the while we were edging closer to the vortex.

I could feel it as we approached, its energies sparking and sizzling. Mixed, though, just like the vortex at Cathedral Rock, currents swirling around one another in patterns as elegant and complex as a twisting helix of DNA.

Lance made a chopping motion with one hand, apparently indicating for Michael and me to huddle behind a particularly large boulder as he slipped, insubstantial and fleeting as a moon shadow, from shrub to shrub, maintaining his cover with a skill I knew I'd never be able to match. I held my breath, clinging to Michael's hand, waiting for the inevitable confrontation.

And waiting, and waiting....

And then I realized something was horribly, terribly wrong, just as Lance stopped in the center of the knoll that was supposed to be the nexus of the vortex energy. No one came to confront him, or seize him.

The aliens weren't here.

CHAPTER NINETEEN

MICHAEL AND I EMERGED FROM OUR HIDING PLACE AND went to stand next to Lance. Even as I did so, I wondered if this was some kind of trap, if the aliens were still hiding because they didn't care about Lance—I was the one they wanted.

But even as I paused a foot or so away from Lance and gazed around in bewilderment, I somehow knew that was not the case. This place was deserted.

"What the hell?" Lance looked from side to side angrily, as if the aliens had somehow let him down by not being where they were supposed to be.

Even Michael, the usually imperturbable, frowned, then stared up at the sky. Clouds were beginning to drift into the area, hiding the stars, making the scene around me somehow more indistinct, more surreal.

The icy night air made itself felt then, finding its way past my warm wool coat, the scarf I had wound around my throat, my fuzzy hat. Or maybe the chills going up and down my spine had nothing to do with the temperature outside.

How could I have been so wrong? This was the vortex closest to the aliens' base. This was supposed to be where they would make their move. I knew they couldn't have abandoned their plans. Everything I had seen and felt told me this was the place, the night, the time.

Or almost the time. We'd given ourselves a little padding; I pushed up my coat sleeve so I could squint at my watch in the uncertain starlight. Two minutes after four. Twelve minutes until the apocalypse.

"Talk to me, Kirsten," Lance said, the words gritting themselves past clenched teeth. He was wound up very, very tight.

Not that I could blame him.

"I don't get it," I replied, my tone wild, breathy. "This is the vortex next to their base. They should be here. It's the safest place for them to work, so they don't reveal themselves...." And my sentence trailed off as a sudden, horrible idea came to me.

"What is it?" Michael asked. "What are you thinking?"

The words came pouring out of me, as if prompted by a sense of intuition I didn't even know I had. "We—I—just assumed the aliens would come here, because all this time they've worked so hard to conceal themselves, to make sure as few people as possible knew anything about them or what they've been doing here. But it's make-or-break time tonight. They don't care if anyone sees them, because in their minds, they're going to wipe out the entire population. So they're not going to go for the *safest* place—they're going to go to the most *powerful* place." And I faltered then, recalling what Martin had said to me only a few days earlier.

Courthouse Butte is the strongest vortex in Sedona...

Oh, my God.

I swallowed, fighting the dryness in my throat. "I know where they are."

"Where?" Lance demanded, eyes piercing silver in the moonlight.

"C-Courthouse."

He didn't blink, but he did say, distinctly and viciously, "*Fuck.*"

I knew exactly how he felt. Courthouse Butte was approximately eight miles from where we now stood. Even if we were in the parking lot of Enchantment and not stuck out on a hillside about a half-hour's walk from the resort's boundary, there was no way we could drive all the way back through town and reach the butte in time, let alone climb up it to reach the vortex. No one climbed to the top of that formation; it was too difficult.

We'd lost.

Maybe this should have been the time for me to fall to my knees, scream at the universe for its capriciousness, tear my hair and sob. For some reason, though, all I could do was stand there and stare at Lance and Michael, at the fury on the face of one, the resignation on the face of the other. My whole body was still, freezing, calm. If someone had touched me in that moment, I would have shattered into a million pieces of ice.

And then it seemed as if the moon was falling on us, a white glow bathing the knoll where we stood, illuminating Lance's strained features, Michael's dark, sad eyes. Which wasn't right, because there was no moon on this, the darkest night my world had ever seen.

Out of that glow stepped a figure in flowing black robes.

No.

My eyes adjusted, and I saw Martin standing there, his long wool overcoat blowing in the wind. Blue eyes caught mine, and held.

"There's still time," he said.

I could only stare at him, not sure I believed what I saw. Not the manner of his arrival—I knew he wasn't human, so the concept of him materializing out of a pool of nonexistent moonlight didn't seem that strange. But the fact that he was there at all.

"Kirsten." His voice was firm, calm. "We have to go. Now."

The words tore themselves from me. "You left! Where were you?"

Lips tightening, he said, "We don't have time for this now. Please. We must go." His gaze flickered past me to Lance and Michael, who were staring at him as if they couldn't believe the evidence of their eyes. "All of us."

And I realized he was right—we didn't have time. The recriminations would have to wait. "But how?"

In answer, he extended his hands. I took the right, while, coming to him almost in a daze, Lance and Michael gripped his left. Light enveloped us. I shut my eyes, worried that the brilliant glare would blind me, and Boynton Canyon disappeared, pulling away in a rush of wind stronger than anything I had ever felt before.

My feet hit rock, and I stumbled. I opened my eyes and saw that we stood on the windswept heights of Courthouse Butte. Thunder rumbled off to my left, coming closer. Wilder, stronger than the approaching storm were the vertical columns of energy all around me, shimmering in the night air, something about them feeling somehow wrong, the edges of their luminosity shading red, not white-gold, the way every other upflow vortex I'd ever experienced had been.

We weren't alone.

I barely had time to register the shapes of our enemies, a blotch of darker black against the Stygian skies. Barely had time to see the glow of red eyes focusing on me before I felt the piercing edge of *his* will running through me, baleful and inhuman as the stare of a dragon.

A scream tore itself from my lips, and at the same time, the energies of the vortex were somehow warped and twisted, hurled at me like Zeus's lightning bolt of old. From somewhere I heard Michael shout, "No!" even as he threw himself in front of me, pushing me to the cold, rocky ground, the red-tinged light enveloping him, tossing him backward like a rag doll, his large body falling limp and lifeless, dark eyes glassy and empty.

Martin's voice then, urgent. *Shield yourself, Kirsten! Now!*

And through my agony and sorrow, I reached inward to summon the white-gold light that had sheltered me before, pulling it around me, not like a blanket this time, but as a shield, armor to defend me from my attackers. Just in time, because the alien leader threw another of those energy bolts at me, only to have it bounce off my cocoon of golden light, dispersing harmlessly to all sides.

No words then, just a sense of Martin's approval, his encouragement. I pushed myself to my feet, choking back tears, forcing myself not to look at the body of the man who was the closest thing to an uncle I'd ever had.

A snarl, and the ranks of the aliens began moving toward us, obviously intending to do by physical force what their leader hadn't accomplished by using the vortex against me. Out of the corner of my eye, I saw Lance pull out a pistol and fire, dropping one alien soldier, then another, calmly picking them off like targets lined up at the range. At first, I wondered why they weren't shooting back with whatever weapons they had, but then I realized the golden light bathed Lance as well, and Martin, too, and somehow I knew the aliens were shooting, but their bullets or energy bolts or whatever they used weren't making it through the shield I'd created.

They're trying to distract you, Martin breathed into my mind. *The time has come. You have to stop him.*

And I felt it then, a sensation almost as if the world had stopped to catch its breath, and I realized the solstice was upon us, the tipping point at which the planet balanced before falling back toward the light. I knew it was in the darkness of this moment that the alien leader would make his move.

I had to stop him, but I hesitated, looking at Lance, looking at how the light I'd conjured was somehow protecting him. If I left, moved to stop my foe, wouldn't I be leaving him vulnerable?

I'll watch over him, Martin told me, and in his voice I heard the sorrow that he hadn't been able to do the same for Michael, that things had happened too fast even for an advanced multidimensional being. Light radiated from him, wrapping itself around Lance, who paid no mind, only slammed a fresh clip into his Ruger and kept firing.

And then I was running, feeling the whispering energies of the vortex tearing at me as my adversary twisted them in on themselves, seeking to use them, not to heal and uplift, but to murder and destroy.

But in doing so, he had to open himself to them, and I sensed it then, felt just the smallest tremor in the power flux around me. That flicker told me he wasn't invincible.

Even so, I heard him in my mind, invading my

thoughts with an intimacy only Martin should have had. *So she thinks she can fight me.*

Yes, she does, I flung back at him.

You aren't strong enough. You will fail, just like that fool who lies dead on the earth behind you.

Rage flared in me then that he would dare to call Michael—strong, caring, quiet Michael—a "fool." For I knew he'd taken the brunt of the attack out of love for me, out of love for this world. And with that realization, I understood how I could prevail.

I loved Michael, loved the quiet laughter in his eyes as he watched our little group of UFO hunters tease one another, loved the awe in his face as he looked on this land he adored. And I loved Lance, and the way he watched over Grace, the child of another man, and the way he'd bend and kiss Kara softly on her cheek when he thought no one was looking. I loved Paul and Persephone, how their eyes always sought one another's from across a room, and how they'd smile, as if acknowledging that all they needed to be happy was each other. And I loved my sister, her strength, her caring heart. I even loved the way Jeff would scrunch his nose when he was concentrating on something, or how the members of our local MUFON group would watch over the ones without family, would drive one another to doctor's appointments or sit up with those bereaved, or even make sure single moms had a babysitter when they finally managed to get a date.

I loved them all.

And I loved this place, the red rocks and the

green trees and the quiet creek that flowed through it all, bringing with it protection and life and strength. Sunlight on the edge of a leaf. Water sparkling under a full moon. Snow on the ridge lines, wildflowers in the spring.

All of it so wonderful, so perfect.

I had to save it.

Somewhere in that split-second between one heartbeat and the next, I felt the power blossoming in me, and I knew it wasn't really me, but this world —*my* world—giving me its energy, letting me take those vortex energies in my hand, pulling them away from the alien leader and his hateful intentions, seeing those rivers of light turn pure white-gold again, just before all that power, all that strength, seemed to gather in me and then burst outward, bathing the top of Courthouse Butte in pale fire, surrounding him before he turned to ash and blew away on the wind, rushing outward to engulf those of his followers who still remained, sending them from this existence like a windstorm scattering autumn leaves.

Gone, all gone.

I sank to my knees, gasping for air as the energy swirled around me, warm and clean, seeming to caress my face, my hair, then dwindled, returning to the earth that had given it birth. Men's voices in my ears as Martin and Lance ran to me across a hilltop now empty save for the three of us.

"Remind me never to get you angry," Lance

remarked, although something in his tone told me he wasn't quite as flip as he tried to sound.

Martin bent and took my hands, lifting me up. *Are you all right?*

I'm fine. Well, at least, I thought I was fine. I still couldn't quite absorb what had happened. In time, I might be able to wrap my head around it. Maybe. *You could get us down off this butte, though. I'm freezing my ass off.*

He grinned, teeth flashing in the moonlight. The smile abruptly faded, though, as he looked upward at a white glow appearing somewhere above us. I sucked in a breath, wondering what was coming next. I was so very tired. I didn't know if I could defend myself against yet another attack.

The glow resolved itself into the form of a man, one I recognized…and wasn't all that happy to see.

"Otto," Martin said in resigned tones.

Persephone's spirit guide came to rest on the rocky red earth. Well, almost. I noticed he hovered a few inches above the ground rather than actually standing on it. Maybe he didn't want to get those glowing opal-white robes of his dirty. Beside me, I felt rather than saw Lance's eyes widen, and I guessed that somehow, despite everything, he hadn't quite believed that Otto really existed.

Unfortunately, I was all too aware of his existence.

Otto shot Martin a disapproving glare. "You interfered."

"You left me no choice."

A purse of those perfect lips. "Nevertheless, you disobeyed a direct order, came here—"

I broke in. "Wait a second. Is that where you were, Martin?"

Mouth unsmiling, he replied, "I was brought in for a little talking-to."

"For what?" I demanded, and then sent an accusing stare in Otto's direction. "Are you trying to tell me that you yanked him away when I needed him the most, just because he broke some stupid arbitrary rule?"

His lips tightened even more. Voice cutting, he said, "It is not stupid, and it is not arbitrary. We do all things for a reason, a higher purpose, Kirsten Swenson, even if such things are beyond the limits of your admittedly narrow perception."

"Now, just a minute," Lance said. "You might want to watch what you're saying."

Otto raised an eyebrow, then continued as if Lance weren't even there. "It is not for you to pass judgment on our actions."

"No, you apparently just want to do that to us." I planted my hands on my hips, weirdly glad for this chance to be angry with him. That way, I wouldn't have to think about Michael's broken body lying on the other side of the hilltop. "Doesn't it matter that we won, that the Reptilians were defeated? That we're *safe*?"

"Of course it matters," Otto replied, this time sounding distinctly waspish. "The order of the universe would have been disrupted if your foes had prevailed. However, there was a good chance you could have succeeded without Martin Jones' interference. You didn't need him."

Didn't need him? How could Otto even say that, when every moment Martin was gone had felt like agony, when we could never have gotten here in time without him? "You don't know what you're talking about."

"I'm afraid I do. You're thinking that you required his assistance to get here in the small amount of time you had left before the solstice. That power also lay within you, if you had only attempted to tap into it."

I didn't believe that for a second. Channeling vortex energies was one thing. Folding the very fabric of reality so we could hopscotch across miles within the space of a single breath? I didn't think so.

Beside me, Martin crossed his arms. His breath sent white puffs into the icy air as he said, "Get it over with, Otto."

"Get what over with?" I demanded.

Without looking at me, Otto said, "Because you, Martin Jones, ignored our primary rule and interfered directly with the people of this world, thus possibly changing the course of their history forever, you have brought down your own people's harshest judgment."

Because he stood so close to me, I felt a tremor go through Martin. I reached out and took his hand in mine, wrapping gloved fingers in gloved fingers, wishing I could feel his flesh. Maybe that would have given him the reassurance he needed.

"From this day forward, you are exiled, your powers stripped from you. This world will now be your only home, and you may not appeal to us for aid, or counsel, ever again."

Martin stood straight as his sentence was handed down, eyes fixed on Otto, jaw set. He didn't even blink. But I could sense how tense he was, tightly stretched as a bowstring. "Anything else?"

"I would think that would be sufficient."

An awful silence descended. Lance held himself still, as if knowing he'd just been witness to something he would rather not have seen.

But the anger still swirled in me, and I held on to it, using its heat to give me the courage to speak, since it was clear Martin would say nothing else. "Well, that's a pretty shitty thing to do after he helped save a world and everything."

Otto's dark eyes bored into me. "We have our laws for a reason."

"Maybe so, but being so inflexible on those laws tells me you aren't quite as advanced as you think you are."

"Enough." I could tell from Otto's tone that he would have dearly loved to pitch me over the edge of Courthouse Butte. "Your foolish arguments will change nothing."

"Okay, fine," I said, and tightened my fingers around Martin's. "But I still need to ask you a favor."

This time, both of Otto's eyebrows went up. "*You're* asking a favor of *me*?"

"Well, yes," I admitted. "If Martin's powers have

been stripped from him, then *someone's* going to have to get us off this butte."

It was a sad procession that made its way up the front walk to Michael's house, Martin and Lance carrying his body between them, with me following a pace or two behind. Somehow, I'd managed not to cry on the way over, mostly because I was so exhausted, I didn't think I had the strength left for weeping. And something about the tight, closed expression on Martin's face kept me from saying much of anything to him, either.

Otto had left us here, whisking us away from the windswept butte without a word, then disappearing. Just as well. We'd all had enough of him by that point, even if he did grudgingly rescue us from being trapped a thousand feet up in the air with no way to get down.

Kara must have been watching out the front window, because she opened the door as soon as Lance and Martin approached. The relief on her face died as she glanced down at Michael's limp form. Slowly, Lance shook his head.

Her breath went in, and then she burst into tears, sobbing in a way I somehow couldn't as Martin and Lance pushed past her so they could lay him down on his bed. Past them, I heard Paul's and Persephone's worried voices, followed by a shocked silence as they took in the situation. And Jeff sat at the drop-leaf table, hands finally stilled on the keyboard, as if he'd just realized there was nothing more he could do.

I looked down at Michael as they took off his boots and pulled the covers over him, and somehow it felt as if I couldn't breathe.

I might have saved the world, but I knew it would never be the same again.

CHAPTER TWENTY

I WENT WITH LANCE TO RETRIEVE OUR THINGS FROM THE suite at the Enchantment Resort, mostly because I knew if I had to sit around while Kara and Persephone called the ambulance for Michael, I'd go crazy. Martin had melted away, saying he would come to see me once things had settled down a bit. His leaving hurt and worried me, but I knew he had his own losses to deal with. I had to trust that this time, his absence would be temporary. At least I knew it wasn't coerced.

It didn't take long to gather the meager items we'd left behind in the suite. I picked up Michael's Bible from the table and opened it at the little red ribbon he'd used to mark his place. *"I will lift up mine eyes to the hills, from whence cometh my help,"* I read. Then I looked over at Lance. "I didn't think Michael was religious."

"He wasn't," Lance replied, zipping up his rucksack. "He was spiritual. That must have been what he needed to read before...well, before."

I glanced back down at the closely printed words on the page. No wonder Michael had needed those reading glasses. ...*The Lord shall preserve thee from all evil: he shall preserve thy soul. The Lord shall preserve thy going out and thy coming in from this time forth, and even for evermore.*

And then the tiny print blurred, and the tears welled up from nowhere, splashing down on the fine paper, sobs tearing through me, blinding me. I felt Lance take the Bible from my hands, very gently, and then he held me, rocking me back and forth, not saying anything, just being there, solid and strong and unwavering, and I knew he was glad I wept, glad I could do this when he couldn't. After all, he'd loved Michael, too.

The memorial service was two days later. We'd put out the story that Michael had died of a heart attack in his sleep, and because he was sixty-two, no one commented on it too much, except to say it was a shame he'd been taken away so soon, and that he'd always seemed so healthy, and how these things were always a surprise.

Because it was Sedona, and because it was Michael, the people gathered to celebrate his life—not to mourn, Kara had told me fiercely, because Michael wouldn't have wanted that—were an eclectic crew, to say the least. Michael's older brother, in from Payson, boots shined and a look of pure sorrow on his face. I knew Michael had no other family; his wife Anna had died more than a quarter-century earlier, and they'd had no children. Well, he was with her now.

Shamans and psychics and palm readers, UFO chasers and bookstore owners. Everyone knew Michael. No one wore black, and the crowd had a gaudy cheerfulness, what with the bright jewelry and spangled skirts and multi-hued scarves. Paul was the only one wearing a sport jacket.

Well, strike that about no one wearing black. Martin stood off in a corner of the Creative Life Center facility where the service was being held, his black suit marking him as something different, something other. I saw a few glances cast his way, but no one made a move to approach him, wrapped in their grief as they were.

After the service ended, I made my way back to him. "You could have sat with me."

"You were with your family," he replied, with a brief nod toward where Kara and Lance stood talking with Michael's brother. Grace slept on Kara's shoulder, pink fleece onesie an incongruous note against the dark blue dress Kara wore.

I wanted to ask, *Don't you want to be with my family?* but was too nervous to be that bold. Ever since Otto had laid down his sentence, Martin had been quiet and withdrawn. He'd returned to the cabin at Forest Houses, while I was staying with Kara until I could get my apartment sorted out.

"Still," I said, and paused. I hated this feeling of not knowing what to say to him, not knowing how to make things right.

He was silent for a moment, then asked, "Will you come with me somewhere tomorrow?"

"It's Christmas Eve," I said stupidly.

An almost-smile. "Just to Flagstaff. You'll be back in time for dinner."

"And will you come to dinner?" I hadn't dared to ask him before this. "We're all going to squeeze in at Kara's—Paul and Persephone are, I mean."

Jeff had left for Los Angeles the day before. I'd tried to get him to stay, at least for Michael's service, but he'd just mumbled that he didn't want to be here anymore, wanted to get back to L.A. I supposed I couldn't really blame him. It was pretty clear that the standoff between Martin and me wasn't going to result in my suddenly transferring my affections to Jeff. And besides that, everything had gotten a little too real for him. Better to go back home and hole up in his house and bury himself in code. Return to ignoring the real world the way he always had. I wondered what conspiracy theories he'd immerse himself in this time, now that the Reptilians had been routed.

"We'll see," Martin told me, which could have meant anything. "Let's go to Flagstaff first."

I didn't know what was in Flagstaff that could be so important we'd have to go see it on Christmas Eve day, but as long as he had me back in time for dinner, I couldn't see the harm. My skills in the kitchen were limited at best, so Kara wasn't expecting me to help out much beyond polishing the silverware and making sure she had all of Grandma's china platters and serving pieces ready to hand.

"All right," I said.

"I'll pick you up at noon." And he reached out and touched my hand briefly before turning away and heading out the door, leaving me to endure the rest of the memorial gathering without him by my side.

I'd worried that the weather might not cooperate with our planned drive to Flagstaff, but the sky was clear and serenely blue, dotted with clouds, though not enough to threaten any kind of precipitation. Martin pulled up to Kara's house precisely at noon. She hadn't been thrilled by the outing, but since I swore I'd be back by five at the latest, she hadn't protested too much.

"So they let you keep the car?" I asked as I slid into the Taurus and buckled my seatbelt.

He pulled away from the curb before answering, "Yes. And my job, if I want it."

I didn't know what to say to that. As far as I knew, in his "Man in Black" capacity, Martin had been based in Phoenix. So did that mean he wouldn't be hanging around much longer?

Suddenly, I found it difficult to swallow.

Neither of us said anything as he drove through town, traffic light because of the impending holiday. Not many people were heading up 89A into Flagstaff, probably because the interstate was faster. Somehow, I was glad we were going this way, though, glad I could watch the trees pass by, could catch glimpses of Oak Creek rushing over its boulders and feel the sparkling beauty of its energy even from inside the car. I didn't know if Martin could sense it or not. Otto had said Martin would be stripped of his powers, but did that mean everything, or just the ones he could use to play with time and space? He hadn't attempted to communicate with me mentally since then, but whether that was from reticence or simple inability, I couldn't be sure.

When we passed the turnoff to Forest Houses, I drew in a little breath, wishing we were going there. Maybe if we could be alone together in that place where we'd first come to explore our love, we could make things better.

But we whizzed past the scattered collection of cabins and up the switchbacks that climbed the thousand-plus feet to take us out of the canyon, and then we were driving through ponderosa forests with snow thick among the trees. Up here in the winter, when it snowed, it generally stayed.

Then it was into the heart of Flagstaff, past the cute downtown area where my friends and I used to hang out in the summer when the heat in Sedona got to be too much, then heading north as if we were going to pick up the road that led to the ski areas. But before we got that far, Martin turned off the main road and into a residential area where both the lots and the houses got bigger and bigger as the street climbed upward, until we finally stopped in front of a handsome stone and log house, its eaves blanketed with snow. A pine wreath hung on the front door.

"Here we are," Martin said, somewhat unnecessarily, and unlocked the doors and got out.

Mystified, I followed suit. Was this like one of those reality shows where the guy acts all cool and mysterious and then surprises his girlfriend with a new house and an engagement ring or something? I didn't think so, but, on the other hand, I couldn't imagine why we were here.

I followed Martin up the steps to the wide front porch. "You going to tell me what's going on?" I asked in an undertone.

"You'll see," he said, and rang the doorbell.

Well, since I hadn't known where we were going or who we were calling on, I was glad that I'd done my holiday beauty prep before we left—just in case I didn't get back to Kara's until right before dinner. Actual makeup, and a dark green cashmere sweater over black skinny jeans and black riding boots, a paler green scarf shot through with silver threads wrapped around my throat. At least I looked presentable, even if I didn't know why I was here.

Maybe all that had been for Martin's benefit, although he didn't seem to have really noticed.

The door opened, and a handsome older man,

probably closer to sixty than fifty, looked out at us. He was smiling, but when his gaze rested on me, I saw something in that smile freeze, as if he couldn't quite process what he was looking at.

"May we come in?" Martin asked.

The stranger blinked, then said, "Of course—of course." He stepped out of the way so we could enter, and we moved past him to stand in a foyer with polished wooden floors and dark wood wainscoting rising to meet walls of a warm butter color. All those walls were covered in plein air paintings of the landscapes around Flagstaff and Sedona, and of the Grand Canyon and other places I didn't recognize but guessed must also be in Arizona, or maybe New Mexico. They were good, too, and faintly familiar in their style, as if I'd seen other works by the same artist in galleries around town.

"Come in," the man told us, pointing toward a room off to the left.

We followed him into a living room decorated with Arts and Crafts–style furniture, and more of those gorgeous paintings. A fire blazed away in the stone hearth, and for a second, I was reminded of my mother's house in Taos. But there had been something of artifice in that place, as if every piece had been chosen specifically for its value or because it went with the other furnishings, and not because she loved it. Here, I didn't get that impression at all.

I didn't see much in the way of holiday decorations, except a simple pine garland draped along the mantel, and found it sort of sad that this stranger would be here alone in this beautiful house on Christmas Eve and have apparently no one to share it with. Once again, I had to fight down that thickness in my throat, trying to tell myself that was silly and that I was still emotional after the loss of Michael and everything else that had happened the past few days.

But then I looked up to see the stranger still staring at me, watching me with silver-blue eyes almost the same shade as my own, and I felt my breathing halt. No. It wasn't possible.

He said, "Oh, Kirsten. My brave, beautiful girl."

Unable to say anything, breath still strangling in my throat, I looked over at Martin.

He met my gaze, not flinching. "Yes, it's true," he said quietly. "Kirsten, this is your father, Gabriel."

I'd had my world turned upside down too many times over the past week. "I don't—I don't understand."

Martin came to me then, took my hand in his, as if he knew the thing I needed most in the world right then was the comfort of his touch.

Gabriel—my father—paused for a few seconds. Staring at him, I could see the similarities between us, beyond our eye color. The determined little cleft in the chin, the high cheekbones. His hair was so pale that it was hard to tell which was his original hair color and which was silver starting to come in. He took in a breath, as if groping for words.

Coming to his rescue, Martin said, "He was exiled here, for what they liked to call 'gross interference.'"

"Just like what happened to you."

A grim nod. "He was not allowed to reach out to you, to approach you. This was as close as he dared live, knowing that if your paths should cross, he might face even further punishment."

"Is that true?" I asked. Once again, I questioned the wisdom of these greater beings, who would judge those who acted from their hearts and not the colder wisdom of their minds.

"Yes, Kirsten," my father said quietly. "I didn't dare approach, but at least I knew that once you were with your grandparents in Sedona, you were safe. Once I think I even saw you a few years ago as you were here in Flagstaff, sitting in an outside cafe with some friends, laughing and talking about your boyfriends."

That sounded like Lindsey and me, our senior year of high school. "But you didn't say anything."

A shadow passed over his face. "It was forbidden for me to approach you. If you had met me by chance, of your own volition...say, at a gallery show, or a restaurant here in town...that would have been different. But that never happened."

"So these are all your paintings?"

"Yes," he said simply. "I had to do something to pass the time."

I thought of him then, alone in this house all these years, knowing the daughter he'd never met was so close and unable to do anything about it. Painting, trying to re-create some of the beauty he saw around him in an attempt to forget the life that had been taken away.

"And now?" I asked, but the question was directed at Martin.

"I thought they'd kept you two apart long enough. I've already been punished—what else can they do to me?"

It seemed tempting fate to even ask such a thing, but Martin didn't seem particularly worried.

"Why?" I whispered.

And I heard his voice in my mind, almost making me sob with relief in the realization that this connection hadn't been taken from us. *Because I know things didn't go well with your mother, and I thought you should at least have this.*

How he had realized I still had that little hole in my heart, the one my parents should have filled, I didn't know.

Actually, I did know.

It was because he loved me.

I went to my father then, arms outstretched, and let him fold me into a strong embrace, hug me fiercely, as if trying to make up for all the years he'd been kept from me. They weren't a stranger's arms, though. Going into them, I felt as if I were going home in a way I certainly hadn't when I met with Marybeth in Taos.

At length, though, he released me, but only to stand back and gaze down at me, as if trying to memorize my features in case this was the only opportunity he'd get to see me. Not that I was going to let that happen.

"Do you have any plans for tonight?" I asked him, and he looked surprised at the question.

"Not really. That is, I had an invitation to a friend's house, but I hadn't confirmed for sure."

"Well, good," I said. "Because you're coming to Christmas dinner with us. Isn't he, Martin?" And I shot a look in Martin's direction that told him I wasn't going to take no for an answer—from either of them.

"Yes, I suppose he is," Martin replied, and I saw it then, the hint of a smile around his mouth that had been missing for the past few days. "Don't bother to argue with her, Gabriel—you'll only lose."

The blue eyes that were so like mine twinkled. "I was beginning to get that impression. Well, let me fetch my coat."

We waited while he went upstairs. There were so many things I wanted to say to Martin, but somehow, I knew this wasn't the time. Instead, I pulled out my phone and called Kara.

"What, Keeks?" She sounded harried, and I couldn't really blame her. Cooking Christmas dinner for even a smallish group wasn't a walk in the park.

"You'll need to set two more places for dinner. I'm bringing a couple of guests."

"Two...?" she began, and trailed off. I could tell from the confusion in her voice that she wouldn't have been all that surprised if I'd brought Martin along but couldn't figure out who the second person might be.

I had a feeling she was about to be very surprised.

"Two," I said, a little flutter of happiness stirring somewhere inside me. Maybe things were going to turn out all right after all.

"Okay." Resignation was clear in her tone. "I'll have Lance put another leaf in the table. Of course, that means we'll have to set it all over again—"

"I'll be there in about an hour. I'll take care of it." I hung up, and saw that Gabriel—my father—was paused in the doorway to the living room, pulling on a pair of gloves. "Are you ready?"

"Yes," he said, and smiled at me. It was like watching the sun come up over the mountains.

Then it was the three of us driving back down to Sedona, my father asking about Kara, about the shop and my web design business, showing that he'd been paying attention to what we were doing, even if he couldn't approach me directly. Sad that he seemed to care so much more than Marybeth had, even though Kara was none of his flesh and blood.

The look of astonishment on her face when we came in the door and I introduced Gabriel as my father was so extreme that I had to keep myself from bursting into laughter. But then she recovered herself and made the introductions, as Paul and Persephone were already there, and everyone was so relaxed and easygoing about it that I blessed them all silently, knowing that this peculiar, wonderful group of people could take almost anything in stride.

That happiness was dimmed a little when Lance held up his glass at dinner and said, "To absent friends." We all repeated the words, and my eyes stung, but I thought of Michael looking down on us, seeing where we'd started and how far we'd come, and knew he would be happy for all of us, and I vowed to be happy, too, even in the midst of missing him.

Martin and I didn't have much chance to talk, and after the food was eaten, the wine drunk—well, sparkling cider for Persephone and Kara—he said quietly that he needed to drive Gabriel back, but that he would see me the next day. I had to be content with that promise; at least he wasn't going to abandon me on Christmas Day.

It felt good to clean up the mess afterward, to stand in companionable silence with Kara as she washed the dishes and I dried them, Grandma's china and silver being too sacred to be placed in a lowly dishwasher. After a while, Kara remarked, "He seems very nice."

I didn't have to ask which "he" she was referring to. "He's the best present Martin could have given me."

She gave a little nod but didn't say anything. I wondered if she was thinking about her own father, who had divorced Marybeth when Kara was barely four. From certain things she'd said, I guessed that she remembered him, but they'd had no contact beyond a few visits before I was even born. He'd paid child support, one of the only reasons Marybeth had ever been able to hang on to an apartment for any length of time, although I had a feeling that the support stopped soon after we came to live with our grandparents. I didn't even know his full name, as Marybeth had taken back her maiden name after the divorce.

"You okay?" I asked, and Kara nodded again.

"Sure. It was good to be with everyone. I guess...I guess I'm just feeling a little at loose ends. Here we've won, and I thought it would be this big celebration and we'd all be dancing in the streets or something. But...."

"But?" I prompted.

"But Michael's gone, and things are settling down, and we're just sort of...living."

"I think that's the most important thing of all." I set down my dish towel and gave her a quick hug, ignoring the soap that dripped from the bowl she was holding. "That we all...live. That's what he would have wanted."

Christmas morning was quiet enough, although I did have fun watching Kara and Lance unwrap all of Grace's presents for her. Of course, she was too little to do much more than just stare, big-eyed, at all the toys and bows and torn wrapping paper, but I couldn't deny how adorable she was as she sat in Kara's arms, wearing a green plaid onesie, a red bow perched precariously in her already thick dark hair.

Martin had said he'd come by around eleven, and he was right on time, looking particularly gorgeous in his long black coat with a sapphire-blue sweater knotted around his neck.

"Hi," I said, still not sure exactly where we stood with one another.

"Hi," he replied, and bent and gave me a chaste kiss on the cheek, since Kara and Lance were watching from the living room.

I followed him down to the car and got in. He drove us eastward from Kara's, and for a crazy moment, I thought maybe we were going to Persephone and Paul's for some reason. But he took an earlier turnoff, climbing up into the hills, winding through narrow residential streets, until he pulled into the driveway of an impressive-looking Santa Fe–style home built on the crest of the hill. Then he unfastened his seatbelt and got out.

Frowning, I did the same, then paused next to the car and asked, "So...are we here to meet another of my long-lost relatives or something?"

"Not exactly." He took off his sunglasses, squinting a little in the bright morning sunlight. Today, there wasn't a cloud to be seen from Mingus Mountain to the Mogollon Rim. He added, apropos of nothing, "Forest Houses closes after the first of the year."

I gave him a wary look. "And?"

"And you probably don't want to crash in Kara's guest room forever, do you?"

I managed a head shake, while at the same time my heart started to beat a little faster. He couldn't mean....

From his inside coat pocket, he pulled out a small gift box and handed it to me. Small enough for…

…yes, small enough for a ring.

Fingers shaking, I opened the box. A brass key lay inside.

About all I could do was send a mute, questioning gaze upward, into eyes that seemed in that moment the same color as the sky, as the scarf he wore.

A smile—no, a grin—and he plucked the key from the box and led me to the front door, then inserted the key in the lock and brought me inside. The house was empty, except for a few lone side chairs in the dining room. On the granite counter in the kitchen, I saw a couple of flyers—*Beautiful Southwest property! Lease with option!*

Finally, I found my voice. "This—this place is yours?"

"Well, technically, I'm just renting it right now, but there is an option to buy. It's a little big, though, so I was hoping you might want to come here so I don't rattle around in it quite so much."

Joy welled up in me then, bright water rising from a very deep spring, and I launched myself at him, felt his arms go around me, his mouth on mine, kissing me wildly, tongues meeting, every cell in my body seeming to spark with happiness and need. I held him, tasted him, smelled the scent of wood smoke in his hair and coat and scarf. My worry was gone, melted away like ice under a brilliant, blazing sun.

He pulled me away from me slightly, eyes still twinkling. "I take it that's a yes?"

"Yes," I said. Then I looked around again. Not that I was the type to track every up and down of the Sedona real estate market, but I knew this place was way above an FBI agent's pay grade. Not that he was really an FBI agent, but—

"I know what you're thinking," he told me, and brushed a lock of hair away from my cheek. "But you don't need to worry about that. We exiles aren't exactly cast into the outer darkness. Look where your father ended up."

Well, that was true. "So, what…they just gave you this house?"

"'Gave' is probably too simplistic a concept. Let's just say they arranged it so it would be mine."

"Wow," was about all I could manage.

Another one of those grins, and he took me by the hand and led me across the living room to the sliding glass doors that opened onto a huge wraparound concrete deck. From there, you could see a huge swath of the valley, from Schnebly Hill almost all the way out to Capitol Butte. I couldn't begin to imagine what it would be like to stand out there at sunset and watch the red rocks blaze with hidden fire.

We stood there in silence for a moment, the brisk wind blowing our hair, the air fresh and clean and alive. Even knowing he wanted me here with him, that he wanted me in his life, I found I had to ask. "And it's—it's all right? Being here? Not—where you came from?"

Martin turned away from the red rocks to stare down at me. Those blue eyes held mine, clear and calm. He smiled, and took my hands in his, and I knew then that he had no regrets. He told me,

"I can't think of anyplace else I'd rather be."

The Sedona Files series continues with Grace's story in *Star Crossed*.

Darknight

Darkmoon

Sympathetic Magic

Protector

Spellbound

A Cleopatra Hill Christmas

Impractical Magic

Strange Magic

The Arrangement

Defender

Bad Blood

Deep Magic

Darktide

Books 1-3 and Books 4-6 of this series are also available in two separate omnibus editions at special boxed set prices. Chronicles of Cleopatra Hill includes the series' two "back in time" novellas, *Bad Blood* and *The Arrangement*.

Or get the entire series in one enormous, specially priced boxed set! (Not available on Amazon.)

THE DJINN WARS

(Paranormal Romance)

Chosen

Taken

Fallen

Broken

Forsaken

Forbidden

Awoken

Illuminated

Stolen

Forgotten

Driven

Unspoken (June 2019)

Books 1-3 and Books 4-6 of this series are also available in two separate omnibus editions at special boxed set prices!

THE WATCHERS TRILOGY*

(Paranormal Romance)

Falling Dark

Dead of Night

Rising Dawn

The Watchers Trilogy is also available in a specially priced boxed set!

THE SEDONA FILES*

(Paranormal Romance)

Bad Vibrations

Desert Hearts

Angel Fire

Star Crossed

Falling Angels

Enemy Mine

Get the first three books of this series in an omnibus edition, or read the complete six-book series in one super-low-priced boxed set!

TALES OF THE LATTER KINGDOMS

(Fantasy Romance)

All Fall Down

Dragon Rose

Binding Spell

Ashes of Roses

One Thousand Nights

Threads of Gold

The Wolf of Harrow Hall

Moon Dance

The Song of the Thrush

Books 1-3 and Books 4-6 of this series are also available in two separate omnibus editions at special boxed set prices.

THE GAIAN CONSORTIUM SERIES*

(Science Fiction Romance)

Beast (free prequel novella)

Blood Will Tell

Breath of Life

The Gaia Gambit

The Mandala Maneuver

The Titan Trap

The Zhore Deception

The Refugee Ruse

Books 1-3 of this series are also available in an omnibus edition at a special boxed set price!

STANDALONE TITLES

Hearts on Fire

Sympathy for the Devil

Taking Dictation

Night Music

Golden Heart

* Indicates a completed series

ABOUT THE AUTHOR

USA Today bestselling author Christine Pope has been writing stories ever since she commandeered her family's Smith-Corona typewriter back in grade school. Her work includes paranormal romance, fantasy romance, and science fiction/space opera romance. She makes her home in Arizona.

Don't miss out on any of Christine's new releases — sign up for her newsletter today!

Christine Pope on the Web:
www.christinepope.com

facebook.com/ChristinePopeAuthor
twitter.com/ChristineJPope

www.ingramcontent.com/pod-product-compliance
Lightning Source LLC
Chambersburg PA
CBHW071245250626
47163CB00002B/336